T0367868

The Viper

The Viper

LARRY PRYOR

authorHOUSE®

AuthorHouse™ LLC
1663 Liberty Drive
Bloomington, IN 47403
www.authorhouse.com
Phone: 1-800-839-8640

Published by AuthorHouse 07/17/2013

ISBN: 978-1-4817-6743-9 (sc)
ISBN: 978-1-4817-6742-2 (e)

Library of Congress Control Number:2013911396

This book is printed on acid-free paper.

For information address: Larry Pryor larrypryor8@gmail.com

PREFACE

The urge to write this novel hit me soon after watching the first Long Beach Grand Prix, held in 1976, an astounding event for starved U.S. Formula 1 fans. The Long Beach street race wasn't the "American Monaco" but it came close enough. The entry field for the first F1 race had been restricted to 20 entries for fear that high-speed traffic congestion would result in a demolition derby. As it was, three drivers—Carlos Reuteman, Gunnar Nilsson and James Hunt—went into the walls and out of the race. Only 12 cars finished. This was the era of four-wheel drifts on narrow, hard tires. Safety measures were minimal. Watching Ferraris, Tyrrells and McLarens dive down the steep hill from Ocean Boulevard to a hard left at the bottom made for stories to tell the grandchildren.

It took me a few years to get the novel down on paper. I was an environment writer for the *Los Angeles Times*. Air and water pollution threatened to submerge the L.A. region in a sea of toxics. No one could say where a Grand Prix race through the streets of Long Beach fit into the pollution picture, nor did we care. It was a glorious diversion. I wove in the terrorist plot, since the Black September attack at the 1972

Munich Olympics was fresh in all of our minds. Arab oil boycotts made the American public aware that some people in the Middle East did not wish us well, but it was not clear to us who in the Arab world wore the white or black hats.

Enthusiasm for F1 racing, which now generates the world's biggest TV audience, plus today's dread of terrorist acts, prompted me to rewrite and update parts of The Viper this year. And thanks to AuthorHouse, bookstores and e-book platforms, it's possible to share these emotions again with a new and wider public. Global society faces big, potentially depressing, challenges, especially in the domain of the environment. But it's my belief that escape, if not overdone, can be a welcome antidote.

■ Larry Pryor, June, 2013

Grateful acknowledgment is made for permission to reprint the following material: Extract from Hermann Lang, *Grand Prix Driver*. By permission of G. T. Foulis & Co., Ltd. Extract from Prince Chula Chakrabongse of Thailand, *Dick Seaman; Racing Motorist*. By permission of G. T. Foulis & Co., Ltd. Extract from Rudolf Caracciola, *Caracciola*. By permission of G. T. Foulis & Co., Ltd. Extract from William Court, *A History of Grand Prix Motor Racing, 1906-1951: The Power and the Glory*. By permission of Macdonald and Jane's Publishers Ltd . Extract from R. J. B. Seaman, Motor Racing. By permission of Seeley, Service & Cooper Ltd. Extract from Rodney Walkerley, *Grand Prix Racing* 1934-1939. By permission of Motor Racing Publications

Ltd. Extract from Laurence Pomeroy, *Grand Prix Car*. By permission of Motor Racing Publications Ltd. Extract from Count Giovanni Lurani, *Nuvolari*. By permission of Cassell Ltd. and the author.

1.

> Why, then, are these Continental firms, especially the Germans, spending such vast sums on racing every year? The reason is, of course, for national propaganda. Much as one may dislike the fact, there is no denying that Grand Prix racing has become a political force on the Continent. Anyone who has seen the enthusiasm and publicity accorded to the German teams, the lofty hall, rather resembling a cathedral, in which the victorious German racing cars were enshrined at the last Berlin motor show, and the keen interest taken in the cars and drivers by the Führer himself, must admit this fact.
>
> R. J. B. Seaman
> *Motor Racing*
> Lonsdale Library Seeley Service & Co., Ltd.

The sound penetrated gradually, a dawn insect attack. Then the part of my brain that has charge during half-sleep rejected the mosquito theory, deciding the intrusion was mechanical. With my eyes still shut, I began to track the rising and falling notes of a motorcycle as it wound its way through the narrow lane outside Senlis. It seemed headed toward our rented cottage.

Since I was sleeping naked and spoon-fashion with the woman I had married eighteen hours before, I favored the idea of staying in bed, though I knew my occupation would eventually force me before breakfast to jog down the road toward Chantilly and double back through forest paths and over pastures.

For a moment, I thought I could watch the approaching machine from some sort of mental hiding place and then, as a matter of will, guide it past our gate and down the road. The country smells and sounds took me out of the room. Gus Walter, young American Formula 1 driver and expatriate, standing alone in a wicker basket under a large red-and-white balloon, surveying all of France. The heavy rapping on the front door deflated my dream.

"Herr Ffalter?" said a goggled messenger, a specter of black leather, buckles, and hard plastic, on the front stoop.

"You bloody bastard," I muttered, hunched in terry cloth. I could hear a rooster crowing in the farmyard across the lane.

"Es tut mir leid," said the rider, extracting an envelope from a leather case and handing it to

me. I ripped the heavy bond paper and unfolded a letter, to which someone had thoughtfully clipped three $1,000 bills.

“Stop by any time you’re in the neighborhood,” I told the man and motioned him to come into the house.

I wasn’t up to German that early in the day, but I felt a bond with a fellow professional. We went into the small kitchen with the well-worn brick floor. I offered him the stool by the butcher board and started water for coffee while I scanned the typewritten page.

Gustave Walter
RN 33
Senlis, France
Thursday

Dear Mr. Walter:

Please excuse this intrusion into your vacation, but time is critical. I find no other way except to intervene directly and ask your indulgence in being given such short notice.

The enclosed sum is yours. Call it a disturbance fee. However, we hope that you will view it as an indication of our financial stability.

At this point, there is no possibility of my elaborating on what we propose to offer you. If, however, you follow instructions set below, we will pay you another $3,000 for what should be no more than a commitment of three days. You are welcome to bring your new bride, since we have set aside accommodations for you both at our test site.

Without elaborating further, we would ask that you report noon Friday (October 4) at the private terminal at Le Bourget. Please bring your driving kit and be prepared for one day of tests.

Your signature on the messenger's form will assure us of your arrival.

Very truly yours,

Willard Schwandt
Weltumspannend GmbH
77 Claridenstrasse Düsseldorf, Deutschland

The stationery indicated at the bottom that the Weltumspannend company had offices in Paris, Milan, and Jubil, Emirate of Qataban. The name of the firm was vaguely familiar. It fit someplace in the constellation of motor racing, but I couldn't place it.

I poured out the coffee and chatted with the messenger, who said his name was Josef, about motorcycle races. My German has always been inexplicably poor, considering we had spoken it in our home in San Diego when I was growing up. The constructions continued to elude me, but I could handle adjectives, I knew the names of the top riders and circuits, and I substituted hand-waving for the verbs. When I got sufficiently warmed up, I queried Josef about Weltumspannend, but he said he knew nothing. So I signed the form, showed Josef out into the newly arrived sunlight, and went back to the kitchen to reread the letter. Who the hell was Schwandt?

"He's a Boche," said Aimee as we drank coffee on the small enclosed patio behind the farmhouse, where a promising fall sun did its work as we sprawled on *chaise longues* in bikinis.

"I knew it would happen sooner or later," she said. "The Boche want you to drive for them because they buy the best and you are the best."

"I'm best, all right. Best at insulting sponsors, giving migraines to mechanics, and parking cars upside down in the scenery. It's a special talent."

She sat up, leaning on an elbow, and looked at me. "German teams have always been made up of known entities, isn't that right?" I agreed. That was true as it applied to the non-Germans they recruited. I could tell she had been reading up on the history of the sport. To split hairs would invite an argument.

"*Bon*," she said. "That settles it. You are a *known* unknown entity. You're a ripe cherry for them to pick out of the middle-back-"

"Front-middle-"

"Yes, front-middle ranks." She was quick to make me feel good because I had just finished a terrible summer of driving and I was still without a contract for the new season. The team I had driven for, a two-car Formula 1 *équipe* sponsored by an undrinkable stout, had finally folded when sales declined, and an accountant had convinced Sir Horace Biddle, chairman of the board, that the drop in sales was mainly due to some madmen who were crashing cars with Sir Horace's name and seal on them at a record rate across Europe.

Biddle's car, a bastardized design to start with, defied improvement, no matter how many days we spent testing and fiddling with it at Silverstone. It was unpredictable and foul when we started the season, and then it got worse. The engineers and mechanics were underpaid and had turned surly, blaming me for the relentless string of bad accidents, which became almost predictable as I began to push the car harder in a mistaken effort to make up for its bad qualities.

The driver of the team's second car was a heavily muscled Swede by the name of Jon Brunnsen, whose greatest show of emotion had been to cluck his tongue after he took off his helmet in the pits, although the car had just tried eight ways to kill him. Brunnsen had stayed on the road, but his times got steadily slower at each race until things had caught up with him at the Nouvelle Chicane at Monaco, where he had hit the steel barrier at the outside of the second turn a massive clout during practice and had gone into a coma. He'd finally recovered, three weeks later, but it was the end of the season for our second car and no one felt motivated to build another copy.

This was supposed to have been my season to become entrenched in the front ranks of Formula 1 racing. Instead, I had received, in succession, a crushed finger, three broken ribs, a burned right foot, and scorched lungs. Somehow I had collected a solid sixth in the Grand Prix of Sweden and a fourth early in the year in the U.S. Grand Prix at Long Beach—good but not that much to show for a season of mortal risk, sweat and pain. That I was still alive seemed like an afterthought.

It now looked like a year of pickup rides in lower formulas, wrestling matches with overweight saloon cars and odd drives in endurance sports-car events, trying to make up the time lost by the Brazilian Sportsman who co-drives—and owns—the car. It would be a search for prize money again, the life of a bounty hunter.

"On the other hand," said Aimee, seemingly weighing the possibilities, "*I* don't think you would be happy at all driving for the Germans. Why don't you scout out some nice, friendly Belgian or Swiss team with an extra car?"

"You're getting too much sun," I said, amazed at her hesitation. Schwandt's letter could spell deliverance.

"The Boche will want to turn you into a machine, Gus. You'll have to drive for men in long white coats with stopwatches. And this gross team manager will shout at you if you are a hundredth of a second off. *Tu adoreras ça*."

I wondered for a moment what it would be like to marry someone who knew nothing about motor racing, who had not been an Olympic athlete and UCLA language scholar—somebody suitably dumb, a vacant-faced crumpet, like the camp followers we attracted.

Aimee and I had met in a Latin Quarter Trattoria during my first season in Formula 1. She'd been in the company of people I knew to be musicians, first-chair players with Orchestre de Theatre des Champs-Elysees. I was hosting my chief mechanic, a bantam Welshman with broken front teeth, to his first hot meal in days. We had just finished racing at Zandvoort, where I had placed fifth. After having been in the top echelon of two forms of motorcycle racing, and made a lot of money at it, I shouldn't have considered fifth in a Formula 1 race as being extraordinary, but the competition was so exquisite, the cars so difficult to drive to their full potential and the costs of running a team so vast that fifth place in a year-old car I had financed with the last of my motorcycle winnings had seemed like a two-wheel championship.

"Gus Walter proved to be the best of the new breed," a columnist for *Autosport* had written that morning. "His style is unorthodox, a hangover from his Motocross background, but he places his car in the corners with exceptional authority, exacting the most from his less-than-competitive private entry. As I watched him sweep through the difficult bends on the back part of Circuit Park Zandvoort in the kind of teeth-clenching power slides we haven't seen since Froilán Gonzáles's first season on the Continent, I wondered how this young man's career would develop in a new medium. Surely his well-deserved fifth place here at Zandvoort, after starting from 14th position, indicates the blond American is going upward, and we will be watching to see how far he can negotiate in four wheels instead of two." The unspoken caveat was: ". . . if he should live so long."

The mechanics and I had driven the transporters back from Holland to my garage in the Billancourt section of Paris, a suitably industrial area for our noisy operation. I was almost logy from fatigue that night, but a vibrant young woman with a black pixie haircut was sitting an arm's length away at the next table. The musicians pulled me into their orbit, knowing me to be a celebrated driver who could talk about something more than suspensions and gear ratios. I had lived in Paris for two years by then, my French was passable, and I was admittedly something of a rarity, a racing driver who loved opera. The feature stories in the racing press played that up, especially when paparazzi caught me squiring young divas.

Wine seemed to be arriving at both tables in buckets, and my chief mechanic and *confidant* soon nodded off. I made him as comfortable as could be expected and reminded myself to get him to the food earlier next time, and then I joined their table, where string players were giving imitations of tenors of the day. They were flush from a recording session, and we shared our success. I pitched in with an imitation of Jussi Björling.

"A racing driver who can sing *'Che gelida manina'* can't be all bad, except your high notes have a bit of a whiskey quality," the young woman in the next seat said to me. Corners of her mouth curled up in jest. Her cheeks were broad, eyes green and her nose thin, long and delicate, like a Florentine Madonna's portrait—the only suggestion about her of virginity. Her rich contralto voice and self-assurance said something else.

We introduced and I soon had her life story. She was Aimee Fouchard, born in France, raised in California. She had excelled in high school and college track, competed in the javelin in the Montreal Olympics then turned from a career in professional sports to study the cello and live in Paris.

She was sitting next to an older gnome-like man wearing thick, black-rimmed glasses whose ugliness hit new levels of beauty. She introduced him to me as her cello instructor, but I wondered how his gnarled hands dealt with the instrument. Something about the arrangement between them didn't ring true. But neither he nor anyone else at the table seemed particularly possessive of Aimee, so I cheerfully filled the vacuum.

Two weeks later, after considerable effort on my part, Aimee and I bedded down in a rococo hotel room outside of Versailles and made thrashing love under the knowing eyes of *putti* painted on the ceiling. We were like two experienced dancers who had finally found the right partner, both being athletic and intense.

Aimee joined our caravan the next week, the middle of the Formula 1 season. She showed up without warning in the paddock at the Paul Ricard circuit, offering to do any type of work for our team, which I had nostalgically named *Écurie* USA. I found a hotel room for her in town and set her to work doing timing and lap charts. Aimee not only did that, but once she was familiar with the other teams, she began to pass along useful tips of pit row information about the tire temperatures, fuel consumption, and gear ratios of rival cars. She picked it up and fed it back to me and the chief mechanic in succinct reports. By the next race, she and I had given up the pretext of living apart, and we rearranged the equipment and bedding in my van.

We were competing in the British Grand Prix the weekend after she joined the team. The transporter was parked in the paddock at Brands Hatch. I couldn't afford hotels then, and we had too much work to do, anyway. Aimee and I were sharing the cot in the back of the van the night before the race, when I asked her why she had left Paris.

"The cello arrived too late in my life, but you didn't," she said. Her tongue was creating seashell sounds in my ear, making it difficult to hear.

"Stop the crap," I said. "I want to know why you dumped your musical training to join up with a gypsy Grand Prix team and its driver-owner, who is rapidly going broke."

"My training wasn't only in the cello," she answered slowly. There was a long pause. It was dark in the van. She put her head in the crook of my naked arm. I could see her features only dimly, but her eyes were open, staring at the ceiling. I sensed she was calculating how long she wanted to be committed to me. Apparently it would be for a while.

"My training was also in espionage at the CIA farm at Camp Peary. Light weapons, explosives, surveillance, and locks and keys. I majored in locks and keys."

"A spook," I said in wonder.

"Not just any old CIA employee, Gus, *mon amant vigoureux*, but a full-fledged officer of the Clandestine Services, a GS-13, and, until three weeks ago, a career woman."

"Then what happened?"

"It's too soon. I can't tell you because it still hurts. I'll do it some day. Basically, my case officer, the man sitting next to me the night we met, and I disagreed on how to handle a problem, and I took a walk. But it had been building. I just wanted out, a long way out."

We talked late into the night. She told me more, how she had been recruited as an agent while training for the Olympics at UCLA. It was unusual. The Agency, she said, seldom recruited Americans as deep-cover agents, preferring to use foreigners who could be dealt with at arm's length by U.S. case officers. But she had a French passport, a legacy from her father, Emile Fouchard, who, as a young diplomat had been posted to the consulate in Los Angeles, had married a young American actress, and then had left the French foreign service for a career as an executive at Twentieth-Century Fox. He'd retained his French citizenship and doted on his only child, speaking to her invariably in French, a language I had found she lapsed into when stressed or affectionate.

"I was alone and vulnerable. My parents both died in a car crash, a drunk who lost it on Sunset Boulevard and hit them head-on," she said quietly. "I was 23. At first, my superiors didn't want me to get data. They wanted contacts, especially among the visiting Russian and East European athletic teams. I had good Russian and German, a bit of Arabic, as well as fluent French, so they used me as a recruiter. I gave promising names to the case officer, and he followed up. A check from the Falls Church Language Academy arrived in my account once a month. It seemed so easy."

I stayed silent.

"After the Olympics, when I got my training and was assigned abroad, I did more for them, a lot more. It's amazing what the analysts can tell from a good color photograph of smoke coming from a factory near a Russian athletic field. They can figure out the product, the volume, and whether the foreman missed the last Party meeting. I needed the money, and I did all that on a contract basis. Then they asked me to join as an intelligence officer and keep working as a deep-cover agent. I said sure. It gets easier, or at least it seems to. That's the problem with it. You take more chances, get further in the open, and then all of a sudden somebody's dead, and it was your own stupid fault. Then the pendulum swings in the opposite direction and everyone goes by the book, even when you know you shouldn't. Then everything gets by you, and Langley wants to know why they didn't get their answer yesterday. Either way, you can't sleep if you care. I cared. I really, really cared. *Maintenant bonne nuit*."

The following day, my car's engine let go with a great spray of metal, oil and white smoke on the third lap. *Écurie* USA went into the red another $20,000. The strains of team management and financial worries, and maybe thinking about my new love, weren't doing my driving skills that much good, and I concluded it was time the Number One driver got some R&R. The mechanics took the transporters to Germany for the race the next weekend, while Aimee and I flew to the south of France for a two-day break. We found a room in a small inn outside Nice. I told Aimee over a late bottle of champagne on the terrace overlooking the Mediterranean to drop discussion of the CIA or related topics until after the season was finished. If she wanted some therapy, she could concentrate on the plight of our team. I was going to run out of money, despite what the press said about my being an heir to a beer fortune. I needed to attract a berth on a sponsored F1 team for the next season, or my racing career might be finished.

"From now to winter, I want you to focus on cars. *And* on me, of course," I told her.

"In that order?"

"Wednesday to Sunday. Then reverse the priority the two days before we have to be at the next circuit. And tonight's almost Monday," I said, taking her arm and leading her upstairs.

Between rounds of lovemaking that night, as the smooth sea breeze moved through our bedroom, she wanted to know why I had followed a sport with such a high mortality rate. It was a question that had dogged me from the day I had gouged the lawn at our home in San Diego with a new mini-bike. Since then, almost every distraction in my life, including school, had been erased as I concentrated on motor sports. My parents turned me out of their enormous ranch house, hoping I would run out of money before I killed myself. I became an outcast from their second generation of gentility, a backslider into the primitive ways of my grandfather, except he had accumulated capital and built his Heidelberg Beer empire, while I was investing in uninsurable and fragile machines.

The only legacies I retained were my father's fascination for hunting and fishing and my mother's passion for classical music. My ears seemed to require something to balance the rasp of engines. I also liked to read. College came in a laundry bag, a white canvas book sack that I drew from at random when idle at race tracks. *The Portable Faulkner,* assorted S. J. Perelman, Aristotle's *Politics,* a Samuelson text on economics, and a parade of others. I read them in hunks, motivated by the uncomfortable thought that motor racing might be, after all, an empty pursuit.

Before I left home for good at 18, my parents had tried to distract me, investing enormous sums in backpack trips to Alaskan trout streams, elk hunts in Colorado, concert weekends in Europe, sailing lessons with Cup contenders. In the process they succeeded only in convincing me that competing with a 250-cc factory-sponsored Motocross machine at Carlsbad Raceway topped any other human activity. In response, they cut me off without a dime. But grandfather didn't.

I knew then that I had a body, reflexes, balance, and, above all, eyes that could drive a motorcycle as fast as, and perhaps faster than, anyone else. These were talents that couldn't be parked or misappropriated.

I read the chroniclers of motor racing—Pomeroy, Walkerley, Monkhouse, and Jenkinson—and marveled at the giants of pre-war Grand Prix drivers, men like Caracciola, Rosemeyer, and Nuvolari. By 1936 their cars were topping 200 miles per hour. They had taken racing technology into new territory, somehow stayed on the road as much as they were off it, and relished the challenge as much as the money and fame.

The lure of Grand Prix in the '50s had attracted American drivers to Europe in successive waves, some to die in obscurity before they developed their skills, and others, like Hill, Gurney, Revson, and Andretti, to become celebrities on the Continent. At the age of twenty-two, already in the top ranks of U.S. motorcycle riders, I had left for London to plunge into international Motocross, switching later into 500-cc road racing, where our lap times on the European courses were beaten only by the fastest sports-racing and formula cars. I drove three Formula 2 races and then leaped into Formula 1, gambling my motorcycle winnings that I could drive my way onto a top team.

But this apprenticeship, three long years abroad, had exacted a toll. By moving to Europe as a professional, I paid a penalty of loneliness and vague anxiety. It was a vagabond life in mildewed hotel rooms and dank garages, with time left over for only the crudest friendships with other riders, and later drivers, and the women we attracted. It had been an endless succession of nightlong engine overhauls, hard racing and then back to the transporter vans for another racing circuit. Even the lucrative advertising endorsements and the initial thrill of living on a continent where professional drivers are idolized did little to relieve the constant fatigue and hollow sense of detachment.

Then, soon after meeting Aimee, I finally ran out of money and felt lucky to be picked up by Sir Horace to drive for the rest of the season. I had folded my own *Écurie* USA for the security of commercial sponsorship and found my employers to be crass and incompetent and their cars to be un-drivable. Now I had one more chance, perhaps. Willard Schwandt to the rescue. I didn't know who he was or what kind of a car he had, but I had the feeling it would be Formula 1 and that, judging from the letterhead, he had the money to be competitive in that league.

Thinking about his offer that morning at Senlis, I developed a severe urge to be on Schwandt's team. Teutonic discipline was suddenly the one quality I had been seeking for a lifetime.

"I'm getting weary of crummy hotels and that idiot of a race engineer," I told Aimee, turning onto my stomach to absorb the surprisingly strong fall sun of central France. "Last year we ate gristly sausages and cold fries and now life with Biddle's stout is only a niche up. I could feature first-class hotels, gourmet food, and then all I have to do is drive."

"You'll get soft," she said. "You've lived right on the edge and gotten away with it, Gus. You sign with the Germans and you'll lose that."

"It's your Maginot Line mentality showing again, Aimee. For some reason, you despise everything Teutonic, which makes me wonder how people named Gustave and Aimee could have gotten married."

She leaned on her elbow again and gave me the Bardot pout, a blank look of female consternation that usually led to further jousting. But the strengthening sun seemed to be claiming her energy.

"The problem is," I said, "if I'm going to test-drive for Herr Schwandt—whoever he is—we'll have to leave for Le Bourget now."

"*Rectification,"* she said, flopping back and closing her eyes. *"You'll* have to leave for the airport now. We rented this cottage for a three-week honeymoon, as it is so quaintly termed, and . . . as far as I'm concerned . . . you can go to rotten Germany and drive for Herr

Schwandt until he loves you to death . . . *Moi . . . je reste . . . ici . . . au . . . soleil.*"

Someone was slowly pulling the plug to her brain. She turned her back to the sun, and I craned my head to scan her broad-shouldered, almost masculine, upper body. The skin glistened. I traced a finger down the musculature to the two deep indentations in the lower back where the terrain turned decidedly feminine. The bikini top was held by a delicate knot, the kind fishermen never tie. It unraveled with a slight tug.

"On second thought," I said, "an F1 driver should be able to get from here to Le Bourget in no time."

An hour later, we emerged from the large brass bed, showered together and then I packed. I had wanted her to join me on the trip but I knew that the calculated tension of test sessions, dealing with unknowns and mechanical things that might fail, plus the pressure of winning a seat on a top team could be torture. I didn't try to talk her out of staying.

"I'm back in a couple of days. Don't moon too much," I said at the door, holding the equipment bag. She was sprawled on the sheets, her face buried in a pillow, her long, tapered legs spread slightly. But her mumbling—what the hell language was it?—sounded encouraging.

* * *

On October 4, the CIA Chief of Station in Paris and the COS of Jubil both received cables from the Deputy Director of Operations at headquarters in Langley. The messages dealt with a query from the Director of Central Intelligence:

/
TO: COS PARIS
FROM: DDO
TOP SECRET

DCI WANTS UPDATE ON RECRUITING AND TESTING NOW PROCEEDING AT QATABAN. NEED TO KNOW NATURE OF PROGRAM. SOURCES THERE IN CONFLICT. DCI ASKS IF THISTLE CAN BE PUT BACK ON PAYROLL AND HOW SOON NEW SOURCES CAN BE PLUGGED INTO TEAMS. EVALUATE THISTLE STABILITY.

TO: COS WBIL
FROM: DDO
TOP SECRET

DCI WANTS UPDATE ON QATABAN AUTO INDUSTRY. NEED TO KNOW TERRORIST POTENTIAL OF RACING DEPARTMENT, LEVEL AND TIMING OF FUTURE AUTO/TRUCK OUTPUT.

THISTLE MAY GO BACK ON PAYROLL. ASSESS RISK TO THISTLE AND BALANCE WITH UTILITY TO YOUR STATION.

~:~

2.

> I was quite nervy, and no wonder; the final decision was at hand. Neubauer started the tests with the charming remark: "If one of you runs out of road, he might as well buy a train ticket home."
>
> Hermann Lang
> *Grand Prix Driver*
> G. T. Foulis & Co., Ltd.

Le Bourget airport, scene of Lindbergh's arrival, lies along the route from Senlis to Paris, and it took me about twenty-five minutes in moderate traffic to reach the terminal. Unlike most of my colleagues, who drive luxury supercars or brawny sports-racers, I prefer a vintage car, a 1952 Frazer-Nash Le Mans, a two-seater that is finicky but quick and gives me a sense of being part of the motoring tradition.

I parked in a covered garage on the perimeter of the airport and walked toward the front of the terminal with a small valise and the bulky kit bag, trying to remember if I had ever met Schwandt. A man wearing a mountain of khaki raincoat stepped through the main door and headed to intercept me. The cloth began its outward angle at the chest, continued more steeply over an expansive midsection, and fell downward almost to the ground at a considerable distance from the feet. If he went on a dehydration diet, he couldn't get under three hundred. But the face, although full, was noticeably hard and had no trace of suet. His slate gray hair was combed straight back. The eyes focused like black beams. I once knew a half-mile bike track owner in Gardena who looked like this man. The promoter looked cumbersome but could win $100 bets by jumping onto the bar from a squatting position on the floor.

"Herr Walter?" He had a true English "W." I had feared that I would have to speak German and wave my hands to substitute for verbs again.

"Yes, and you are Schwandt?"

"Natürlich, natürlich. So good of you to come. It should be worth your while, and I don't mean necessarily in terms of money. But your wife, Herr Walter?"

"She prefers what is left of the French sun to what she says will be the drizzles for sure in Germany," I said.

"Ah, but Herr Walter, I didn't say in my letter that we were going to Germany. Because of a certain amount of necessary secrecy about this whole enterprise, I couldn't be explicit, but we are flying this afternoon in the personal jet of the Emir of Qataban. We will land at the coastal town of Marib on the Persian Gulf, where we will conduct tests on the Emir's track."

Our plane, a hyped-up version of a Dassault-Breguet Falcon, took off in mid-afternoon. Schwandt and I were the sole passengers, and he had become extraordinarily uncommunicative. I got out of him that he had been one of the up-and-coming Mercedes-Benz reserve Grand Prix drivers but only had a chance to test and practice during 1939, when it all came to an end. He had served as a motorcycle courier during the war and caught a severe leg wound that had finished him as a competitive driver. He had become involved with a number of engineering projects, earned a degree at Hamburg, and ended up on the technical fringe of motor racing, supplying custom-made electrical and fuel systems for various racing teams.

Any questions about Qataban were deftly turned aside. The nimble jet had the Emir's stamp on it, figuratively and literally. The body was painted flat black, and on the plane's tail was the Qataban flag, a bright orange rectangle with inscrutable Arabic messages in the middle. Inside, the decor was Contemporary Emir, including a couch that went almost from window to window. There was no liquor aboard, and since

Schwandt was being so unhelpful, I pulled out a new book on dry-fly fishing, a thorough English treatment of my hobby, rivaled only by my love of firearms and hunting, and read about Low-Water Stream Techniques, as the batlike plane flicked across the Aegean.

The copilot, who appeared to be Dutch or Swiss, emerged from the cockpit, opened a refrigerator compartment, and retrieved trays of cold food. He opened bottles of Badoit mineral water and poured them into cut-crystal goblets for us. He and Schwandt conversed rapidly in a German variant, which I guessed was Schweizerdeutsch, while I watched blankly.

"Are you political, Herr Walter?" Schwandt asked as the copilot retreated and we began to probe a pheasant aspic, accompanied by unassuming boiled eggs that concealed a heart of Beluga caviar.

"Political, Schwandt? You mean am I a Republican or a Democrat or a closet Socialist or something like that?"

"Political, Herr Walter. I mean do you care about such things? Are you interested in the Israeli conflict, for example?"

Now I could see the shoals more clearly. A condition of employment would probably mean sticking strictly to the cars.

"Does it make a difference?" I asked.

"Not entirely, of course. We wouldn't expect you to act differently than you do now. But if you drove for the Emir, we would expect you to be cautious about such things."

"Such things?"

"You would leave political statements to the diplomats. We want our drivers to drive. Nothing else."

I couldn't see a problem with that logic, though I wondered if Aimee might have a problem. Before the Second World War, Richard Seaman left England to drive for a Mercedes-Benz team that was directly subsidized by Hitler. But then I couldn't remember whether Seaman gave the Nazi salute from his car during parade laps, as the German drivers did.

"Neutral means we don't have to go either way—right, Schwandt? No parade laps in fezzes for the Pan-Arab League."

"Precisely."

A wall of humidity met us when the copilot opened the door and let us out onto the ill-lit pavement. An orange van pulled up, and a young Arab in a black jump suit with orange piping put our bags in the back and drove us around the one-story terminal.

"An onshore breeze comes up around midnight," said Schwandt. "It sends this humidity inland, and we have about four hours in the early morning to drive the cars. Then we hide in the air-conditioned garages."

I wondered how long this project, whatever it was, had been going on. There are few secrets in auto racing. If a car is being developed, word inevitably gets around. After about two minutes, we drove up to what appeared to be a motel on the outside, and lived up to its billing on the inside.

"This was built by one of your American chains," Schwandt said, handing me a key that he had obtained from the Arab clerk. "It is run for the exclusive use of the Racing Department, but unhappily there is no bar. You will find your room on the corridor on the right. Breakfast will be brought to your room at five o'clock, and we leave for the track at five-thirty."

The clerk came around and took my bags, and I headed off down the hall with a vague feeling that I had wandered into something more structured than a German team could create at its Kafkaesque worst. The room was Holiday Inn with few surprises, although there was no piece of paper stretched over the toilet and the bed was of an enormous size.

Only in sleep do my subconscious fears of racing come from hiding. I'm driving a Formula 2 car at the Nürburgring in the rain. That had been my first professional race behind a wheel. A fanatical team manager had shouted at me for poor times in the opening practice. I couldn't see through the rooster tails of cars ahead and didn't know where the 14-mile course went. *"They're* supposed to drive in *your* spray, laddie!" The big man had hunched down to cockpit level, curly hair matted by the rain, dark patches of wet showing beneath his plastic raincoat. A raindrop had fallen from his nose to a jutting chin, which was pitted with a deep dimple. His head grew large and disproportionate. He shouted more, but I couldn't understand . . . Then I'm out on the track, still not able to see. The car slides viciously, and I'm heading downhill, backwards, towards some trees, then banging over a ditch, the car rolling over. Noise, flying dirt, grass clumps, the smell of fuel, and I'm upside down, held in by the belts, muscles tensed, waiting for the flash of mortal pain.

I could hear the windowpanes, framed in aluminum and anchored in concrete, chattering in the wind, and I mumbled a few low-key *merdes* into the pillow. Schwandt hadn't mentioned how strong the onshore breezes were, which was a topic of some interest to me, since wind, like rain, has a terrible influence on race cars. Under the best of conditions, the cars teeter on the edge of control. A gust of wind from the wrong angle or at an awkward moment can be what safety engineers so wonderfully call the Initiating Event, or the reason the car hit a tree at 200 miles per hour.

The watch dial looked like 4:55. I turned on the light and read some more on the Values of Underwater Obstructions, which didn't do as much to slow the pulse beat as I had hoped. Breakfast came on the second of 5:00 A.M. in the hands of a silent and effacing young Arab in white. The fare was Spartan—coffee, rolls, jam—but excellent. The butter tasted as if it had been churned that morning in Paris.

I began to pull on the Nomex fireproof uniform of the trade, which seemed to grow more bulky and difficult to get into as the layers of underwear and outer suit increased each year. At times, usually when dressing, I long for the days when drivers like Alberto Ascari drove in natty short-sleeved polo shirts. Then I recollect the burn victims, the drivers who crashed brutally but might have lived if they had worn fireproof clothes. Nomex and injected foam at least give us about forty seconds to save ourselves, if we are still conscious and able to move. Considering the number of times I had had to call upon them the previous season, I valued my Hinchman overalls, which have sewn-on grab handles on the shoulders, sides, and legs. These allow course workers to get a limp body out of the cockpit without strangling the driver. The suit has an outer system for injected foam and an inner system for body coolant, both of which hook into the car. Or at least they are supposed to. I wondered about the plumbing in a car made in the Middle East.

Schwandt and I met in the lobby and walked out into what was still total darkness. He had exchanged his raincoat and suit for a white tunic with epaulettes. He looked like a couple of elephant hunters.

“What will we be driving in this wind, Schwandt? It makes a difference.”

“Patience, Herr Walter. You will find out in a moment. The wind dies down, leaving us with about an hour to work with before the heat returns.”

We climbed in another orange van, and I thought about Teutonic precision and how it even extended to controlling the winds. I really didn’t want to drive in those tropical gusts, but it often isn’t easy for a driver to say no, particularly when he is well paid. Deep-sea divers have the same problem when an oil company foreman tells them to leap off an offshore rig and fix something when the wind is blowing a gale and the currents below are churning the mud. Their chances of surfacing again are poor.

We went through a high steel fence, taking a sharp turn after the manned gate into a brightly lit concrete courtyard with white garage doors surrounding it on all sides except the entrance. The guard at the gate had an M-10 LISP slung from his shoulder. No wonder word of the tests had not gotten around. Wind raked even the protected yard, rasping our faces with sand as we stepped from the van.

"If the wind persists, I will ask my clients to postpone this for a day," Schwandt said, "but I doubt they will agree. They say they do not have the time. I think it is an unrealistic position, you understand, but I am only the middleman."

"Fortunately, I'm not a middleman," I replied. "I wouldn't even drive a taxi in a crosswind like that."

"Yes, of course," he said, stiffening up, "but there are others in this as well. So, please, come with me, and I will show you with whom you are dealing."

We went through a small door into one of the garages, a fluorescent-lit room where folding chairs had been arranged in ranks five deep and five across. The three back rows were filled with mechanics in black overalls and orange piping. The men had uniformly swarthy complexions and aquiline faces. The next row was filled with technical types in open white shirts with ballpoints and slide rules clipped to their shirt pockets. One man was Asian, the others Caucasian. In the front row sat a driver I knew from our motorcycle days, Heinz Brunditz, two times the European 500-cc champion and a recent convert to formula cars. At the front of the room, four men dressed in traditional white mufti over black robes sat at a banquet-length folding table facing the rest of us. They had the look of the raptor-faced Bedouin sons who made it through the prestigious business schools.

Schwandt guided me to the front row as if it were a church service. The men at the table appraised us silently. I shook Brunditz's hand with what I hoped was disguised relief at seeing a familiar face. We had diced in the middle and the back of the field in several Grand Prix the previous season and knew each other off the circuits. He had not established a professional pattern yet, except that when his machines ran he was blindingly fast. He had also gained a reputation as a car-breaker and so far had not found a permanent berth on a major Formula 1 team.

Before we could talk and break the god-awful silence of the room, Schwandt arrived with another driver, Rachid Mohammed Bashir, an Algerian who had surfaced quickly to become the least understood, most undecipherable man in auto racing. For the past two years he had campaigned in Formula 1 in a privately sponsored car and had done well against the factory and commercially sponsored teams. He was reliable, steady, progressing professionally as if on a timetable, but not yet first class. He'd remained aloof during the season, and we'd all wondered where his team got its money.

The drivers shook hands, and Schwandt sat with us in the front row. At the front table, the second man from the left, who exuded the most authority, began to talk.

"Thank you for coming. I am Sheik Abdel Majeed el Sayed, Finance Minister of the United Emirate of Qataban. With me are my cabinet ministers. Plans call for conducting our business in two sessions today, here and out on the track. The object is for you to get to know us and our cars and for us to get to know you."

I thought of dropping a pin. The noise would have been shattering.

"This morning, we want to show you a car, a new Grand Prix car, and let you drive it or, to put it more bluntly, see if you can drive it. The car, I am told, has peculiar handling characteristics. My concern is mainly with the auto industry we are developing here in Qataban. We plan to build a line of trucks, passenger cars, and sports cars, all based on the same engine design and with the same name as the racing machines, Vipers. The Grand Prix cars will be our salesmen, our ambassadors.

"Our car operates at exceptionally high engine speeds and cannot be driven like a piston car. But it also has enormous output—about seven hundred and twenty horsepower—and I think you will at least enjoy that aspect. Rachid has already driven the car extensively and has been doing secret testing here for several months. Since I am merely a money man, I'll let him tell you about the car."

Rachid rose to his feet, enormously tall, like a powder-blue Nomex pillar. "Let's adjourn to the next garage. It will be easier to talk about the reptiles while we're looking at them." I caught the hint of his British accent. Not London School of Economics, like Sheik Abdel. Perhaps a heavy dose of tutoring in London before his climb through the regional racing clubs.

There were two cars, jet black with no insignia or sponsor stickers except the orange Qataban flag on the side. Aerodynamically, the cars looked like thinly sliced cheese wedges with wings balancing them fore and aft. The tires had a lower profile than I had seen before, like Go-Kart wheels. The cars looked like conventional Formula 1 machines that had been stretched by a mighty taffy puller.

"Jesus Christ," I muttered in Brunditz's ear. "We'll have to be mashed flat to fit in."

"Do you know the German for pancake?" asked Heinz. Like many drivers, he was a linguist with a good vocabulary in food, sex, and racing in about eight languages.

"Pfannküchen." We had begged for them for breakfast from the large cook at our grandfather's California ranch, the home that Heidelberg Beer and a tough geezer of an immigrant had built.

"You notice," said Rachid, "that the engine is enclosed in the frame back here. It is not part of the chassis, as in conventional Formula One cars."

"I never would have noticed," I said, and saw Sheik Abdel lift his head among the circle around the cars to scrutinize me. "Rachid, this is the damnedest thing I ever saw. The engine couldn't be more than a foot high."

"The inner works are still largely a secret," he said, shrugging imperceptibly. "The patent has been bought by Qataban from Schwandt's firm; that much is public. But the engine has been modified for racing purposes in ways known only to Schwandt, his technicians, and the Race Car Liaison Department for Qataban. I tested the thing, and they wouldn't even let me look inside."

"We'll reveal details to the FIA for certification when the time comes," said Schwandt. "In the meantime, no one needs to know except us. I can tell you this. It's a rotary-vane concept. The engine looks like a sawed-off washing machine. Around the perimeter are two ports. The fuel comes in one port, explodes between ports, then is expelled through the other port. Between the time the fuel comes in and ignition, there is a compression step, which acts like a turbocharger and greatly increases output. That step is highly classified, as are the metals used in the vanes. As you can imagine, they are under tremendous stress, as is the central shaft they are attached to. If there is a weak link, it is in the metal, and as drivers you will have to take certain precautions to prevent breakage."

"What he means is, you can't shift down," said Rachid. "It's bloody tricky. You've got all the horses in the world to get you going, and none around when you want to stop."

I had once driven a turbine machine for a couple of laps at Riverside and had almost died. A Grand Prix car with no compression for braking would be awkward to drive. We have to pull them down from over 210 to 30 miles per hour in a matter of 250 feet. The drivers, with the ball of the foot stamping on the brake and the heel deftly blipping the accelerator, downshift through five gears in about as many seconds. The tendency in recent years has been to rely more on the brakes, but no downshifting seemed unnatural.

"Those brakes better be classified, too," I suggested.

"The disks on all wheels are made of a new braking compound. The unit design is also revolutionary," said Rachid. "And when all else fails, you can put these cars sideways and scrub off the speed."

"Thanks," I mumbled.

"My ass is getting homesickness," said Brunditz under his breath. He enjoyed translating his native Bavarian argot literally.

Schwandt found a need to sound reassuring. "The car and the tires have been designed to accept that type of handling—more than the open-wheeled cars you are used to. And, I might add, we selected you for this tryout because each of you has had a background in motorcycles. This car requires a style like Tazio Nuvolari's or Berndt Rosemeyer's—people who are willing to let the back end hang out quite a bit, instead of trying to drive around the comers or rely on understeer. We also believe the crowds will like it. We intend to exploit this characteristic when we market sports and touring cars—a machine that can go right through the limit and still stay on the road."

"Are you going to sell us as accessories, just in case they go through the limit?" I heard myself ask. It was an insane jest. I was desperate for a job and here I was putting down the employer's product. The rigidity of the session was getting to me. Only Brunditz smiled.

"The engine is extraordinarily efficient," Schwandt said. "Therefore, you get almost no pollutants, and our mass production cars can meet any air-quality standards the Americans come up with. Now I believe it is getting light, so let us move to the pits."

In that spirit of good public health, a new goal in a sport that lacks for all but the most elemental motives, the group left the back of the garage and followed a concrete path toward a bluff and what I could dimly perceive as the Persian Gulf. We crossed a wide macadam apron and approached what appeared to be the rear of a row of pits, a low concrete-block structure with an aluminum roof. There seemed to be a road on the far side. We filed through a back door into a large pit enclosure, open on the other side, with our equipment and helmets waiting for us on the counter.

I leaned out and scanned the most impressive track surface I had seen anyplace, outside one or two circuits in Europe. It was the proverbial billiard table—wide, graded, and cambered to perfection. The concrete immediately in front of us tailed off into asphalt to our left, a surface that looked as if it had been sanded and painted.

"Where does it go? How long is this thing?" I asked Schwandt as he leaned next to me.

"It is a mix. To our left is an exact duplicate of the Südkere at the Nüburgring. One of my favorites. Also very instructional. The track doubles back, and you can make a U-turn to the right over there and it leads back to the pit straight. But take a left over there," he said, pointing almost opposite the pits, "and you will plunge down a steep hill and find yourself on an exact replication of the Grand Prix course at Long Beach. The Emir has decided we should introduce the cars at Long Beach."

"You're joking."

Schwandt ignored that and watched the two race cars being rolled toward us along the pits by the mechanics, then straightened up, his mammoth hands still on the counter, and watched the sun rising over the Persian Gulf. "The Emir's net oil revenues last year were seventeen billion dollars—for a country of less than half a million people, most of whom can't read or write. We—those of us hired for the auto project—have been told we have to change this from a country of camel breeders to automobile producers in a matter of months. We are to spend whatever is necessary, so I can assure you that the million dollars it took to build a couple of miles of tar and concrete to duplicate Long Beach wasn't even noticed."

A mechanic fired up one of the cars, and the sound was astonishing, a high-pitched wail in the night. It was more electrical than mechanical, a cross between ripping bed sheets and a Moog Synthesizer in top register. Schwandt tapped Brunditz on the shoulder and motioned us both to join him out back.

"The object today is to see if you can handle these cars and if you can improve on Rachid's lap times. I want you to go down to the ersatz Südkere and back up to the U-turn here a couple of times before you go out on the Long Beach circuit. Just get things sorted out and warmed up. If you have a question, stop.

"When you are out on the course, keep in mind that we have spotters. We will be in communication with them, and they will be taking pictures of you on videotape, as well as timing you over various parts of the course. We won't be talking with you by radio."

Radio communications between drivers and pit crews had been suspended in Formula 1 the previous year after a slick scandal involving intercepted transmissions and counterfeit transmissions. It probably cost one team the World Championship in a crucial race. The tendency now was not to rely on radios for anything, even during testing, until the FIA could sort out the security and bandwidth problems. It had been a debilitating electronic jag, and the radios had never been fully successful because Formula 1 cars are so insufferably noisy. Language was also a barrier. Some tapes of an Argentine ace trying to communicate with his Scottish crew chief are still replayed at parties along the Grand Prix seasonal circuit.

"Each car is worth more than a million dollars," Schwandt said, "so we would be most appreciative if you brought them back the way you find them. Lap records will not be necessary. Now that the sun is up, the wind is going away. There may be sand left on the course, so be cautious."

He went back through the door into the pit and then, with extraordinary grace, used his arm as a fulcrum to vault over the counter. The jet-pitched whine of both cars was utterly numbing. Heinz and I scrabbled for our earplugs, then put on helmet and gloves. We joined Schwandt on the pit apron, and he pointed to our cars. Mine had an orange strip around the nose. Two mechanics helped me in, a procedure that called for jackknifing under the instrument panel and steering wheel. I found myself almost flat on my back with my helmet propped more or less vertically. Nonetheless, the cockpit felt comfortable, with padding in the right places to keep me from rattling around under the intense G-forces of cornering, braking and acceleration.

"Comfortable?" asked Schwandt, shouting over the idling whine and through the layers of helmet and a Nomex cap. They must have known my measurements and used a lookalike for the cockpit dimensions.

I nodded. A mechanic reached in and helped me with an elaborate safety harness and coupled a hose from the foam protection layer of my suit to a discharge bottle in the cockpit. A second hose led to the coolant. So much for Qataban's plumbing.

"Be cautious," Schwandt mouthed. "There's still wind," and he flopped his hand around to indicate turbulence. I selected first gear, eased off the clutch, watched in awe as the engine revolutions soared up to the red line at 22,000 RPM, and felt the seat kick me in the back. I quickly snatched second gear.

The power and responsiveness of Grand Prix cars put them in a class by themselves, dragsters that turn corners. But this car was clearly on another plateau. It is about a quarter of a mile from the pits to the South Curve at the Nürburgring, a circuit I had raced on twice before it was shortened and ultimately boycotted by the Grand Prix teams for safety reasons.

Without really trying, I found myself heading into the duplicated corner in about seven seconds, so quickly that I almost wasn't ready for the left-turning entrance and the long right-hand loop, which is normally taken about 90 in a Formula 1 car. If a driver took time to think in a situation like this, he wouldn't survive. My instinct was to go easy on the car because its many complex systems were not yet warm—the tires, brakes, transmission, shock absorbers, and springs. Nor did I know how the car had been set up or balanced. I went into the corner standing heavily on the brakes, but not locking them up. The trick is to bed the brakes in without making a bald spot on the tires or losing control of the twitchy car. This also knocks the sheen off the rubber and gets the tire temperatures up quickly.

Halfway through the long right turn the car was still on the road and coasting along at about 40. I put it into first gear and accelerated back toward the pits, moving through the gears with deliberation.

The low black car almost flew down the short pit straight. My rear end recorded the slight snaking motion at the back of the car, and my in-built computer estimated the percent of weight the wings fore and aft were putting on the wheels. I arrived at the Südkere too fast again. I braked the Viper hard through the left-hand entrance, and the car started to slide wildly to the right. I snapped the wheel to the right, into the slide, deliberately overdoing it. The car now slid out to the left, and I cut the wheel to the left, meeting the slide and holding the car sideways as it went through the start of the right-hand turn. This smacked of dirt-track style—sloppy, perhaps, but an effective way to slow a car that has arrived at a corner too fast and a dramatic, if risky, way to get a car through a left-right comer.

Rachid had been correct. The car scrubbed speed perfectly. The apex went by, and the exit of the turn had opened up. By applying power, judiciously this time, and with the front wheels cocked in toward the grass, the slide became a drift, with all four wheels sliding at the same rate. At the exit, I applied more power, the rear wheels broke loose, and I entered the straight with full lock to the left.

The car snaked up the back straight toward the pits, and I could see in my mirrors that the rear tires were smoking as they alternately lost and gained traction. It occurred to me that the whole sequence through the comer must have sounded awful from where Schwandt stood, screaming tires and ragged engine notes.

I have always prided myself—a perverse delight—in being able to drive unfamiliar cars almost flat out, a habit that sometimes made team managers and racing engineers feel faint. As I backed off the throttle for the U-turn at the end of the straightaway, I heard the engine freewheeling. The gears and differential had been set up in some way so that compression and stress on the vanes was impossible. Schwandt was standing near the outside of the turn, pumping his hand up and down like a bird with one wing. Slow down, hell, I thought. Tell the car that. Instead, I ripped off down the pit straight, ready to finesse the Südkere with style. The ride, which had given me some apprehension, was now turning into a real joy. This time I planned to dive left before reaching the U-turn and join the Long Beach circuit.

The Long Beach race had been shut down for a year over a civic squabble but had reopened in newfound glory, the United States' only true road race, and around a harbor, at that. It lacks the *premier cru* quality of Monaco, and the 2.2-mile course with its twelve turns is not as challenging to the drivers, while being more brutal to the cars, but it has its place. The sharp downhill after the pit straight sucks the stomach up into the head, and it is desperately hard to get a car positioned correctly for the left tum at the bottom. After a less complicated right kink, the course opens up into a long left sweep that must be taken crisply to get the maximum benefit from the short straight up to the right hand hairpin. The cars blast out of this, accelerating fiercely from 40 to 190 miles per hour on the three-quarter-mile-long back straight, which has a blind, right-hand bend in the middle of it. A driver must go perilously deep into the next hairpin at the end of the straight, putting brakes down and throwing the car through the right-hander at the last tenth of a second. Another looping left, taken at about 90, is probably the crucial corner of the course. The car has to accelerate through it but somehow stay in position to enter the S-turns properly. They are difficult to take tidily in a Grand Prix car. The cars have too much power, and the road is too narrow. They spill out into a sharp right that must be taken under full power, never minding the solid retaining wall at the exit that is there to collect anyone who overcooks the speed. A climb back uphill and a sharp right puts the car back on the pit straight, a slightly more than quarter-mile run that brings the car back to the sharp downhill right. All of this takes a short breath more than a minute.

The Qataban version of the course pitched over a bluff and ran along a sandy plain next to the gulf, climbing back up to the bluff, the pit straight running along the top. I decided to run one tentative lap to see if it indeed was an exact duplicate of a course that I knew well. And it was uncanny, complete with the new curbs and a concrete block wall at the exit of the right turn at the bottom of the course to simulate the concrete wall that was sitting there in Long Beach. I hadn't yet had time to get a clear message from the car as to what it would do if the limit were irrevocably reached in a corner—would it snap into a viciously uncontrollable spin or fail to respond as the front wheels lost all traction and the car plowed nose-first off the course?

THE FORMULA ONE CIRCUIT AROUND THE STREETS OF LONG BEACH

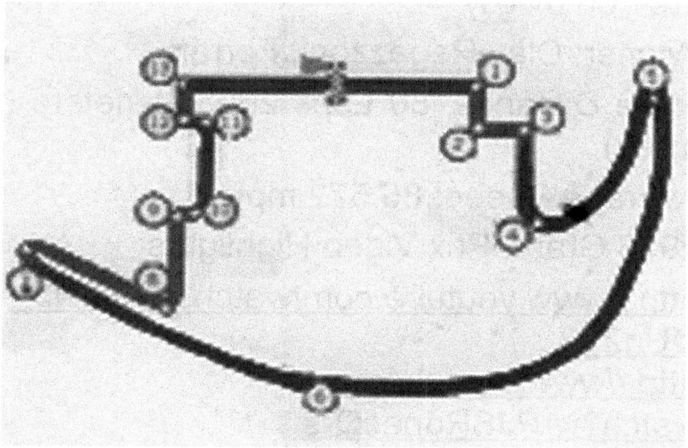

- Status: Temporary Road Course
- Course Length: 3.251 kilometers (2.2 miles)
- Features:

  - Pit Straight: Ocean Boulevard
  - Turn 1: Downhill Right
  - Turns 2 and 3: Sharp left and right
  - Turn 4: Looping left (About 90 mph)
  - Turn 5: Hairpin right
  - Turn 6: Right-hand kink in the backstraight (Fastest part of the course – 190 mph)
  - Turn 7: Hairpin right
  - Turn 8: Looping left (About 90 mph)
  - Turns 9-12: The Esses
  - Turn 13: Right onto the Pit Straight

- First F1 Race: March 28, 1976
- Course Distance: 80 laps, 260.08 kilometers (161.60 miles)
- Winner: Clay Regazzoni, Ferrari
- Race Distance: 80 Laps 260 kilometers (161 miles)
- Average Speed: 85.572 mph
- 1976 Grand Prix Video Highlights:

  http://www.youtube.com/watch?v=BCN5_QUgZ_8
  http://www.youtube.com/watch?v=PJSRgnecQ-s

By the time I got back up on the bluff, I had some of the answers, and I let the car out, blasting past the pits at about 160, a good ten miles faster than I had ever been able to get a car down the pit straight at Long Beach. The rotary engine felt like an afterburner. I caught a glimpse of Schwandt, no longer flapping his arm. I braked hard and literally hurled the car around the sharp right and down the bluff, but the car had predictability in its abandon. I swept through the next three turns in full-lock slides, using the car like a motocross machine. The wings were highly effective, the immense down-force steadying the car before the corners, a moment of poise before the impossible angles that followed. The inability to shift down allowed me to concentrate on the acrobatics, freeing me to enter a new level of intensity. Even in sandy sections of pavement, there seemed to be no limit to the car's tractability.

On the second lap, I discarded Schwandt's advice and went for a fast time. The qualifying lap record at Long Beach last season was 1:08.3, or a twitch more than one minute and eight seconds. The curbs had been modified, making the course much quicker. To break that might cost me a berth on the team just on grounds of insubordination alone, much less if something let go and the car ended up in the Persian Gulf. But I was bored with being humble and driving nicely for the half-dozen people around the course who were hunched over the videotape cameras.

Screw it, I thought, if they wanted to bring back the days of screaming, crossed-up Auto Unions, they were going to have to get used to sweaty palms in the pits. At moments like this I also recollect that in four years, when I will be thirty-two, I get a check for a quarter-million dollars from the Trust Department of Heidelberg Beer. Not a fortune, as the press was so fond of calling it, but enough of a cushion to allow me to risk early retirement. It could buy the proverbial farm, which is what I envisioned, one with a trout stream through it and deer that conveniently stepped out of the woods at the far end of the pasture, waiting to be bagged.

I cursed at myself for letting the mind float, even for a split second. Driving at speed requires concentration to an abnormal degree, like bringing a jet fighter in for a night landing on an aircraft carrier.

As I passed the pits on my first flying lap, I saw Schwandt standing as if listening to "Deutschland über Alles." It occurred to me that this was probably the first time, except for the initial tests by Rachid, that they knew for sure whether the Viper would go straight, sideways, or up in the air. This was opening night for a billion-dollar production, and the critics could judge the rotary cars by matching their times against the lap record at Long Beach.

The next time past the pits, a sign told me that the previous lap had been 1:06.7, well below the Long Beach qualifying record but perhaps not fast enough to compensate for the differences in track surface. The car was superior, but the track was fast. After another precise lap, if a chain of smoking power slides and fishtailing straightaways could be considered precise, I logged a time of l:06.4, probably enough to account for the difference in pavement. Then I decided to do a few things differently. I tried new approaches, different lines through the comers, deliberately defying the conventions to find out what the soul of the car was all about. But at this extreme limit the car became balky and too skittish going into the corners. It needed more work. It would have to be better set up for a full-fledged Grand Prix campaign.

After climbing back on the bluff, I put the car in neutral and coasted toward the pits. The car rolled to a halt, and a mechanic reached in to switch off the engine.

Schwandt stood by the car, unsmiling. "Sheik Abdel is in the third pit down. He wants to see you."

"That's fine, Schwandt, just fine. That car is a nice piece of work."

Brunditz went by the pits at a terrific rate. I remembered a documentary that recorded the sound of a rocket attack on the Russian front near Stalingrad. Brunditz outdid Zhukov by several decibels.

Sheik Abdel was seated at a cloth-covered card table in the center of the pits. A battery of television screens glared at him along the back wall. He turned from watching Brunditz's progress as a cabinet minister smoothly poured a steaming, viscous liquid into a small glass with a spoon in it. The air had a mint smell.

"Mr. Walter, Schwandt tells me you are totally undisciplined, that your antics on the course this morning were outrageous, and that you broke the lap record. I would like to offer you a contract for this season for three hundred thousand dollars, plus forty percent of the winnings. Does that suit you?"

* * *

On October 5, the CIA Deputy Director of Operations at Langley received brief memoranda from the chiefs of station at Paris and Jubil:

> To: DDO
> From: COS Paris
> Top Secret
>
> Because of delays, the Formula 1 target is still poorly penetrated. Two mechanics remain from the original net, but their reliability is severely limited by the difficulties of their work. Four other

mechanics have been recruited, three in England and one here, but none has yet been assigned to Formula 1 cars. After our unfortunate accidents, no drivers have been approached and we have made no effort to train an agent for this work. Electronic surveillance possibilities are circumscribed by the constant movement of the teams and their cohesive nature.

Due to our position at this point, I would recommend using Thistle. Phone contact indicates her negative attitude is unchanged, but she recognized the precarious nature of the situation at Jubil and wisely decided not to follow her husband there until she had made contact with us. Since she is highly motivated to protect him and has an excellent degree of familiarity with the target, Thistle would be most useful.

To: DDO
From: COS Jubil

Reliable Western business contacts report serious bottlenecks prevent auto and truck production from going ahead on schedule. The foundries and tooling appear to be progressing under German guidance, but lack of labor may set everything back at least six months. Local government sources say that managers are looking for new ways to automate.

The German firm apparently calls all the signals, under the review of Abdel. The chain of command is less clear with the Racing Department. That operation is separate and under tight control. Our usual contacts are unable to supply data. Terrorist possibilities are still a subject of rumor in Jubil, and our source in Marib reports unusual security beyond anything required for the racing effort.

If Thistle's driver joins the team, she would face a high degree of risk once inside their compound. But lack of data production by almost all standard contacts suggests her high value. Her secure cover should be sufficient.

~:~

3.

> Grand Prix racing has always been regarded by Continental nations as one of the highest exercises of professional skill in design, construction and driving. Large numbers of companies have exerted immense efforts and spent vast sums, drivers have been retained at high fees, and have driven under strict team orders—not, it may be mentioned, always obeyed.
>
> Laurence Pomeroy
> *Grand Prix Car*
> Motor Racing Publications, Ltd.

The black disk spun out over the sand beach, wobbling slightly from the wind, and disintegrated into a puff of black clay dust. An identical disk, coming from the opposite direction, met the same end. The twin reports from Aimee's 20-gauge Purdey were almost one blur of sound.

"You don't have to hit them that square," I said, moving off to reload the traps. "A knick here and there will do."

"No comments, please," she said, breaking open the over-and-under breech and looking obviously happy about her performance.

During the month we had been in Qataban—the entire month of January—our skill with the matched Purdeys, wedding presents to each other, had improved to a level that neither of us would have believed possible. But then neither of us would have believed how long and tedious the effort to set the cars up for the season had turned out to be.

Despite their initial show of speed and deft handling, the Vipers proved to be frail and temperamental. Under sustained testing, we hit one technical snag after the other. I had driven the cars off and on during November and December, while commuting from Paris. Aimee and I had vacationed over Christmas at St. Anton, where I did mostly cross-country skiing to keep my legs in one piece, and then we had flown to Marib on January 2 to take up what seemed like permanent residence in the Racing Department's motel.

On our first day there, after the morning test session, Aimee and I had borrowed an orange van and had driven into town. Marib had the charm of a government project.

"Take all our schlock traits, bundle them up and export them, and you'd have this," Aimee had moaned as we drove down the near-empty four-lane boulevard past slabs of concrete apartment buildings arranged like an urban domino bone yard.

"Here's some color, tepid but authentic," I said as we drove up to the focal point of town, the mosque. We could hear the muezzin calling the faithful to prayer over a scratchy loudspeaker. Three large cars—two Cadillacs and a Lincoln, all driven uncertainly—turned into a gate and disappeared into an inner courtyard.

"Lovely, Gus. What's the next high point?" I turned toward the waterfront. It was growing hot, and the acres of cement around us seemed to be quivering. Marib had once been a coastal fishing village, and it was supposed to have a commercial fleet. We pulled onto an esplanade and had a good view of the hefty breakwater and harbor the Emir had built with oil revenues. Tied up along the quay were the new fishing boats bought by the government, snappy white seiners with racks of radar masts. But except for a few deckhands who were picking desultorily at some nets, there was no activity. It looked as if the fleet had been quarantined.

"That's truly exciting, like Newport Beach or Saint Malo," she said.

I kept looking for more signs of life. The oil industry had literally passed the town by. There were no oil rigs or petrochemical plants in sight, but a continuous parade of supertankers glided by offshore, headed for Selal, Qataban's deepwater port somewhere up the coast.

I thought I had identified something human when we passed a large, block-long lot with an impromptu open-air market. Awnings and tents had been propped up in a field, and people were arriving and departing in older cars. We got out and walked through the stalls, surrendering ourselves as objects of curiosity and what I sensed was animosity.

"Not a very happy market," said Aimee. "I want more highlights."

I drove on. We had found the town dump, an enormous pile of crud on the other edge of town. I'd hawked that as a highlight, but I'd run out of ideas and headed back to the motel wondering how I could ginger up Aimee into accepting Marib as home while we drivers did the necessary test work on the cars.

The track headquarters, garages, motel, and airport were all located on the bluff overlooking the harbor. The plateau of sand and rock stretched from there to a horizon of low hills. The capital city of Qataban, Jubil, was located a hundred miles inland, connected only by Air Qataban and by camel. The assembly plants and manufacturing superstructure for the Qatabani auto industry were being built there, but Brunditz and I had not been taken to Jubil yet, although Rachid had made several trips. Schwandt mentioned something about Jubil's being a holy city and our being shown the works at the proper time, although I failed to make the connection.

Meanwhile, parts and freight flowed into our airport on an Air Qataban 707 freighter that seemed to be at our personal disposal, as Schwandt would order it off to Europe or Jubil at a moment's notice. The buildup of materiel at the garages looked like a Panzer depot. And still the cars broke down—vanes, brakes, suspension, transmission, frame. Over a period of two months all three cars, and the training spare, were rebuilt several times over. We drove them during the early morning hours according to lap times strictly set by Schwandt; then we sat for the rest of the day at the motel, sometimes getting in an evening test session if the heat dropped below a hundred degrees, which wasn't often.

Aimee and I didn't do any more sightseeing. We found we hadn't seen much on our first tour because the Qatabanis in Marib stay air-conditioned and tuned to government cable television. The open-air market was attended only by the foreign labor force, who were doing the buying for Qatabani households. None of the servants we had been dealing with at the hotel were even Arabs, but were part of the corps of workers brought from Iran and Turkey to do the scut work. The Qatabanis received an oil royalty income per capita, which I heard pegged at between $25,000 and $85,000 per year, though nobody around the hotel was terribly open about these things.

Aimee and I tried to use the swimming pool, but it was as hot as the air and suffered from an algal slime. We had briefly tried playing tennis with Brunditz and his girl, whom he had introduced simply as Mimi, a stunning Indonesian from Amsterdam. But after one set we were done in. So we kept to our room, read books, did calisthenics, and made long and undistracted love. But even this had begun to pall, and after the second week Aimee and I agreed to abandon the air-conditioned cell of our room and ignore the heat.

I'd had Schwandt order three cases of shotgun shells and an elaborate trapshooting set complete with ten thousand clay pigeons. They'd arrived a day later from London. We'd unlimbered the Purdeys, which we had originally brought with us just to admire and keep clean; then, dressed in pith helmets and desert tunics, we'd set off along the beach in a borrowed van and had quickly found the ideal spot to set up our range. Since then we had plunked about five hundred clay birds a day, critiquing our own shots and getting better by the hour, hitting about ninety-six out of a hundred.

We came back from our shooting session on February 1 dank with sweat, as usual, and ready for champagne, which Schwandt made available to us in our rooms, and a shower, which was always a letdown. The fixture looked promising, but there was almost no water pressure. Maintenance didn't seem to be Qataban's strong point.

Schwandt must have gotten by another problem, I thought as I saw the label on the bottle of the day, Dom Pérignon. I took a glass to Aimee, who was in the bathtub trying to extract hot water from a fretful faucet while reading the latest batch of newspapers brought in by the freight plane. She read them inveterately and indiscriminately—*The London Times, Le Monde. Frankfurter Zeitung*. The sections on motor sports she translated for me; the rest she digested. Politics, fashion, crime, fads, furniture, theater.

Sometimes she had left me. Over the year we first lived together, she would fly to London or Vienna for two or three days between races and attend the theater, ballet, concerts, eat at the new restaurants, visit shops. She was a dedicated correspondent and wrote a steady stream of letters to friends, mostly female. I had used the time to work with the mechanics, long nights in cramped garages, eating poorly and drinking too much coffee. Without notice or comment she would return, a migrating animal who would appear at the door of the van, enigmatic and somehow fulfilled. I'd asked her once after a three-day trip to Salzburg if she had been sleeping with another man. "I don't care for quickies," she had said. I'd also asked if she were doing some designated hitting for her former government employers, and she had replied with a rich mixture of expletives.

"The whole world's gone absolutely bonkers," she commented in the bathtub from the depths of *France-Soir*, its bold headlines signaling something about a *crise*. I admired the sleek long black hairs of her crotch, still high and dry, and resisted the temptation to jump in, throwing confusion into a placid twilight.

"Here, have some Dom Pérignon, courtesy of the Protector of the Faith, and let those little bubbles bombard your delicate palate."

"India just exploded another H-bomb, and you've got to get all excited about a bubbly drink."

"Beats *le rouge d'Algerie*," I said, perching on the sink and turning to *The London Times* sports section to see if it carried the practice times for the Brazilian Grand Prix at Interlagos. We were skipping the first three Grand Prix to make our team debut in California. The pages were filled with a ritualistic New Zealand cricket tournament.

"As if H-bombs weren't bad enough, get this," she said.

"'New Wave of Terrorism Hits France, England.' Within two weeks, some group—it's believed to be the same one—has blown up a large solar collector power plant in the Pyrenees, a wave motor power project on the Brittany coast, and then tried to do in a gas-cooled nuclear reactor in Scotland. That caper didn't come off, fortunately, or the Loch Ness Monster would have been glowing like Big Ben."

"Trivia. Just some of the boys having a little clean guerrilla fun."

We both read on. The hot water surged forth from time to time and then declined. "Dom Pérignon makes me feel guilty," Aimee said, holding her glass out for another refill. "If the whole world can't drink it, then nobody should."

"It isn't like having the *Mona Lisa* in your den, you know. It's just that you have no concept of merit—the big payoff for risking one's ass, or reputation, or health, or whatever."

"Ah, you're getting soft, Gus *chérie*. Only a few months ago a cold beer in the van was like nectar. Next thing you're going to need is a valet, someone to fold your undies."

“Not a bad thought,” I said, pouring out the rest of the bottle, wondering why the indentation at the bottom seemed to accelerate the end so unfairly.

We met Brunditz in the hall after our bath. He was dressed in a stark black turtleneck and white denims, a blond Druid god with hair to the shoulders bearing his girl in tow. Mimi had been mostly silent, comfortable in the Dutch she spoke with Heinz, but melting every man in sight with large ripe-olive eyes that came out of *Geographic* articles about Bali. Aimee had broken through Mimi’s barriers a few times and picked up some of the singsong and liquid-sounding German of the Dutch language, but both couples found a need to preserve some distance, as if fearing that since there was so little else to do, there would be nothing left but each other.

“Punctuality is our national stereotype,” said Heinz as we headed down the corridor toward the small private dining room. “But I’ll bet Schwandt is waiting for us at the door with his stopwatch ticking.”

We entered a low-ceilinged dining room, the kind the Rotarians and Lions have their Thursday luncheons in, except the drapes were velvet and the wall sconces came from Venice. Schwandt presided at one end of the polished mahogany table, china and silver arranged within millimeters. There were no Arabs at the table except the solitary, enigmatic Rachid, a pattern that had begun when the team had first assembled in October. The Qatabani mechanics and technicians lived in a separate wing and ate in their own dining room. Schwandt said they were observing Islamic law.

Rachid had opened up somewhat under constant kidding and prying by me and Heinz when we met for dinner. He told us he first drove as a cabdriver in Oran, started racing motorcycles, and quickly established a reputation along the North African coast. A benefactor, whom he left unidentified, had selected him for further training in Europe and England. Another sponsor, whom he also left obscure, but I suspected was an Arab country, had financed him in Formula 2, then Formula 1 last season. He'd walked away with ten championship points, exceptionally good for a first-year private entry stacked against the commercially sponsored and factory cars.

On the test track at Marib he became steadily faster, although our lap times were carefully circumscribed by Schwandt's orders. All three of us cheated by screaming through certain sections of the course and dogging it at other sections so that each lap time would average out to a slower speed. I wondered what would happen when Schwandt let us go.

"We have a calculatedly light repast for you tonight. No heavy stomachs in the morning," Schwandt said as the group assembled and found seats. The non-Muslims included a German tire technician, introduced by Schwandt as Herr Heubner, who spoke only in High German monosyllables. To his left was a Belgian suspension specialist, Petre Priest, voluble but creative when it came to cars. Across from Aimee and me sat a Japanese engineer who had done some sort of early development work on the vane engine and shared in the patent. The incongruous Herr Osawa, as Schwandt called him, spoke all languages, all of them badly, but his capacity for staying with a problem for days and nights without sleep until a flaw in a part had been reworked and tooled out of the engine made me feel Sybaritic. Mimi and Aimee were the only females attached to the team. Drivers presumably were the only personnel with the time and temperament for dalliance.

At times like this, I speculated about the Spartan lives of the Qatabani mechanics. Since I came out of a motocross background, I knew what team discipline could mean, although even in my brilliant teens, as I liked to think of them, the rules seemed to apply last to me. At nineteen I was on one of the hot Japanese teams, and it put me off the way the Japanese mechanics were drilled like gymnasts. The slightest lapse brought a one-way ticket to Tokyo, and the factory sent a replacement within twenty-four hours. Even then, the Team Mitsawa mechanics seemed at least quasi-human. The Qatabani men, uniformly in their twenties, struck me as alien beings. But all of this was the pimple on top of a professional problem that had been nagging me for weeks. My train of thought suddenly surfaced.

"Schwandt, I don't like this distance from the mechanical side of the operation. Some of the most crucial rebuilding work has been going on in Jubil as you fly the cars back and forth. They come back the same way they were sent. Patched up, maybe, but with a lot of the same handling faults." A pair of Iranian servants brought in dishes of clear soup and poured flinty white wine.

"You're paid to drive," said Schwandt, but he seemed to pull back, since the value of the driver in the testing process would be difficult to argue against. Some drivers are simply unimaginative throttle stompers, fools who could go fast in the rain or drive flat out through an accident scene, weaving between the ambulances, but their part in the sport had always been limited, usually by an untimely end against something obdurate, like a fence post.

Most top drivers in Formula 1 are sensitive about setting up cars. They have engineering degrees or have worked under cars enough to tell the mechanics and designers precisely what it felt like when the machine twitched at the entrance of a l40-mile-per-hour curve, costing them two-tenths of a second on the lap time, or how the engine lacked 300 revolutions per minute in third gear between two corners, or peaked too early between two turns, forcing an upshift and immediate downshift, the whole thing taking place so fast that it sounded like three notes on an organ, a trill, but also cost precious hundredths of a second, the stuff of competitive lap times. Despite my love of the tail-out power slide, I knew I was in the sensitive camp and had built up enough of a reputation as a test driver to fend off Schwandt if he counterattacked.

"I still think you ought to cut out the middleman," I said, which I suppose wasn't all that diplomatic, since I meant him. "When I pull in, I want to talk to the people who are doing the final work."

"They won't understand. Terrible English."

"German? French? Swahili?"

"Unfortunately, you will have to learn Arabic, and classes in language are not part of our schedule."

I turned to Brunditz. "Are you getting through?"

"It makes no difference," Heinz drawled. "The car goes. If it goes, it goes."

"And goes," I said, reckless chemicals starting to pound through the head. "Maybe we should learn which way Mecca is and leave it at that. Which way is Mecca, Schwandt?"

The servants were passing a tureen of seafood, a vast pot of claws and shells and white hunks of fish sloshing in a wine sauce. All the food was flown in from Europe, I had found. Schwandt heaped his dish, following it with rice and asparagus.

"Herr Walter," he said slowly, "your humor is often appreciated; it is good for our nerves. But the religious theme must be studiously avoided. I'm sure Herr Rachid Bashir will confirm that our employers feel most strongly about their image in the Western world. It is one reason—perhaps the primary reason—this team has been formed and that you were hired. Therefore, as their employees, we have an obligation to promote that image, or at least to do nothing to detract from it. Above all, we must respect their religious beliefs."

Brunditz and I exchanged a flick of the eye. The technicians were picking at crab meat.

"This is probably an excellent time to bring up conduct," said Schwandt. "We will live in our own quarters this season—no hotels except those we have to ourselves. The necessary houses and garages have all been rented for the rest of the season. Two days a week you are all free to go where you wish, do what you want, as long as it doesn't get in the newspapers in a negative way. From Wednesday through Sunday you are subject to team rules. We are all being paid generously."

"This wasn't made clear in October," I said in a way that I hoped was even. "There was no mention of lockups or living apart according to the Koran."

"Aha, you go too far again, Herr Walter. You are now sipping Pouilly-Fuissé 'seventy-one. That is not on the recommended list of the Koran. There will be many perquisites and comforts. You will each soon get your own Viper road cars, which are very fast indeed, I understand from preliminary reports. You will have ample cash for your two-day vacations. But as a team we will stay apart. We are working with a new, largely secret technology, with highly sensitive employers who are anxious to industrialize their country while they have the capital to do it and before the oil runs out. You may choose to drop out, of course, Herr Walter, but it must be now, before the first race."

Aimee's sandal nudged my shin. It was an ambiguous nudge. Go ahead, you coward, advise this totalitarian *cochon* to blow it out. Or, keep your irreverent and foolish tongue silent. My peripheral vision caught Aimee slowly relishing a taste of Pouilly-Fuissé '71.

"Ah, well, Schwandt," I heard myself say, "it's only for a part of one season, and we can adapt to a few months of anything, short of bed checks. Just give us fast, reliable cars."

"Let's make deals, Herr Walter," he said, lifting a glass. "We'll give you the fast car. You keep it in one piece and win us a championship."

"How was I supposed to know what that kick meant?" I asked Aimee in our bedroom.

"It was a simple Keep Quiet kick."

"But look at it logically. By your standards we should have thrown crab claws at him and walked out. Now we've totally abandoned our freedom and become the charges of a Prussian wet nurse."

"You're so good with machines and so dumb with people," she said, rolling her body against mine in the hard but massively accommodating bed.

"Besides," she said slowly, "I like the idea of going to bed instead of dancing in the discotheques and drinking with your friends. I'd like to have your Pan's body exclusively mine."

Her short but well-formed fingernails drummed a light tattoo on my stomach, moving inexorably lower.

The next morning, I committed the ultimate sin, the defilement of Schwandt's most sacred canon, by setting a lap time around the test course that was considerably faster than he had assigned. It felt faster than the lap record I had set during the October trials and far below the qualifying lap record at Long Beach set last year by Ushi Tifumo, the Japanese ace, shortly before he died at Spa. The Viper did it with surprisingly little flap and dust, although I knew as I turned it that I was on the knife edge of disaster each foot of the way. Driving through the long right-hand bend on the back straight at almost 200 was like going into orbit. The car seemed to launch itself out the exit and fly at the waiting hairpin. I sensed that if something snapped, the car would soar off across the beach and skip out into the Persian Gulf like a properly flung river stone.

Evidently Schwandt sensed this, too. When I pulled in to answer his angry pit signals, Osawa said I was to join Schwandt in his office in the garage.

"Incredibly stupid, Herr Walter," he said as I took a seat on the opposite side of the metal desk. "Totally unnecessary, and by all laws you should have lost control of the car."

"I didn't."

"It's risky. None of us yet really knows what these machines are doing at the limit. When I want you to let things out, I will tell you. Until then, you will drive the lap times I give you. Clear?"

"Clear." It seemed dangerous to tell him I was bored by the whole autocratic operation and we had three more weeks before leaving for California, three more weeks marooned in Arabia.

"Otherwise, you will spend the rest of the season driving Go-Karts in Argentina! I will not allow you to disrupt our planning."

"But you know there's still a hell of a lot left in these cars. They're just picking up speed at two hundred."

"Moderation, Herr Walter. Steady, informative laps in the one-ten to one-fifteen range. No risks. No thrills. Not yet. We are not ready yet."

"Just one more point, Schwandt. I'm curious. Our employers—where the hell are they? We haven't seen Sheik Abdel and the contingent from Harvard Business School since the trials."

"In the first place, Sheik Abdel is not our employer," Schwandt said, sitting up a bit straighter, wary, it seemed. "The Emir of Qataban, Protector of the Faith, and the ultimate check-signer for our racing team, is the person we answer to. He arrives *this* weekend, for your information, and we will provide him with a demonstration. He will arrive by boat—a very large boat, you will find."

Schwandt had excellent information because the next morning there was no argument about the size of the Emir's yacht.

"This you have to see," said Aimee from the window. "It must have come in overnight."

I left the bed and peered into the weak morning light that made Marib's harbor look like a dim color slide. In the center of the harbor stretched a coal-black yacht with the orange Qataban flag on its large, rakish funnel.

"It's like a cruiser. Must be five hundred, six hundred feet."

"I've seen pictures of it in the fashion magazines," said Aimee. "Gold faucets, mother-of-pearl bidets, compasses in every stateroom to keep a permanent fix on Mecca."

The breakfast trays arrived and I fetched them at the door, since apparently the very glimpse of Aimee in night clothes was enough to give young

Iranian waiters paralysis. As we ate, I began pulling on the first layers of fireproof clothing.

"This opens up a whole new world," said Aimee. "I think Mimi and I will angle for lunch on that floating mosque out there."

"Remember, the bidets are there to wash your feet in," I said, turning toward the door. "And don't handle the food with your left hand or I'll be driving Go-Karts in the Argentine."

I should have anticipated the problem. Schwandt, I'm sure, thought he had such control that it could never happen. But then, racing drivers are probably some sort of human mutation, a variant of the species that has branched off bravely but is bound to exterminate itself through sheer folly.

Schwandt had coached us on how to greet the Emir—an awkward protocol session in the pits—and then he drove the drivers, with Mimi and Aimee, down to Turn One in an orange van. "*Emir,*" he had instructed us, means "head" or "king," and we were to call him "Your Highness." Schwandt's attitude had been totally humorless, the heat was breathtaking, and I could feel pools of sweat accumulating beneath the Nomex.

We saw a line of a half-dozen black limousines parked on the apron of the track, to the right and out of our line as we would be entering the tight downhill right-hander. A wide red carpet stretched across the sand and stones to the Emir's open-sided tent, which was on a small rise. It overlooked much of the track, where the road plunged down the bluff and into the first series of turns. The back straight disappeared to our right.

The Emir stood in front of a deep couch draped in thick ocher fabric. His face, framed by headdress, had a desert bird's eyes, locked on prey miles distant, and a nose that hooked like a child's elbow. Below it was a compact gray beard that summed up his aging appearance into a piratical conclusion. His black outer robe was stitched in gold on the sleeves and down the front. The white inner garments were infinitely pleated and cold white.

Sheik Abdel stood to the Emir's left. He seemed reduced in stature since I had last seen him, but the Emir was one of those political leaders whose presence reduces everybody. To the Emir's right was another, younger Arab, extraordinarily tough-looking, his narrow almond eyes beneath slashing eyebrows and his cropped black beard giving him a look of disciplined symmetry.

The Emir shook Brunditz's and my hands wordlessly, and as he reached Rachid they embraced and spoke briefly in Arabic, his rolling basso resonating from the rich garments. He nodded to the women noncommittally. A pause followed; then the Emir turned to me.

"You hunt, I am told."

"When I have the time, Your Highness."

"You have had the time here, I understand. You have been shooting shotguns."

"My wife and I practice with traps out on the beach. We use twenty-gauge Purdeys, but the birds are strictly clay."

He looked at Aimee, lingering this time. "I have several Purdeys. You must hunt with me one day. Although I prefer rifles. I can pluck the eye from an antelope at three hundred meters with a Mannlicher, as can any of my tribesmen," he said, nodding obliquely toward the dozen or so men standing around the rear of the tent platform. "We practiced as children on RAF fighter planes and could hit them on the wing with matchlock muskets. When the Raj left, we lost our targets. Perhaps our aim has suffered."

The elegant man with the Oxford overtones was involved in some metaphoric message that I didn't follow.

"I like your bird," I said. It sat on a low perch near the couch.

"The peregrine makes us all mortal, my dear fellow. He kills as cleanly as Allah meant us to. Would that we could dispense justice as well as this one does."

I had been told about the chopping block in Marib's police courtyard, and there were rumors about how the Koran was being upheld in Jubil. I could see advantages to being slammed from out of an empty sky by a falcon.

"Drive well," he said, resuming his seat and giving us Allah's blessing. We left for the van to return to the pits. Schwandt gave us our marching orders as we drove back:

"You get one parade lap. Stay nose-to-tail with Rachid in the front, Walter next. Then pick up the pace for a second lap together. After that, give yourselves room. I want two hundred yards or more between cars in case someone loses it. Put in three good laps in the one-ten to one-twelve range, whatever feels comfortable in this heat. But no faster. The tire compounds will not take it. Understood?"

We moved out with the cars quickly before the air-cooled engines seized up. If it hadn't been for the coolant in our driving suits, we would have passed out in the cockpits. The noise from the three cars traveling at such close quarters could have shattered steel plates. We yanked the cars from side to side to scrub the tires and heat them.

We cut out the sluicing back and forth and pitched to the right over the hill, staying in second gear until the back straight, when Rachid began to accelerate deliberately up through the five gears. The lap was boring, and I didn't feel we were accomplishing much that morning, except to make noise for the Emir and his entourage. The length of the parade lap gave me time to think about the significance of Rachid in the lead. I had the uncomfortable feeling that we were setting a precedent for the year and that the Son of Muhammad was going to be getting the nod.

In times past, a team manager like Alfred Neubauer of Mercedes-Benz could select a race winner and make his team orders stick. It was still possible for a team to favor one driver, but there were limits, particularly if the favored one was not an indisputable Numero Uno, a Jackie Stewart or Niki Lauda, who commanded total respect. But Rachid and I were equals at the wheel. His style was slightly more conservative than mine, and while he saved time through his tidiness, my tail-smoking audaciousness canceled him out. Brunditz was only a shade slower, as if still reluctant to let the new car out fully.

We reached the top of the bluff and began to space out along the straight as Schwandt had ordered. Rachid accelerated away, and I held even, while Brunditz fell back. By the start and finish I was going full tilt, ready to show the fellows in the tent how we intended to take the first turn at Long Beach.

We had studied the turn for hours, and the technique we settled on required an almost complete rebuild of the cars. The hill is so steep that Grand Prix cars have a tendency to become airborne as they round the corner and plunge downward. Most drivers back off to keep the cars on the ground and the suspensions from breaking on impact. We rebuilt the suspensions and deliberately put the cars in the air. Since they were off balance from the right turn at the top, they tended to thrash sideways when they landed, which left them pointing the wrong way for the left turn at the bottom of the hill, about a hundred yards away. That was solved, after several nervy excursions off the road by me in the training car, by landing with a trailing throttle and full lock to the left, which snapped the car sideways the other way, leaving it pointing into the left-hand turn. It looked and was a highly dangerous maneuver, but, like motocross technique, it was predictable in its insanity.

I did it now, leaving a trail of dust and smoke, and continued to let the car hang out through the next series of turns, taking the looping right onto the backstraight like a yo-yo being spun at the end of its string. On the straight we unleashed the Vipers, and there could have been little doubt up on the bluff that we were going to stir things up abroad. At the end of the straight I braked the car and snatched a look in the rearview to see Brunditz closing in. At the last fraction of a second he put the car sideways and somehow made it through the hairpin. By the time we reached the next turn he had closed the gap. I let things out through the Esses, even grabbing a higher gear for an instant in the middle of the turns. We screamed up the hill, nose-to-tail, and hit the pit straight with a vengeance, closing on Rachid by the end of it.

At the end of the back straight we both swept by him as we entered the hairpin, a maneuver that I vaguely realized might have repercussions, but my body was too full of the absolute tonic of the chase. The shrieking cars and animal grip of their power made everything else irrelevant, a mental block-out of sexual proportions. Schwandt stood, hatless in the heat, at the edge of the track, well out from the pits and almost in our path.

For an instant sanity prevailed and I began braking earlier than usual for Turn One, but Brunditz darted by on the inside and by the time we reached the bottom of the hill I was on his tail again. Rachid was nowhere to be seen. I couldn't get by Brunditz for two more laps, although not for lack of trying. On the last lap we entered the hairpin at the end of the back straight side by side, and I nipped him on the inside of the turn under heavy braking, forcing him to swing wide.

He crowded me through the Esses, and I plowed into the right-hand turn that headed up the hill with my right foot firmly into it. The car drifted toward the concrete wall on the outside, which had been placed there to keep our lap times honest, when something let loose. I clobbered the concrete at well over 80 miles per hour, caving in both left wheels and scraping noisily and ignominiously up the hill, coming to rest almost at the top with cement dust filling the cockpit and a ringing in the ears, as if a blood vessel had been jarred loose deep in the cranium.

Then silence. I had flicked off the ignition at the instant of impact. Brunditz wailed down the distant pit straight. Rachid slowed for a moment, looking over at me, and I waved him on with a quick snap of the wrist. I almost preferred to be injured, since that might give me some means to drum up sympathy and divert attention from my stupidity.

I took off my helmet and sat, nauseous from the heat and jarring contact with the wall, trying not to think. From past shunts during testing, I knew it would take Schwandt, driving the course backward, about two minutes to reach me in his van. In case of something serious, he had an ambulance with trained Qatabani paramedics ready to roll and the doctor in the clinic in town on standby at all times we were on the track. We could be flown to a hospital in Jubil, if necessary, and he kept a 727 jet at the ready.

Just as I was beginning to enjoy the solitude and will myself into unconsciousness, I saw a black car, an inspiring Rolls-Royce Silver Wraith, loom up in the rearview. It stopped inches from my wheels, the windows being so much higher than my position that I had to tilt my head backward. The rear window hissed down, and the Emir looked down at me.

"Perhaps this will help, my dear boy. Our heat can be punishing," he said, handing down a black umbrella. I opened it, admiring its true silk and the texture of the warthog tusk handle. It brought an air of Edwardian civility to the wreckage. I thanked him.

"You take too many chances," he said. "You can afford to be mellow at your age. Now that you have a chance to be the best, you should be deliberate, like my falcon here."

"Thank you, Your Highness, but it's hard to keep things in hand when you have seven hundred horsepower to work with in a thirteen-hundred-pound car."

"We are all troubled by excesses. I have a treasury that is turning this country into a nation of pleasure-seeking, indolent imbeciles. We all have to remember discipline and the existence of higher purpose. Good-bye, my friend." The head retreated back into the car like a detached figure in *Alice in Wonderland.* I heard his bass voice invoking Allah as the window whizzed up. The Rolls pulled away noiselessly, as if it had no engine at all, and I was left under my umbrella to think about higher purposes.

"Where did you get that umbrella?" asked Schwandt in flat tones a few moments later. "You carry one with you, no doubt, for when you stupidly crash the car."

"It's the Emir's. He asked me to return it to him when we get to Long Beach." For the moment I thought I might have had a trump card to stop Schwandt's formidable long suits. At least I didn't think he could fire me before Long Beach. He got back in the van, wordlessly inspected the streak of scraped black paint that ran for over a hundred yards up the wall, and drove away, while I waited under the shade for the tow truck.

* * *

On February 9, *the CIA Deputy Director of Operations called a communications man into his office and then entered into a direct, coded teletype conversation with his Chief of Station at Jubil:*

>DDO HERE. THE DCI IS PREPARING A REPORT ON THE QATABANI AUTO

QUESTION. THE INTEREST IN BOTH THE ECONOMIC AND TERRORIST ASPECTS IS INTENSE. CAN YOU CONTACT THISTLE AND FEED US BY WEDNESDAY?

>COS: OUR LOCAL GOVERNMENT SOURCE WILL APPROACH THISTLE TOMORROW. YOUR CASE OFFICER SHOULD HAVE HIS REPORT BY EVENING.

>WHY HAVE YOUR SOURCES FAILED TO PRODUCE? WE MUST KNOW MORE ABOUT WHAT IS GOING ON IN THAT RACING DEPARTMENT AND WHY THE HELL A BUNCH OF CAMEL RIDERS WANT TO START AN AUTO INDUSTRY. WE THOUGHT SHEIK ABDEL WAS MORE SAVVY ABOUT INVESTMENT THAN THAT.

>COS: PLANNING IS TIGHTLY HELD AND EVERTHING NOW SEEMS TO FUNNEL THROUGH PRINCE HASSAN, RATHER THAN THROUGH ABDEL AND NORMAL PALACE CHANNELS. THISTLE SHOULD ENLIGHTEN US.

>THAT IS THE PROPER VERB. SEE TO IT. GOOD NIGHT.

>COS: GOOD NIGHT.

~:~

4.

For their private use all the Mercedes racing drivers were provided with Mercedes touring cars which were entirely maintained at the Company's expense. Seaman had a 2.3 litre saloon, given to him early in 1937, and he was pleased with it . . . .

A letter to Dick from the Mercedes Company regarding the touring car lent to him gives a good idea of arrangements made. "We herewith beg to call your attention to the General Rules as to how the cars are to be handled and attended upon, so that the cars may be in a state to render best services to you at any time, and be a good means of propaganda for our make. Above all, the car must be submitted regularly to the inspection of our Customers Service. Specially we ask you to have the oil changed at the right time."

Prince Chula Chakrabongse of Thailand
Dick Seaman; Racing Motorist
G. T. Foulis & Co., Ltd.

Word was out in Europe. The Qatabani Racing Department had applied to the *Fédération Internationale de l'Automobile* for an exemption from the rules limiting standard engine sizes. We were approved for Formula 1 competition under a new rule that encouraged the entry of exotic engines and weird fuels. One car this season was supposed to be powered by a flywheel, and another by steam, although they hadn't been seen on a track yet, and maybe never would.

Nevertheless, the world's desire to escape from Middle East oil had spilled over onto the racetracks. Our cars used a special blend of methanol fuel refined from Qatabani crude, a step in the other direction. But our rotary-vane engines would be watched carefully as designers sought new ways—any way—to get away from inefficient piston engines.

The announcement in Paris of the existence of our team and its proposed debut at Long Beach brought the media down upon us. The Marib airfield became loaded with chartered planes as journalists and film crews sought us out. They were housed at the motel, and Schwandt told us to be polite. Some of the writers I admired; others were insufferable slobs. Schwandt threw a cocktail party the night they arrived, and Aimee and I showed up to answer the questions that we knew would be repeated several thousand times over the next weeks. Soon after dinner, Brunditz and I commandeered a van, put Mimi and Aimee in the back, and drove off into the night to escape. I screeched through the Südkere, the van tilting like a sailboat on the wind, Heinz urging me on with shouts in several languages. I slowed and parked on the edge of the track at the exit of the turn, while Heinz fished out a champagne bottle from the silver bucket he was clutching with his feet. When glasses had been poured, we drove off sedately with the windows up to keep in the air conditioning. I joined the Long Beach course and watched it roll by our headlights in slow motion, all of us knowing how crucial the track in California would be to our careers.

"If Schwandt doesn't drive us nuts, the press will," I lamented.

"To hell with them, to hell with all of them," said Aimee. "The guy you've got to watch out for is the Emir."

"Why?" asked Heinz, swiveling to watch her.

"Because he's probably a madman—depending, of course, on your definition of sanity and when I'm driving with my spouse in a top-heavy van, I have to keep revising that all the time."

I accelerated for a second, and she had to pause to keep from spilling.

"As I was saying, look at it this way. Mimi and I were out on the yacht today, and we got a good look at his operation. He's living back fifty years ago. The harem is out there, his old Bedouin buddies. The place is paneled like the *Queen Mary,* and all they can talk about is hunting and camel racing. I couldn't find anything about the country being modernized, but they're supposed to be running things."

"I have to tell you something that has to stay among us," said Brunditz with uncharacteristic seriousness and fluent English. "What you've seen so far is not what it seems, and I must add that I'm not what I seem, nor is Mimi. We are both Israeli agents who work for the Mossad."

I drove even more slowly. He had upped the ante.

"I'm telling you this because you should know that you are caught up in something immensely complicated, and it could also be very dangerous for all of us."

"Why worry about us?" I asked. "From what I know of the international game, you play strictly for your own team."

"Beyond the fact that we like you both," he said, "it is going to get sticky for Mimi and me when we get to Long Beach. Your people know us, and we will be there at their sufferance. So we have agreed to cooperate with the CIA and FBI, and part of the deal is that we are supposed to help you if you need it."

I thought about all this for a few moments, and I could tell Aimee was doing the same.

"You'd better tell us some more," she said, "or we might just bail the hell out of all this." I tacitly seconded that. "We don't know much, dammit."

"Hold it," I interjected, "is Mimi in this conversation? Does she speak English?"

"No, honest to God. She's a North African Jew, and speaks fluent Arabic, which is most helpful, but she's not fully trained and it was all we could do to teach her Dutch so that she could pass in Europe as Indonesian.

"Here's the thing," he continued. "Our intelligence reports indicate Sheik Abdel is a lot more than he says. We know he's the financial brains for the Emir and behind the auto industry, but he's got something else in mind for this team."

"Like what?" I asked, driving slowly up the hill at the back of the test circuit.

"That's what you may be able to tell us. Any approaches by him, any deals or proposals, I want you to pass on to me. We can pass them on to your people because we're in daily contact with CIA in Jubil. We can evaluate the situation and advise you if things get at all hairy."

"What do you mean 'hairy'?" I asked. That adjective has a particular meaning in racing terminology. If properly used, it means you are one hair away from getting killed.

"Things are very complicated in Qataban at the moment," he said. "A lot is going on; heavy pressures are on many people. And not everyone agrees which way Qataban should go. Since this team is the country's most visible activity in the Western world, if you don't count the investment of billions of dollars each day in the stock markets, it's bound to get caught up in the cross pressures. And as the drivers, we are the most visible part of the team and could hardly expect to escape the infighting. What I'm saying is that we could find ourselves in a real pickle this season, and you will very definitely need the Mossad behind you."

I pulled through the pit enclosure and headed back to the Racing Department's motel. "I'll think about it," I told Heinz. "But I wasn't trained to snoop or poop around, and, frankly, I don't give a damn. So don't expect me to do your work for you."

"Of course, but you haven't got much choice. Maybe you didn't realize it at the time, but when you signed on to drive for a bunch of Arab nationalist fanatics, you made a serious commitment, one that they're not going to let you out of very easily. Do you remember what happened to Richard Seaman?"

"He died in the rain against a tree at Spa in 'thirty-eight. So what?"

"He drove for Mercedes-Benz, as a British citizen. But he also drove for the Third Reich. And it got very sticky for him. The Führer himself said that Formula One racing would be the measuring stick for German knowledge and German ability. He went crazy when he heard that Seaman won the German Grand Prix by beating von Brauchitsch, the darling of Goebbels and the man Hitler wanted as champion. The next season, Seaman's car spun while leaving a corner he had driven a thousand times and then hit a tree. Does that make sense?"

I was figuring. A Grand Prix car is a brittle, highly stressed machine. Seaman was supposed to have been pushing too hard at Spa, but if your own crew or anyone who had access to the cars wanted to do you in, it wouldn't be hard.

"You're going to need help, Gus," he said. "Lots of it, but maybe you don't see that now."

We parked and got out. I would have preferred using a side entrance to reach our rooms in case any of the press was waiting in the lobby, but there was only one entrance and exit to the motel. The lobby was empty. We could hear raucous hoots and laughs coming from behind one of the conference room doors as we headed down the corridor. Schwandt must have cut loose a whole bin of Dom Pérignon for the press.

The four of us bade perfunctory good-nights as Aimee and I walked past Heinz's door and went to our room. I sat on the edge of our bed for a moment, distracted and depressed.

Holy God, I thought. All I wanted to do was drive Formula 1 cars and live with Aimee. Shoot birds with our friends in Scotland, bag an occasional elk or goat, and fish when we felt like it. Join her in the capital cities and eat onion soup after the opera. International intrigue struck me as being a huge pain in the ass, particularly if it was going to cost our lives, which I now believed it might.

I pulled out of my funk with the realization that Aimee was swooping around the perimeter of the room like a bird, alighting on this light fixture, flitting to a nearby sconce, landing on the bedside phone. I watched her at work, realizing that this was the first time since we had been living together that I had seen her put her covert CIA skills to use.

She was quick, quiet, and systematic. After a few minutes, she joined me on the edge of the bed, and I could tell she was mad as hell. She scrabbled in her purse on the bedside table for a pen and paper and began writing energetically. Her characters looked like enlarged typewriter print, anonymous but practical. She passed me the note.

"Bugs are probably built into the walls or furniture. They had plenty of time. Let's go shooting tomorrow at regular hour and talk then. Meantime, trust no one."

I took the pen. "Gratuitous advice."

She snatched back the paper and walked to the bathroom. A moment later I heard the toilet flush. We later exchanged a few noncommittal words and read in bed. I was plowing through an anthropological treatise on hunting, a book I liked because it reinforced my prejudices. The world, said this scholar, had once been divided between the hunters and the gatherers. The hunters were lean, athletic, and bestowed with keen instincts for survival. The gatherers were agricultural types with heavy builds, a placid manner, and a methodical, safe approach to life.

I counted myself a hunter. I valued the instincts, the ability to outwit game and predict the course of nature, the patience and cunning it takes to be a part of that magnificent system but also be able to use it, manipulate it for survival. I liked to anticipate, the very stuff of fast driving. I had developed my senses, the delicate nerves along the spine, to tell me when I was being watched, when I was heading into danger. I could see the same instinct in the game and fish I stalked, and it seemed at least prudent to imitate nature.

Auto racing might be as far as one could get from the natural order, but the ways of the hunter, I was convinced, had kept me alive. The hunter instinct explained why the fastest drivers in the past had endured. Fangio was known for his uncanny ability to predict disaster around the next blind corner. Time after time, he wove his way through multicar crashes, missing spinning race cars as they bounced across his path like hundred-mile-per-hour billiard balls. He'd done it at Monte Carlo, at Le Mans, on the open road. Fangio looked like a hunter. He had the eyes. So did Stirling Moss, who drove his incredibly powerful Mercedes across the mountain passes of Italy in the rain in one long series of power slides and won the Mille Miglia. Stewart had it, too, driving his March Tyrrell at speed in fog and rain on the Nürburgring, Europe's most dangerous circuit, to win the German Grand Prix.

The anthropology book confirmed my theory. I planned to continue to stalk animals, edible ones, and bag crafty trout. Hunting and fishing were important to my career, vital to what had become my paramount goal, to be World Champion in Formula 1. I saw, for the first time since I had started competing in motor sports, that the goal was not fantasy but could be reached.

I nodded off to sleep but revived as Aimee reached across to turn out my bedside light. Her athlete's small but sculptured breasts had nailed me to the mattress.

I wondered how sensitive listening devices could get and decided they were probably scientifically positioned to pickup whispers in bed. Nor did the room have a radio or television to drown out a microphone. I led her quietly from the bed, taking a pillow and light blanket. We stretched out in a far corner of the room, wrapped the cover around us, and put the pillow under our heads. Our nude bodies fit together from toes to ears.

"Tell me, great technician," I said in her ear, "can they hear everything we do in bed?"

"I suppose, but they've heard quite a bit already, and besides, we aren't in bed now, anyway."

"Good point," I said. She slowly massaged my buttocks. My hands roamed up and down her back, mostly down, and then I entered her without changing position. I didn't want to think about anyone listening; it shouldn't have meant a damn, but we continued to copulate silently as if being overheard by small children.

My member stayed erect, but it didn't seem to be mine. There was no sensation. The indignity of a Qatabani agent monitoring us had ignited a seething anger deep in my gut, or roughly the same area where the impulse for orgasm begins to build before rushing down the base of the spine and out the stem.

"I don't think I'm going anywhere," I told her after about five minutes. "What would you like?"

"It's known as the Russian Embassy Disease," she whispered as we stopped our movement. "If you're stationed in Moscow or any of the hard-target areas like Eastern European capitals, you get used to sharing your bedroom noises. Most people do, anyway. It's diplomatic."

I withdrew and sat up, cursing. She punched me lightly in the kidney, and we went back to the bed to sleep.

The next morning, Schwandt led us through another lesson in technical tedium, an entire practice session devoted to spring adjustments. Our suspension specialist, Petre Priest, rotated the cars through ten-lap segments, adjusting the balance of one car while the other two drivers were out putting in their times. The grosser suspension problems had been solved, and we were down to fine tuning. This meant we had to turn faster, near-competitive lap times.

The combination of minute changes to spring lengths, anti-roll bars, and wings called for a hypersensitive rear end on the part of the driver to detect what the car was doing. It's one thing to detect a car that wallows from coil to coil and another to appreciate whether another tenth of a second could be squeezed from the braking zone of a crucial corner. The driver also has to be sufficiently articulate to tell the specialist what went wrong.

My times got consistently lower and the car gained stability as the Belgian engineer made adjustments. His full, pink cheeks and Gallic cupid mouth made him look like a Parisian butcher as he waited for us at the pits, except his long white technician's coat had black grease stains on it instead of beef blood. He and I could talk about the car in French, and over the weeks we had built a useful understanding. He knew that I could make the most of the car's tendency toward final oversteer, where the rear end swings out at the end of the corner, overtaking the sliding front end and pointing everything the right way for the exit. Deliberately inducing this, though, leaves no margin for error. There are safer ways to set up a car.

While Rachid's and my lap times got lower during that practice session, Brunditz's didn't.

Priest seemed to have trouble finding out what was going on. With about a half hour left before heat would drive us off the course, Schwandt hung out a pit signal for me, and I pulled in behind Heinz's car in the next lap. Heinz sat sullenly on the pit counter as the mechanics removed his seat and padding. I got out, and my mechanics began stripping out my cockpit. Ten minutes later, I was driving the big German's car, which, indeed, had bad handling problems. It seemed a miracle to me that he had kept it on the road.

Priest and I tinkered and adjusted Brunditz's machine for the rest of that session, although I was acutely aware that one driver's preference may not be another's. I felt badly about how Schwandt had handled things. But then, if Brunditz preferred to live off his reactions alone and have a sloppy car, that was a luxury that a first-rate team couldn't afford. When I pulled in after the final few laps, I was going to tell him what the car now felt like, but he had left the pit area.

I went back to the room to shower and sleep. Aimee joined me later, and we had buffet lunch with the remainder of the press corps, the stalwarts from the specialty publications, and then we commandeered a van for an afternoon of trapshooting.

We set up the equipment on our favorite sand dune, about a mile from the coastal village at the end of an oiled dirt road. I moved the van out of earshot, and Aimee checked our equipment for bugs, including the big beach umbrella and folding aluminum chairs. She set up one of the traps with a clay pigeon and triggered it when I spoke the magic word: "Mark." I looked at her and shot straight into the air.

"Now that we are out of range of the *écouteurs,* would you kindly explain what the hell's going on? What's Brunditz up to?"

"If you wait a few minutes, I can give you a better explanation."

"What the hell do a few minutes mean," I said, breaking open the over-and-under breech. "Are you collecting your thoughts? Just give me some raw data and I'll sort it out. Start with you, for openers. Why were you so eager to have me stay with the team?"

"So we could make a half-million dollars in one bloody year. That's reason enough."

"But there's another reason. You've been too happy sitting around that motel for most of the winter. You should have been struck dead by boredom."

"Not happy, just mentally engaged," she said slowly as she adjusted the spring on the trap and changed the height the clay bird would rise.

Several times, I noticed, she had looked back toward Marib. There was a squeal of brakes from that direction, and she looked as if she were expecting it. A black Mercedes sedan had pulled up behind our orange van, and a man in the local khaki police uniform stepped out, a corpulent Arab in white headdress. The shiny Sam Browne belt and decorations told us something about his rank. As he approached I noticed he had a remarkably amiable face, with two or three chins. He looked like one of the few Arabs who had the capacity for a good laugh.

"The heat gets unbearable almost as soon as the sun is up," he said to Aimee as he approached.

"Sometimes it's unbearable even before dawn," she replied.

He grinned broadly. "Mushkir, my name is Mushkir. How much have you told him?" he asked, flicking his head in my direction.

By now my male ego had been so badly wounded I figured I'd never function, never drive again. "She hasn't told me a goddamned thing. But we're all about to spill our guts out now, aren't we? Every last little sliver of explanation."

Aimee took one of the traps off the wooden shotgun case, which we had used as a platform, and moved the crate under the umbrella across from the two metal chairs. "C'mon in, Mushkir, it's only a hundred and ten degrees in the shade," she said, leaving the chairs for us. My ego appreciated the gesture.

"Jubil Station must be under considerable pressure from Washington," he said in a high, lilting voice. I wondered whether he guarded the harem.

"Well, tell Jubil Station their worst fears are realized," said Aimee, turning to me. "OK, I've re-upped with the Agency for another tour, but I did it because I wanted to make sure you stayed in one piece. Langley has had considerable doubts about Qataban's true intentions with the racing team, and no one is quite sure why the hell they want to go into auto production. They started investing in auto racing as long as six years ago. Rachid was their driver. Qataban trained him and sponsored him. Then we began to get signals that a new terrorist organization was being set up in Qataban, one of those arm's-length groups, like Black September, that the Emir could deny having any contact with when it was convenient.

"The theory developed that the racing team would be used as a cover. It would be an ideal mechanism for flying around technicians and complex equipment to any continent in the world. But the theory got somewhat shaken when the Agency found that Sheik Abdel was actually planning to build an auto industry. That's for background. Tell him the status in Jubil, Mushkir."

"We have sources all over the factory complex, since it's no problem for me to recruit the foreign laborers," he said. "There's no question the Emir has invested billions into building an industry. There's a foundry, assembly plant, warehouse, storage lots. It goes on and on. But whether it's a full-fledged, serious development effort is difficult to tell. We had even less success in penetrating the terrorist camp. None, in fact. Overflights show barracks, obstacle courses everything. The Racing Department is in an adjacent area, completely run by the Germans, and it is also a mystery. The Qatabani mechanics are all recruited from Prince Hassan's family and are highly paid. We have yet to get anyone in there. Their security is the best. We've never seen anything like it."

"Has Washington found more on Schwandt?" she asked.

"He's bought. The Zurich people say the Qatabanis paid a hundred and fifty million for the engine patent, which was about three times too much. That's to get Schwandt to play along. But Schwandt doesn't get to collect the bulk of it until after the end of the season. The racing operation has to come off right or they don't get the money."

So much for secrecy in Swiss banking, I thought. "And what about Sheik Abdel," I asked, beginning to warm to the game.

"A total blank," said Mushkir. "His relationship with the Emir is extremely complicated, and grows more so with the rise of Prince Hassan."

"Think back to that day we met the Emir in the tent," Aimee told me quickly. "The man on the Emir's right, the one with the tough looks, was Prince Hassan ibn al-Razi, a real comer and the Emir's nephew and maybe heir apparent. He's an Arab nationalist, a Muslim fanatic. Virulently anti-Israel but capable of siding with the Russians once in power."

"He has KGB support now," Mushkir said. "They contact him constantly both in Jubil and in London. He was in Moscow two weeks ago."

"This is all of more than academic concern to Washington," Aimee continued. "Prince Hassan may be shouldering Sheik Abdel out of the way. But Abdel is the leading pro-Western force in Jubil and the country has done very well by him. Abdel is considered the shrewdest oil negotiator going and has made a lot of shrewd investments for the Emir and the Qatabani treasury in Europe and the U.S."

"So you don't know what clout Abdel has anymore," I said. "That's rather awkward, considering he hired me."

"It's worse than awkward," Aimee said.

"Please, my friends, I must go and we are probably being observed," said Mushkir. "I came here officially to ask you if anyone on the motel staff had been stealing your ammunition. But that's a rather short question."

"The answer is maybe," said Aimee. "We'd have to count our shells, which anyone knows takes time." She made a show of counting boxes of ammunition. "Tell Jubil Station that Brunditz unexpectedly surfaced last night, representing himself as Mossad and asking Gus to feed him any information on what Abdel is doing. He also promised to protect us in Long Beach. The girl was with him. He said she was North African, a Mossad Arab specialist not trained yet to operate in the West. We now know he's more than a Grand Prix driver and his Mossad ties are a pack of lies, and since they've both been around, they must have left plenty of tracks.

"Ask Washington to do a computer check on Baader Meinhof links with Brunditz and all ties between the Munich group and the Qatabani Arabs. They might pick up the woman. My feeling is that Brunditz and his girl represent the first evidence we've had of an international tie-in among the terrorist organizations. That would be evidence, then, that Prince Hassan is bankrolling something on an international scale, providing a mechanism for every dissident group from

Libya to Ireland. The Munich intellectuals are apparently the catalyst. But it's hard to operate around here. I haven't got anything hard."

"Pity," he said.

"Pity, yourself. What are you getting out of the motel?"

"We have labor sources, of course, but they've turned up essentially nothing. Our bugs get swept out nightly. Whoever runs that operation is very, very good." I was bleary from the heat. Mushkir, I noticed, didn't perspire. He heaved to his feet.

"I will be back at this time tomorrow. It would be helpful if some of your ammunition was missing, you filed a complaint at the desk and I was forced to question you. The imported labor is so untrustworthy, you know."

"Tell Washington we leave for Long Beach in ten days, and I hope they are ready for us there," said Aimee. "And make them get Munich Station off its ass. We need to know who we're dealing with."

He shuffled off through the sand while tripling off pleasant good-byes. We resumed shooting, this time in earnest.

The next morning, March 16, we drivers began to get intense pressure from the technicians. They questioned us at length on each system in the car. Instead of having time on our hands, we suddenly found ourselves desperately pushed to ready the team for the flight to Los Angeles. The more knowledgeable journalists were permanently encamped at the motel and watched our every move from the pit counter as we attempted to perfect the cars and settle on the right tires, which had been our most consistent headache. They were made specifically for us by a small firm outside of Munich. Schwandt gave the company exacting specifications, which were never met. Tires blew or threw their treads at awkward moments, and Rachid had crashed badly on the back straight the previous week during a tire test, not injuring himself but leaving the training car dented and pranged beyond hope.

After the early morning test, Aimee and I sat on the pit counter drinking coffee that was sent to us in thermoses from the motel. We watched the Air Qataban 707 freighter making a final approach. It seemed to be winging in twice a day from somewhere with new loads of goods as Schwandt pulled his resources together for the final assault.

"I think you should see this shipment," he said as he walked by the pits and headed toward his office. "Most unusual."

We picked up one of the ubiquitous orange vans parked out back and drove over to the airfield, where a couple of writers from *Motorsport* and *Road and Track,* Nikons at the ready, were waiting for the wide cargo doors to open. Two low-slung sports cars, wrapped in cloth covers, were off-loaded from the plane. Sheik Abdel appeared from the jet's front quarters, which were designed for long-distance passenger use. He was dressed in Western clothes, a Bond Street blue suit, except for a white headdress held by a gold-braid band. His compact, full-boyish face, set off by the thin mustache, prompted the Nikons to chatter as the Sheik helped the mechanics push the cars out on the runway apron, parking them side by side. Two more vehicles, still tantalizingly wrapped, were off-loaded and parked. Rachid and Brunditz arrived from the tire tests, and Schwandt pulled up in another van, accompanied by two film crews. I sensed a media event in the making.

Sheik Abdel greeted us and assembled us around the cars. "The plant at Jubil has finally disgorged. These are the prototypes for our sports machines. The first four go to Schwandt and the three works drivers." The writers scratched madly on their pads. "We will take them with us to California and will use them in Europe during the season as well."

"When do you expect production?" interjected the writer from *Road and Track,* an engineering graduate with a deep, almost religious, love of cars.

Abdel smiled wryly. "If I tell you it will be this summer, I'll be proved a liar. Realistically we're talking about an assembly line start-up next fall and worldwide marketing a year from now."

"And in what price range?"

"Eventually under thirty thousand dollars, a mass-produced performance car. The first model, based on these, will be more exotic and sell for perhaps double that." He pointed a finger at the cloths on two cars, and the mechanics stripped them away. The cars were powerful, coal-black, with a Qataban flag unassumingly on the door. A metal emblem on the hood showed the factory symbol, a Viper that could have said Don't Tread on Me. The cars were low, wedge-shaped two-seaters with a rear engine and a hell of a lot of pizzazz. They were in the open, Targa-style, with the rear roof doubling as a roll bar. One had my name on the door, and Aimee and I got in. The interior, like the exterior, was progressive and well-finished but not radical. Qataban, like Japan with the Datsun, was going after an identifiable market. I started the engine, and it sounded like the Grand Prix car with mutes on. We drove off down the runway, gathering speed. It was a glorious car. Despite the pounding heat we—the three factory drivers and Schwandt—moved over to the track and the rest followed in vans.

We drove the sports cars around the track at a modest pace, letting the writers take a turn and generally having a pleasant time with these new gifts that seemed to have fallen from the sky.

As I commandeered my car back from a journalist, Sheik Abdel detached himself from a group inside the pit, vaulted over the counter, and asked to join me in the car. Aimee waved a quick good-bye, and the Sheik settled in the passenger seat. His boyish good looks fit well with the playboy image of the car.

"Slowly, Gustave," he said as we pulled out. "Another time—perhaps at night when it would be more dramatic—I would like you to take me around here at speed. But right now I have a difficult topic to broach to you."

Oh, Christ, I thought, more revelations. All I want to do is drive race cars.

"To get to the point: Out on the yacht, which is somewhere in the Atlantic and heading toward Panama, sits our leader, Sahal Abdallah al-Shaibi, the Emir, a man who is growing elderly. Strong opinions, monumental prejudices. He has personally designated Rachid Mohammed Bashir as Team Qataban's Number One driver. Since Rachid represents Islam to the world, the Protector of the People, Crucible of the Faith, and Embodiment of the Law has decreed Rachid must win."

“He’s out of his fucking mind,” I said, turning the car down the steep hill. “We made no deals when I was signed on.”

“Of course, the Holy Protector is not being realistic, Gustave. And that is why this conversation is so delicate. As his Finance Minister, I see the two strongest markets for our product being the United States and Western Europe. It is patently obvious, if not essential, that you and Brunditz come out on top this season—preferably you, since the Europeans can relate to you.”

“Keep going, Sheik. We may have found a common language.”

“To put it bluntly, we will have to deceive the Champion of the Faithful. You and I must work as a team for our own self-serving reasons.”

“What about Schwandt?”

“In the dark. This must be between us.”

“He could fire me.”

“You must act cautiously, diplomatically. Don’t provoke him. But somehow, win. Your image, if you can be World Champion this season, is crucial to our advertising, promotion, goodwill, and brand identification. The sales value would be immense.”

"How much are we talking about?"

"For our brand, perhaps half a billion dollars in free promotion and added sales; it's hard to say. There is some disagreement among my economists. Nevertheless, I'm willing to pay you another five hundred thousand if you can win the Grand Prix at Long Beach and earn more than twenty points in the championship standings, with a bonus if you carry off the championship—all without being fired, of course."

"And if Schwandt fires me? I want to avoid the Argentine Go-Karts."

"The—"

"I need a guarantee. It won't be easy to pull off, and it may not work."

"A quarter-million has already been set aside for you in a bank in Zurich. Here is the number of your account." He passed over a slip of paper. "The other quarter will be deposited at the end of the season, assuming you are still on the team and have fulfilled the requirements."

I put the number in my pocket and accelerated down the straight, hitting 140 without really thinking about it until I saw Abdel begin to grow rigid. "Sorry." The car rolled listlessly toward the Südkere leg as I tried to parse out the problems. "What happens," I asked slowly, "if we're in the closing laps at Long Beach and I'm on Rachid's tail?"

"Pass him, Gustave. Make him make a mistake, a plausible slip. You must come in first. You are our best hope for quickly penetrating the American market."

"All right. It's insanely stupid, but I'll agree. I probably should have signed on with some friendly Swiss team, after all."

"Ah, but you have, Gustave. You and the Banque de Suisse."

Aimee and I met in the bedroom before lunch. We were both in a foul mood, our sex lives obliterated, having to weigh each word we spoke in the room, the immense complexities of Team Qataban become an increasing burden. For a moment I thought of not telling her about Abdel, but she was too deeply entwined. I knew we could talk best out on the trap range, and so we headed for there soon after the meal.

"Do you believe all this crap about making sports cars?" she asked, squeezing the shotgun and shooting behind the clay bird by at least two feet.

"Abdel could be genuine, you know. He could be building an auto industry, and the people who want to use the team as a means of shipping terrorists around could be coming along for a free ride. He may not even know about it."

"Well, at some point you might want to confront the turkey with what you know. *Pull.*" Another miss.

We heard brakes squeal behind us. Aimee leaned her shotgun against one of the wooden crates and began to arrange the seats again under our limited pool of umbrella shade as Mushkir made his way to us, his feet burying themselves deep in the sand with each step.

"Where do you find the Mushkirs?" I asked when he was still out of earshot.

"It's not hard in Third World countries," she said. "He's probably been to CIA-sponsored seminars at every police academy in the U.S. If he wants eventually to emigrate, the Agency can handle things like that. He's safe; that's all we need to know."

"How did you contact him?" I now realized we had been under fairly tight observation at the motel.

"The letters I got from my old roommate, Heline. I asked her to turn them over to my Paris case officer. The Agency used her letters to write me in special ink, literally between the lines. We still go in for that kind of mumbo jumbo, as well as those phony-sounding recognition procedures." Then Mushkir was upon us.

"Washington has news," he said. "Munich was finally teamed up with the computer. Brunditz's real name is Klaus Effron, a graduate of an anarchist group in Wuppertal. He was with them from 'sixty-seven to 'seventy-two. Dropped out of sight. Was arrested the following year in the Netherlands on an arms-possession charge and held in Scheveningen prison. He participated in the taking of hostages in 'seventy-four when the Palestinian Adnan Nuri pulled that ransom caper."

"I remember," said Aimee. "But Nuri and the others were captured after the shoot-out and put back in Scheveningen."

"All except Effron," said Mushkir. "In the confusion the police lost track of how many prisoners had escaped, and the hostages were unsure how many captors there were because they were blindfolded. Effron hid and later escaped. He dropped from sight again."

"That's the year he started motorcycle racing," I said. "I met him that season in Italy."

"By then he was clean-shaven and with a new identity," said Aimee. "What about the woman, Mushkir?"

"Else Farah, twenty-nine. Turkish father, German mother. The father was one of the first labor imports of the late fifties. They were badly abused. She took up the Arab cause, met Klaus at Wuppertal, and converted him from anarchism. She has been active in a number of Palestinian cells. We don't know when they joined up to come here, and they aren't man and wife, by the way, probably not even lovers, judging by our observation of their bed clothes."

He paused, apparently to think about that for a moment. I could hear the breath whistle through his nose. Mushkir wasn't a well man. The flesh accumulated in pools under his khaki uniform and extruded into pouches of cloth in unlikely places, such as the outside of his thighs. His face suddenly became animated once more.

"Ah, yes, another point," Mushkir said. "Jubil Station asks that you pay attention to how people here use the term 'Viper.' The Qatabani radio traffic is getting hard to cipher. At times they seem to be referring to the car and other times to something else—the terrorist cell, perhaps."

"They may be using the code word interchangeably," said Aimee.

"It fits the pattern of Black September," Mushkir said. "The leadership can use the racing team as cover and recruit specialists on an ad hoc basis for certain tasks and then disband. The dossiers on Effron and Farah indicate they both have the experience to coordinate the gangs. He was trained as an assassin, by the way, and she developed a specialty in letter bombs and plastic explosives. Very, very bad people."

"That's wonderful news," said Aimee. "Thank Jubil Station and tell them I haven't got anything new for you, except someone in Jubil was able to build four of the fastest-looking street machines you ever saw without your unimpeachable industry sources catching wind of it."

"Pity," he said, with the detached resignation of someone who has been paid well in advance. "Some heads will roll."

He wished us a good trip. It was apparently the last we would see of this conduit. Aimee resumed shooting when he had left.

"This peripheral stuff is beginning to get to me," I told her. "I've got to concentrate on what I was signed on to do, which, if I remember, was to race a Formula One car for a season and contend for the championship."

"I'd settle for that," said Aimee, putting down her shotgun. "Just keep one thing in mind. Their names are Klaus and Else, both of them extraordinarily competent at what they do. They're tough, crusading terrorists. Like many things the Arabs do, Team Qataban seems to be turning into a multipurpose project. They keep mixing up religion, politics, and technology. That isn't going to make your job as a driver any easier.

"And there's more at stake here than just you and me. We've apparently run into a new dimension in the terrorist export business, using sports as a cover for an international linkup. And that leads into a national security problem, since Qataban is an OPEC country and about half of the U.S. oil comes from the Middle East. Any confrontation with Qataban could lead to another oil boycott."

"You tend to national security," I said, growing more testy by the minute in the heat. "All I know about Qataban is that they have bankrolled a racing car that is one of the fastest and most difficult to handle that the world has ever seen and they've hired me to drive it. If I concentrate on what I'm doing, I may be able to take the Formula One championship with it. So from now on, just keep your spooky friends out of my life. They're a distraction."

"Listen to me, Gus," she said, her voice shaking with emotion, which was a rarity for Aimee. "You can't just turn your back on this, on me. You're going to need me and the Agency, because if Prince Hassan is gunning for Sheik Abdel's job, and if Hassan is linked up with the Russians and the KGB, you've got more than a peripheral problem. Hassan is taking over that team for his own purposes. He's apparently been planning this for a long time. I think he wants you out of the way, and there's no question in my mind they already tried to do you in once."

"Ridiculous."

"Think back. Did you find anything wrong with your car the day you hit the wall?"

"It's hard to tell sometimes," I said. "The left suspension got mashed in from the impact. Could have been any one of a half-dozen things."

"It's also possible that Brunditz got a wheel against yours and shoved your rear end out, isn't it?" she persisted.

"Possible. I might not have felt it, but that is about the least likely explanation."

"Just think about it."

"Thanks. That's not what I want on my mind when I'm driving a car at over two hundred. It's like wondering if someone is going to throw a javelin in your back when you're about to make a record throw."

"You can quit, you know."

"No chance. Just tell your cloak-and-dagger people to leave me alone." I wasn't sure I meant that, but my ego applauded.

* * *

On March 17, the Deputy Director of Operations sent a memo to the Director of Central Intelligence:

To: DCI
From:DDO
For Your Eyes Only
The Qatabani circus moves to Long Beach next week. As you know, we have been totally stymied as to the Emir's intentions, despite moving an agent into their racing headquarters and an all-out effort by our source at Marib, not to mention our sources at Jubil. Whoever set this terrorist cell up—and we are quite sure it was Prince Hassan—departed from normal channels and worked independently of the Emir's usual entourage. German technicians have been instrumental in putting the racing team together and providing long-term racing training and development for their terrorists.

The Qatabani cell under Hassan is small, well-disciplined, and gets active KGB support. We have picked up ties with Baader-Meinhof, the Palestinians, Pakistanis and possibly the North Koreans, Japanese gangs, and the Sicilians. We feel it imperative that these associations be severed at the earliest possible opportunity and that Sheik Abdel once again be given the full support of the United States government. The Long Beach Grand Prix may be our best chance to take out Hassan's network, since we can exert maximum control there. I have been assured fullest FBI coordination.

Our strategists are working on a scenario that will provoke Hassan into overreacting and exposing the guts of his organization, which will be quickly ripped out. However, this calls for maximum exposure of our deep-cover agent. The plan also calls for a maximum effort from her husband, the American driver. I realize you have a policy against using people with close emotional ties in a situation like this, but I feel we have no alternative.

I believe the racing driver's instinct to win at all costs can be put to good use. Our reports show he performs well under pressure, is exceptionally gifted with firearms, and is more than a touch mean when pushed. He should suit our purposes well and will get maximum aid from our agent.

Adding to our difficulties, the White House, without consulting us, of course, has invited the Emir to DC for a state dinner after the race weekend. This will have to be our best work or POTUS is going to hang us all by the balls.

~:~

5.

Jim Burge, Seaman's former mechanic, attributed his success to "his phenomenal patience and ability to remain unruffled by the many disappointments and hard luck which beset the best of racing motorists from time to time."

William Court
A History of Grand Prix Motor Racing 1906-1951: Power and Glory
Macdonald: London

The wall, the real wall, a long line of tall concrete slabs, had random craters and streaks of paint from errant race cars. I ran my hand along it and walked up the hill toward Ocean Boulevard, squatting down now and then to study the road surface. Track employees worked in a single-minded frenzy as they readied the Long Beach course for the first morning's practice. Concrete blocks, fencing, and rubber tires were being stacked and bolted together to cage the uncivilized cars that would soon be turned loose on the streets.

My black Nomex suit with orange piping brought stares. The attention of maintenance crews and die-hard fans who turned up early for a Thursday morning practice I could deal with, but at least one of the onlookers behind the fence was not there out of curiosity. As best I could tell, the surveillance had been constant since we'd flown in with the cars from Qataban two days before. Schwandt had staged an airlift with two Qatabani 707s, assembling in one orderly pile in a hangar at Long Beach airport the three formula cars, the four sports machines, parts, tires, and people, presenting Customs and Immigration with a six-hour exercise.

We had taken over an entire motel downtown. We used it as if we owned it, which was probably the case. Once again, the rooms and phones were suspect. Aimee and I fled from the room without even unpacking, heading off in the sports Viper for a late dinner at a crab restaurant we knew that was strategically positioned across the street from the San Pedro fishing fleet. I started to keep track of the car lights behind us as we headed through the Long Beach Naval Complex. Our car was probably the most distinctive one in North America, leaving a trail of bent necks behind us. We wouldn't be melting into any freeway traffic or slipping up side streets. To use the car's performance would only bring down the California law, which escalates in efficiency from eager city cops to the deadly cool State Highway Patrol.

At the base of the Vincent Thomas Bridge, I swung briefly into the parking lot of a restaurant, a converted steamer that is tied up among the freighters and turns out good seafood and nostalgia. The parking lot links up with the next wharf and a second parking area. I pulled through to the wharf and out an unmanned gate. As we drove back on the road, we saw a car backing up in the *S.S. Princess Louise* lot, scattering two men and their dates as they were heading toward the boat canopy.

"That guy's pretty frantic," said Aimee as we drove up over the humped bridge to San Pedro. "Suppose that means he's alone?"

"I don't get it," I said. "I thought we were going to be watched by real pros, and they send us people from the Gang That Couldn't Shoot Straight."

"Yeah, but I wouldn't be so sure. If they're desert Arabs, they can shoot. They just can't drive, that's all."

By the time we reached the restaurant, I had picked out at least two cars that were sticking with us. One peeled off in downtown San Pedro, and the other pulled past us as we turned into the parking lot. Whoever was directing the nether side of Team Qataban must have decided that if I confronted them with a protest about being followed, which I would, they could handle it. For your protection, Herr Walter. Threats from Zionist extremists, you know. Can't be too cautious. Should be grateful, Herr Walter.

"Let's just drop it, Aimee," I said as we shuffled through the sawdust to an empty table. "Does it make any difference if the Emir or Prince Hassan or anyone else wants to know where we went for dinner?"

She thought for a time without talking, then picked up a sourdough breadstick and broke it as though it were someone's neck. "Now I see why they don't like to have husbands and wives work together in the field. I look at your situation two ways. For your own good, I would advise you to ignore their surveillance and do what they tell you, or else quit. From the professional point of view, I want you to hang in there and bust things open. Up until a few hours ago, the professional in me was winning, but now that we're here I'm not so sure. The wife is having doubts."

A waitress came, and we ordered cold Dungeness and a good bottle of California Chardonnay. "Surely it wasn't those clowns following us that changed your mind," I prompted, after the waitress brought the chilled wine.

"Hardly. They're probably from the Emir's security team. Country boys on the fringe of the Viper group. But wait until you meet Hassan. Here's a man who apparently has the ability to infiltrate his people, a bunch of trained terrorists, right into a Formula One team." We had leaned forward until our heads were only inches apart and our voices didn't have to carry. "That takes some doing. If he wants to get rid of us this weekend, there's probably not much we can do about it. Our people can't keep us that well covered."

The crab arrived, cold and sweet to the taste, and with a mound of coleslaw that carried some hidden clout, probably fresh horseradish. For a moment we could forget the food we usually ate in Paris.

"We've got to stick it out—for now, anyway," I said. "We've got a lot to lose, including a substantial hunk of money."

"You're telling yourself that because you want to drive," Aimee said. "Oh, hell, I don't blame you. I'd probably do the same. But I'll tell you one thing. I'm getting the impression we're digging ourselves into deep, deep trouble."

I also had the impression that Aimee was becoming less of a help to me. She had useful skills, and I knew I might have to call on them, but I needed to be in a position to make my own decisions, quickly if necessary. She represented the encumbrance of government, decision by committee. I decided to keep my own counsel in Long Beach. If I botched the job, I would do everything possible to see that she didn't pay a penalty.

The first day of Grand Prix practice, any Grand Prix opening practice, is a study in delay, and the Long Beach officials saw no reason to break decades of tradition. By 10:00 A.M. Thursday, an hour after we were supposed to be out on the track, parts of the circuit still needed to be padded and wired shut. I started to walk down to Turn One to look at the track surface there. Brunditz slid off a pit counter and joined me.

"You've been followed, too, I take it," he said as we looked down the incline at Turn One. I told him about the past two days, the irritation and clumsiness of it all.

"We are in contact with your people now," he said, moving close enough so that his voice wouldn't be overheard. "We're getting ready to handle whatever might come along. We have no reason to believe the Qatabanis will waste any time taking advantage of their cover, but we don't know yet what they might try, maybe something specific, like the headquarters of a pro-Israeli organization here. It may be something major, more symbolic, like a skyscraper."

I didn't answer. I was more intent on making sure the road hadn't been resurfaced or the turn hadn't been changed in some way since the previous year. It hadn't.

"I told you, Gus, we could help you, and things are likely to get very dicey here. I'll give you a Los Angeles number. You can call it anytime and somebody from the Mossad will be there to pull you both out. Dial five-five-two-JONA. Don't worry about introductions. They know your voice."

"I don't need all that mumbo-jumbo crap," I told him, turning back to the pits but filing the number away nevertheless. "I'm here to drive cars."

"Sure, sure," he said, his broad Bavarian face with the high cheekbones breaking into a smile. "It's five-five-two and then the man who got swallowed."

I studied the track, flicking pebbles and small shards of glass off the surface. We could hear the various cars being fired up outside the garages, the brawn of the Ford engines in the Marches, Wolfs, Tyrrells, Shadows, and others, the tense rip of the Ferraris and Alfa-Romeos, the eccentric blast of the Matras, and, suddenly soaring over them all with an ungodly high note, the wail of the Vipers.

It was an outrageous chorus of sound to visit on a city. I had visions of pacemakers being short-circuited throughout the apartments of the elderly, the staunch folks who held their ground and spurned the promoter's free weekend offer in Palm Springs. By all standards, it seemed, everything we did in Grand Prix was illegal, a trait that had lent the sport a certain enduring charm.

Long Beach and Monaco share the same improbabilities as auto racetracks. On several corners, the world's fastest road cars virtually come to a halt. At spots, they tear open, hurtling toward casinos and hotels, parapets and restaurants, or, in the stunning case of Long Beach, a pornographic movie theater. The turns skirt harbors and twist through the urban scene in ways that seem to invite mistakes.

At Monaco, exquisite creatures in tailored pants follow the action from balconies. Their men watch from the shadows, eyes veiled, wondering if they have the nerve to drive that fast and bothered by the notion that it is probably too late to find out. At Long Beach, the flesh is wrapped in bleached denim and is out in the sun. The men, more quickly into their wealth, look as though they could handle any car around if they took the time to knuckle under to the dedication. But their time is firmly booked.

The five of us—three drivers, helmets in hand, and the two women—sat on the Team Qataban pit counter, watching the first cars burst from the other pits, engines cleaving the morning quiet and reverberating through the walled canyons of the city. Schwandt arrived along the pits like an act from the Moiseyev Dancers. His long white smock showed no sign of his legs, yet he glided down the pit row briskly, hair slicked back and clipboard and watches in hand. A tangle of technicians followed behind, their legs pumping to keep up. Photographers switched to wide-angle lenses to group the entire team, the mystery phenomenon of the sport.

"The cars are all coming," said Schwandt. "Vane problems again last night, but they're all coming."

Qatabani mechanics appeared at the back of the pits and began breaking open crates, laying out parts and tools in patterns on canvas cloths. I watched the men disinterestedly over my shoulder, trying to keep my mind off the rival cars as they came by on their first lap. The practice games had begun. If a team could afford it, one car could be designated to put in a blistering series of opening laps and scare holy hell out of rows of team managers. The drivers without healthy cars sat and fidgeted.

Today was no exception. This year's Formula 1 crop had a full complement of seasoned but young and talented drivers. Moreover, they'd already had three Grand Prix this season to set their cars up. Perry Unseld, the young ace from Australia and the surprising choice as Ferrari's Number One driver, was out in his blood-red car seconds after the track opened. He was pursued immediately by the other front-runners:

Kevin Dair, the aging Irishman at a full thirty-four years; Dirk Seutenbach, the Dutch dentist who drove quite a bit faster than Dutch dentists were given credit for; Eugenio Braccio, the eccentric Italian who lived up to everyone's stereotype of a touched Sicilian. Out of earshot we called him Kamikaccio.

We didn't call the new Japanese drivers that. They were precise and fast, although their one claimant to the front ranks of Formula 1 had died the previous year. One of the young Japanese drivers, Ari Tomaka, had already accumulated nine championship points this season. Unseld led with twenty-one, followed by Robin Askew with twelve. Braccio, driving with an overabundance of adrenaline, had eleven points, and Seutenbach nine.

More Qatabani mechanics, each of them appearing to be interchangeable, rolled up our black cars. A doughnut of photographers, motorized lenses singing, moved with the machines. Once at the pits, they turned their cameras again on the drivers, sitting in a row on the pit counter, dressed in black driving suits with orange piping. "This is no time to be so somber," Schwandt said, waving his arms like a bandleader. "We must reflect an air of joy, an image of constructive optimism."

"Schwandt, for Christ's sake, just get the cars going," I said. Brunditz mumbled Bavarian argot that was too convoluted for anyone to comprehend. Something about opening pickled pig's feet too late. Rachid remained impassive, then reached back over the pit counter and drew a bottle of Pepsi from a cooler that had been placed there by the mechanics. Slowly, casually, he put the cap in the wedge of his eyetooth and pried it off.

"Good God, how'd you do that?" I asked appreciatively.

"An acquired Muslim talent," said Rachid. "We take oceans of Pepsi with us to the desert, but nobody seems to remember the opener."

"I'm going to try that one night at Huber's," said Brunditz. "Greatest thing they'll have seen since pig-sticking with bayonets."

The cameras wheezed and captured constructive, optimistic images: two blond Aryans and an Arab ready to do battle on the circuit.

"Rachid goes first," said Schwandt. The tall driver jackknifed and disappeared into the black metal envelope. The engine started.

"You guys have got to be kidding," shouted a racing journalist who had been standing behind the car. Pit crews near us covered their ears or sought frantically through kit bags for a set of earplugs.

Rachid pulled out, moving deliberately until he reached the green signal at the end of the pit row. Then the car broke loose, as if on a prearranged signal by Schwandt, the rear end snaking as the car lurched over the hill at Turn One and accelerated down to the esplanade and the sea.

"You're next," said Schwandt, pointing at me. A mechanic helped with the belts and hoses, and I marveled at the man's nose, an awesome rival for the Emir's. Then, annoyed at myself for failing to concentrate, I watched the instruments as another mechanic reached in and fired the car. Gauges popped up and told their messages. Schwandt leaned in as I adjusted my helmet. "Don't feel you must overcook things. We'll put in our fast times later."

I dawdled on the first lap, getting the feel of the car again and scruffing the tires. The texture of the track surface varied at places from the track at Qataban. I needed to shake the memory of the dummy track before driving at speed. Once back on the pit straight, headed toward the start and finish, I let the black machine wind up through five gears at full pitch. I looked forward to Turn One like opening curtain, arriving there sideways, then taking to the air through the corner. The downhill landing and counterslides unfolded in a shattering scene of noise, dust, burning rubber, and distillate fumes.

Unseld and the other drivers who had gone out early with serious intentions had immediately gotten down into the high 1:08s, which was enormously fast for the opening sessions of practice, only a few tenths above the race lap record. It seemed certain that someone would break the qualifying lap record of 1:08.3. On my fourth practice lap, I almost did, setting a time of 1:08.41. The others made a run for it at the end of the session, and Dair came close to my time in his March, 1:08.57. The cars still needed fine tuning, and the track surface had problems, which meant that my time held, scaring hell out of everybody else.

For the next two days we would be working with tenths and hundredths of seconds as the field of cars sorted itself out, the fastest cars being placed on the front of the starting grid. A mere second in time on a short course such as Long Beach can separate the first-rate cars and drivers from the ranks of mediocrity. A small adjustment by a mechanic or a maneuver by a driver that can save a tenth of a second is considered an enormous advantage.

At these speeds, working with such fine margins, at the rate top drivers are paid, errors are inexcusable. To make them is to invite replacement, if not oblivion. Only about a half-dozen drivers each season can be counted on not to make mistakes. However, names at the top change from season to season since no one is perfect.

I found Brunditz sitting on the pit counter Friday morning reading the morning paper. *"Schön, schön,* you flashy bastard," the German muttered. "You're all they can write about."

"You were only a half a second slower. It wasn't as if you were pedaling your grandmother's wheels," I said, looking over his shoulder. The press was ecstatic. Team Qataban and a new technology, an obscure sponsor, a mad-dog American driver two-tenths of a second off the lap record in the first session of practice, a disciplined pit crew, hellish engine sounds, a dictatorial team manager. The *Los Angeles Times* sports section had a prominent photo of Schwandt festooned with stopwatches and scowling out at the track. A second photo showed me power-sliding through the left-hand bend before the Esses, the car cocked at a suicidal attitude. For the dazzled press, Ferrari, Lotus, Wolf, Tyrrell, BRM—the teams that had been turning out searing lap times since the season opened in January—did not exist.

"Mr. Walter, follow me, please." I looked over my shoulder into the pit to see a young Arab, London School of Economics, one of Abdel's cabinet ministers. I vaulted the counter to join him and walked out into a narrow alley that led to the paddock area. Off to one side of the roped-off lot sat a compact recreational van, a bullet-shaped silver vehicle with ominous antennae on top. The young Arab opened a side door, and I entered alone.

"Gustave, I apologize for not having contacted you sooner," said Sheik Abdel as he rose from behind a teak desk built into an alcove in the rear of the van. The desk held three small gun-metal telephones. A teletype machine clattered mutely inside a Plexiglas enclosure. We shook hands, the Arab standing almost toe-to-toe. Why was it, I thought, that they always seemed to want to smell you, like a predator assessing the kill. I caught a tinge of SenSen and returned a volley of garlic. Drivers were meant to be uncouth.

Abdel motioned me to sit on a banquette opposite the desk. His Arabic headgear over the gray pin-stripe suit looked uncomfortably anachronistic. His boyish face was unlined, alert. An air conditioner and generator sent in distant mechanical noises. The carpet, apparently some sort of desert lamb, almost covered my narrow black driving shoes.

"I've been preoccupied with the internal aspects of this development program, the production side. Our factories have been tooling, and we expect production in five months now, but some of our bankers have little faith and grow nervous. That is under control now, and we can turn to publicity—the more enjoyable side. Tea, Gustave?"

"Coffee, please."

Abdel touched a button and one of the ubiquitous cabinet ministers opened the door and glided in on ball bearings of efficiency. "Coffee for our guest. He must drive in a few minutes. We want him conscious, alert."

The young Qatabani stepped behind a partition and produced an egg-like cup that held a Java blend, probably ground that morning. Always first cabin, I thought. The man vanished.

"In case you're curious, the Crucible of the Faith arrives tonight. His yacht is a hundred and fifty miles off San Diego. After the race, he takes his entourage in the 747 to Washington for a state visit."

I nestled the cup and waited.

"There is something else you should be aware of. It could affect the success of the racing program if we don't deal with it properly. The Emir is a clever man and keeps his dominion well divided. Those of us in one wing of his government seldom know what's going on in any of the other wings."

Here comes the revelation, I thought.

"I do know, of course, that Hassan has been training terrorists," he continued. "I have financed the camps, although reluctantly. They can only hurt us abroad. The point is—and you must believe that I have just learned this—that certain members of the Racing Department also received terrorist training, and Hassan and others who have the Protector's ear on this matter have infiltrated their agents into the team. I blame myself for not having watched matters closely enough."

I stayed neutral as a stone. "What about Schwandt?"

"He sold to the highest bidder. I thought a hundred and fifty million would at least buy his loyalty, but I hadn't counted on the size of the personal bank accounts pitted against me. Suffice it to say that he allowed the team's purposes to be subverted and somehow neglected to tell me about it."

"How did you find out?"

"Qataban is also divided along bloodlines, and the lineage is not always obvious. I have a second cousin in the Emir's immediate circle, but because of some fluke of genealogy he is old enough to be my grandfather. The ties between us go back to a small village in the Empty Quarter, but they are enough to secure his eyes and ears. I joined the yacht when it put in at

Port-au-Prince on its way here. We were able to take a walk, and he described the dimensions of the problem for me. And believe me, it is very, very serious."

There goes another one, I thought. As if driving the cars wasn't close enough to doomsday.

"What I had thought was merely misplaced chauvinism on the part of the Emir, which spilled over into his blind support for a Muslim driver, now appears to be part of a well-planned strategy by a group of paramilitary people. Even my cousin, one of the Protector's closest confidants, has only a slim grasp of what is going on. It is possible that our leader himself is being used. I will know more after the ship arrives. In the meantime, you must be extremely cautious. Trust no one." That phrase was beginning to sound like a litany.

We watched the Emir's yacht loom through Angel's Gate harbor entrance like an ocean liner as we drove along Ocean Boulevard on the way to the motel late Friday afternoon. The ship didn't exactly arrive with flags at half mast, but word quickly spread that there had been a death aboard. Schwandt said before dinner that Sheik Salah Fasil, a member of the Emir's inner circle, had had a fatal stroke off Baja. A 707 would fly his body back to Qataban that night. Diplomatic string-pulling apparently assured a minimum of medical oversight.

Abdel must be frantic, I concluded. His best source—and I had no illusions about who the dead person was—had been removed. I fell into a morose funk thinking about this as we assembled for dinner, but only briefly. Alcohol brought a helpful gift of memory blank.

We ate in a private dining room of a restaurant that adjoined the motel. The restaurant's symbol was a plastic medieval coat of arms. The menu offered steak or lobster or both, a custom that I hadn't adjusted to, having lived mostly in Europe for the past five years. Brunditz joyously ordered the combination and had glasses of both red and white wine before him, taking alternate pulls. Aimee's Dutch had grown into specialized vocabularies and structured tenses. Mimi's English had budded after she landed in the U.S., and the four of us, holding down one wedge of the table, set standards for boisterousness. Even Rachid that night drank more than his customary solitary glass, and Schwandt began to glow at the end of the table like some figurehead revolving over a nationwide franchise of German sausage stands.

The team took an upbeat from the second practice session, which was held Friday morning. My car had soured after a couple of tentative laps—a flapping vane again—but Rachid put in the best time of the day, 1:08.22, a new qualifying record, and Brunditz the third fastest, sandwiching Unseld's Ferrari on the starting grid. Although the positions were sure to change, we were fairly certain that on Saturday, when more rubber had been left on the porous surfaces and the track was broken in again, giving the racing machines better traction, one of the Vipers would end up with the record and be on the pole position. No other team had done this well so quickly since Mercedes-Benz had come out of retirement in 1954.

We guessed with raunchy humor what the other teams were doing that night, the frenzied adjustments and bickering among specialists. Our technicians convulsed with laughter at their rivals' predicament. Unsmiling waitresses imported a stream of wine bottles into the rowdy room. Brunditz stole a white cap off Petre Priest's lap, and we scaled it up and down the table like a Frisbee as Priest scrambled after it, so amused that spittle dripped from the corner of his mouth.

A man with an accordion, a hired musician, burst into the room squeezing out a polka. He was tall, with a pink face and enormous forehead. His fixed smile looked like another keyboard. Schwandt positively radiated with the success of his social planning while Brunditz hauled Aimee to her feet with an animal grunt and they danced a polka around the room as the rest of us shouted and clapped. I waited until the tempo went to three/four, bowed, and asked Mimi to waltz, which we did with exaggerated decorum. Her small body felt as strong as a leather whip.

"All right, my chickens," said Schwandt finally, signaling for the music and flow of wine to halt. "This is your leader speaking." We didn't pay any attention. For one inebriated moment I felt fond of the man, the provider and thinker who anticipated our needs down to the last ignition wire and thirty-pfennig clamp. "Tomorrow we go all out, but I want no bent cars and no katzenjammers in your delicate heads. A toast!" We jumped to our feet. "To the Vipers. And may they stay friendly."

"Hear, hear."

"Snakes in the grass."

"Grass in the snakes." Faux hilarity. Aimee and I left for the large bedroom with the thick, stringy carpet. In bed we talked in improvised sign language, some of it obscene, like incoherent deaf-mutes.

* * *

On Friday evening, the Director of Central Intelligence sent a memorandum by special courier to the Assistant to the President for National Security Affairs:

To: Assistant to President for National Security Affairs
From: DCI

We now have a taste of how Qataban intends to act in the international arena. Hassan's faction murdered one of the Emir's closest advisers before the yacht arrived at Long Beach. We got the body out and smoothed things over without a flap developing, but the problem is serious. My strategists view the Viper group as a prototype of a multi-country terrorist linkup. That would set a very bad precedent if it is allowed to survive.

The problem is further aggravated by the importance of Qataban to the nation's energy posture, and the Emir's position among Third World leaders. Since he arrives here Tuesday for the state visit, we need some tangible way to impress on him the importance of not financing terrorist cells.

Moreover, Sheik Abdel's position appears to be seriously weakened. Either we back Abdel to the hilt and keep our close ties with Qataban or we'll have to live with Hassan for a long, long time. We have firm reports that the Russians want our share of Qatabani oil. That might be good news for the Candle Lobby on the Hill.

If all this is going to be properly nipped in Long Beach, we should convene the

Special Committee tomorrow morning, at the earliest convenience of the Secretaries. I ask that this be given the highest priority.

~:~

6.

There were people who smiled and shrugged their shoulders when one risked one's life to be a few seconds faster. For me it spelled happiness! To sit in the car, huddled behind the screen, waiting for the starter's flag to drop and then roar off, perhaps a fraction of a second quicker than the others.

Then the hours on the circuit: the wind whistling past and the engine's boom, there is even a booming within yourself, for you are no longer a man with a painful leg and broken heart, but master over three or four hundred horsepower. Yours is the will that rules this steed of steel, you think for it, you think within its rhythm. Your brain works with the same speed and precision as its steely heart. If not, then the monster will master and crush you.

Rudolf Caracciola
Caracciola
G. T. Foulis & Co., Ltd.

The fraction of letup Friday night promoted more than a hangover on Saturday. In fact, alcohol played little part in our difficulties the next day, since Schwandt steadfastly discouraged hard booze and the daily wine ration was less than we made it out to be. But we had discounted the sheer momentum the other teams had built up by racing first in Brazil, Argentina, and South Africa. Saturday was divided into two one-and-one-half-hour qualifying sessions at 9:00 and 3:00, the city streets now being closed off until Sunday night.

Portable garages had been set up out in the paddock area this year. They were large white aluminum structures, like outsized chicken sheds. We met in our garage at 8:00 for a strategy session. Schwandt said Team Qataban would wait before nailing down fastest time. It was up to the other teams to beat our marks of the previous session. If they bettered our times, we would go out and take them back. The cars themselves were ready for Sunday's race, and the less we had to extend them, the better.

Schwandt's strategy seemed reasonable, except Unseld, in the Ferrari, went out when the course finally opened at 9:35, and on his third lap set a qualifying record of 1:07.26, almost a full second better than Rachid had done the previous day. Schwandt stood before us at the pits, stopwatches in each hand, marking the passage of the cars with ferret eyes. We sat on the pit counter, the Vipers in front of us, covered with dust cloths. Kevin Dair came by in his March at full chat. Schwandt's hand flexed, and when he glanced down at the watch face, his chins vibrated, which for him was a major show of emotion. Another car in the low sevens. Giovanni DeMarco in the Brabham-Alfa-Romeo joined the below-eight club, and for the next twenty minutes it was like a parade past us. With a half hour left in the morning session, six cars stood ahead of us on Sunday's starting grid. It became quickly obvious that the other cars had most of their quirks worked out.

Schwandt motioned to the Qatabani pit crew, and his finger ended up pointing at my car. So I would be the hare. I would have to go all out to find out how genuine the other times were and, if possible, grab back the advantage. Not exactly a distinction, this. The chances of bending the engine or the car, not to mention myself, were close to even. And with the race practically on top of us, I would rather have seen someone else make the suicide run while my car stayed pristine for the main event.

I sat in the car, blipping the throttle. Schwandt waited. With eleven minutes to go in the morning session, enough for about three flying laps, he jerked his thumb and I gunned the car. The light beamed green at the end of the pit row. The black car nosed out on the almost-deserted track as if smelling the spoor. By the time I got on the back straight I let everything out, the rear end still yawing from acceleration at 160 miles per hour. In that brief moment of relative inactivity—time for one long inhale and exhale—I realized that this was the first time I had driven the car without some sort of limit placed on me by Schwandt, so the car could be driven flat out without inhibitions or guilt.

Drivers hone their ability to concentrate, each settling on a pattern that serves specific needs. My pattern is that I simply black out. With a sound Formula 1 car, I become the eyes and reflexes of the machine. That answers a number of problems because there is no place in the driver's universe for human emotion or conscious physical movement. Nor for memory, a loss that is usually beneficial.

At the end of the fourth lap, a Qatabani pit crew member held out my last time, a qualifying lap record of I:07 flat. A course official signaled that the morning practice session was over. I slowed the machine to a crawl at Turn Three as my spirits returned and found everything intact. In the wonder of it, I looked around and then up at the tall, round apartment building that towers over that section of the course. Balconies loaded with spectators rose above me like ranks in the company of heaven, and ranged around the fifth-floor balcony was the entire contingent from the yacht. The Emir must have rented the floor. The Arabs stood immobile, almost threatening and accusatory it suddenly seemed to me, with knuckles sticking out of black sleeves, grasping the balustrade.

Even going at a crawl, I almost missed the right turn at the top of the hill. The apparent suspicion, if not hostility, of my employers, after I had just spent the past ten minutes on the knife edge of disaster on their behalf, threw me into a paralyzing rage. The antiquated princes and sheiks arranged along the balcony seemed to me clearly in one camp of the human condition while I lived in another. And that wouldn't have bothered me, except I was now convinced they were going to try to bring me down.

From the looks of them, there seemed to be no question that Abdel was right. The Qatabanis were there to see Rachid drive. I was a Western encumbrance thrust on them by the need to modernize their country. And if Aimee and her CIA sources were correct and racing was the ancillary goal of a terrorist group, then I was more than an encumbrance. I was a distinct threat. I didn't understand the Emir's people, but even as a remote reactionary force they were no less the enemy. I had confined my life to perfecting one facet of technology. I was dedicated to motor racing but without a strong sense of purpose. My blue-eyed face was on the cover of *Sports Illustrated* that week, but I didn't recognize it. The person in the car and the public property in the media were not related. And I wasn't sure that either of them was really me.

I was forced to concentrate on driving again when I got to the back straight. The course had opened, and the track was suddenly loaded with roaring tow trucks, ambulances, and a squadron of Official Pace Cars. The drivers all seemed eager to show off their skills, which made me feel more than uneasy. I could see myself explaining to Schwandt how I got rear-ended by an off-duty Chevy dealer. I continued in first gear and eventually made it to the pits unscathed. Schwandt, festooned with stopwatches, was waiting for me.

"Beautiful, beautiful, Herr Walter," he cooed as I took off my helmet and sat limply in the car, feeling my muscles tick and cramp the way a machine does after it has been driven hard

"You got your bloody time, but it probably won't stick this afternoon. The track is very fast."

"Leave that to me, Herr Walter. We shall be ready."

By now my rage had modulated into a tranquil hatred. I just sat in the car and thought about how much I wanted to be off the team and the hell away from there with Aimee, to be free from being used, risking my life for so little purpose. The money didn't mean anything just then. The winner's purse at Long Beach this year was $350,000, 40 percent of which could be mine, plus my salary, plus my payoff. The morbid total made me ill, knowing how much of a mortgage I had taken out on my life.

Aimee came over the pit counter and stood by the car as I extricated myself, bumping my knee on a sharp switch box and getting a foot tangled in the safety harness. We walked quietly out into the paddock area and found a grassy strip that was home to a couple of placid trees. I flopped down and leaned back against one and plucked a long blade of grass that had the taste of new-mown hay.

I told her about driving past the balcony after the final practice lap, and how hostile the contingent from the yacht had seemed. "It gave me the creeps," I told her. "This team is shaping up as some sort of battleground, and I'm beginning to feel like the ignorant grunt, the guy in the trenches who's been told over the field telephone to move over the parapet and face the machine guns."

"The best damn grunt I ever met," she said, leaning her head on my shoulder.

"I've got a feeling that I ought to quit while I can, but then this other voice—I can't tell if it's my good voice or my bad voice—keeps saying, 'Don't do it. You haven't got a good reason to pull out, and you have the fastest machine of your career under you and a chance to win the championship.'"

"If you desert too early, you'll never know," she said, looking up at my face. "You'll spend the rest of your life wondering."

"And if I stay, I may not have much of a life left to find out, either."

"You've ridden on this edge for a long time."

"Nowhere near like today. That's as close to the brink as I've ever been. After I went by the pits on the last lap, I came out of it, sort of woke up, and I looked down at the entrance to Turn One and saw these incredible snaking black tire marks on the road and then realized they were mine. I must have been crazy to try that."

"Crazy is probably the right word, but it's pretty impressive, too." She looked straight into my eyes. Hers were lustrous green. "Please stick it out, at least till tomorrow. You can always dog it in the race, tell them you don't feel well or a vane is sticking, and then you can chuck it. But if you cut out now, I think you're going to regret it."

I got up slowly, gave her a hand, and we walked back to the motel for a shower and some rest.

For me, cleaning firearms steadies the nerves almost as well as tying trout flies. We broke down the Purdeys and worked them over methodically while we flopped on the rug watching a 1938 George Sanders gaslight drama on one of the seemingly infinite TV channels that operate in Los Angeles. The banana-tinged medicinal smells of the solvents finally overwhelmed the vinyl-and-detergent environment of the motel room.

According to Schwandt's long-term schedule—which was no longer necessarily mine—we had a week free after the Long Beach Grand Prix before having to assemble at Monza, Italy, for tire tests, since he had decided to cure our tire woes by inviting three major companies to make tires for us. The winning firm would be selected in a drive-off at the Italian track, and we then would have another short break before the next Grand Prix, which would be in Spain.

Aimee and I had planned to drive to San Diego after the Long Beach race and stay with my sister and grandfather at the green and sprawling ranch, the sight of which made housing developers go weak in the knees. My sister and her husband, a psychologist whom I had met once, on their wedding day, were coming up for the race. My parents had moved to Maui to escape the aging-parent scene, and my grandfather was now detached from the kind of realities that concern the rest of us. He'd refused to come to the phone when I'd called about the race and had passed the word through his housekeeper that he would stay home and weed his zucchini patch.

After helping in my grandfather's vegetable garden, Aimee and I were going to fly to Panama for two days of snook fishing. Then my business agent, a San Francisco attorney who coordinated a collection of professionals, had me booked into appointments in New York and London before we were due in Milan for the tire tests. In the rush to sign with Team Qataban, I had failed to resolve my status with other sponsors, and it wasn't clear how much extracurricular work Sheik Abdel or Schwandt would tolerate. One vitamin pill company was threatening to sue if I didn't show up for the taping of a television commercial.

We still had an hour before I had to be back at the track for the Saturday afternoon scare show. The TV was pumping out a jangly used-car commercial, a lot of good 0l' boy glad talk from a cowboy with a lion on the hood of his come-on car. I turned the volume up.

"Have you gone mad?" asked Aimee.

"No, that's in case someone's listening in," I told her as I looked through my kit bag for a roll of aluminum tape. "Look, just for the sake of argument, should your worst predictions come true and this turns out to be a difficult weekend,

I think we should make sure we have custody of these shotguns."

"Um-hm. Now you're talking sense," she said, and we both started to prowl the room, looking for a likely hiding spot for a pair of 20-gauge Purdeys. Finally I took a screwdriver from a gun case into the bathroom and started unscrewing fixtures. Ten minutes later, the job was done.

I sprinkled my body with baby powder and re-donned the driving suit. The Team Qataban drivers had had a serious confrontation with Schwandt over our having to abandon our own driving suits for the black-and-orange uniform. My argument was that dyed fabric was unclean. If it got ground or burned into our skin during a bad shunt, it could be toxic. The other two drivers simply wanted to keep the suits they were used to. And we also didn't want to lose all our sponsors, whose patches covered our chests like regimental colors.

But Schwandt had overriden us in a significant power play. "I will remind you," he had nearly shouted in the garage in Qataban, "that you are paid like crown princes and you can therefore spare me this safety cry-babying. You will drive where I want, wearing what I want. Driving has always been and will continue to be dangerous." His chins had started to vibrate. "If you can't live with risks, become—become—*Bibliothekar.*"

For once his English had left him, but we got the point. We were at least allowed to have the black suits made by our own tailors. I had gotten hold of Hinchman Racing Uniforms by transatlantic phone and ordered a new pair made with more handles for the emergency workers. Risk is one thing, but stupidity is another.

Aimee and I walked back to the paddock through the radiating California sun. Schwandt had arranged a small theater of seats in the garage, as if it were test day again, back in Qataban. Now he had replaced Sheik Abdel at stage center.

"This afternoon is likely to be difficult, but I'm confident in the cars and your ability," Schwandt said. "Herr Walter has proved once again that we can still stay ahead of the rest of them."

Brunditz, sitting on one side of me, gave a few silent claps and whistled quietly through his lower teeth.

"Please, please, hold your applause until he has finished," I answered behind my hand.

"The other teams will be pressing hard this afternoon. We'll see what their times look like and then do ours about halfway through the session. Hopefully there won't be any last-minute scrambling. Clear?"

"No," I said. "Why are we busting ourselves to set such fast times? It's going to be a long season."

"True, Herr Walter. But from the start our employers have been looking for maximum publicity from this event. That means pole position, fastest lap, and hopefully the race. Anything less might not be worth the investment."

Ah, I thought, there's that ugly word. Even if this team were what it said it was, we would still be a capital venture, with the drivers taking the risk. Sport was an investment for them, and we had to produce dividends, or else. I began to think about buying a trout-fishing ranch in Utah while Schwandt yammered about gear ratios.

We moved to the pits again and began our vigil as the other cars went out. The first laps didn't go well for some of the teams. A few events that took place between Formula 1 qualifying sessions, a race between historic formula cars and another race between identical Corvettes driver by some loopy celebrities, left patches of oil on the course. Three qualifying Formula 1 cars spun, two crashing badly in the Esses, but not seriously enough to injure the drivers, all of whom were back-markers who had been pushing too hard. The times gradually came down, though, and Unseld put in a wild lap with the Ferrari at 1:06.94, breaking what had once been believed to be an impossible barrier. This time gave him the pole—for the moment.

Schwandt sent Brunditz and Rachid out together. They immediately went through the eight-second barrier but found it hard to get down to the time I'd set in the morning, much less to catch Unseld. After four laps, Rachid came in and asked for new tires. He had that possessed look of someone who is about to make the ultimate effort. He left the pits under full power, the new tires giving off smoke. A wake of angry officials waved their fists, but he probably didn't know there was anyone else alive.

I started to follow him vicariously around the circuit, my own inner clock being well enough calibrated that I could tell second by second where he was. That way lay madness, so I went in search of a Pepsi. Rachid shrieked by as I rummaged in the ice chest. Aimee was off in another pit with Mimi and several drivers' wives, and I knew they would throw me out if I tried to smuggle my case of nerves into their midst.

Brunditz was late. Schwandt got word almost immediately that he had gone down an escape road backward with shredded tires but no damage to the car. Rachid posted a lap of 1:07.002 and then 1:06.5. When he pulled in, he whooped with glee. Qatabani mechanics, smiling broadly, helped him from the car, and Schwandt gave him a loud smack on the back. Rachid swung over the pit counter, brushing past me, and headed out toward the paddock. I waited while Schwandt and the chief mechanic went over the car, which seemed to be in one piece. The telltale needle on the tachometer was stuck on 24,000 revolutions per minute, or 2,000 above the limit, but even that didn't seem to deaden their joy at now having Rachid on the pole.

The other cars rushed out on the track in response, Unseld leading the pack. Only twenty-two minutes remained before qualifying ended. I told Schwandt I wanted to go out, and as I feared, he was noncommittal, mumbling something about the car being cold.

"Well, let's warm it up, for Christ's sake. If any more of those cars out there get into the sixes, we're in bad shape."

"But I don't think they can, Herr Walter. And it wouldn't be very productive if you bent your car trying to bump a teammate off the pole. As it is now, you are well placed on the second row."

"That's a matter of opinion, Schwandt, and there's still time to make a run for it." The competitive juices were coursing like hormones as the urge to get back out on the track left me recklessly addled.

The closing moments of practice can sometimes be hairier than the race itself. Cars peeled off from up and down the pit row, intent on one last charge at the front rows. On a short, tight course like Long Beach, where passing is difficult, it helps to start up front and stay there. By now, the qualifying times were dangerously fast, with less than a second separating the top seven cars. DeMarco, driving smoothly, moved ahead of me in the Brabham-Alfa at a time of 1:06.79, and the veteran Dair, also driving with remarkable economy of steering-wheel motion and no theatrics, took the outside of Row Two at a rate of 1:06.92.

Then Jon Brunnsen, my former teammate, crashed badly on the back straight. Someone said in the next pit that his car had smashed from wall to wall for a quarter mile before coming to a halt in pieces. That chopped several minutes from the waning qualifying session as tow trucks and the ambulance went to work. No sooner had the track been cleared than Raul Casteňeda in the new Brazilian Condor braked too late in Turn One and lost it going down the hill. Reports came back that the car was demolished but he was already standing next to what was left of his aluminum tub of a cockpit. Brunnsen apparently had not been as lucky and had been taken to the hospital.

There were now only eleven minutes left, and the Team Qataban position worsened. Robin Askew, who until then had put in very few practice laps, suddenly took his cobalt-blue Tyrrell out and did a remarkable series of quick laps, getting into the high sixes and moving me to the outside of Row Three on Sunday's starting grid. Then Ian Campbell, who had also practiced lightly, did 1:07.62, and Ari Tomaka, the Japanese ace, improved his time of that morning, turning 1:08.09. Seutenbach, the Dutchman; Campbell; and Braccio, who literally ripped up the course, all did faster laps than they had previously turned, which pushed Brunditz to the outside of Row Six. Unseld, meanwhile, was driving so smoothly that he went unnoticed, until the official clock registered his second-to-last qualifying lap at 1:06.47 and Team Qataban no longer had the pole position.

Schwandt, now tactically on the defensive, suddenly nodded at me and signaled our chief mechanic, who got in my car and fired it up, blipping the throttle, until I put on my helmet and gloves and replaced him. I headed out for one warm-up lap before trying for a good time.

Almost from the start, the car felt wrong. The front end was too light and tended to wash out in the comers, and I had to back off or risk plowing off the course. I went to the pits.

"Bad understeer," I shouted from the car before it had even stopped. "The front wing feels like it's messed up. Maybe the shocks, too."

The car popped up in the air as Qatabani mechanics levered it with jacks front and rear.

A couple of men pored over the front end with wrenches in hand as I watched cars streaking by.

"Screw it," I shouted at Schwandt and Petre Priest, who were supervising the front-end work. "Just get the car out. Get the bloody car out."

Mechanics still bobbed up and down. The car stayed up on the jacks. A minute. A minute and twenty seconds. Then I felt the car pitch forward, and the crew chief signaled I could pull out. I hauled out of the pits fast enough to make Rachid's earlier departure seem like slow motion. I was out on the course, pushing for a fast standing lap in order to get a flying lap in before it was too late. But the car still didn't respond; it twitched and veered, the front wheels chattering across the pavement. An utter pig of a machine.

"Goddammit, Schwandt, what happened?" I asked, lying still as a corpse in the car after qualifying had ended. My instinct was to pull the top-heavy man into the cockpit and then systematically smash his teeth in.

"These things happen, Herr Walter," Schwandt said with a professional, almost condescending tone. "The wing must have gotten out of adjustment. We can set it up again tonight and test it in the morning."

Maybe I was becoming paranoid, but wings don't just suddenly readjust themselves.

Somebody had wanted me up on the jacks during those final, crucial minutes of qualifying. We were to be allowed a half hour on the course on Sunday before the race to make final adjustments, but the laps would not be timed, and the starting places had been established.

Schwandt was leaning over me, one arm resting on the roll bar behind my helmet. I began to follow my instinct and reach for him, but the consequences of getting fired acted like a fuse and my arms went limp. By exercising control, I might actually get a sound car to compete with, but there were limits to the crap I would put up with.

"Next time something like this happens to me, I'm coming out of here with a tire iron," I told Schwandt. "The photographers from *Motor Sport* and *Road and Track* will burn up their shutters."

"You push the limit, Herr Walter."

"Always, Schwandt." He straightened up and walked away.

Aimee and I went toward the paddock and our Viper street machine. I felt like driving in the general direction of Denver, although the team was due for a reception out on the Emir's yacht starting at seven-thirty. We hadn't walked far before we were intercepted by Sheik Abdel's underminister. This time, I told him, she comes with me.

We found Abdel behind his desk in the motor home reading papers in a manila binder. He greeted us tepidly and asked us to sit, Aimee on the chrome-vinyl chair and me semi-stretched out on the banquette, where the smells of grime and desperate exertion reeked from the zippered opening of my Nomex uniform. When he offered drinks, I settled for tea, a sweet, minty brew served in a tall glass with a silver spoon that radiated heat.

"She knows everything," I said. "We don't talk so that we can be taped, and I don't think we've left any tracks. But Aimee and I work as a team."

"Of course. It's just difficult for me to adjust to this sometimes," he said. Too bad for him if they keep their women locked up, I thought. They probably should be waging war with Women's Lib instead of the Israelis.

"That was your man on the boat, I take it."

"Unfortunately, yes."

"Murdered?" I asked.

"Probably. The timing was a great coincidence—let's put it that way. The important thing is why, what did they know, what do they know about me—or you?"

"Me? How could *I* fit in that? I never met the man."

"If they know that you are aware of the terrorist potentials of the team, you could be in serious jeopardy. The Western members of the team were not meant to know."

"Does that mean Rachid knows?" I asked.

"Yes, he's one of them. That's why he flew so much to Jubil. He was being intensively trained in explosives and assassination, among other things."

"Is he the Viper?"

"Where did you learn that?"

"Rachid mentioned the word to me one night in a strange context. It could have applied either to our cars or to a trained murderer." Fluent lying was coming more easily to me.

"That was a serious slip on his part. No, as far as I know, Rachid is not the Viper. The leaders function as a group, each possessing unique skills. My sources tell me that one of them is perhaps the most accomplished hit artist, as they put it in your country, that an Arab nation has ever recruited. Sheik Fasil was going to identify him for me, which is why his loss is a disaster, for both of us."

"Maybe for all of us," said Aimee.

"Quite so, and if you see it that way, then you will side with me and convince your husband it is essential that he accompany me below decks on the yacht tonight. Fasil knew the peril he was in. We agreed in Port-au-Prince that in the event he didn't make it to Long Beach he would leave some sort of message for me in his cabin, Stateroom Six. We have to get in there and find it, and I have to have you because if I were found below decks alone or with one of my aides, I probably would never make it back up. With you, I have a plausible excuse, showing you the sights, the gold faucets. Together, we have a chance."

* * *

At approximately the same time Saturday, three thousand miles to the east, the tall, distinguished Director of Central Intelligence took a towel to his aquiline features. He was soaked with sweat after having played his seventeen-year-old son three sets of tennis in their indoor tennis court on the Director's spacious farm outside Fredericksburg. He heard the phone ring in the nearby dressing room and reluctantly left his son to the pitcher of lemonade, which a servant had brought to the edge of the court. Only three people had access to that phone number, and he had a feeling which one this was.

"You get whipped?" The President was an avid player.

"Are you ordering me to reveal the score?"

"Thought so. Send him out to Camp David Sunday afternoon. We'll see who's still got the young legs around here. I'll lob his butt off."

"If you can touch his serve. These kids get so damn much spin on it." The DCI shut up. He sensed the fun was over.

"I just saw the staff report on the Special Committee meeting this morning to discuss the Qataban thing," the President said. "I'm not happy about this one damn bit, or the way you people are handling it. Do you realize that Arab is my guest here Tuesday night? You bungle it in California tomorrow and we're going to be eating crow at that state dinner."

"I understand your concern, sir."

"Do you? Do you really? Well, you just put your strategists to work, then, writing me a toast to give Tuesday night if some of that Arab's people are shot up and it gets out in the press or on national TV. That race is on national TV, for God's sake."

"Yessir, I'm aware of the exposure."

"Have you got enough people on it, you and the Bureau?" He sounded more contrite.

"Yessir, the DDO has set up the twenty-four-hour command post at the Pit in Langley. We've called in field people from Paris and Jubil and we've got substantial forces on the ground with a fleet of helicopters ready to go. We'll coordinate through the Bureau's Los Angeles field office. I believe it's under control."

"Better be, Richard. Or it could be more than embarrassing on Tuesday night. Like this country might find itself in an OPEC boycott and without fifty-two and a half percent of its oil by Wednesday. Got it?"

"Yessir."

"Don't forget to send that kid over for tennis tomorrow—two o'clock sharp."

The line went dead.

7.

> After the hours of practice we all sat down together for a tactical conference . . . . I think these occasions were Neubauer's favorite ones. Like a general he sat ensconced among his soldiers, or rather like a good shepherd among his flock.
>
> Rudolf Caracciola
> *A Racing Driver's World*
> Cassell: London

The launch made its sleek way toward the black yacht that was silhouetted by the lights of the *Queen Mary*. Ballroom music met us over the water as the helmsman throttled down the engine.

"We could run the Grand Prix around the decks. Save everyone trouble," I said.

"The wonders of oil," mused Aimee. "I wonder how many tanks of gas it took for us to pay for that."

"Last Fourth of July weekend was the down payment," I said as the boat pulled abreast of the platform and gangway. Aimee leaped over the low rail faultlessly in a short black formal dress, ignoring the proffered hands of two crewmen in black-and-orange uniform. I landed on the balls of my feet, feeling comfortable in a veteran tuxedo. We moved up the teak stairs, led on by Cole Porter. No hard metal for this host.

The ballroom—there is no other word for it, even on a yacht—could hold about a hundred. Guests were following us aboard in a steady procession of launches and private boats. Sheik Abdel had said it would be an eclectic grouping of the racing world, the diplomatic corps, and West Coast utility executives and oil importers. Each bloc wanted a slice of Qataban and its Emir, who was greeting guests in a reception line. Behind him on the wall was an outsized version of the Qatabani flag, the only decoration in the room. I wondered what would happen when the Arabs turned seriously to art collection. Whole walls of Giotto's frescoes would be carved out of Italy.

"I still maintain that you push too hard, my dear boy," the Emir said when we reached him. "You must learn to relax."

"If I relax any more, I'll be starting on the last row, Your Highness. And the car wouldn't like that. They're like animals. They quit on you." I introduced Aimee. He greeted her with equity, almost warmth.

"When the race is done," the Emir said, "you both must join me for some falconry. I have bought a ranch south of here, near President Nixon's estate, and it is filled with gophers. But it won't be before long."

He turned to the next couple, and we moved past the unsmiling members of his entourage, the balcony contingent, their heavy eyes giving away nothing. Prince Hassan stood among them, watching us as we walked past. His face had that fullness that comes with power. We locked eyes for a moment, not breaking contact until a group of people walked between us. He was clearly a tough young bastard.

"That's rather nice—buying a ranch for your bird," said Aimee as we took a turn on the uncrowded dance floor.

"What's wrong with that? You don't like birds or something? I'm going to put him up for the Audubon Society's Man of the Year award."

We hunted for the bar, but there was none, at least not in the Emir's presence. A corridor led to an adjoining room, paneled in rich knotty oak, where champagne, the best of Veuve Cliquot, was being poured by waiters from bulging magnums.

I fetched a couple of tulip glasses. Aimee had been collared by one of the young promoters of the Grand Prix, who gushed about the size of the gate so far, and the keen interest generated by the black Vipers. The team had probably gotten him out of debt. I took in part of the conversation while scanning the densely packed room for Abdel. I finally spotted him against a far wall in animated conversation with what appeared to be utility executives, a group of close-cropped, middle-aged engineers who were probably wondering if this chance moment over champagne might get them the oil they would need to turn their turbines that summer.

Eventually, Aimee and I broke away and headed toward Abdel, stopping to check with friends—drivers and car designers—we had not seen for the months we had been sequestered in Qataban.

"You like driving bloody blowtorches, do you?" asked Ian Campbell, the clipped-mustached Guardsman, now driving for Surtees and one of the infamous five I had shared a pad with in London three years before.

"It'll be handy for you, Ian, if you need a light. You'll be behind me all afternoon."

"But what about these Wogs?" he asked, *sotto voce,* moving closer in mock conspiracy.

"Cheeky of these minorities getting into Formula One, if you ask me."

"Ask the Emir, Ian, and he'll write a check big enough to buy your team, your farm in Cornwall, and your girl friends—and that's for openers."

"Filthy lucre, old boy. Ostentatious. Besides, I sold the farm to some Saudis last month. That's all we have in Cornwall now, you know, Saudis. They're going to turn the village parish into a mosque, I hear."

"Serves you right, you bigot," I said.

"Bigot. I sell my inheritance to the blighters and he calls me a bigot." We agreed to meet after the race, a reconvention of the remnants of the Kensington crowd, three of us now being in Formula 1 and two being dead, which was in accordance with the law of probabilities. The carnage on the tracks acts as a drumbeat. About one-third of the pre-World War II Grand Prix drivers, the sport's Golden Age of the 1930's, had lost their lives in race cars.

Abdel saw us coming and broke away from the utility types. "Yes, well, here it is, one of our national monuments, the world's largest yacht. I suppose we should have a tour."

"Lead on," I said, although I wasn't happy about having Aimee this deeply involved. We were heading into an unknown. In a car, I could evaluate risks to within decimal points, but probing below decks was a murky void. Abdel looked at Aimee and then me.

"Just keep going, gentlemen," she said evenly. "I wouldn't miss this for anything."

The three of us moved out of the room and down a passageway away from the music. There was traffic to and from the toilets and considerable congestion, since there weren't toilets enough to handle the demand from a shipload of Western champagne drinkers. The women in particular were backed up, and Abdel took advantage of the commotion, quickly opening a small, unmarked door. We followed, closing it behind us, and found ourselves on a dimly lit platform, metal rungs tailing off into the well below.

"The classical back way. Since I had to put up the fifty-three million to pay the shipyards, I got a copy of the blueprints. But I must ask you, Mrs. Walter, to join the ladies outside. We should be only a few minutes."

"Sorry, boys, but I'm in on this. I've been below decks here before, and I know my way around. Besides, it'll look more natural to be giving both of us a below-decks tour."

"Lead on, Sheik," I advised. "Your case is futile."

"Aai-yai. Western women," he muttered. He swung around and rattled softly down the rungs. We followed to a door at the bottom. Abdel slipped it open. I could see a slice of the sparkling white paintwork of the passageway and strips of teak handrails.

"Empty," he whispered. We stepped out, turned right, and began to amble forward. The corridor kinked left ahead, blocking our view. I wondered about electronic surveillance but could see no cameras. The staterooms had Arabic and cardinal numbers on them, an accommodation no doubt to the oil customers who came aboard on cruises. Likewise, security would have to be low-key or the oil men, a paranoid lot to begin with, would be put on guard or antagonized unnecessarily.

Abdel moved swiftly. We turned the corner without meeting anyone and stopped halfway down. Abdel tested a stateroom door, Stateroom 6, then produced a small wire and slipped it in the lock. No wonder oil men are paranoid, I thought. Abdel can probably read contracts across a desk upside down better than most of us can read them right side up with a magnifying glass, and he is no doubt a graduate in lip reading. Racing was close enough to the oil industry so that we heard weird stories about marathon negotiations with the Abdels of OPEC.

We slipped noiselessly into the dark stateroom. Abdel popped out a pen light that produced an astonishingly big beam. He held it obliquely to his face and signaled for silence, waving his finger airily around at unseen microphones. I exhaled, and it sounded like a whale breaching. Each crinkle of fabric or footfall on the carpet seemed to echo like a cathedral choir. Abdel reached again into his pocket, this time producing a two-foot-long, snakelike wire that must have extended into his coat lining. He grasped the end of it, which was shaped like a hypodermic plunger. He pressed his thumb, and four claw-like wires popped out the other end. I remembered a nightclub manager using one to retrieve a gold ring from a sink.

Abdel picked up the bathroom in his beam and moved into it. We watched from the door. The faucets were gold plated, and the bidet was lined with mother-of-pearl.

It was obvious now that Sheik Abdel and his distant relative had left few untied threads. Rather than a bumbling cohort, Sheik Fasil must have been a highly efficient operative.

Abdel quietly threaded the wire down the sink and into the trap. He pressed the plunger, maneuvered for a second, and slowly withdrew, pulling out a small aluminum cylinder shaped like a miniature cigar container. One end had a screw cap. Abdel didn't bother opening it but pocketed the wire and metal tube swiftly and aimed his light toward the door. We had got halfway across the stateroom when we heard furtive noise in the corridor. There must have been two of them. We heard them testing door handles down each side. They couldn't have picked us up on a bug. The ship was probably rigged with some sort of electrical beams that had been cut by our passage down the corridor, which had us narrowed down to one section of the ship but not the exact stateroom.

Abdel had doused the torch at the first whisper of sound. We took up station around the door and waited, our breathing and heartbeats seemingly outrageously loud. The searchers moved past us quickly, testing doors, then stopped at the end of the passageway, four doors down, and moved back, more methodical this time, opening the staterooms and presumably scanning with a flashlight, then closing and locking. The next sweep would probably be more thorough still.

"Move when the doors open," Abdel whispered. We listened. They had opened two doors simultaneously, a signal for to Abdel flick open our door. We stepped out in one motion, Abdel drawing the door closed. They had heard us, but by the time they stepped back out into the passageway, we had already taken three strides toward them.

"What luck," said Abdel. "They have a key. We can go in and look at the faucets and bidet.

You must see the bidet." He then spoke swiftly in Arabic, and they hesitated.

The one to our left, a hefty Arab in a black jump suit with orange piping uncomfortably reminiscent of my driving gear, began to move toward Abdel, and it looked as if the Sheik would be put against the wall. The second man, smaller and apparently in charge, shook his head almost imperceptibly, and Abdel slipped by into the opened stateroom. If these two didn't have the authority to nail us, I wondered who else was on the way who did.

"The wallpaper was custom-made," Abdel said in guided tour patois. Speed was essential, but both guards were watching us from the door. Haste had to be avoided. "The backing is fourteen carat, and the flock is actually animal fur, although that turned out to be not such a good idea because it gives people with allergies all kinds of problems. We'll have to replace it."

We did our best to look impressed. The room was ornate but somehow cautious, as if the decorator hadn't made up his mind. Except for the fixtures, there were no bold strokes, no Picassos or poetic pen-and-ink renderings of rear-entry positions. We made it back out to the corridor, the two Arabs in black suits backing up a pace. Abdel led the way to the main staircase, a sweeping circular shaft that looked as though it came from a Paris town house. As we reached the midpoint, we saw Prince Hassan poised on the top step. His raptor eyes bored into mine; then he turned back toward the ballroom.

Conversation in the narrow champagne room had reached unacceptable levels, which gave us a chance to talk briefly in the babble. "I must study the note," said Abdel. "Meet me in the trailer after your team meeting tonight."

"We want to hear it all, Abdel," I told him. "It's our necks, too."

"You will get it, but take care. They obviously know we are onto something."

Aimee and I finished a quick glass and headed for the gangway. We had an hour and a half before a meeting with the drivers and technicians at the motel. I smelled the salt air on deck and felt almost light-headed that the venture had gone so smoothly.

"Do you think we were smart or lucky?" I asked Aimee as we stood alone on the fantail of the launch, hunched against a cold sea breeze.

"I just can't tell how good they are," she said. "I get a feeling we haven't seen the first team yet."

"That's one game I'm hoping we can skip."

"It's the intuition bit again," she said slowly, "but it hasn't failed me yet in twenty-seven years. I think they're going to try to kill us."

We stood side by side, out of earshot of the helmsman. She had raised a more than valid possibility, but I didn't want to deal with it.

"Call it selfish or foolish," I said, "but I really don't care what they're planning at this point. We will deal with them when we have to. Taking first things first, the real problem now is whether I'm going to be able to tame that car tomorrow and use it."

My first goal was to drive a black machine through the streets of Long Beach faster than any human had done before. If that was egocentric and essentially suicidal—which it was—it was also intensely invigorating, a perilous ambition experienced by few other professionals, the bullfighters, downhill racers and aerobatic performers of this world, not to mention Evel Knievel.

My second goal was still less specific. It operated at a level of animal cunning and cold vengeance. I was sure now that Aimee had been right. Brunditz had tried to get rid of me in Qataban by nudging my car into the wall. When cars are running at that close quarters, with the open wheels mixed together, the drivers trust in each other's judgment and skill. I had relied on the wrong man. If Brunditz had done it once, he would do it again, and I knew why: I had learned too much, and I was in the way of a well-financed international criminal organization. The only questions were when would he try again and how.

The uncertainty of it rankled. Drivers confront death every instant they are on the course, and learn to deal with probabilities of survival. I had always counted on, at the last conscious instant, being able to see what was going to kill me, something familiar like an overpass support or drainage culvert. But the thought of getting unexpectedly spiked in the back of the head with an ice pick or shot through the tender underarm with a silenced bullet presented another problem. The alarm mechanism along my spine seemed permanently activated.

I stood next to Aimee in the stern of the trim launch, watching the profile of the Emir's yacht grow smaller. We didn't talk any more since, in the tricky marine air, it was difficult to tell how much the Qatabani helmsman could overhear. I put my hand on her hip, eminently grabable through the thin dress, and pulled her close.

The return to shore began to take on symbolic overtones for me, like being rowed across the River Styx. From now on, I would have to think differently, model myself after the most dangerous type of game when it is on the defensive, wild cattle. The wounded Cape buffalo will often double back and take the hunter from his blind side, so quickly and with such calculated preparation that the hunter has no chance to react before the horn slams under his ribs and opens him up. It struck me as being the appropriate time to imitate nature. The Cape buffalo succeeds because it is patient and blends well. Until the race was done, I intended to do the same.

Schwandt called the team meeting in his motel suite, in an executive room with sofas and a small conference table. There weren't many of us—two race engineers, three drivers, and our leader, still resplendent in tuxedo. The rest of us were dressed casually, except for the engineers, Osawa and Priest, who were in overalls and stood by the door.

"All right, my chickens," Schwandt said, pulling a desk chair from the conference table and putting it to the test. "We have one last rehearsal of our début."

He took out a sheet of folded paper from an inside pocket and scanned it. I guessed it was the final starting grid and our qualifying lap times.

"I will admit I miscalculated this afternoon. We lost the pole, and Herr Walter is now in the third row, but our position is still excellent. And it may even be an advantage to have Herr Brunditz in the sixth row."

Brunditz, sitting next to me on the couch, whistled, almost inaudibly, "La Marseillaise" through his lower teeth.

I was impressed by his jocularity. He could have been a Jekyll-and-Hyde type, a crusading terrorist this hour and carefree driver the next, but the better bet was that Brunditz was the most calculating operator I had ever met.

"Unseld is on the pole, and he will no doubt want the lead," Schwandt said. "I want Herr Rachid Bashir to stay with him and the rest of you to hold position. Above all, I don't want you to push hard in the opening laps. Rachid will have to cope with Unseld as best he can. This circuit is notoriously hard on cars, so by forty laps—which is halfway, in case any of you have forgotten—it will be more than fortunate if two of you are still running.

"We will assess the situation at that time, and I expect you to follow orders. Remember, only one car in the pits at a time, and then only for fuel and tires or the most dire emergency. We must avoid the pit stops if we wish to win. Everything else is the same as we worked out in Qataban. Watch out for the tires; they are our weakest link. Any questions?"

"What happens," I asked, "if by some miracle in the final ten laps we're one-two-three?"

"You will stay that way. No passing. We have a long season ahead of us, as you pointed out, Herr Walter, so each of you will have your day of glory."

That was factory team procedure, which wasn't always followed, and I was certain it wouldn't be by Team Qataban. Brunditz was reckless, Rachid had Islam to worry about, and I was being paid off under the table. Schwandt was in for interesting times.

Aimee and I walked over to the garages about ten-thirty, six blocks through downtown Long Beach, an area that had once been tired and frayed but was suddenly seeing better days, as if the suburbs had exhausted themselves and progress had no other place to go. We stopped for a few minutes at an outdoor cafe, drinking espresso and marveling at what was happening to urban America.

The Qatabani guards let us through the garage door, and we saw that one of the cars, Brunditz's, had been stripped to the frame. His excursion up the escape road seemed to have wrenched the suspension badly, even though he hadn't hit anything, and, in the course of events, the engine had been, no doubt, over-revved, bending the vanes and central shaft. With these cars, it took only a stab of the toe to rearrange everything.

Petre Priest broke off from the knot of mechanics working to re-install the engine and joined us. My car was to one side, under a dust cloth, which we peeled back. I climbed in and reached for familiar controls. The mirror of black lacquer stretched out toward the front wing, which was inches from the ground and almost out of sight. The front wheels stuck up like the notches of a gunsight, and I used them that way on the track, aiming at the apexes, constantly leading ahead of the dizzying motion. Each detail of the machine had the mark of polish. It was fit for pagan gods.

"You were right about the wing," said Priest. "It was off a couple of ticks, enough for understeer. Somebody must have pulled on it when it was pushed back from the garage at noon. But the tires were correct. It was the shocks that gave you some difficulties. You must have been bottoming going into the corners." I had been, slightly.

"What's the status now?"

"It's finished. Wing adjusted. New shocks. Everything is *au point.* Drive very hard the first laps. We have only the half hour to make adjustments, and Brunditz's car will need a lot of attention. If we know your car is satisfactory tomorrow, we can concentrate on him."

"It takes only a minute to get around, Petre. You'll get a report in a hell of a hurry."

We pulled the dust cover back over the car, as if covering a graceful body, and went to the guarded door. Osawa was still bent into the engine compartment of Brunditz's car, oblivious to all but the task. He would probably be doing it all night.

The cold air smelled like mussel broth, since the tide was out, exposing the harbor's concrete jetties. We went through the garage area, cutting up and down alleys between the temporary buildings in the Long Beach Arena parking lot. After several minutes, we were sure we weren't being followed and ended up at the door of Abdel's trailer, which was probably under Prince Hassan's surveillance, anyway.

Abdel let us in himself, dressed in polo shirt and slacks, the first time I had seen the Sheik in completely Western dress. He looked like a young Arabian professor of hotel management, precise but worldly, boyish yet capable.

"I have bad news," he said, closing the door.

"Wait till we sit down. It's been a long night," I said. We moved to the office part of the trailer.

The teleprinter still lurched silently inside its Plexiglas home. I saw something about arbitrage profits in the Geneva office and a gaggle of financial figures. We sprawled in the same seats we'd had at noon, which must have been several epochs earlier. Aimee and I both felt an affinity for Abdel, as if a firm alliance of interest finally had emerged.

"Now what? The tube had a cigar in it?" I ventured.

"Not quite. But decidedly not what we had hoped. Fasil didn't find out who the principals of the Viper group are or very much about the organization. It is an entirely self-contained operation. I know that from the financing side. The whole organization funnels directly through Prince Hassan to the Emir, who unfortunately shares little of it with his cronies.

"Fasil confirmed, as I feared, that the Viper organization is international in scope and is behind the terrorist attacks on energy facilities in certain countries. Two years ago, I strenuously advised against creating such an alliance because it is fruitless and will invite retaliation, but I apparently lost. Hassan was able to convince the Protector that it was a meaningful weapon to discourage the Israelis from blowing up our own energy facilities. Israeli commandos have been quite active in our oil fields and port facilities, you know. They blew up a crude-oil storage area last year that put our biggest field out of production for four months. They did the same to the Saudis a couple of years ago and destroyed Qatar's natural-gas loading facility, a sixty-million dollar loss there alone. We were told through diplomatic channels it was because of our financial support of terrorists. What irony!

"That only strengthened Hassan's position, and he has been able since to talk our Protector out of more than half a billion dollars to bankroll the Viper group. And Hassan's been able to point to one success after another.

"With one exception. A team of saboteurs organized by the Viper group almost got caught trying to blow up a nuclear plant in Scotland and had to escape by submarine. That's our navy, you know. A submarine that acts as a terrorist bus. Such a waste. Anyway, Fasil said the Emir's yacht was going to be used as an observation post to time the entrance of the liquefied propane gas ships into Long Beach. It was moored to give them a clear view of the storage tanks and off-loading area. The intent is to eventually blow up a loaded LPG ship in port, probably with limpet mines.

"That would make quite a fireworks display, let me assure you. If a hundred thousand metric tons of LPG got loose and went off, you might as well have dropped an H-bomb."

"What if it's traced to the Emir?" I said. "That won't exactly buy you the best publicity, Abdel."

"Don't talk to me about reasonableness or diplomacy," he said. "And by keeping the Viper organization at arm's length they can always disown it. That's been the pattern in the past with the PLO and the Septembrists, and it's worked very well. You didn't see anyone canceling their oil orders after the Munich Olympics."

"It still seems self-destructive," Aimee said. "Sooner or later this insanity is going to catch up, and then, no matter how much money you people have, you'll never make it into the twenty-first century."

"My dear people," said the young Arab, leaning intently over the desk, "your concern for our mental health is touching, but the Islamic world, one billion believers and the fastest-growing religion in the world, is doing very nicely. The treasuries of four countries around the Persian Gulf, if combined, would make it the richest nation in the world. And you might remember where the word *algebra* came from: *al-jabr.* Abu Mohammed ibn Musa al-Khwarizmi invented it in the ninth century. He was calculating the square roots of numbers when Western Europeans were still learning to scratch their armpits."

Abdel leaned back in the tall leather chair, his eyes almost closed. "Trigonometry, spherical geometry—they were ours. We had physicists, astronomers, physicians, chemists, and navigators. We are the source of today's technology. Without Islam, you wouldn't have a car to drive.

"Granted, the Arab nation fell prey to marauders and went into a long period of decline, but talk about brain drains, it wasn't that we weren't producing creative people over the centuries; we just lost them, many to your country. At least thirty thousand of our best professionals have gone to the U.S. alone over the last forty years.

"And because you've systematically bled us to death, we now have to use our oil money to hire people like you and Schwandt and the loudmouth Texas engineers who drill our production wells, and the arrogant, nicotine-addicted, drunken swine who build our roads and ports and oil refineries. If we had our technicians and scientists back, we would gladly boot you out. It's our fondest hope."

He sat up, his pupils dilated, the first time I had seen Abdel indicate the possibility of fatigue. "You still don't understand, but it's partly my fault. I never instructed you about Islam, took you inland to meet the Bedouins, to shoot with them, to watch a race between the white *mughathirs,* the world's finest camels. All you saw were the slothful idiots in that coastal village. I didn't think it was necessary to take you to Jubil. I wanted you on the outside, driving our cars. You were never meant to be drawn in. The Prophet once said, 'When an epidemic strikes your land, if you are in it, stay there, and if you are outside it, stay out.'"

"Do you still want me to win tomorrow?"

Abdel waved his hand at a stack of newspapers and weekly magazines on the desk. "I have a meeting with the Emir in the morning, and I will show him these. Our effort in practice today and photographs of our cars are in every newspaper and publication in the country. You were on all the television networks tonight. The publicity is incalculable. Hassan has one of the Protector's ears, but I still have the other. I invest his money well, and I have made our country grow. I can make Sahal Abdallah the most important man in the Third World, and it won't be by blowing up LPG ships and the Alaska pipeline. I know I will prevail. There is an Arab proverb: 'A soft tongue can take milk from a lioness.'"

We left on that note of mysticism and walked slowly back through the night to the motel. It was after 10 P.M., but I didn't sleep well before races, anyway. I had a tendency to anticipate the day, thinking through the start, mentally pacing the course in search of new places to pick up a hundredth of a second, although Aimee and I frequently took the edge off with roaring sex.

It seemed the closer we timed intercourse to the start of a race, the better I drove. It simply eliminated one more human element.

The door to our room was ajar. I motioned Aimee to stay in the hall and entered slowly. Prince Hassan, his almond-shaped eyes and trim black beard framed by all-white headdress and robes, made a mockery of the bland motel. He sat immobile in an armchair, a mean, unsmiling visitor.

I backed a step into the hall. "We've just run into the first team, Aimee, come on in." She closed the door behind us and we sat on the bed, a few feet away from his chair. I had never heard Hassan speak and didn't even know if it would be English. The pause sort of hung there.

"Yes, I speak English. And Arabic. *As-salaam alaykum."*

"Wa alaykum as-salaam wa rahmat Allah wa barakatu," said Aimee. His predator eyes didn't move a millimeter.

"We seem to have a problem," said the Prince, "and that, of course, is you, Gustave Walter, wealthy young American who delights in driving fast. You don't seem to want to do what we ask you to do."

There was that Oxford accent again. They must have imported packet boats of nannies and tutors, a chorus of Annas of Qataban. But their genteel manner clashed with their feral Bedouin instincts.

"Are you here to lecture on the abstract virtues of obedience, Prince Hassan, or shall we look at my contract?" I asked. "I don't recall the fine print required that I kiss anybody's ass."

"I've made a study of you in the last few months, Mr. Walter, an investigation if you will. You seem to need ego satisfaction as the rest of us need calories. Why else do you do it? You could have worked in a brokerage house in San Diego or done something risky like becoming president of the Philharmonic Society. Well, I'll tell you, our rich American, you have great talent as an F1 driver. But I have also been studying this field of sport. Sheik Abdel made a terrible mistake hiring you. He hired an artist, and we needed a technician. He wanted publicity, and we wanted discipline. Do you see the conflict?"

"The conflict I have came about because you submarined my car," I answered. "One mechanic putting his hand on a wing and quietly pulling it until it lost its down-thrust. That's all it takes, you know, if you've been studying Grand Prix. And that kind of opportunity will always work to the benefit of excrement who are outside the sport and use it for their own purposes."

"Excrement! Prince Hassan ibn al-Razi, perhaps with a net worth of two to three billion dollars, being called excrement by his employee. I shouldn't be surprised. You see, I've watched the young Grand Prix drivers at the other races. Some of you are quite good, but none measures up to what I have read about the disciplined drivers like Lang and Fangio. You are all dilettantes. You are in love with your sports images and your vitamin pill sponsors, talking about outside influences. If Sheik Abdel had had a chance to hire Fangio, which unfortunately he didn't, he would have rejected him because the man was bald and spoke Spanish in a high, squeaky voice. That wouldn't go over in the American market."

By now I had moved to the edge of the bed. He was discussing my calling, after all. "I've been very polite, Your Highness, but let me enlighten you a bit. The drivers who come up out of the garages are fine, but if you really want Team Qataban to prevail in the long run, you'll need brains and lots of them. It's going to take an extraordinary combination of driving and engineering talents to test and develop your Vipers and keep them competitive in Formula One.

"There aren't many drivers who are sensitive about what a car is doing and can articulate it, but I'm one of them, a technician *and* an artist, and there are more of us in Formula One now than anytime before."

"What we want from you is discipline," he said. "You must follow team orders."

"You mean I have to play hind tit to Rachid?"

"You are the support car. Whatever Sheik Abdel intended you to be is changed now."

"On whose authority?"

Hassan looked deliberately at his gold wristwatch. "Sahal Abdallah will tell you himself. He is here by now. Let us go."

I rummaged around in the closet for a moment until I found what I needed. Aimee picked up a book and sullenly watched us leave. The Rolls-Royce Silver Wraith was in the motel parking lot, over by the ice machine and soda vendor. It must have had its own stateroom on the Emir's yacht. Hassan opened the door of the car and motioned me in. The Emir sat in the shadows, and I joined him on the deep bench. Hassan unfolded a jump seat, facing me. The Emir sat opposite his hooded bird, which rocked on a low perch with a gravel tray beneath it for its monumental droppings. A Qatabani driver in black-and-orange uniform and an Arab in a large raincoat, who I assumed was a bodyguard, sat on the other side of the glass window.

"Thank you for the umbrella, Your Highness." I held it out.

"Ah, my dear boy, you are one of those rare persons who remember to return things to the wealthy," he said in his sibilant and tapestried bass. The Rolls murmured off, turning south onto Ocean Boulevard, onto the Grand Prix course itself. "I prefer the texture of boar's tusk to anything else," he said. "There are so few of us hunters left, Gustave. We may be the last elite."

"I admire fishermen, too," I said. "Particularly the commercial ones who take such enormous risks in the North Sea and around Alaska."

"Our drilling crews are working in those same waters, but somehow we are not perceived as heroes. Look at that oil rig out there," he said, pointing out to a small island in Long Beach harbor, where the pumping rigs are disguised to look like apartment houses. "To me, that is desecration. Why cover up progress?"

"Prince Hassan has indicated that my status on the team has changed. Could we be more specific?"

"Of course, dear boy, I must tell you exactly where we are. But you must understand how difficult it is for us in Jubil at the moment. The concept of generations is more cultural than biological, and a new generation with new values seems to come into existence in Qataban every three or four years.

"Sheik Abdel's generation made a total commitment to Western technology. He brought in talent, brains, hardware. But he forgot that while factories can be imported, industry cannot. I gave him power as my chief minister and then watched him give away our true Islamic heritage. As of tonight, I have given that power to Prince Hassan, who will put Qataban on a course of development that is compatible with Islam."

"And that means," said the Prince, not wasting a second, "that you must go. I want Rachid to be World Champion in our car, and that won't be possible with you on the team. I have already arranged through one of our oil outlets to get you a berth on the Uaxco team, same salary and guarantee for another season."

If he wanted to buy me off, he couldn't have done better. Uaxco was a new team of Anglo-American entrepreneurs with exceptional resources.

"And what about Brunditz?"

"He goes, too, to another team."

"Out of curiosity, Hassan, who do you plan to replace us with? Rachid can't carry the team by himself, and it would probably take two seasons for you to get the championship under the best of circumstances."

"We built Rachid from a taxi driver in Algiers into a World Champion contender, and we can do it again," Hassan said. "We already have three young drivers from Jubil in the Road California Driving School, and they will drive the rest of the season on the Continent in Formula Five Thousand."

"If they live," I said, as we continued to glide down Ocean Boulevard toward Seal Beach. "You would be lucky to get one out of three back in one piece at the end of the season. And he would need at least two or three more seasons to handle the Vipers. I don't think you know what you have spawned—probably the most powerful and unmanageable racing cars ever designed."

"Are you rejecting my offer?"

"Of course not. No offense, but I'd prefer to be away from you people. You're badly screwed up. But tomorrow is different. The publicity's built to the point that I don't see how you can prevent me from starting—and with a car that hasn't been jiggered with, I might add. The organizers can make life difficult for you."

The limousine, as if directed by unseen powers, threaded its way back through Long Beach to the motel. We fell silent until the car had been parked by the swimming pool, the engine ticking over quietly, the air system a faint pneumatic hiss.

"You will start tomorrow," said the Emir in his deepest bass voice, making it clear this was law. "But under no circumstances are you to finish ahead of Rachid. You must drive within political constraints."

The conversation seemed to halt there. I could read into his words what I wanted, and I couldn't find much that augured well. Hobbes once made it clear that the root of politics is violence. I said good night and left the car. Aimee was watching a Marx Brothers movie on a 24-hour film channel when I let myself in. It was now close to 11 o'clock.

I turned the volume up. Chico's and Groucho's staccato repartee would screw up any bugging system made. I joined Aimee on the bed, where she was propped on her elbow, dressed in an oversized T-shirt with a big Ferrari Prancing Horse stamped on it. This was psychological warfare waged because I hadn't insisted she come along for the ride in the Rolls. It would be no easy task to persuade her to strip out of it.

"We're caught in a palace coup," I said in her ear. "Prince Hassan is in. Sheik Abdel is out. And so are we."

“Sue them,” she said, still watching the damn movie. I pulled her elbows out so that she fell back on the bed.

“I’m sorry about tonight, but a woman would have spooked the Emir when he was making deals. They’ve got this hang-up.’

“What deals?” she asked, warming a few degrees.

“I’m fired as works driver, but they’ll give me a clean car for one race, this one. They say they’ve got a berth for me with Team Uaxco, which wouldn’t be bad at all. No more black uniforms and bed checks. There’s one hitch.”

“I suspected.”

“I have to finish behind Rachid tomorrow, no matter what, for the glory of Islam.”

“Are you?”

“The question is whether I want to go out with class. It’s like deciding whether to take a dive in a fight. What do you think?”

“Dumb question. But don’t let them know you aren’t going to be a good boy or they won’t give you a sound car.”

I rummaged around in my bag until I found a T-shirt with a more appropriate message, a German gasoline brand that advertised with a scatological slogan. I held it up, moved to the bed, and then slowly stripped off the Prancing Horse. Her limbs were now pliant and akimbo, inviting me to make up for having left her behind, a task I willingly initiated.

Later that night, we lay together naked in the bed facing each other, our arms finding those dents and hollows where lovers can embrace in sleep without losing circulation. Our need to stay silent made the night seem ominous.

"I didn't mean what I said back in Qataban about you being a softie," she whispered. "I think you are very tough and smart."

"Thanks, so are you."

"And I think we're going to need everything we've got tomorrow," she said.

"We'd better sleep or we'll doze through it all," I answered. "Remember our motto: Trust no one."

"Except each other."

I wished I could. She still had the taint of government, and even if that were to our mutual benefit, the CIA wasn't going to be able to help me make the split-second decisions I might be called on to make out on the track or later. I wanted to be free to act with an animal's instincts.

On the edge of consciousness, I speculated about what the Viper group might try to do if I broke the Emir's ad hoc law. I opened my eyes and stared at the ceiling, thinking about whether they could shoot me. I had spent enough time looking down the barrel of a rifle to appreciate the difficulty of picking off a driver in a fast car. The problems seemed almost insurmountable, although the noise of the engines would probably cover the sound of a rifle shot. The best place to get at me in a closed cockpit would be from an elevated trajectory. The International Tower, the building where they had the rooms overlooking the track, would be a poor perch for an assassin. The balconies were too far above the pavement, the car would be passing at an angle.

They still might try something with the car, but I felt Schwandt and his technicians and mechanics were highly motivated to win and had put too much of themselves into developing the machines. It wouldn't be easy to get them to act against their instincts and destroy their own creation, let alone me, no matter how much money was thrown at them. Someone, though, *had* gotten to the front wing. The possibility of a filed-down torsion bar snapping under a critical load was real. I had to convince them that this kind of drastic policy, with all of its risks of subsequent detection, wasn't necessary.

Then there was the possibility that Rachid or Heinz might try to put me through a wall, claiming later that they never saw me in the mirror. Many drivers—too many—have cut off a passing car's line through a corner and pleaded this hollow case later, when the wreckage of the opposition has been scraped away. Who's to say, when they're driving at those speeds, that it wasn't true? Both Rachid and Heinz would deserve special care. Expect the worst, I told myself.

* * *

The scene in the Pit at CIA Headquarters early Sunday was typical of a transitory crisis. The team, handpicked from several divisions in the building and two stations abroad, roamed around the periphery of the enclosure, coffee cups in hand, reading the teletype machines and occasionally conferring in groups of two and three. From time to time they would step to one of the Octopus terminals, the entry points into one of the most powerful pieces of computer machinery in the world, and make a request.

In many respects, the operation differed little from the mobilization that was necessary during the visit of any chief of state. The Emir required an extra effort, since he not only had to be protected but had to be defended against. Any false move by the Agency, any overreaction, however, would bring down the fierce ire of the White House. That had been made abundantly clear by the Deputy Director of Operations before the twenty-four-hour vigil had begun.

The routine sweeps were being conducted—tedious checks of lists of unstable persons in the community, the arrival of anyone suspicious at Los Angeles airport, a blanket alert to all police departments within a hundred miles to report any event, no matter how innocuous or trivial, that might relate to the presence of the Emir. The West Side of Los Angeles alone, after all, had more Jewish residents than Tel Aviv itself.

One teletype, connected to the temporary CIA office in downtown Long Beach, spat out a routine request. It would transmit the names and former addresses of the tenants at the Riviera Building, an apartment house on the outside of Turn Five. Octopus would be asked to cross-check the names through its almost infinite memory banks to see if anything read Tilt.

An intelligence officer ripped off the list of present tenants when the sender in Long

Beach was done and took it to a pool of computer clerks, who converted the data into punch cards and fed them into Octopus. Almost as an afterthought, he went back to the teletype and asked Long Beach for a list of previous tenants of the Riviera Building, going back one year. Long Beach hesitated, then agreed to find the names and transmit the extended list.

~:~

8.

> Overlaid upon the peculiarities of every race, however, there was, common to all, a strong suggestion of the gladiatorial. Side by side with the color and movement, the eager chatter in the packed grandstand restaurants and the slowly moving streams of vehicles and people along the roads leading to the enclosures around the course, there was always a tense undercurrent. It was as if the multitude exhaled a nervous tension which became palpable to those who realized that the actors in the great drama of skill and speed might at any moment become figures in a tragedy, for Grand Prix racing was, like all motor racing, balanced on the very brink of life and death.
>
> Rodney Walkerley
> *Grand Prix Racing 1934-1939*
> Motor Racing Publications

The bow of the boat headed up a point too high in the wind, nudged there by a wave, and the leading edge of the jib started to luff. I tugged the tiller, and the sloop fell off until the forces of wind and sail were once more properly balanced. The boat thrust forward the way a racing car drifts through the apex of the corner or how skis knife past the crown of a mogul. The laws of physics are irrelevant at these moments, since the whole becomes greater than the parts.

"Have a Beck's," said Heinz, his head sticking up from the cabin. "It'll be worth more than half a second a lap this afternoon."

"Sure, sure. If I had a Bavarian liver. Just pass up an apple juice."

We had agreed to take a pre-race sail in the Cal 30 that I had been borrowing from a friend of one of the race promoters. We had brought along a cold brunch to see us through the afternoon. Some drivers fast before a race, but my metabolism is such that I stoke up in the morning and then lose seven or ten pounds in a couple of hours during the afternoon.

"I warned you it would be Byzantine," he said, passing up the juice. Aimee and Mimi were stretched out in bikinis on the weather deck under a potent spring sun.

"Hassan gave me my walking papers last night, too, and paid off another team to avoid trouble. Sent me to Condor. They want a German driver for their third car, for some reason. What do you plan on doing today?"

"Drive bloody fast, but not faster than Rachid. He can have the show, for all I care. I want out. And without us, they're headed for disaster."

"We aren't out of it yet," he said. "Do you realize how hard it may be for us to stay behind Rachid? What if his car sours and he starts to slow? We're lost, then—in deep trouble. The Mossad knows how powerful the Qatabanis are in this country because we come up against them here more and more. You should have seen how they got the body of Sheik Fasil to the airport and out of the country before the Los Angeles coroner even knew the boat had docked.

"And guess who was assisting in the body export program?" he said. "Your own CIA and FBI. With your oil imports running about fifty percent, and most of that coming from five Middle East countries, including Qataban, they just don't want to mess with them."

"Pass up some chicken and get off this morbid kick, for God's sake, Heinz. We do what we have to do today and then we're out of it. At least I'm out of it. If you make a double income as an Israeli agent, that's your problem."

I threw the tiller leeward, backing the sails momentarily and swamping water across the deck and over the two women. The swear words came at me in eight languages, but it was time to eat. I wanted the calories out of the stomach and into my blood by noon.

We headed downwind, towards the sloop's marina. Tension gripped us, and we talked little. Several times I caught the small, olive-skinned woman scrutinizing Aimee, as if matching her up with a picture in a long-forgotten file. Beneath the veneer of a racing driver's pit bird, I felt I could see Else Farah, a specialist in letter bombs and plastic explosives.

"That was a waste of effort," said Aimee later, as we headed up the Long Beach Freeway in our sports Viper. "We didn't learn a damn thing."

"Didn't expect to. He was trying to catch us out."

"What was the point, then?" she asked.

"I made it abundantly clear that I intended to follow team orders. I want a solid car for this race."

Aimee flicked the radio to a classical station, and we let the tactile chords of a Schumann symphony fill up the car. Then I spotted Hassan's men tailing us again, trying to appear unobtrusive. I signaled to Aimee. "Hold on a minute. We'll have to give them a little crash course."

"Very funny, Gus. If you do something crazy, I swear, I'll—"

By that point I had already pitched the Viper into the freeway off-ramp, a long downhill turn. Anyone growing up with sports cars and motorcycles in California becomes proficient at greasing through freeway exits and entrances. It's the state's least-advertised pastime. We arrived at the bottom of the turn with the car sideways and the brakes almost locked, shot under the bridge and into the looping uphill on-ramp back onto the freeway, while I held the Viper into the uniform turn in one controlled slide.

"I want a lawyer," said Aimee. "I don't care if it's Sunday and the bastard charges triple, I want the divorce papers."

"That's nothing," I said, only half in jest, as we headed back to Long Beach. "You ought to see what it's like from a Formula One car."

"Now I know why racing cars don't carry mechanics around with them anymore," she said. "No one could be paid enough to watch that."

"It's just like magic," I reassured her. "Racing drivers pick up these little tricks of the trade, which makes our work look suicidal, but if we let the public in on them, no one would come watch." I didn't think she believed me, but it was a good try.

"I'll take the next off-ramp and we'll drive on the back streets and sneak through the alleys. I want to get some gas and find a safe parking lot in case we need this machine later."

"Sneak? With this car?"

"They can't cover the whole town."

The gas station came first, a hydrocarbon palace that was designed and landscaped better than most homes. No less than three gas station attendants dropped what they were doing and approached the strange black car with undisguised respect. I told Aimee I would be back in a minute and went to a nearby glass telephone booth. I fed the beast some coins and dredged up the memory-aid phone number Brunditz had given me It answered after the second ring.

"Yes." A cautious man.

"This is Walter."

"Ah, yes, Gustave. What can we do for you?"

"Nothing. Perhaps never." The voice was unfamiliar, unaccented, and told me nothing. "Have we met?"

"You wouldn't recognize me," he said. "Where are you?"

"On the way to the track." I hung up quietly. At least they were there. The Viper group was more than a figment of the imagination, and I had a way of getting to them if it suited my purposes. It was a contact I didn't want to share. Aimee's people might clean out the other end of the line before I made my move, before I could erupt silently from behind the clump of thorns and hit from the blind side.

I paid for the gasoline and noticed that a full tank would not get us far if the Viper were driven at speed. The engineers would have to look around for more space for fuel.

"What was that all about?" she asked as we drove off.

"Looking for a parking garage."

"You didn't use the Yellow Pages."

"I have a good head for numbers."

"Liar." She could say that word with such good nature and trust that I let the challenge go.

I had already scouted out one promising two-story garage about four blocks from our motel. I knew the owner-manager, a large black man in his early thirties, had a suitably hang-loose attitude. Charles didn't care much about racing, but if we wanted to rip around in those flitty cars, that was all right, too.

Aimee and I pulled in. The race-day crowd was giving him good business. "Say, now, that car's more like it," he said, walking up to us. "Color's not bad, either."

"This may be too much to ask, Charles," I said, "but if you can resist the impulse to drive this car to Tijuana, I can make it worth your while."

"This is Charles Whitsun, high-priced car watcher, you're talking with." I pulled a hundred-dollar bill from my wallet. "I'd like to leave the car next to that door to the alley and cover it," I said. "There are some people, nosy press types and maybe some engineers from the auto companies, who want to know where this car is today so they can look under the hood and kick the tires and find out stuff they're not supposed to."

"Just park it by that door," he said with reassuring detachment. "Anyone touches that hood gets his knuckles broken. Any kicking will be ass kicking."

Aimee and I pulled the dust cover over the black machine. Before we left the garage,

Charles had backed several cars next to ours, blocking it from view but not walling it in. I didn't want the sports Viper at the motel, and I now felt reasonably sure Hassan's people wouldn't find it.

We left through the back alley. The back streets of residential Long Beach, even on race day, were empty, as if Civil Defense had given an alarm. I saw only one elderly lady, with nylon socks rolled to the top of her calves, watering her lawn, and she didn't look up as we went across the alley.

We arrived back at the motel with about forty-five minutes to get ready. When we had locked the door to our room, I turned the faucets on in the bathroom to make noise, retrieved a Swiss Army knife from my shaving kit and unscrewed a metal plate by the sink over a hole that housed some plumbing. It left a remarkably large gap in the bathroom wall, which had been wide enough to admit the butt and barrel of our disassembled shotguns in the gap between the tile and the wall. I reached in as far as I could and groped until I found a loop of tape. The pieces to the two guns came up in a string, followed by twenty shells, taped like a Chinese firecracker. We wrapped the parts and shells in two motel towels, taped them, and put them in my kit bag, along with my helmet, gloves, spare shoes, extra tape, and the bric-a-brac drivers accumulate.

As I put my uniform on, somehow the layers of Nomex seemed even more cloying than before. I didn't think it was possible to develop claustrophobia by wearing clothes, and drivers aren't supposed to have phobias, anyway, but today the routine of wearing chemically soaked clothes was getting to me.

Aimee and I hadn't talked much in the room, but we usually didn't before a race. It was like waking up with a hangover. Conversation, whether idle or profound, felt like a bodily violation. And today we had more to think about than how well I would do or whether I would come back in one piece, which I wasn't prone to dwell on before a race, though Aimee frequently did.

"Ready?" I asked. She looked spectacular in white denim jeans and a shirt embroidered with Indian symbols.

"I guess." She smiled at me, reassuringly, more or less. "Just remember how tough you really are and that you've got the best car under you that you've ever had." We went out into the hall, down the stairs, and out into the street, with me toting the kit bag. We still couldn't talk freely. The streets near the course were now jammed with people, and my driving suit drew stares and eavesdroppers.

She had been right. This would be the best chance of my career to win a Formula 1 event, a *Grande Épreuve.* Historically, this is the event a young driver needs to secure his rank in the international racing world. American drivers in particular are seldom taken seriously until they have taken a first place, no matter how competent, brilliant, or consistent their driving performances have been.

But it seemed likely that if I won today, the opposite would occur. I had tried to work out all the combinations of retribution by Hassan if I didn't follow orders; at a minimum he would wipe out the deal with Uaxco. That arrangement had been so unusual to begin with—I could only imagine the bargaining in hotel suites that must have gone on among the netherworld negotiators of the oil industry to nail it down. I knew any violation of the agreement would rebound harshly on me. Word would go out among the network of team managers that I was unstable, dangerous, a poor investment. There were too many other fast team players to choose from.

Not that any of that mattered. It also became clear to me that as long as Team Qataban stayed intact and the Viper organization was a part of it and therefore deeply embedded in the world of Formula 1, I was a dead man. Even if I played it cool today, finished dutifully behind Rachid, and transferred to Uaxco, I still knew too much. If it weren't today, the group would make a move at Jarama or Monaco or Aintree. I would never again be secure in the sport without bringing the

Qataban-sponsored terrorists out first. It seemed like a classical no-win situation for me unless Team Qataban could be spread out across the countryside for the contrivance it was.

And Aimee shared my vulnerability. It seemed likely they would remove her, assuming, quite rightly, that I had shared my concerns about the team with her. If they even suspected she was a deep-cover CIA officer, the Viper group would probably be more concerned about her than me, but the evidence, so far, indicated her cover was still intact.

Aimee and I reached the paddock area and walked past the slot where Sheik Abdel's trailer had been parked. The morning mist from the marine layer had left faint marks on the pavement, a template of the trailer. "Makes your bloody skin crawl," I said.

"Wonder what they did with him," she mused.

"It's the Qataban Air Lift. One passenger per seven-oh-seven, not necessarily alive."

"Come on." She pulled my sleeve, and we turned to the garage, where Schwandt had scheduled yet another team meeting to drive home his lessons on the virtues of restraint. We met him at the garage door, and he immediately began a lecture on the length of the race and how he didn't want it to end for me on the first lap. Aimee stayed outside, sitting on a folding chair, her foot propped on the kit bag.

"I've got it, Schwandt," I said as we sat in the corner of the garage he had staked out as an office. "Rachid wins, and Heinz and I drive the course backward—like going the wrong way on the freeway."

"Just so you understand what *I'm* saying, Herr Walter. This race is a hundred and eighty-one miles long, and I want you to make it beyond Tum One. Clear? And save your technique on that corner until the road is free. No acrobatics in the traffic. Clear?"

I nodded appreciatively and shuffled my feet—anything to get hold of that gleaming black car. Schwandt motioned Rachid and Heinz over to join us at his corner desk when they arrived. Schwandt went over the same points with us again, like a coach who believes in repeating the fundamentals, and I found it difficult to concentrate or stay civil, so I remained silent and thought about what it would be like to knock off a straight one hundred clay pigeons. I shoot shotguns left-handed. I wondered if that could make a difference in championship competition. It couldn't.

We shouldered our way through the pack of bodies in the paddock, an extraordinarily fit-looking mass of people, living testament to the

California health cult. Shirtless men with haltered women reveled under the topaz late March sky. Aimee opened a wedge through the crowd, and I steered the heavy kit bag behind her, not really focusing on anything until we filed through the gate onto the tarmac of the pit lane.

The three Vipers, black, sleek, and compellingly menacing, were parked at an angle in front of our two pit enclosures. Qatabani mechanics bent over them, making fine-tune adjustments and last-minute inspections. The untimed practice session was scheduled to start in twenty minutes, but governments would topple if anything in Grand Prix went according to schedule. Aimee and I sat on the counter and waited, listening to the scratchy public-address system as it cajoled, commanded, reminded, wheedled, and pitched, a train of mindless annoyance.

We didn't take the cars out until 12:30, which meant the 2:00 P.M. start would probably slip a half hour. I was first out and had the road to myself, which isn't necessarily an advantage since it's possible to slide through a blind comer and find a course worker with a broom standing directly in front of the car, or a tow truck making a U-turn. A course like Long Beach is built one day and gone the next, making communication among track personnel untrustworthy. I nevertheless had a need to get an instant feel for the car in case the Viper group had been able to fritz it. After Turn Three I stood on the power, flying through the long left at Turn Four with an armful of lock. I shot by the round apartment building, sensing the eyes of the princes and sheiks on the balcony as they followed my progress.

The car responded like a trained animal, the torque going instantly into the road, the brakes bedding and holding deep into the comers. The suspension components had been readjusted overnight, but instead of the front end washing out, as it had the day before, the back end was now too loose. I went through the Esses at less than the limit, hoping the car would understeer or drift neutrally, only to feel the back end whip out in a vicious slide, almost uncontrollable. At the top of the hill I threw the transmission into neutral and coasted back to the pits.

Other cars surged by. Some teams were running in fresh engines and trying out new gear ratios, but several drivers were sorting out ugly problems, knowing there was no hope of being competitive.

This time I felt confident my car hadn't been gimmicked. The previous night, Petre Priest and the mechanics had set the car up close to the complex balance we had worked out on the test track in Qataban. It remained only for them to use a bit of technical magic and finish the job.

"It may be in the torsion bar spring," I had told the suspension specialist as he weighed a diagnosis and cure. "The back end snaps out under less than full power. I don't want that oversteer until the very end of the corner." He'd nodded and set to work, ordering adjustments to the tires, wings, and torsion bars.

Back at the pit, I leaned on the counter next to Aimee, trying to think of nothing, going through a well-established prerace dehumanizing process.

Schwandt waved Brunditz out onto the course. I knew he faced a far more serious problem than I did in making his car competitive during the short run-in period, since it had been so badly yanked out of tune during his off-course excursion the day before. Then the mechanics dropped the high-speed jacks under my car and Schwandt motioned me to get going.

I did two more fast laps, concentrating on the two or three crucial corners on the Long Beach course. This time the back end didn't swing out until the last possible moment as I let out the full 720 horsepower. I coasted back into the pits. "It's done, Petre," I told the suspension specialist. "You can't improve on that. The gearing is also perfect," I added for Schwandt's benefit when he joined our conversation.

During my final test lap, I had had a chance to look up at the balcony. The sheiks and princes were sitting this time, a gallery of white and black cloth and impersonal dark glasses. One of them would be Hassan, but the Emir, we were told, planned to watch the race through a special television hook-up on the yacht, as a security precaution.

After the last test lap, I sat on the pavement, my back against the pit wall, next to Aimee's feet. I kept an eye on my own car in front of the pits as Schwandt and the technicians worked feverishly to make Brunditz's car faster. Rachid sat on the next counter, also silent.

The run-in session ended, and the public-address system picked up rhythm as the moment to start approached. Mechanics rolled the cars out onto the grid while bands played and white doves were let free in a cloud that shelled one grandstand with dung.

Then Aimee gave me a mock shove, and I walked out, helmet under my arm, to look at the two-by-two grid alignment. Unseld's Ferrari next to Rachid's black machine on Row One seemed appropriate, like contrasting backgammon pieces. The color scheme ended on Row Two, where Dair's shocking green-and-orange March on the left was paired with the red-and-white of DeMarco's Brabham-Alfa-Romeo. My black car, which had the orange stripe around the nose cowl for quicker identification, sat behind Dair and to the left of Askew's cobalt-blue Tyrrell.

Behind me was Seutenbach's orange-and-white McClaren. The rest of the twenty cars tailed away in a blotch of color. Brunditz's black car was two rows behind Seutenbach, where I didn't think Heinz could do me any harm during the start or the close quarters of the opening laps.

We climbed in our cars. The impassive Qatabani mechanics strapped me in and hooked up the various fluid systems to my driving suit. Heat sensors could shoot fireproof foam into my suit in less than a second, and as the mechanic reached in and fired the car, I could feel the coolant drawing my body heat off through the network of flexible tubes in the uniform. The engine howls penetrated my helmet and Nomex hood as I blipped the accelerator. The revolution counter, tilted in front of me so that the highest numbers were visible, registered what was going on in the engine immediately behind my head, while the needle wagged back and forth hypnotically.

The space-age comforts and safety devices, I knew, were only a way to reduce the percentages. There were more than a hundred gallons of high-octane methane derivative wrapped around the cockpit in a fuel cell. The speeds we would be going at in a matter of minutes were enough to rip the car into flaming, isolated pieces if anything went wrong. As stray thoughts on safety intruded, I forced them aside. The dehumanizing process was almost complete. The body was the machine, the machine the body, and Gustave Walter had become irrelevant.

The field of cars was allowed one warm-up lap under the control of the pace car before lining up again for the start. It gave us a chance to bring the tires back up to running temperature, thin out the oil, and bed things in, which cut the possibility of a first-lap pileup. We circled the course, yawing from side to side in first gear. I watched Askew out of the corner of my eye. I wasn't sure whether racing drivers developed superior peripheral vision or we became drivers because we had it.

The pace car peeled off and left us out on the grid. Theoretically we would sit there only sixty seconds, but several cars overshot the paint marks. I saw mechanics running out to push the machines in place, and the battery of lights ahead of us, suspended by a wire over the start-finish line, stayed red. The red light would start blinking at the twenty-second mark, flash to orange at the five-seconds, and then turn green. It was a primitive starting system compared to other Grand Prix courses, but this track wasn't permanent, and we took what we could get.

First laps In Grand Prix are always a brutal display of pushing and shoving with lethal machines. It is neck-wrenching driving and unspeakably dangerous. The light hit orange, and I selected first gear. Instruments fed my eyes the data. The oil temperature was near the red line. I had to get going before the engine seized.

We drag-raced through the green light to Turn One. I saw dust, smoke, heat shimmers, flying papers, and the green and orange of Dair's car millimeters in front of my right wheel, and exhaust fumes made my eyes water. I saw no blue to the right, which meant Askew had fallen back a few feet. I cut across the apex of the hard right, lurching downhill, tucked behind Dair, who was half a car length behind DeMarco, to Dair's right.

Unseld was already entering Turn Two ahead of Rachid. I still could barely focus as we powered through turns Two and Three. The fumes and dust cleared slightly as we headed up the hill, and I could drive on more than reflexes and guesses.

By the back straight, physical laws and driver ability had already begun to sort the cars out. At the end of the lap, Rachid and Unseld, running nose-to-tail, had pulled out about twenty yards ahead of Dair, DeMarco, and myself, all three of us tearing by the start-finish in a tight clump. I fell back slightly under braking, running fifth at Turn One. They had the advantage until I had more room to slide, bringing out the black car's remarkable qualities.

Drivers often know little about what is going on in a race except the car ahead and behind them and what little information the team manager chooses to share. Pit signals are like illiterate semaphore. The Team Qataban mechanics flashed me a lap time as I passed on the third lap: "WALT 094" or "Walter did the second lap at 1:09.4," which was searingly fast for a car loaded with fuel. The second board they held out said 1 UNS, Unseld leads. The second line read :5 BASH, which meant my teammate was in second place, a half second behind. The third line said +4.1 DEM, or DeMarco was third, slightly more than four seconds behind Unseld.

Halfway through the third lap, Dair's March nipped past DeMarco's Brabham-Alfa-Romeo as we braked for the hairpin at the end of the straight. I dogged them both through the Esses. On several parts of the course I could glimpse Unseld's Ferrari struggling to stay ahead of Rachid's black car. The young Australian was plunging deep into the corners and taking the width of the road to stay ahead of the phenomenally quick Algerian.

On lap eight, Seutenbach crashed badly behind us against the wall on the uphill leg, the same spot that I had plastered on the ersatz course in Qataban. Flags waved frantically as we came by on the next lap, and we pulled to the right to avoid the fire crews and tow truck. They had him out, but flames shot twenty feet high, and black smoke rolled across the straightaway, forcing us to punch through, hoping for the best.

Two laps later the road was clear, but on the next lap DeMarco made a serious error, using the whole road as he left the same right tum and hitting the residue of extinguishant on the road under full throttle. His tail slammed the concrete wall just ahead of me, and he rocketed back across my path. I cut left, purely a reflex, and the Viper squirted through, the wheels just ticking the wall. I was too busy collecting things to see what happened to the Italian.

On the next lap the same emergency crews were out, this time on the right side of the road. There was no flame, but DeMarco didn't appear to be moving. The entire front of the car—wheels, wings, suspension, and cowl—had ripped off on impact, and his motionless feet stuck out from what was left of the nose of his car.

I was now fourth. Somewhere deep inside, where thought processes still functioned, this news was well received. The pit signal read: 1 UNS/+.5 BASH/+4.6 DAIR/68 laps.

Races are like operas. The arias are galvanizing, but between heroic moments there is a lot of noodling by the strings and some necessary but routine dialogue engaged in to move the plot along. For me, the race had entered a stage of unremarkable development.

The burden was being carried by Rachid, who was trying to worry Unseld into making a mistake. I tucked in behind Dair, a steady veteran, for a series of fast laps, and waited for the inevitable mayhem ahead.

Dair and I could see the red and black cars ripping through the long turn on the backstretch as we pulled out of the looping right-hand turn behind them. The front-runners already faced new obstacles, the rearguard of slow cars, young drivers, and sour machines, among them Brunditz, who waved me past in the Esses. Passing them made lap times unpredictable, and I had to give Brunditz a wide berth as I went by, which slowed me even more.

I was trailing Dair's green-and-orange March by less than a foot three laps later when I saw the cloud of dust and tire smoke ahead of us as we rounded the fast bend in the backstraight. We both went to our brakes as the course marshals began flapping their Caution flags.

Unseld, under extreme pressure from Rachid, had pushed too far into the hairpin at the end of the straight and had locked up his front wheels, letting the black car past. Unseld was frantically U-turning as we slid through the hairpin, and on the next lap our jubilant pit crew held out: 1 BASH/ +5.1 DAIR/+5.6 WALT/52 laps. Schwandt stood with his own pit signal for Bashir and me. HOLD, said the small sign.

We reached the two-thirds point with the Vipers running first and third. My car still felt as if it had power to spare and showed few signs of mechanical wear, with one important exception—my sensitive backside began sending reports of excessive tail-twitching. The car had a tendency to slip to the left, more than to the right.

Most of the turns at Long Beach are to the right, putting heavy stress on the left tires. That, combined with the peculiar handling of the Vipers and the way we used final oversteer out of the comers, was causing excessive tire wear, so I pointed to my left-rear tire as I passed the pits and swooped in on the next lap, lap fifty-nine.

It took nine seconds to get the new tire on, plus a blast of fuel, and eleven seconds to get in and out of the pits, enough time to drop me to eighth place, about twenty-three seconds behind Rachid.

When I entered Turn One I fell in behind Braccio and Campbell, who were dicing for sixth and seventh. I caught them both in one pass, keeping a tight line through the looping right turn onto the back straight and blowing by them as we accelerated out of it, making good use of the Viper's power advantage.

It took another twenty laps to work past Askew and Tomaka, who were nose-to-tail in fourth and fifth position. I caught them on the pit straight as they slipstreamed each other on the left side of the road; then I dove to the right and arrived at Turn One on totally the wrong line, the car sideways. They were so horrified they backed off to avoid what appeared to be an inevitable accident. By then the Viper was soaring through the air and down the hill, and Unseld, now third, was nowhere in sight. On the next lap, the pit signal read: 1 BASH/+6 DAIR/+8:2 UNS/19 laps.

The field of cars had become widely spaced out as others darted in for fuel. With a clear road ahead, I let the Viper out, driving almost in a trance, and the car slid through the whole course. A sign given by the Qatabani pit crew said WALT 07:2, which meant I was driving about a second and a half faster than Tifumo's lap record of the year before and approaching the qualifying record set by Rachid, but Rachid had put in those fast qualifying times the day before with a light car and special tires.

I had Unseld in sight on the next lap and passed him a lap later in an impossible spot, the right-hand entrance to the Esses. I slid around him and took his line going into the next left-hand bend. I saw Unseld shake his gloved fist at me as we reached the pit straight and he was able to get an arm free. Dair was now twenty feet ahead and wary, and his pit crew urged him on with a big "V" for *véloce* sign.

With ten laps to go, I tucked in behind the March to collect myself. The Team Qataban pit crew had stopped communicating with me; by comparing Rachid's and my lap times, Schwandt could see what I was capable of and must have suspected what I had in mind, so I had become a pariah.

I looked up at the tower. The Qatabanis were standing now, clapping, enjoying a moment of true Islamic glory as Rachid appeared to have the race in hand. They weren't privy to Schwandt's stopwatches and were unaware of the narrowing gap.

I slipstreamed behind Dair down the first part of the back straight and shot by him on the inside. The next three laps were only a question of mathematics. With the good left rear tire and a lot of attention to what the car was trying to do at the limit of adhesion, I was able to lap at below the magic six-second barrier, and I knew that Rachid couldn't. In three laps I cut his lead in half, and two laps later I was driving in his slipstream. Schwandt stood at the side of the pit wall, hands jammed in his ankle-length coat, while the crowd waved me on with a sea of white shirts and caps.

The two cars were like one going down the back straight. Thinking I would pass to the right, Rachid edged toward that side of the track. I waited until the last tenth of a second to pull to the left, throwing the car sideways to scrub speed as we approached the right-hand hairpin.

Rachid cut to his left to block my line, but made his move an instant too late. His left front wheel slammed my right rear tire, which was already feeding out power as my car began to point toward the exit of the turn. The contact succeeded only in propelling my car out of the hairpin, and I looked in the mirror to see Rachid scrambling to stay with me. Then I hurled the Viper through the Esses and saw Rachid fall back as his worn tires drained off the hundredths of seconds. When I passed the pits twenty feet ahead of him, the Algerian was helpless.

It wasn't my nature to observe political constraints, unless they were set down in writing. I had always been a lousy team player, and nobody could tell me to finish second.

As I slid out of Tum Four, I looked up again at the balcony. The Qatabanis were now sitting. I drove on for another lap, stretching the lead in the closing minutes of the race, but a warning instinct was robbing me of my concentration. My spine overrode the other circuits and told me that something was clearly wrong. I could feel the skin on the rib cage pinch, making it more difficult for a predator's teeth to penetrate. The surge of adrenaline was almost intoxicating. I took a closer look at the balcony on this go-round. Then I looked up once more, straight ahead into an open window on the third floor of the Riviera Building on the opposite side of the track. The window was a black void in the light-brown wall.

My brain caught the message. A marksman with a scoped rifle sandbagged on a bureau could get a straight-on shot as I accelerated up the hill. I swung the car on instinct and it spoiled his shot, so I felt the impact on the top of the shoulder instead of the throat. The car waltzed out of control, and all I could think about was having dyed fire retardant chemical punched into my muscle and blood by the bullet. Curiously, there was no pain.

The car went through two quick gyrations and smashed headlong into the outside concrete barrier, favoring the left front wheel, which came off and slammed my helmet. I felt the blood leave my head.

That would be the Viper group's plan. Have someone—their best shot—put me under with a small, fast-caliber rifle. The car had come to a rest, but I couldn't see. My mind still functioned, and I continued to think through the problem. It would take a 30-06 rifle with a military ball and light hand load to get a small, neat wound. If the car burned, the wound probably would never be noticed, and even if it didn't burn, the course workers wouldn't be looking for a bullet hole when they lifted me from the cockpit. Blood in racing accidents is not uncommon. Later, they could turn up a doctor to complete the work before I was conscious. They wouldn't want me to come out of it.

The pain in my shoulder asserted itself now, and I welcomed it perversely. I had lived with it all my life through a long series of accidents. Pain was now my one tenuous touch with the world, a goad for the faculties.

I could hear the rescue crew approaching, but I couldn't open my eyes. My tongue was numb.

"You want him out?"

"Jesus, yes. There's fuel all over the road."

"It may be his neck or his back."

"Out. This could go off any second."

"Straight up, and when his knees clear, pass him my way."

They lifted me with the handles on the uniform, and I could feel their muscles shaking slightly. The man took me in his arms and lowered me. I felt the canvas cloth and fingers closing around the underside of my wrist. They propped my head a few inches to take off the helmet and Nomex hood.

"Blood all over. Get him in. I want to start an IV." The sweat on my cheek cooled as the ambulance started, and the siren whooped the way they did outside the apartment in Paris. The ambulance rolled violently, and he missed the vein.

"Slow down, Bill, for Christ's sake."

"No way. I'm getting off this track."

My Grand Prix colleagues snatched gears and roared past as the ambulance lurched through one of the holes in the concrete barrier to reach the field hospital in the paddock. Then there was suddenly an abnormal quiet. I needed more to hold onto. Or had I slipped off? Could I think while I was unconscious? I already was. It was the next level, the switch-off, that I feared. I began to play mental games in an attempt to claw my way out of what felt like a deep, dark well. My body was too lazy to move up into the light.

"Let me look at him. We may be better off going straight into Memorial." Flat accent. I concentrated. Maybe Omaha. Did his internship at Boston General. I conjured up the diplomas with the cramped signature of the Chief of Staff. His coat crinkled like paper.

"Don't want to keep him here concussed like that. I'll tell them you're on the way."

"Here's his wife. His wife's here. Let her by." The doctor backed out, his soles scraping.

"I want to ride with him." Good woman. Deliberate.

"Sure, lady. Let me in first." He had no smells or sounds. His neutrality wasn't good, not stimulating. I heard the kit bag clink on the metal floor. The ambulance moved. Up-and-down notes. Up, down. Then I smelled her, strong animal smells from heat and fear.

"Put some water on this towel." Cold on the forehead. "Come on, Gus baby. Come on." Her hair was stuck on her forehead and fell over her green eyes.

"Yeah. Now you're cooking."

"I want to sit up."

"Don't," she said. "Don't move. We're on the way to the hospital. How do you feel?" She pressed my hand.

"Good. Pain in the shoulder. Lot of metal was flying around."

"We're really in for it at the end of the straight," said the driver. "Should have sent him out by helicopter."

We were back out on the course, and I could see the grandstands along the backstraight from my perch on the high gurney. The race was evidently over. Then I heard the whining pitch of the Viper as Rachid took a victory lap. I propped up on an elbow and watched out the long side window. He looked up as he drove past, and for an instant our eyes locked. Then I gave him the finger.

But I did it with the right arm, and it hurt like mad, and I collapsed back on the gurney. I wanted the Viper group to know they would have to do it all over again. This time it would have to be on my territory with my timing, which meant there was still some small possibility that we might get out of this alive.

"Quel beau geste, Gustave," Aimee said, smiling. "You're really a rotten loser." The man in starched white looked as if he didn't comprehend. I thought he would be more at home comforting the geriatrics, and I swung my feet over the edge and sat up, gesturing to the needle in my arm.

"Have it your way, buddy. I'm just a flunky EMT." He withdrew the IV and moved forward through the narrow door and sat with the driver. "Guy's crazy. Few minutes ago we thought he was dead."

"You were beautiful," Aimee whispered as I held her. "Best damned grunt in the world."

"They shot me," I said quietly. "Right shoulder."

She leaned back, her eyes wider. Then she unzipped my tunic and unbuttoned the middle layer of Nomex. I couldn't see the wound, and my neck had stiffened. It seemed like the entire right side of my body was throbbing.

"*Les salauds*," she said slowly. "But it looks OK. Let me see your back."

I bent forward slightly, and she rose above me in the cramped ambulance. "It went right through the shoulder muscle," she said. "It may have clipped the shoulder blade. Can you move your arm?"

I moved the right elbow back and forth. It felt as though somebody were stabbing me, but it moved.

"*Bon*. Hang on. We'll be there in a few minutes."

The ambulance was firmly stuck in traffic trying to cross Ocean Boulevard. The driver was cursing and blasting his siren, but the departing fans couldn't move out of our way until we got near a cop, who sorted things out and created a path.

"We can't let up now," I told her. "If we take the Viper group on now, we have an advantage. They won't be expecting us to fight back, and they may do something dumb. If we wait, they'll pick us off and there's no way we can stop them."

"Can you drive? You've got to have something left."

"I'll make it. The head's cleared. But we need our car and I don't want to have to strong-arm these ambulance guys."

"We'll have to," she said. "If we're going through with this today, there's a lot more at stake than your skin or mine."

"Ah, yes, national security. But keep your spooky friends out of this. They'll get in the way." She didn't answer but watched me closely, evaluating my usefulness. Apparently I passed.

"Put one of the Purdeys together while I talk with them," I told her. The dashboard clock said 4:10. We didn't have much time.

She could assemble a shotgun without a chink of sound. In the room, under threat of sensitive microphones, her ability with the weapons was uncanny.

"What happened to Seutenbach and DeMarco?" I asked, leaning through the doorway into the cab.

"It wasn't our section, so I don't know that much," said the attendant, a chunky man with a curiously fine profile, like the cameo of a Roman senator. "I heard the Dutchman got some burns but was supposed to be OK. The Italian, I don't know. One guy said he was dead, no pulse. Another guy said he showed some signs in the helicopter on the way to Memorial. Bad, though. You guys take a lot of punishment."

"We're well paid."

"Couldn't be enough."

The ambulance had finally broken loose across Ocean Boulevard and was heading east towards Pacific Coast Highway. I felt the pressure of the shotgun against my calf and reached back for it.

"We are also mean bastards. So that's why you are going to do just what I tell you."

The attendant turned his head and saw the blued over-and-under barrels of the Purdey. Even a 20-gauge at close quarters looks like the forward battery on the Missouri.

"He's got a gun, Bill."

"Right, Bill. I probably won't kill you, but I will cheerfully plug you in the knee or the foot if you so much as make the wrong twitch. That would be terribly painful, and my aim might be bad. Now turn off the siren and lights and take a right at the next side street."

Bill did as he was told. It must have been something about the dried blood caked all over the black uniform and the desperate way I smelled that grabbed their attention. I looked for a likely side alley and found it. Aimee had put together her own shotgun and had drawn the curtain around the windows in the back. We needed only a moment of seclusion, and I saw it in a back driveway, which had a couple of unfetched newspapers and a political flyer stuck in the garage door handle. Weekend escapees.

"Pull in here. And now do exactly as we say because it's the only way you're going to get your asses out of this in one piece. I'm going to back up against the windshield, and I want you"—I nodded to the attendant—"to stretch out on the gurney. OK, move slowly."

The attendant moved deliberately past me, watching both barrels that Aimee had leveled at him while I covered the driver. Then I moved sideways with my back against the windshield where I could see them both. Aimee put down her shotgun.

Trying to accomplish all this in tight quarters was like staging a ballet in a closet, and sooner or later the choreography was bound to fail.

As soon as the attendant sensed Aimee was between us, he made his move. All I could see was her back. She was on her own.

"Just blink, Bill, and you're dead," I reassured the driver.

His partner must have started awkwardly because he didn't get far. The groan told me a lot, and even in the cab we could hear muscle and cartilage parting in his shoulder.

"It's cool, Gus. Isn't it, *mon lapin*?" she said to the EMT. "I'm very good with both hands, and the next move will be to your neck and you won't survive that. Now give me your other arm, and we'll try this again."

I could hear him heaving for breath as Aimee took several quick turns with a torn sheet she had earlier taken from the gurney and shredded. She took the tape from the kit bag and locked up the job, turning to the feet next and easing him to the floor, a bundle of hatred.

"You're next," I said. "Slowly." She trussed the driver the same way. I got behind the wheel and backed out of the driveway, laboring against the weight of the ambulance. Aimee joined me in the cab.

"I didn't count on being shot."

"You need a painkiller?"

"That will probably screw up my brain. I'll make it."

I had to drive only another four minutes to reach Charles' garage. I'd have to humiliate him, but there didn't seem to be an alternative. I wanted to make sure Charles didn't get nailed by someone for helping us. We drove through the front door. As he stepped from his glass booth in the corner, I leveled the shotgun at him, while Aimee went over and pushed the button to close the large door.

"Hey, man. What's all this?"

"Sorry, Charles, but we're in a big hurry. Just lean over the fender and put your hands behind your back." He didn't move.

"You didn't have to do that, man. I would have helped you. Just looking at you I can see you got a bit of a problem."

"Do it, Charles. We haven't got time."

"Shit," he said eloquently, and reached one hand slowly into his pocket and pulled out a wad of bills. He peeled off five twenties and dropped them at my feet, put the wad back, and held his hands behind his back, staring at me impassively. Aimee moved behind him with sheet strips and tape. She sat him down on the open side door of the ambulance and bound his feet.

"Next customer who comes looking for his car will call the cops or find a way in," I told him. "But we need a jump. You're better off not being an accomplice." Aimee rolled him into the ambulance before he could reply. I went over to the Viper and stripped off the cover. I patted my pockets for the keys, but Aimee walked up with them. She slid open the garage door to the alley and I fired the car and pulled it out as she closed up shop, bringing the first-aid kit from the ambulance with her. We paused for a moment to take the shotguns apart and stash them inconspicuously at Aimee's feet. Two minutes later we were heading down the Long Beach Freeway, sedately this time, because I didn't want the Highway Patrol to get a good look at me.

But we also badly needed time. I wanted to draw the Viper group into my territory with enough light to do the job.

The shoulder hurt, and, added to the post-race fatigue, I was beginning to fade out again. I turned my focus to vengeance. Blood—mine—would have to be paid for.

"You sure you're OK. We just have to call the right people and they'll take over," she said.

"I'm going to make a call, but it will be to the wrong people. This is our chance to catch them off guard, to crowd them."

"Be serious. How do you plan to smoke them out?"

"Brunditz gave me a number to call if we were ever in trouble. He said it was the Mossad. The number answers. I gave it a trial run this morning."

"Where are we going to meet them?"

"I'll tell you on the way there." I didn't trust her yet not to bring the government in with us. "We've got about an hour of light left, and that will be enough if we push them."

"I want time to dress your wound," she said. "It isn't bleeding badly, but I can get some of the soreness out of it."

We were on the San Diego Freeway, moving south through suburban Orange County. I pulled off in Fountain Valley and looked for an isolated pay phone.

After a block, we turned into a shopping center, acres of tarmac surmounted by a Sears' tabernacle. There was a pay phone at the empty end of the parking lot. Aimee fished out change for me.

The same cautious voice answered after the first ring. "Yes?"

"Walter."

"We were waiting for you, Gustave. We heard you didn't turn up at the hospital. Terrible consternation there."

"I'm taking you up on the offer. I want you to pick us up and stash us someplace for the night. I'll need a doctor."

"We can arrange that. Where are you calling from?"

"It doesn't matter. We have to keep moving. Be at the El Cariso fire station at the top of Ortega Highway at five-forty-five."

"We can't move that fast. Give us another hour to do it right. We can also talk with your people."

"The ambulance crew will call out the hounds. It's five-forty-five up there or we'll find another way." I hung up. They would have to scramble, and their work might be sloppy.

We pulled back on the freeway and drove to San Juan Capistrano, where the Ortega pulls off eastward into the coastal mountains toward Perris. It's a unique piece of road, perhaps the most challenging and best engineered in the country. An enlightened government would close it to all but enthusiasts and charge admission. There isn't a competitive driver or motorcycle rider I've heard of in Southern California who hasn't had an all-out midnight go at the Ortega. Some were not ready or serious about it, driving on alcoholic courage, and died young, flattened against concrete abutments on the bridges or crushed at the bottom of the tall cliffs, not knowing, at the last conscious instant, why they did it.

It's twenty-three miles from the bottom of the road to the Forest Service fire station, a long climb up the gentle western face of the escarpment, long flowing turns that gradually tighten toward the summit in the Cleveland National Forest. From there the road dives straight over the sheer eastern face, over the upheaval of sandstone, to Lake Elsinore. The tight switchback turns closely resemble some of the great stretches of Apennine road, the Raticosa and Futa passes to Florence, where for mile after mile there aren't more than fifty straight yards, with vast drops on one side or the other. During motor sport's better days, they were the setting of the blood-stirring Mille Miglia.

I needed to test the sports Viper. Except for a few laps in Qataban, I hadn't driven it all out, and I wasn't sure how the car would behave now at the limit or how well it had been set up after we arrived at Long Beach.

"Hang on," I said as we left the edges of San Juan Capistrano and headed toward the ridge. The street Vipers were not in a league with the Grand Prix cars, but I knew they could hold their own with the best road machines now being built—the newest Ferraris, Lamborghinis, and Porsches, all in the mid-$150,OOO price range.

I drifted through a sharp left in second gear, passed two vans and a camper at over 100 in the short leg to the next right turn, and took that in third, going in impossibly deep with the confidence that only a few drivers in the business could allow themselves. The car twitched a bit, threatening to plow into the oncoming lane; then the rotary engine kicked in:, sending the tail out. Priest had set it up with final oversteer, like the Grand Prix cars. That's all I needed to know, and I slowed the car to a more sedate touring pace.

"Doesn't your stomach tighten even a little bit when you do that?" she asked as the speed dropped.

"It used to, but now it's like walking downstairs. I don't get nervous anymore until I feel the fire coming through the Nomex."

"I'm not wearing Nomex."

"You were supposed to think of everything," I said, turning to her with a smile. She gave me the Bardot pout.

Just before the summit the road flattens out. I took a side road I knew well, pulled off the pavement into a meadow of short grass, and parked under a hulking oak tree, where we collected ourselves in the failing light. Aimee dressed the wound, putting anesthetic and salve on it from the black bag; then we rebuilt the shotguns, parceled out the shells, and talked through what we wanted to do.

Then we waited, as the Cape buffalo that had doubled back blends into the acacia thorns and waits for the wary hunter. The buffalo now has the element of surprise and the advantage of being on the offensive. The odds favor the animal's being able to do considerable damage.

* * *

The Deputy Director of Operations walked briskly into the Pit at Langley, having been called from the dinner table at his nearby suburban home. Matters in Long Beach were far from under control.

"We put a hundred and thirty federal agents into the field to keep track of one man, including one agent right at his side, and you lose him" he commented to his

Project Director, who handed the DDO a batch of the latest teletypes. "You couldn't even keep him from being shot."

"It was an obscure link. Octopus didn't make the correct match on the alias names in the Riviera Building until the race was almost over," said the Project Director. "We busted in one minute too late, and he shot his head off. Another Baader-Meinhof graduate."

"This is absolutely marvelous," said the DDO, who had begun reading a teletyped interview from an indignant ambulance crew. "Does anyone have an opinion on what Thistle thinks she is doing?"

Head of Western Europe Division, who had recruited her, did his best. "Given the pressure put on Walter by the Viper group, she probably has limited control over him at this point in time. She is being forced to extemporize, and it should be only a matter of minutes now before we locate them and move in the shield team."

"We *are* being optimistic tonight," said the DDO. "The planets must be in a favorable alignment. And that hothead driver could cause an international fiasco while our people who should be doing the job right are sitting around with their thumbs up their ass someplace. Where the hell are they?"

"In the helicopters at Long Beach airport," said the Project Director.

"Get them airborne." said the DDO. "Get them out of Long Beach. Thistle won't hang around there after assaulting an ambulance crew. Tell the shield team to head inland and south because he's probably heading to the border. And start betting what's left of your pensions that we can tell them something more concrete before it gets dark out there."

~:~

9.

Tazio Nuvolari: "It is better to die pasted on a wall than to be burned like a chicken."

Count Giovanni Lurani
Nuvolari
Cassell: London

The sun had set when Aimee and I rejoined the Ortega Highway. The sky was faintly overlain by wispy, flaming-pink clouds and the light had a peculiar caramel-colored quality as we pulled into the El Cariso fire station's parking lot. A sign said the fire danger rating was Very High, but I couldn't recollect when it had read anything else. We pulled up by the door of the white firehouse about fifteen feet from a phone booth. When the Viper's whine had died, we sat for a moment to assess the mood of the place.

A window in the fire station was open. The Forest Service district radio on the sill was quietly spitting static, suddenly punctuated by some 10-4s and an abbreviated transmission about an 0D in the Blue Jay Campground. The rangers were out cleaning up the weekend mischief.

Aimee sat impassively, a hand on each shotgun, which lay at an angle under the dash. We had lowered the windows, and the soft evening breeze moved through the car.

"I'm going now," I said.

"*Sois prudent.*"

The booth looked like a small pagoda. I stepped in, dialed the JONA number, and waited four rings before hanging up. I walked slowly back to the car on the balls of my feet. The screen door opened as I was halfway back. They stepped out quickly, two of them, both Qatabanis in the orange and black of the ship's crew, both armed with machine pistols.

And that meant we had the advantage. If they had had Magnum handguns or shotguns, it would have been different. But not knowing for sure what they were headed into, they had picked the most versatile weapon, the one they could spray. Except the start of the burst isn't accurate unless the weapon is first brought to the shoulder. Either way, it is too slow and imprecise for this type of encounter.

The movement in the car drew their eyes, but that meant they were looking the wrong way. The shotgun flew for seven feet, hard and at the precise angle. I leveled the barrel with the right hand while tucking the butt in with the left.

The two reports sounded hollow in the evening air. They both took the charge of shot full in the face. One had already started to loose his clip, and metal was ringing off the tarmac. The other was simply too slow. At twenty feet, the charges almost took their heads off. The first one yanked around and snapped a metal support, pulling down the white metal awning above the door. The other simply sagged into a growing reservoir of blood.

The third report followed the second in an uninterrupted cadence. As I looked back left to the far corner of the fire station, I saw the third Qatabani falling to the grass near the fire-rating sign, his chin shot off and throat gaping. It had been a longer shot over the driver's door but still within the thirty-foot range, where I didn't think Aimee could miss if she used her toes.

I moved quickly around the car, hauling myself back into the narrow cockpit, as Aimee calmly but quickly reloaded.

"*Tiens,* switch," she said as I started the car. I handed her my weapon for new shells and tried to find someplace to stash hers. My hands were shaking, and I could feel my heartbeat knocking the chest wall. The wheel kept getting in the way. I finally wedged the shotgun against the door, pinning the barrel against the seat with my left shoulder.

We tore back out the parking lot, Aimee just finishing reloading, and I wrenched the car hard right onto Ortega Highway. An approaching camper in our lane ground its brakes, and the driver leaned on the horn, which he stopped blowing when the shotgun flipped out my window, skipping across the road. The second sports Viper pulled out from the side road opposite the parking lot, rounding to the left of us so that we accelerated up the road door-to-door.

Aimee was up on her knees, swiveling around like a turret gunner. The tremendous speed we used in pulling out must have thrown their timing off because the woman leaning out the Viper's passenger side with a machine pistol was still aiming a foot behind us. As she caught up and started to squeeze, now about two feet from my left elbow, Aimee aimed over my head and shot Else Farah with both barrels, knocking her back into the car against Brunditz.

"*Reste avec lui,*" Aimee shouted and reached around me to get the second shotgun to finish him off.

"It fell out," I shouted back.

"*Ah, merde!* Well, go. *Vas-y*," she said, kneeling down to pluck out two more shells where she had wedged them into the upholstery. "Why didn't I use one barrel on *him?*" she complained to no one in particular. "I was still afraid she would get off the burst."

I could see him trailing us by a few feet, but his steering was erratic.

"He's trying to get untangled from her and get her weapon," Aimee said, watching over the rear deck as she snapped the bore shut. She poked both barrels over the deck and as she did, he braked hard and sawed the wheel, spoiling her shot.

I snatched another look in the rearview—we were accelerating hard toward the Ortega Summit and the sharp turn just beyond it—and I saw the windshield of his car disintegrate, but the car stayed on the road . . .

"*Ah, merde!*" she wailed. "Why aren't these water-cooled cars? I'd just shoot his radiator out and we'd be done with it." The front wheels were virtually hidden by the aerodynamics as well. No shot there.

Brunditz held back now, and I tried to concentrate on the difficult piece of road coming up.

"I think he's got the machine pistol in his lap, and he's putting his helmet on," Aimee said as we dove hard left into the first turn. She was holding to the top of the windshield with her right hand while leaning down to shout in my ear over the wind. He would need the helmet and visor at the rate we were driving. A couple of startled drivers went by the other way. I had a feeling we were about to horrify a legion of citizens. A beige Jeep loomed up on our side, and I cut around it just before sliding into the next turn, a hard downhill right. I honked the horn to warn the driver there was more to come.

"He's got the advantage," she said, which is about the way I had reasoned, under these circumstances the machine pistol beating the shotgun, "but we're OK if we can keep our range." I looked in the mirror on the next straight to see Brunditz scream around the Jeep, which was pulling to a stop by the right-hand embankment.

"I was hoping for a quick resolution back there," I shouted over the wind. "Is there enough national security to justify this?"

"You bet," she shouted back. "We get these two and we've got the brains of the Viper group. Keep 'em quiet for a good, long time."

We passed a scenic turnout on the left, and a few sunset watchers shifted their gaze from the spectacular valley below to our lawless cars, now about forty yards apart, which were drifting at high speed through the next right turn.

Onlookers were probably writing us off as suicidal exhibitionists. Even knowledgeable fans at Grand Prix races sometimes conclude a charging driver will never live through another lap. But the top drivers get into those ranks by being able to rearrange physical laws and only the participant knows where the true limit lies.

Both Brunditz and I had extended ourselves to the limit and beyond on race tracks. I had occasionally driven quickly on the open road, such as a memorable push from a morning motorcycle race in Ostend to a Formula Two practice at Spa—over 190 miles in less than two hours, including a traffic jam in Brussels. On the whole, though, I didn't like open road driving. Like Fangio, I preferred to take taxis in cities. Aimee had become permanently distrustful of speed after I had once gone all out in the fog with her as a passenger, again when late for a practice. "Don't worry about that cart; I see it," I had told her and we were by it at more than 100 miles per hour, taking to the gravel shoulder, before she had even focused. Later I tried to explain that competition drivers could see and react differently, that there had been no danger, but she slowly shook her head. It did no good to explain.

Under the aseptic conditions of a Grand Prix course, I could pull out the tenths of seconds on Brunditz, but racing on a public road allowed for no such niceties. That he was a trained marksman and capable agent added considerably to our risk. If he hadn't just driven in a race, he wouldn't have a helmet and visor to fend off the buffeting wind. If he hadn't . . . There were a dozen ifs in my head but the blunt truth was, after I had driven as fast as I knew how through another difficult mountain turn, his car remained only forty yards astern.

Aimee looked over the cliff at the road as it looped down the escarpment below us.

"Know anything about fighter-plane tactics?" she shouted. I shook my head. "He's got a chance of getting us on one of those open turns down there. It's called the deflection shot. The lead plane goes into the turn and shows its whole length to the pursuer. All he has to do is lead us, the way we lead birds."

I wrenched the Viper through a long left-hand turn, the rear end inches from the cliff face.

"What's the defense?"

"Put your wheels and flaps down, dive, or tighten the turn—anything to throw off his timing."

"Thanks, especially about flaps and diving."

Another series of switchbacks were coming up, and I wasn't sure we would make it. I couldn't shake Brunditz, who was still holding about thirty yards behind, and the pain and fatigue were making me do dumb things. I missed one up-shift and smashed gears—a sin—and braked too early for a corner and had to go back to the accelerator—worse than a sin.

Two cars motored uncertainly in my lane. A Honda Civic came around the next comer as I was about to pass. I put my headlights on, and he lurched into the bank as our Vipers went through the gap and into the tum. Spastic horns blew behind us.

"He'll rake us on that one," she shouted, pointing to the third turn, a looping right, as we exited from a blind left. "I did him a favor by shooting out the windshield. Clear field."

I braked hard for the right-hand turn and cocked the car into a power slide. Aimee hunched down, expecting the worst. Past the apex, I could see him out of the comer of my eye as he started into the turn; then came the flashes from his automatic weapon in the failing light.

I drove the corner like a parody of performance driving. The Viper skidded and counter-skidded, lost time, shot ahead, hit the inside bank, looped outside into the oncoming lane. But it screwed up his aim, and instead of pouring into the cockpit, the sheet of bullets cut across the door, up the right front fender, and over the hood. They rattled around inside the metal cavities, making clanging noises.

"He let the whole clip go," she shouted, almost gleefully, scrambling to her knees and pointing the Purdey out the rear. "Let him close." I lifted off the accelerator, but he had already dropped back, having taken the turn slowly to get off his rounds.

Aimee let one shot go out of frustration, hoping perhaps that he would drive into the scattering pattern of pellets and one of the BB-sized shots would find its way through his visor, but they bounced harmlessly off the hood, too scattered and spent.

By this time we had both slowed to a crawl, and I was about to do a U-turn and go on the attack when Brunditz suddenly shot forward. I matched him, but not quickly enough.

Aimee held her ground too long. She should have hunched down when she saw he had another weapon. I could see the heavy pistol in the rearview mirror, the butt resting on the dashboard. The first shot came through the window, passing between us and out the windshield, making a small hole with spider-webbing around it. The second hit the rear deck, where Aimee was resting her arms to steady the shotgun, and the impact and flying metal threw her upward and the shotgun clattered back out of her hands, disappearing over the rear deck and bouncing end-over-end along the road, pieces of burled walnut stock flying through the air. She collapsed to her knees on the seat, screaming with frustration.

Speed was now our only defense, and I snatched a higher gear as the road leveled out. He had probably reached the engine limit while loosing those shots and had to put the pistol aside to shift. We were at the bottom of the escarpment now, with one right turn remaining before the Ortega Highway stubbed into the road that circles Lake Elsinore.

I had no doubt that stopping at the intersection at the bottom of the Ortega would be more unhealthy for us than driving through the stop sign. Nevertheless, after years of obeying the damn things, the thought of violating the vehicle code so spectacularly alarmed me. I blew the horn and turned on the headlight, thinking somehow that might help.

"Hold on," I warned Aimee, who had swung around in her seat and was looking stonily ahead.

We entered the intersection under full brakes at about 75 miles per hour. The squealing tires had acted as a sort of siren. One approaching car lurched to a halt, and a blue Oldsmobile traveling from our right was taking evasive action.

We had to negotiate a ninety-degree left turn. The car was going far too fast and started to slide broadside into a store on the far side of the road. At the last instant, the tires bit, and we sliced through the parking area and back out on the road, heading down a long straightaway on Highway 74, the first chance I had had to let the car loose.

I saw Brunditz in the rearview as he came through the intersection, also with his headlights on. He was far neater and would have closed the forty-yard gap except the Oldsmobile was wandering in a catatonic state and briefly blocked his way. Traffic had thinned somewhat, and our speed picked up. I drifted through a right bend at the end of the straight at well over 100.

I'd once known this road, but it was three years since I'd driven it last, though I remembered its character, if not its details. In the last daylight, we drove down another long straight, which was lined on both sides by palm trees. As we approached a four-way intersection at about 120, a line of cars was stacked up in my lane, drivers waiting their tum through the gate of stop signs.

I chose to weave through the lanes, horn blowing, missing one pickup truck that had stopped, paralyzed, in the intersection by probably an inch or less. Brunditz decided to pull over to the right shoulder and drive all the way through on the inside, practically taking the Four Corners Market with him. It saved him time, and he was a scant twenty yards behind as we drove through the open farmland toward the small town of Perris ahead of us.

Under any other circumstances, this part of Highway 74 is a glorious piece of road with long, undulating curves, but my familiarity with them didn't help. Brunditz could drive in my lights, braking when he saw the flashing red. A driver of his class could match me on a strange road as long as the lead driver knew what to do.

A Riverside County sheriff's car came bounding up a side road through an apple orchard, blue-and-white lights flashing, siren ululating. We were probably a half mile beyond him before he pulled onto the road. I thought briefly he might be able to radio ahead for a roadblock, but we were going too fast. We would be on 1-15 before the Highway Patrol even got the message. I wondered how long it would take Aimee's people to figure out who it was who was ripping up the countryside and how quickly they could react. Not quickly enough, I concluded.

"What's that red light flashing for?" she asked, pointing at the dashboard, her tone flat.

"Gas. We're running low. Several gallons left."

"Great. Now what?" We were on the outskirts of Perris. Signs identified Sam's Welding Service and the Petersen Mortuary.

"We're going to take him into home territory."

"Gus, *nom de Dieu*. Stop playing games. Where the hell are we going?"

"Riverside Raceway. That's my briar patch."

"*Tu es fou*," she said, hunching down and jamming her hands in her pockets.

I had trouble getting through Perris in one piece and onto the freeway, which passes by just beyond the town. There was too much traffic in the intersections, and we almost crashed at several points. I had to haul off the road and drive through a shopping center parking lot to get by a string of cars, while Brunditz drove in my tread marks.

We swooped onto the freeway, headed north, a sign pointing the way toward Riverside. The Vipers literally blasted down the four-lane road, topping 150 at one point. Several times cars and campers, struggling back from a long weekend of sunshine and beer, blocked our path, and I pulled over to the broad shoulder on the right and rifled by.

We passed March Air Force Base in the night, and I toyed with the idea of turning in and pulling up to the guardhouse to ask for federal asylum. But knowing the way the Strategic Air Command feels about its B-52s parked out on the runway, I figured we'd never live through the guards' first barrage.

The light on the instrument panel stopped flashing and locked on red, which wasn't good. The car hadn't come with an owner's manual, so I didn't know how much fuel was left, and the gauge said none. At the rate we were driving, we couldn't be getting more than five miles per gallon.

Also, I was almost physically finished. My own reserves were quickly being used up, and the flesh wound had frozen my shoulder. I had to steer with my left arm, and my right could no longer move the gearshift.

"You're going to have to shift for me," I said. "Do you know where the gears are?"

"Five-speed box?"

"With no downshifting. Just move it when I tell you."

We drove into the little commercial strip near the raceway at an appallingly high speed; then I hit the brakes and hauled the car down hard, feeling the high-tech pads turn to mush and heard the screech of metal binding on metal. But it was the last time we would need them, one way or the other.

We slid sharp right, Brunditz closing the gap dangerously, but with too much driving to do to get off a shot. On the long straights on the I-15 he had been close enough to try one, but the turbulence from our rear deck's wing configuration at those speeds probably would have deflected the shot.

"First gear," I shouted, and Aimee rammed the lever forward as I hit the clutch. It was only a few yards to a side road that leads past several houses and up to the track entrance.

"Second!" She raked the lever back, but I had timed the clutch badly. The gears crunched. She hit it again and the lever went into the slot, while Brunditz closed to within twenty feet. Then we flew over a bump in the road, both cars leaving the ground.

The entrance gate is well secured against would-be nighttime Fangios. But I had raced bikes and cars at Riverside off and on since I was a kid, and if the system of parking lots, snow fences, and enclosures hadn't been changed in the past year, I felt sure I could make my way onto the track.

I went past the main entrance to a smaller side entrance, slid the car sharp right, and quickly built up speed, aiming for the midpoint of the wire fencing in the service gate. It flew apart under the impact, not doing the front end of the car a great deal of good, including the headlights, which shattered in a spray of flying glass. I headed back through the parking lot in front of a one-story office building and maintenance area. I couldn't have seen enough in the dark to know where I was going, but Brunditz, who was practically driving up our tailpipe, kept the scenery well lit.

We went through a small enclosure, and I caught a quick glimpse of a blue-uniformed rent-a-cop in Brunditz' headlights. The cop was energetically trying to unholster his revolver.

One more parking lot and we were out on the track, accelerating across the dirt apron on the inside of Turn One. I called out the gears, and we changed up without mishap. I gained a few feet as dirt and dust cut his vision. But it was a marginal improvement. He still had us. A Magnum pistol beats nothing.

We got into fifth gear after Turn Two, and I hauled the car through the serpentine Esses one-handed, the sequence of G-forces feeling familiar.

I was almost sure Brunditz didn't know this course. For him, it was probably just a vague memory from a map in a racing magazine or a book about racetracks.

What I wanted was Turn Six—car-grinding, driver-killing Turn Six—most competitors' candidate for least-favorite corner. The outside of the right-hand loop is virtually solid. It has no escape road, no delicate catch nets, just sheets of heavy plywood backed by three layers of old, unforgiving tires and an earthen embankment. Cars have hit the wall full tilt and just stuck against it, the drivers perishing instantly in telescoped metal.

"When I tell you to pull the hand brake, pull it hard," I shouted. The hand brake wasn't crucial to what I had in mind, but it might help.

She got ready as we made the approach, both hands on the lever. We wouldn't be shifting again, and I drove up the inclined entrance to the corner with Brunditz's headlights casting an ominous shadow of our car against the red-and-white checkerboard of the plywood-surfaced wall. Steep grandstands loomed above us in the night like the Roman Colosseum.

The entrance to Turn Six can be taken at almost 90 miles per hour in a formula car, but we were approaching in a sports car at about 130. I cocked the car inward to the right, starting a slide that I knew would never get us through the turn. The black pavement at Turn Six goes through a double apex, through about 160 degrees of arc, more than anyone should ever have to drive.

In this split-second ballet, with Brunditz twenty yards behind, I couldn't give up any advantage, not even foot-brake lights. Technically, we were all going to die, anyway. He must have sensed that by now. I had led him in too deep, beyond the physical limit.

"Pull!" Aimee heaved back on the handbrake and our car spun, swinging around to the inside, as we sat, helpless, going backwards, staring into his headlights. Then our car rotated back to the inside, across his path, and we were headed towards the wall.

The Viper gyrated one more time, swinging us inward and then outward, just past the lip of the solid wall, as we soared backwards through an opening on the outside of the comer, smashing through a row of orange cones that are used to block the strip of track that stock cars take as a shortcut to Turn Eight.

The sky flashed white from an explosion as Brunditz hit the wall broadside, and we watched a pyre rise as we lost speed, still traveling backward down the road, a bunch of tall plastic cones tumbling after us.

I switched off, and the car rolled to a halt, about a hundred yards away from his flaming car. The night fell quiet except for popping noises from his car, until heat reached the fuel tank and it let loose, sending a wave of flame across the track. Smoke rose through light cast by the burning wreckage.

I felt blood oozing down my chest under the chemical underwear and wondered when Aimee's people would show up.

"Why aren't they here?" I asked. ". . . Your people."

"Oh, well, they're coming, I'm sure. They lost us, and it wouldn't have been easy to catch up. *Dieu ce que tu conduis vite.*"

We fell silent again, and then I picked up the helicopters by sound, coming low and fast, homing on the fire. Their lights shone on us as they skimmed over, landing on the track in front of us like three black geese.

Four agents leaped out of the first machine, dressed in SWAT fatigues and lugging an impressive assortment of weapons. The night was suddenly noisy and chaotic again.

A gnome-like man extricated himself from the third helicopter and, blue suitcoat flapping in the rotor wash, started walking down the track towards us. He was smaller and more gnarled than I remembered him from the restaurant in

Paris when Aimee and I had first met, and his head, dominated by black-rimmed glasses, was disproportionately large. He walked at a slant, ducking under the rotors, which were kicking up sand and old bits of paper.

The sight of him made me inordinately sad. I had never pushed Aimee about why she had left the CIA, and I hadn't wanted to because I had loved her.

"You weren't really a musician," I said, realizing I should have known the answer two years before.

"I was scared to death you'd ask me to play a cello," she said quietly, watching the man's progress. "We had no idea a racing driver would know something about classical music."

"Poor scouting."

"We didn't have time. Both of the people we were trying to get into international racing died within three weeks of each other."

"Where were they, just out of curiosity?"

"One of them was doing well in Formula Two. He died at Auckland. The other had a long way to go. He turned over a sports car at Buenos Aires, and the fire killed him. We had almost as much luck with our mechanics. They could never have made the grade."

"So you settled on Red-White-and-Blue me."

"It would have taken years to get someone where you were. We didn't have a choice."

"Neither did I."

The man reached our car and stood by my door. He was wheezing noisily. His enormously intelligent eyes flicked over Aimee and then me, focusing on my chest, where the blood had soaked through in a large patch.

"We have a doctor on the way. How serious is it?"

"I'll live, no thanks to you," I said.

"My apologies, Mr. Walter. Things got away from us in Long Beach. We did a computer search of the tenants of the Riviera Building, but the Viper group had rented the room over a year ago, then changed names on us. The computer didn't find the alias and make a match until your race was actually on. We got to the room a few minutes too late. He used the next shot on himself, if that's any consolation." I grunted.

Another helicopter landed farther up the track, and a man in white with a black bag got out. An agent pointed him in our direction.

"After he looks at you, we'll fly you by helicopter to the USC Center," the gnomelike man said. "Then you two can go fishing together anyplace in the world, courtesy of the federal government."

"I'm not going anywhere," I told him, "except for a walk."

Whenever I'm in an accident, which used to be quite frequently, I get up and walk around, no matter what's burned or broken. It reassures me that I'll live. Now I had another reason.

Getting out of the Viper wasn't easy under any circumstances. Tonight it was purest agony. The doctor loped up and started to ease me back in the seat.

"Get your hands off," I advised. He stepped back as if he had just met something unclean.

I got out this time and started to walk down the track away from the car and the helicopter lights and the garbled radio messages. Everyone seemed to be either transmitting or receiving, but for no apparent reason.

Aimee joined me as I walked out into the dark along the short stretch of track to Turn Eight.

When she took my arm to give me something to lean on, I shook free.

"Then why did you marry me?" I asked. "You used your beautiful self to get in my sack and get a place on our team. Then you had to compound it by saying some empty vows. They must have died laughing back at headquarters."

"*Faux, faux, faux*," she said. "In the first place, I didn't intend to go to bed with you in order to get on your team and into the Formula 1 clique. If I remember, you had to fight for two weeks to get me to say yes, and it resulted in a certain amount of mutual satisfaction." I couldn't argue about that.

"Then when I joined you at the Paul Ricard circuit and moved into the transporter, I told them I thought I was falling flatly and madly in love with you. My case officer—that's the man back there—had a God Almighty fit, calling it unprofessional and an emotional complication. He threatened to have me kidnapped to get me away from you. I told them I wasn't interested in their games anymore and resigned. By this time I knew I was in love with you. By marrying you I could confirm that, at least to myself.

"When the messenger turned up at Senlis last fall," she continued, "the day after I thought I was done with the whole deep-cover life forever, I could have shot him. The Agency had known for over a year that Team Qataban and Schwandt's people would act as a cover for some sort of terrorist group, but I didn't really think the Qatabanis would hire you."

"Thanks."

"Well, they had about twenty drivers to pick from. But it just had to be you, of course, and that threw us both into the vortex. It just got out of control. I went back to the embassy in Paris when you flew to Qataban for the trials and told them it was too risky for you to be on the team, but they were suddenly delighted that I was married to you. They said the best way to protect you was for me to go back on the payroll."

"Did you buy that logic?"

"Yeh, sort of. Remember, I tried to talk you out of staying with the team a couple of times. I was all mixed up."

We stopped walking, out in the dark. Orion was shining collectively above the horizon, as if trying to signal some advice. "*Laisse-moi rester avec toi*, Gus. I can show this wasn't just an Agency scenario. We can be ourselves and have a good life together."

I didn't answer for a time. I tried to see how, by caving in to this woman I had grown to love, I would be sacrificing some essential principle, but I couldn't find anything that crucial standing in the way. If anything, I had been using her the last twenty-four hours, drawing heavily on her training and coolness under stress. I put my arm around her neck to keep from staggering.

"And I thought I was quick and tough," I said.

"You are, Gus. And you're so gorgeously cheerful about it." She put her arm around my waist, and we moved back in the direction of the helicopters. I was starting to black out.

"Get me a good surgeon and tell him to get all the junk out," I said.

"*Le meilleur.*"

"Then let's go down to San Diego and hoe some zucchini. I feel like humoring an old man."

* * *

On Monday morning, shortly after 10:00, the Director of Central Intelligence received a call from the White House:

"You can take that kid of yours back now. He's done enough damage to the presidency." The DCI's seventeen-year-old son had had a case of nerves and lost the first set, 6-4. "Then he cleaned me, 6-2, 6-1. Sayonara, you old fart."

"I'll instruct him better on protocol next time," the DCI said.

"Do that. And send that agent and the racing driver around to the back entrance after the Qatabanis leave. I want a word with that pair."

The DCI couldn't tell what kind of a word and kept silent.

"I'm going to hang a medal on both of 'em. Now I can take that Arab out on the balcony after the flowery toasts are over and kick him in the butt until he agrees to keep his house clean, and he'll know it won't be just a bunch of damn words."

The President guffawed as he hung up.

###

Also by Matthew "Dr. Matt" Abergel

Work Your Stars! Using Astrology to Navigate Your Career Path, Shine on the Job, and Guide Your Business Decisions

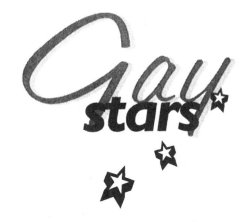

Gay stars

The Ultimate Gay Guy's Guide to Astrology

Matthew "Dr. Matt" Abergel

A Fireside Book
Published by Simon & Schuster
New York London Toronto Sydney Singapore

FIRESIDE
Rockefeller Center
1230 Avenue of the Americas
New York, NY 10020

Designed by Gabriel Levine
Manufactured in the United States of America

10 9 8 7 6 5 4 3 2 1

Library of Congress Cataloging-in-Publication Data
Abergel, Matthew.
Gay stars : the ultimate gay guy's guide to astrology /
Matthew "Dr. Matt" Abergel.
p. cm.
"A Fireside book."
1. Gay men—Miscellanea. 2. Horoscopes. 3. Astrology. I. Title.
BF1728.2.G39 A34 2000
133.5'83067662—dc21 00-03874

ISBN 0-684-86607-2

"It occurs to me that all of gay life is stories."

—Ethan Mordden,

I've a Feeling We're Not in Kansas Anymore

"Know who you are and be that person."

—Kama Brockmann

Acknowledgments

Writing a book is like putting on a show. A lot of behind-the-scenes drama takes place that's juicier than what happens onstage. And a lot of talented people backstage make the people onstage look good and ought to get more credit. I want to thank those people whose names aren't on the cover—but without whom there'd be no cover:

- My editor Carrie D. Thornton nurtured the book with humor and suicide prevention.
- Professor Ralph Johnson, Bart Goldstein, and Howard from Cariboy contributed a dizzying array of gay culture.
- My agent, Daniel Greenberg, and former editor Becky Cabaza believed in the idea, and Marcela Landres and Ted Landry turned it into a real live book—I hope they knew best.
- Christine Young, Tammy Allen, and Rhonda Abrams improved the manuscript's clarity, as well as my own.
- Nadya Giusi furnished wisdom about gay relationships.
- David Cunningham got me online and made my Web site.
- Clients, friends, and strangers on the street showed me their stars and answered naughty questions.
- And our dog, Obi, protected my desk when he'd rather have cruised in the park.

To Bob and Eric
And to every gay man who's had the courage to
"Sing out, Louise!"

Contents

Introduction

In the Beginning, There Was a Poof!

A long time ago, in a galaxy very, very nearby, a runaway meteor crashed into a small planet. Poof! In a cloud of smoke and gas, the meteor sprinkled the oceans with organic molecules, the stuff that life is made of. Pretty soon, over the next few billion years, the planet was hopping with amoebas and jellyfish, penguins and elephants, Neanderthals and disco queens.

If scientists are right—if life's original ingredients came here on a star-sprinkled meteor*—that makes all of us intergalactic hitchhikers. Gypsies from outer space. A whole planet of disoriented Dorothys seeking the Wizard of Oz. This means that we are, in fact, the children of stardust, planted here for God only knows what purpose.

Kinda cool, isn't it?

So if we come from the stars, do we continue to have a relationship with them? That's the question humans have always asked, in many, many ways. Of these ways, the oldest and most enduring is astrology. As old as civilization, maybe older, astrology studies and interprets the relationship between us and the stars we come from. It's part science, part imagination, and totally fascinating.

***Newsweek*, July 26, 1999, "Shoot the Moon."

The Greatest Show in the Universe

Forget the circus. Turn off the TV. Put away your Barbra CDs—yes, *even* your Barbra CDs. You've got front-row seats for a show that's been playing a lot longer than *Cats* or *I Love Lucy*. It's the Great Cosmic Soap Opera, and you're not only a spectator—you're the star of the show. All of us are.

Gaze at the stars. Look at the moon and planets. Up in the sky, the most spectacular performance takes place every night. Long before Broadway or Hollywood, the stars captivated nearly every human culture. These cultures recognized that the stars were telling stories about our lives on Earth. These cultures listened to the stars for news and important events. They watched the stars dramatize myths, values, and dreams.

Gay culture is no different. Our stories are told in the stars—they always have been. But modern astrology has generally overlooked gay interpretations, just as mainstream culture has frequently overlooked, suppressed, or stereotyped gay culture. One popular astrology book, for example, asserts, "The problems of homosexual tendencies and homosexual panic run rampant through these times of permissiveness." Hmm, I didn't realize it was a problem!

Anyway, it's time to change all that. Our culture has come a long way since Stonewall.* We've learned to appreciate gay contributions to world art, history, literature, music—the works. Likewise, we need to rip astrology's closet door off its hinges and reclaim our stories in the stars.

*For more about Stonewall, see "Cancer Event," p. 80.

The Stars Are Out!

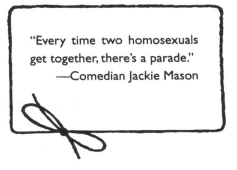

> "Every time two homosexuals get together, there's a parade."
> —Comedian Jackie Mason

Why have so many Geminis become famous gay authors? What makes Aries actresses some of our favorite bitchy role models? More important, how can *you* seduce that aloof but oh-so-yummy Aquarius waiter at the local cafe? Open up *Gay Stars* and explore these mysteries among the stars.

This book showcases the gay characters and stories that the zodiac "performs" every night—what I like to call The Great Cosmic Soap Opera. Like a play, *Gay Stars* is divided into two sections:

1. **The Cast of Characters**: With in-depth character sketches, this section illustrates your sun sign—and all the rest—in terms of archetypes familiar to our culture, drawn from the movies, books, and plays we love—or love to hate. To make astrology less abstract and more hands-on, the Cast of Characters explains the zodiac with real-life examples we can relate to, spotlighting the lives of the divas and heroes of gay culture.*

*This isn't a contest! *Gay Stars* doesn't try to rank the "most important" icons of gay culture. I selected divas and heroes for how well their lives and works illustrate their sun signs. If you think of other examples, e-mail them to my Web site at gaystars@drmatt.net.

2. **The Stars in Action**: Characters don't just exist—they *act* and *interact* with one another. This section offers practical insights and advice on using astrology in the real world. It addresses the issues most frequently on gay men's minds. A final chapter on spirituality discusses the karmic lessons associated with each sign.

A Brief History of Gay Stars

An intimate relationship between homosexuality and astrology goes way back.* According to a manuscript written 500 years before the birth of Christ, the ancient Babylonians believed the constellation Scorpio represented the "love of a man for a man."

> "It's all there—all through history we've been there; but we have to claim it . . . and articulate what's in our minds and hearts and all our creative contributions to this earth. And until we do that . . . we're doomed."
>
> —author and activist Larry Kramer

But it was the ancient Greeks who really started the ball rolling. The Greeks didn't invent astrology any more than they invented homosexuality, but they turned both into subjects of serious study and appreciation.

Plato, Sappho, and many other Greek authors produced

*This history applies only to Western culture. Other cultures—Chinese, Native American, and Indian among them—also related homoerotic myths and legends to the stars but used different astrological systems.

a huge body of literature about the same-sex relationships that formed a cornerstone of their culture. Likewise, having learned astrology through their wars and trading ventures, the Greeks charted sophisticated horoscopes and cultivated the study and interpretation of the stars into an absolutely central part of their revered belief system.

Most important of all was Ptolemy of Alexandria. During the Roman empire's heyday, this Greek wrote the granddaddy of all astrology textbooks, the *Tetrabiblos.* In it, Ptolemy says certain planetary configurations influence sexuality and make men "in affairs of love restrained in their relations with women, but more passionate for boys."

Yep, Aquarius Was Gay!

In one of the most famous Greek myths, Zeus—the king of the gods—was represented by the biggest planet in the solar system, later called Jupiter by the Romans.

From up on his throne on Mt. Olympus, Zeus spied a beautiful shepherd boy tending his sheep. According to the story, this was no ordinary guy: He was Ganymede, "the loveliest born of the race of mortals."

Accustomed to getting what he wanted, Zeus had to have him. Magically turning himself into an eagle, Zeus snatched the boy and took him to live on Mt. Olympus where Ganymede served Zeus as his cup-bearer by day and his favorite (of many!) sweetheart by night. And for all of his good service, Ganymede was placed in the sky as the constellation Aquarius—the water-bearer or cup-bearer. So it's the gods' own truth: Aquarius was a heavenly boy toy!

Not Just for Greeks Anymore

Conquering the Greeks and stealing their culture, the Romans likewise reserved a special place for astrology and homosexuality. A famous example is Julius Caesar. As for sexuality, Caesar indulged his libido so much that he was called "husband to every man's wife, and wife to every man's husband." As for astrology, Caesar received a warning from a soothsayer to beware the Ides of March, a type of astrological forecast. But Caesar ignored the stars, falling victim to a gang-bang assassination on the steps of the Senate. Poor Caesar, he should have listened to his astrologer!

Centuries later, throughout the European Middle Ages, astrology and homosexuality continued to quietly exist side by side with Christianity, sometimes grudgingly tolerated by the Catholic Church, other times fully endorsed by men of the cloth.* But it wasn't until the Renaissance, with the "rebirth" of art and classical learning, that interest in stars and same-sex relations simultaneously took off again.

In Italy, for instance, the philosopher-astrologer Marsilo Ficino looked to the stars to explain sexual and romantic attraction, both homo and hetero. What's more, the artist Michelangelo had an astrologer who reported that "Mercury and Venus were in [Michelangelo's] house of Jupiter at

*For superb scholarship on medieval gay communities, see the work of Yale historian John Boswell. For example: John Boswell, *Same-Sex Unions in Premodern Europe*, reprint (New York: Vintage Press, 1995).

his birth, showing that his works of art would be stupendous"—and that he'd have a soft spot for beautiful men.

The Hapsburg Emperor Rudolf II (1552–1612) was another poofter* who fancied astrology. Refusing to marry, taking little pleasure in war and politics, Rudolf preferred to spend his time in Prague studying nature, promoting the arts, and chatting with astrologers, whom he invited to live at his court. "He preferred the stars to politics, astronomers to politicians, the supernatural to the natural," according to A. L. Rowse in *Homosexuals in History*.

In—and Out—of the Closet

After the Renaissance, both astrology and homosexuality became officially taboo. Branded as "deviant," they were pushed to the margins of society by science and so-called "natural" law. But they didn't go away—they just kept a low profile.

Almost simultaneously, in the late 19th century, astrologers and homosexuals started finding their voice. Oscar Wilde, for example, dared to blurt out "the love that dare not speak its name." Astrology, meanwhile, found new popularity, and many astrological societies were founded and popular books published.

During the 20th century, both astrology and homosexuality gained greater acceptance. The gay rights movement

*Throughout *Gay Stars* I occasionally use the terms "poof" and "poofter" to refer to gay men because they're less clinical than "homosexual" and not as cruel as "faggot."

coincided almost exactly with what was being called the "dawning of the Age of Aquarius" by the 1960s counterculture. In fact, the term *Aquarian Age* was probably coined by San Franciscan Gavin Arthur, a Paris-trained astrologer interested in gay rights, to describe a new era of love and tolerance.*

Have you ever thought you and your friends would make great characters in a book or movie? Of course you would! Real people lead lives even more interesting than those of fictional characters. And that's what this book is about. It starts with the premise, "What if you and your friends all put on a show about your lives?" What a glorious soap opera it would be!

> Hannah: Would you say you are a typical homosexual?
> Prior: Me? Oh, I'm *stereotypical.*
> —Tony Kushner, *Angels in America: Perestroika*

So watch the stars. Listen to their stories and mysteries. Way up there your name is already in lights.

On with the Show!

*Warren Johansson, "Astrology," in *Encyclopedia of Homosexuality*, vol. 1, ed., Wayne R. Dynes (New York and London: Garland Publishing, 1990), 86–87.

Part One

Cast of Characters

Gay Aries

March 21–April 19

The Vicious Stereotype:
Sign of the Bitch

Enter Aries. A cross between Bette Davis and the Marlboro Man, you light up a cigarette and blow clouds of smoke at every schmuck who dares cross your path. Notoriously hysterical, infamously high-strung, you throw tantrums. For you, the whole world's too goddamned slow! A speed demon, a blowhard, you honk your horn and attack rush-hour traffic like an obstacle course. Your idea of an upper-body workout is slapping the barista who can't make your triple espresso just the way you like it.

Costume:
- tight jeans
- shit-kicking boots
- accessories in the shade of Jungle Red, a là *The Women*

Props:
- long cigarette
- riding crop
- copy of *1001 Ways to Say "Fuck Off!"*

Opening line: "Get out of my way! I've got things to see and people to do."

The Real You

Yeah, well, there's no denying you've got attitude. Inside every Aries lies a well-developed Inner Bitch dying to get out, a real Amazon queen. Don't believe it? Consider the historic battle of wills between Bette Davis and Joan Crawford, a couple of Aries divas. Their cult film *Whatever Happened to Baby Jane?* shows the wrath of Aries in action. But let's not get hung up on stereotypes.

So what if you're a bitch? You're also one hell of a good sport. Rams possess a quality of openness and frankness that's beautiful to behold—like outspoken gay Aries congressman Barney Frank, who even called his book *Speaking Frankly.* You laugh, you cry, you express your humanity.

Aries has a refreshing what-you-see-is-what-you-get quality. Quick on your feet, a master of improvisation, you act spontaneously. When you occupy a room, nobody forgets it!

With such megawatt personality, it's no surprise Aries strives for originality. You'd hate to show up at a party and discover you've been outdone in the fashion department—or worse, that you're wearing the *same* outfit as someone else. In olden days, you might have pioneered the Old West. In these gay days, maybe you'll start a fad, trailblaze a gay colony on the moon, or rewrite *The Joy of Sex.* Anything's possible.

Ever youthful, abounding with boyish charm (and maybe just a few infantile behaviors), you approach life with exuberance. "If I have any genius, it is a genius for living," said Errol Flynn, Aries movie star of the 1940s. "One thing I always knew how to do: enjoy life."

Maybe because you retain a childlike glow so long yourselves, you Rams get along great with kids. Not that you have to birth your own, mind you, but it's worth the effort to bond with *somebody's* kids. What better excuse to act silly at Disneyland? Not that *you* need an excuse.

Aries gets a bum rap for selfishness. Sure, you may not always notice if people need your help. But when you finally get the message, you fly to their side, a ferocious rescuer of loved ones in distress. Just think of *Gone With the Wind*'s Scarlett O'Hara—played by Aries actress Vivien Leigh, of course—who saves her war-torn family's plantation. With Aries around, there will always be a Tara.

> "It is in vain to say human beings ought to be satisfied with tranquility: they must have action; and they will make it if they cannot find it."
>
> —Charlotte Brontë, *Jane Eyre*

There's something tropical about Aries. You're hot and sultry. You know what you want. You have a strong sense of self. If you don't, then get one. It's your birthright. But I don't have to tell *you* that. You're on a lifetime self-improvement campaign, constantly striving to be better. One of my Aries clients, for example, decided to improve his self-esteem (not to mention his romantic prospects) by learning to dance the tango like a pro. Another took up ancient languages, mastering several in under a year. Whatever works. Just watch out for excessive self-consciousness. Have you ever considered you might be swell as is, without the makeover?

As a gay man, you're essentially a big poof like the rest of us. But as an Aries, you're a macho big poof. Gutsy and feisty, you Aries have a mind of your own. You rage against impotence—not the limp-dick kind, but that icky feeling of paralysis and powerlessness. Apathy and indifference are insufferable. True, your temper may flare, but you never hold a grudge for long. Who has time for grudges? Not you!

Despite all your independence and individualism, many Aries hate to feel isolated. "Where's the party?" you want to know. Without one, you'll start one—the more the merrier.

Full of self-imposed challenges, an Aries's life is never easy. That's OK. You didn't ask for a cakewalk. On the rare occasion when the uphill battle gets you down, maybe it's time to react like Doris Day, your fellow Aries who played so many of Hollywood's sassy virgins—in her old TV show she simply rolled down the top of the convertible and belted out, "Que sera, sera, whatever will be, will be."

The Secret in Aries's Closet

You pretend to eat fire for breakfast, lunch, and dinner, but deep down you'd appreciate some tea and sympathy once in a while. For inside every Ram dwells a little lamb, too, and despite all your blustery self-assurance, you take things awfully personally.

You're more sensitive and compassionate than you let on. Somewhere in your closet there's a bleeding heart. I wouldn't be surprised if that show-quality Doberman pinscher of yours were really a pound pup that you rescued from loneliness.

Aries hates a vacuum. Afraid of emptiness and silence, you rush to fill it up. So visibly full of vim and vitality, you may not let the world see you recharging your batteries. That doesn't mean, however, you don't secretly crave a little less fanfare, a little more peace and quiet. Who'd ever guess you sometimes whisper, "Take me away from all this."

It's a funny thing about you Aries: You seem to express your feelings easily and even outrageously, and yet you're not the most emotional of creatures. You may squelch many of your subtler feelings, substituting anger for disappointment or randiness for tenderness. When you're feeling blue, don't be afraid to stay with your "unpleasant" emotions. It's OK to wallow a *little*, to fully experience the blueness instead of running from it in a streak of red flames.

So, the next time you want to cry, hold back from telling yourself, "Just deal with it, missy!" Instead, let the tears roll with pride and acceptance. *Then* you can hit somebody!

Gay Aries Growing Up

Did you ever watch the cartoon show *Scooby Doo?* Remember Danger-Prone Daphne? Definitely an Aries, Daphne was the pretty girl who couldn't stay out of trouble. All you Rams-in-training had a funny way of frequently winding up in the emergency room or the after-school detention center.

No matter how bright, you weren't about to let school dominate your entire world. A strong and early interest in the facts of life made you wonder about subjects *not* found in textbooks. Insatiable desires stirred you to run wild. If you grew up in the sticks or the burbs, big bad cities beckoned loudly.

Daring and adventurous, you gay Aries kids struggled to achieve self-reliance. Even if you had a happy family, you needed to break free of parental control—not as an act of rebellion but as a means of test-driving your own identity, hell-bent on proving you could ride just fine without training wheels.

Most gay Aries kids spend their youth conquering fears and uncertainties. But in the process, let's hope you didn't conquer the little boy within. Now that you know you can compete in the Big Leagues, feel free to wear Mom's high heels or be a stay-at-home dad. Because there's lotsa ways to become a *real* man.

Aries in Love

Except for those rare thoroughly jaded Aries, you boys fall in love at first sight. And when you fall, you fall hard, like head-over-heels, flat-on-your-face, scrape-you-off-the-sidewalk kind of falling in love.

After recovering, you still need love's passion to burn brightly. Boredom and *ennui* must never get the best of you. Remember, though, that even the most ardent relationships go through their quiet, docile phases. Staying home some Saturday night doesn't have to doom the relationship, you know.

As your relationships deepen, you find it tough to go

from being a "me" to a "we." Like Jonah in the whale, you fear the relationship will gobble up your hard-won autonomy and identity. You want a leading man, but you also want your time in the director's chair. So you may enter a struggle of egos to see who's on top, so to speak.

Dr. Matt says be versatile—if not in bed, then in love. A little compromise, some give-and-take, won't kill you. Besides, being versatile gives your boyfriend a break and doubles *your* chances for a good time.

Mr. Right—Or Is It Mr. Right Now?

> "It's taken me a lifetime to get here. I'm not going anywhere."
>
> —Aries soul sister
> Diana Ross

Given your thrill of the hunt, you gladly accept a challenge. So Mr. Right *Now* may exude an air of detachment and defiance. He wags his unavailability in your face. He makes you feel good one day, suicidal the next. But hey, you want what you can't have, and who can blame you?

Then comes along Mr. Right *Forever* (or at least a long, long time). He finds you irresistible but can also stand up to you. Your temper and strong opinions don't send him running. Your tendency to blow things out of proportion doesn't make him panic. And he's got his priorities in order—with your name at the top of the list.

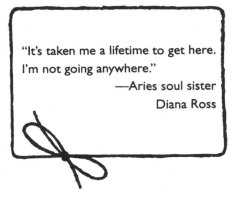

You have zero tolerance for a goody-goody Mama's boy who shies away from fun and adversity. Mr. Right knows how to have a good time and how to deal with a bad time. He can tame you into sharing his life without breaking your spirit. To Mr. Right, it doesn't matter which of you wins the skirmish—as long as you *both* win the fight to share a life.

Finally, Mr. Right can't be a prude. He might look respectable (you can't abide a putz), but he also knows how to rip through a bodice or drop to his knees begging for more.

Aries in the Sack

For Aries, sex is not a spectator sport. You demand full participation. When hormones rage, you tackle the "problem" like a real Don Juan type, an aggressive lover pursuing your prey.

The Ram bulldozes the door to sexual experimentation. Multiple partners, multiple venues, multiple genders, multiple orgasms—none of it lies outside your realm of possibilities. Besides, Aries learns through trial and error, not out of a self-help manual.

You're in good company: Aries artist Leonardo da Vinci chased beautiful young men through the streets of Florence. In Victorian times, when everybody else wrote sappy love poetry, Aries poet Paul Verlaine composed smutty stuff that better reflected his hard-living, hard-loving lifestyle. And Jeff Palmer, the Aries bad-boy porn star, has gone on record saying, "I like it *rough.*"

So we can't dismiss the appeal of a quickie and the satisfaction of a fully stocked dungeon. And yet, you also long for the passion that develops over time. With trust and familiarity comes an easy, free-flowing mutual lust. Gone is the heat-squelching awkwardness of remembering one another's names and fumbling with a bottle of lube. Here's a partner who doesn't need a map to take you to the top of Magic Mountain.

For a few thoughts on helping *him* get there, take a peek at Act One, "Seduce Any Stud in the Universe."

Aries's Fame and Fortune

Career

To Aries, winning matters. The only thing that matters more is failure, which you despise.

So in their careers, Rams aim high. You aspire to make a name for yourself. You attack new projects with enthusiasm, long hours, and too much caffeine. Sometimes I wonder if you really need three jobs to pay off the Ferrari, or if you're just showing off.

You refuse to kowtow to rules and regulations, and red tape makes your blood boil. But that doesn't necessarily make you a high-maintenance employee. For the right boss—a talented boss who can make executive decisions and command your respect—you'll voluntarily climb on a cross and nail yourself to it.

It might help, though, if you applied less force and more

technique. To prevent burnout, strive for an *even* performance at work. Think of a Broadway star performing in a big hit. On opening night you've got to be great. And on the 163rd show—a Sunday matinee—you've got to be great, too. That requires taking care of yourself. So ration your energy like silk stockings during the war. Don't spend all your gusto in one place. And don't believe the Aries stereotypes—because you really *can* collaborate and play for a team.

> "Gangway, world, get offa my runway!"
>
> —Aries lyricist Stephen Sondheim, *Gypsy*

Generic jobs don't work. You need a career that lets you be *you*. Think of Billie Holiday, the Aries jazz singer who became known for her deeply *personal* interpretations of standard songs. And let's not overlook Aries's entrepreneurial spirit. For a be-your-own-boss role model, look no farther than impresario Charles Ludlam. Pudgy and effeminate, he wasn't welcome on Broadway, so he wrote, directed, and starred in his own shows, eventually founding The Ridiculous Theatrical Company in Greenwich Village with hilarious hits like *The Mystery of Irma Vep*.

Whatever you do, watch out for taking too much of your identity from your career or profession. You're more than a job title.

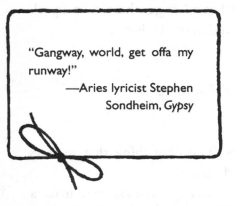

Money Matters

In the game of life, Aries goes for broke. So of course sometimes you really are broke, your piggy bank smashed to smithereens to finance your latest escapade or get-rich-quick scheme. That doesn't stop you. Picking up the pieces is all part of the fun.

Conventionally, astrologers classify Aries as the big gambler of the zodiac. But I've found that gay Aries take risks in so many other aspects of their lives that they don't necessarily line up to shoot craps or spin the roulette wheel. Besides, if you're going to win a jackpot, you'd rather it be proof of your skill than the whim of Lady Luck.

In your youthful days, you may take money for granted, adopting an attitude of "All I need is the air that I breathe." Later, though, after you've proven yourself creatively, romantically, and otherwise, you're likely to get a hankering for a hunk of affluence. Leather sofas, sports cars, and mutual funds take on new importance as you look around and see your more down-to-earth friends acquiring the toys of adulthood. Still, though, planning for the future doesn't come naturally. Save for your retirement? *What retirement?* you ask.

Aries in the Spotlight

Aries Diva: Bette Davis

"Until you're known in this profession as a monster, you're

not a star," said every drag queen's favorite idol, Bette Davis. Feisty and headstrong (some might say hysterical), Bette Davis (like most Aries) liked to take charge. On the set, she often directed her directors, bossing them around with volcanic outbursts and that defiant laugh of hers. Please note, by the way, that *Davis* is the word *divas* anna-gramatized!

Interview Attributed to Bette Davis

Reporter: Miss Davis, what's your reaction to Joan Crawford's death?
Bette: My mother told me never to speak anything but good of the dead. So Joan's dead. Good (puff, puff).

"All right, Mr. DeMille, I'm ready for my close-up."
—Aries actress Gloria Swanson, *Sunset Boulevard*

Aries Diva: Rosie O'Donnell

Could it be? Was the Queen of Nice really born under the Sign of the Bitch? Yes, Rosie exemplifies the warm, outgoing, I'll-try-anything-once side of Aries. But Rosie can also be quite outspoken (another very Aries characteristic), such as when she argued in favor of gun control against Tom Selleck. Go Rosie!

Aries Diva: Celine Dion

It usually takes a gal a long lifetime to earn her divahood.

Not Celine Dion. VH1 dubbed her a *bona fide* diva before age 30. Starting life in a poor Quebec family of 14 children, she exercised that typical go-get-'em Aries attitude and made it big seemingly overnight. Precocious (like many Aries kids), 12-year-old Celine composed a song that got her foot in the door, and by age 16 she'd racked up international awards for singing about the power of her love (Rams often regard their love as a powerful force). Apparently her love is even strong enough to survive a sinking ship—her U.S. career hit new heights with the *Titanic* theme song, "My Heart Will Go On."

Aries Hero: Tennessee Williams

In his plays, Tennessee expressed the *sultry* side of Aries. Think of macho Stanley pitting forces against passionate Blanche in *A Streetcar Named Desire.* Or see the movies *Sweet Bird of Youth* or *Cat on a Hot Tin Roof* with Paul Newman (hubba-hubba!) and feel the hot, humid, raw essence of Aries. In his life, Tennessee exhibited more of the Ram's restlessness and drive. "There was never a moment," he said, "when I did not find life to be immeasurably exciting to witness, however difficult it was to sustain."

Aries Hero: Stephen Sondheim

Some say Sondheim killed American musical theatre; others, that he raised it to new artistic heights. Whichever, this preeminent writer-composer boldly forged his own unique style. Breaking the mold, his shows like *Company* and *Pacific*

Overtures pioneered fresh narrative forms for Broadway musicals, while *Assassins* and *Sweeney Todd* spotlighted villains as misunderstood "heroes." For this Aries innovator, as he explains in *Sunday in the Park with George*, "Art isn't easy."

Aries Hero: Elton John

Rams always like to be at the head of the class, the front of the line, the cutting edge. So it's no surprise Sir Elton John was one of the first rock stars to come out of the closet (as bi in 1976, later as totally gay). He's also brought Aries ardor to his concerts, with wild, extravagant costumes (gotta love those giant platform shoes!) and the Ram's characteristic attitude of "Here I am—deal with it!" Not content with fame and fortune alone (is Aries ever complacent?), in the early 1990s Elton focused on raising awareness and megabucks for AIDS charities.

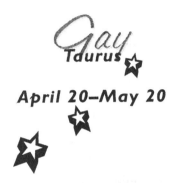

Gay Taurus

April 20–May 20

The Vicious Stereotype: Sign of the Material Girl

Enter Taurus. You've had breakfast at Tiffany's, dinner at Maxim's, and liposuction on Rodeo Drive. When you decide you want something—or someone—you adhere to it like a tight girdle. A gold digger, a fortune hunter, you've got a sweet tooth for a sugar daddy. You're a sucker for any troll with an extralong limo. Your idea of a good time is clipping coupons and watching late-night reruns, buying everything the infomercials have to offer. Like oh-so spoiled Karen from *Will & Grace,* you regard filing your nails as a hard day's work. Have you ever read literature more meaningful than the Gump's catalog?

Costume:

- Italian suit
- Ferragamo shoes
- snakeskin belt (who cares if it's an endangered species?)

Props:

- shopping bags
- 18 matching pieces of Louis Vuitton luggage, plus hat boxes
- gold-plated nail file

Opening line: "I'll take it! I'll take *you, too,* sweetie!"

The Real You

Sure, you enjoy having stuff. Sure, you covet beautiful things. But if the truth be told, you Bulls express your "materialism" in so many ways beside greed and gluttony. You may commune with the earth by running naked through the woods. You may conjure sumptuous flavors by cooking for friends. You may ride the fine line between pleasure and pain by giving a massage with *oomph.* The point is, you're grounded; you live in your body on planet Earth. Not everyone does, you know!

Seldom rattled by the shakes and shuffles of a mad, mad world, gay Taurus generally stays even-keeled, shunning the extreme emotions and high drama so characteristic of our orientation. When stormy weather strikes, you anchor the rest of us to a strong sense of calm and composure, never afraid to slap to his senses the first non-Taurus queen who goes emotionally haywire.

Since you're reading this book, you're probably not a lesbian; nevertheless, inside every Taurus—male or female, gay or straight—there resides an earth mother goddess.

One of the earth signs, you're a natural kind of guy, one who can't abide synthetic fibers or people. Reliable and honest, you try awfully hard to prove your worth with good deeds.

> "*Les garçons, changeant comme la mer.*" "Boys! They change like the sea."
>
> —Taurus author Henri de Montherlant (1896–1972)

You don't ask a lot of dumb questions. Rather than ponder the meaning of life, you prefer to ponder the finer things in life, like a beautiful sunset or the contours of a man in Levi's. Rather than curse your fate, you'll happily hoe the row God gave you. Take, for example, Taurus artist Keith Haring. He got his start in art by painting graffiti in the New York subway—hey, everybody's got to start somewhere.

People may wonder why you always wear such sensible shoes. Do you have an orthopedic condition? Probably not—just a deep faith in practicality. Instead of crying over spilled milk, you cut your losses and call in the dog to lick it up. The Taurus director John Waters, for instance, approached filmmaking with a down-to-earth attitude: "Always put sex and violence in your films. That way, even if it's no good somebody will want to see it."

Taurus poofs make great friends. You guys are easy to be with, great at hanging out. Friends flock to you for the warmth of your company and the sincerity of your sympathy. You have a knack for laying out the welcome mat. In a gay Taurus home, a plate never goes empty nor a glass unfilled for long. You tend to buy in bulk, and the moment a guest walks through the door, you try to fatten him up like a Christmas goose.

Gay Taurus resembles Ferdinand the Bull, the children's storybook hero who preferred reposing under a tree sniffing flowers to fighting the toreadors. A pleaser of people and promoter of peace, you try not to ruffle any feathers. As a result, anger and resentment may silently accrue until—*bam!*—you can't take it anymore. When you do get mad, look out! You snort, fume, stamp your feet—and somebody's going down.

Without a doubt, the Material Girl stereotype comes partly from Taurus's interest in value. But here's the rub: Values can mean *cost*, but it can also mean *beliefs* and, *principles.* What are your values? What principles matter to you above the rest? Figure *that* out, and you're well on your way to Taurean utopia.

The Secret in Taurus's Closet

To most who know you, you're as cool and *tranquilo* as the Fonz on *Happy Days*—and every bit as comfy and complacent in your well-worn jeans and broken-in motorcycle jacket. Yet if we peel away the denim and leather, we might glimpse a wild animal pacing its cage. Aha! The Bull *does* know how to howl and growl.

Occasionally, when the moon is blue and evil spirits conspire, you detonate like a bottle of Dom Perignon on New Year's Eve. On the spur of the moment, for example, one of my Taurus clients up and road-tripped cross-country with a new boyfriend—for three months! It was completely out of character—or so I thought—but the potential for such behavior must have lurked deep inside.

Within every Taurus, the conservative and the carnal seem to compete (or simply coexist, if you're lucky). Case in point: the eminent philosopher Ludwig Wittgenstein. He cultivated self-discipline and solitude to do his work, yet he found the gay haunts near Cambridge University irresistible—even in the restrained 1910s. No, he never wanted to become a boring old professor disconnected from "real" life!

So in a word, what's Taurus's big secret? Danger! You avoid it, yet you crave it. Like chocolate.

Gay Taurus Growing Up

Oh sweet embraceable you! Cute, cuddly, and cherubic, baby Bulls are more like bears—teddy bears, to be precise. Grandparents pinched your cheeks. Mom slipped an extra Twinkie in your lunchbox. But no matter how spoiled, you still took out the garbage and mowed the lawn, a responsible kid whose biggest fault was being a klutz.

Faster, louder, less sensitive kids made you think you couldn't keep up or fit in—until, that is, you realized they all belonged to a club you didn't want to join anyway.

Seemingly self-reliant, you growing Bull boys actually

needed lots of encouragement to stand up for yourselves and chase your dreams. Without it, many Taurus kids (Barbra Streisand, for example) grow up with an ugly duckling complex. Remember, the Taurus soul thrives on affection. That's sometimes tough for a child—especially a gay child—to find, so do your inner teddy bear a favor and make him feel safe, comfy, and loved. Allow yourself to play in the mud and run through the woods and eat with your fingers—and to hell with Miss Manners.

> "I never knew any mere physical experience could be so exhilarating!"
>
> —Taurus actress Katharine Hepburn in *The African Queen*

Physical and tactile, you Taurus kids discovered your bodies early—maybe because there was no one else to play with. If this smoldering sensuality seemed too "naughty," you may have developed inhibitions. Well, grow up and get over it. It's time to explore the animal within. You can't stay an innocent Shirley Temple doll forever. (Yes, she's a Taurus too.)

Taurus in Love

When love knocks on his door, the typical gay Bull may slowly get up to answer it—but not without looking through the peephole first. Cautious, you doubt the staying power of whirlwind romances. Though you may yearn for a passionate, life-altering affair, you worry some guy will rock your world and turn it upside down. If you wanted to feel the earth move, you'd visit San Francisco, not fall in love.

So you resist love's onslaught. A different boy may pass through your bed every weekend (I never called you celibate!), yet your heart remains well protected. Then one of those boys stays a second night, and a third. He learns how to brew your coffee the way you like it. Pretty soon he simply belongs there, like the cat purring on the sofa and the African violet that refuses to die. That's when a Taurus knows he's really fallen in love.

Once you open the door to love, you stick to a fella like peanut butter. You catch yourself singing, "All of me, why not take all of me." Domesticity doesn't give you the creeps as it might a Sagittarius or Gemini. It's the nature of Taurus to care for someone and be cared for.

Too much mushy gooey romance will make you sick, but a loving, easy, steadfast relationship will keep you satisfied and coming back for more.

Mr. Right—Or Is It Mr. Right Now?

A Taurus's Mr. Right has a big appetite. Food and drink, warm cuddles, and sloppy kisses—in all these he likes to indulge, and he indulges you, too.

The rest of the world may not find him attractive in the conventional sense—he's probably too tall, too hairy, too *something*—but at night when the lights go out he communicates in uncanny ways. It's OK if he works with his hands—in fact, all the better! He knows how to push your secret buttons and win the jackpot.

He shouldn't require too much house-training. You can deal with messy but not with absent, so Mr. Right ought to stick around. He's devoted to you. More than that, he's devoted to the long-term durability of your relationship. In short, Mr. Right is a man you can count on.

Mr. Right has a good head on his shoulders. Though generous, he can handle money profitably. Though intelligent, he doesn't disappear into nutty theories and far-flung speculations. Sometimes it takes a tug-o-war champion to drag out your feelings. Mr. Right can do it. Mr. Right draws you out of a rut. He keeps you on your toes, enthusiastically inquiring, "What's next?" instead of expecting the same old thing. And he takes the good with the bad, the mundane with the fabulous.

Taurus in the Sack

Taurus is a Latin word that comes from the Greek letter *Tau*. Like our letter *T*, Tau made a little picture of two people copulating (see, the long vertical line represents the penis and the short bar on top represents whatever orifice one might imagine). Positively pornographic, this only goes to show Taurus has always been interested in *doing it*.

Bodies enthrall you. So do life's little—and not-so-little—pleasures. Extremely tactile, you're a hands-on kind of guy. The smell of leather may quicken your pulse, the odor of a locker room may tickle your taste buds, but nothing makes you squirm like the scent of a man, a real live man. For an even more explicit idea of the Bull's musky sensuality, watch an old silent movie with Taurus heartthrob Rudolph Valentino—he couldn't act, but he didn't need to.

Every Taurus I know stashes a little box of toys under the bed. When your man's away you may miss him terribly—but that doesn't mean you'll go to sleep unsatisfied. The toys, however, can't substitute for affection, and it's affection that feeds the Taurus soul. Whether you come from big Italian families or more reserved backgrounds, you Bulls are all touchy-feely.

One little tip from Dr. Matt: Bulls have stamina. Honey, you can go all night and well into the next morning. But remember, not every studly looking man performs like a stud, so give the guy a break and let him catch his breath.

Taurus's Fame and Fortune

Career

Bulls vegetate—you've seen them lying there in the field, chewing the cud, aspiring to nothing greater than mounting some reluctant dairy cow. This is the impression you may project in the workplace—lazy, smug, faithful to the credo "If it feels good, do it!" But it ain't necessarily so.

Bulls do their fair share—and then some—yet you expect to enjoy your work, too. For Taurus, having a great career plays second fiddle to having a great life. Ambitious, competitive careers attract many Bulls, but you'd rather not put up with stress and internal politics. Bulls turn up their snouts at on-the-job bullshit, no matter how many stock options it yields.

> "The difference between men and boys is the price of their toys."
>
> —Taurus pianist Liberace

Even more than a paycheck, what really motivates you is a job well done. More than the boss's or the public's approval, you need to see the tangible, valuable fruits of your labor. If you want to know what that fruit tastes like, do yourself the favor—if you haven't already—and listen to the music of two gay Taurus composers: Erik Satie and Camille Saint-Saëns. Despite their different styles, all of their music has soul. One note at a time, it's simple, it's powerful, it's fulfilling. What better role model for a Taurus's career?

Money Matters

Let's be frank: You've got money issues. Inside your wallet, comfort and security pull in opposite directions, making things a tad uncomfortable down there. For example, the comfort-loving side of Taurus may want to buy a BMW with heated seats to warm your rump on the commute to work. Meanwhile, the security-seeking side prefers to keep driving the old Ford Escort and amass a mound of money to roll around in. "Buy!" says one voice. "Save!" says the other. What's an inner-peace-loving Taurus to do?

Dr. Matt recommends the financial wisdom of the ancient Greek Hedonists. The Hedonists sought maximum pleasure from life with a minimum of pain. So they drank wine, but not too much. They ate good food but, unlike some of the Romans, didn't vomit and eat more. In this philosophy, moderation guides one's choices. Neither austerity nor desire holds sway. After all, you Bulls burst on a roller coaster of extreme ups and downs.

It's also wise if you invest as well as work. Then you can practice your art or profession how you like, with honesty, integrity, and plenty of coffee breaks, without worrying how you'll keep up payments on the sailboat.

Taurus in the Spotlight

Taurus Diva: Barbra Streisand

"If I could meet Barbra walking down the street just once," said my acupuncturist, "*then* my life would be complete." Indeed, in the pantheon of divas worshipped by the gay community, Barbra ranks damn near the top. A divinely talented entertainer, she embodies some of the Bull's most salient qualities. Determined and headstrong, financially savvy and with a strong sense of self, Barbra won't budge from her values. Undeniably a Material Girl (e.g., the Donna Karan wardrobe), Barbra puts her wealth to work by fighting for social and political causes.

Taurus Diva: Shirley MacLaine

Shirley seems too busy on the astral plane to be a Material Girl. But she's a Bull, all right. In her career, she's hung tough, persistently outlasting fads that come and go. Originally a dancer, Shirley approaches acting with a Taurean wisdom of the body. To star in *Madame Sousatzka*, for example, she got fat! "Once you get something in your body, in your movements, in your gestures and facial expressions, it's always there," she says. Of course it could all be different in her next lifetime.

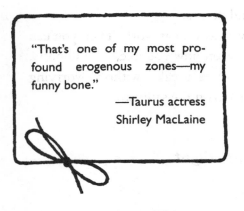

> "That's one of my most profound erogenous zones—my funny bone."
>
> —Taurus actress Shirley MacLaine

Taurus Diva: Audrey Hepburn

Elegant yet unostentatious, an icon of glamour yet still a down-to-earth mother and children's advocate, Audrey Hepburn defined many facets of Taurus—including those of Material Girl and something altogether deeper. Though she commanded huge Hollywood salaries, she gave up acting to raise a family, represent UNICEF, and garden. Why? One biographer asserts, "Some regarded her as a snob. But her isolation grew largely from her need to overcome a desperate sense of insecurity."* Then again, maybe she was simply a Taurus who wanted her peace and quiet!

Taurus Hero: Liberace

When in Las Vegas, absolutely don't miss the Liberace Museum. It's a temple of Taurus, a monument to one man's quest for all things beautiful—and *beyond* beautiful. The clothes, the jewelry, the candelabra, the "hair" (or whatever it was)—all of it delighted a mainstream audience that overlooked this pianist's sexuality in favor of his fabulosity. But don't think for a minute he was a pushover pansy—Liberace valiantly challenged the malicious tabloid press in court—and won.

Taurus Hero: Armistead Maupin

Taurus has a special appreciation for life's little pleasures and everyday triumphs. So it's no wonder that Armistead Maupin turned the deceptively ordinary lives of several 1970s San Francisco apartment dwellers into the blockbuster *Tales of the City* books and movie series. Besides making us laugh, Maupin's *Tales* have offered gay readers a Taurean sense of having a place in the world, a feeling that, yes, we *do* belong to a valuable culture. "Your job," Armi-

*Barry Paris, *Audrey Hepburn* (New York: G.P. Putnam's Sons, 1996).

stead advised, "is to accept yourself—joyfully and with no apologies—and get on with the adventure of your life."

Taurus Hero: Ludwig Wittgenstein

No, he's not exactly a famous household name, but he quietly exerted a huge influence on 20th-century philosophy (that's very Taurus, by the way). A Cambridge University philosopher before World War I, Wittgenstein pondered the nature of reality itself. (Taurus is always interested in what's real.) A down-to-earth Bull, he resisted academic mumbo-jumbo theories, asserting, "Whereof one cannot speak, thereof one must be silent." Born wealthy, he gave away his inheritance so friends would value *him* and *not* his money.

Gay Gemini

May 21–June 20

The Vicious Stereotype: Sign of the Ditzy Blonde

Enter Gemini. What a bimbo! Like a bag of potato chips, your head holds more air than substance. With as many little boyfriends as Smurfette, you tra-la-la through the Pines. Are all your sweaters too tight because you want to show off your chest or because you can't work the washing machine? A big floozy with helium heels, you typically can't remember what floor you parked on—nor, for that matter, whose floor you slept on. Do blondes have more fun? You sure try—even if a genuine blond hair has never sprouted *anywhere* near your body.

Costume:

- See-through blouse
- Short shorts
- Socks for stuffing in strategic places

Props:

- Bottle of peroxide
- Degree from the Copacabaña School of Dramatic Art (just like Marilyn Monroe in *All About Eve*)
- Wind machine (for blowing through your hair and up your bloomers)

Opening line: "Haven't we met somewhere before? You look just like my ex-boyfriend. Oh, gee, you *are* my ex-boyfriend."

The Real You

Blond, brunette, or bald, every Gemini has to put up with the vicious stereotype of bleached-blond bimbo-hood. Actually, though, a true Gemini is terribly clever. Logical and rational, you see objectively. Emotions don't hijack your better judgment. Take Confucius, for example. Was he gay? I'm not sure, but according to his birthday this Chinese philosopher was definitely a Gemini—who else could have invented all those pithy proverbs in the fortune cookies?

Contrary to the clichés, Gemini seeks stimulation beyond tanning salons and *GQ* fashion spreads. A curious soul, you take an interest in the world. Among your ranks are read-a-holics and media junkies, current-events mavens and TV trivia gurus. From all walks of life you make friends. Gemini priest and author Michael Boyd, for example, confessed, "I yearned to open up windows in my claustrophobic life. . . . Could I learn to exercise my intellect and provide oxygen for my soul? I wanted to try." Most Geminis try all their lives.

Geminis are idea people. Above his desk at city hall, Gemini politician and gay activist Harvey Milk prominently hung a quote by Victor Hugo: "All the forces in the world are not so powerful as an idea whose time has come." Though he didn't live to see it, Harvey's ideas about civil rights forever changed our lives.

Like Harvey, most Geminis make the best cheerleaders. Forget the little skirts and pom-poms—I'm talking about a flair for creating excitement about ideas, the ultimate free speech activist. Like President John F. Kennedy. He wasn't gay but he was a Gemini, and more than any other 20th-century president, he convinced generations of Americans they could improve civil rights and put a man on the moon.

> "I've been on a calendar but I've never been on time."
>
> —Gemini diva Marilyn Monroe

Gemini gets around. A restless spirit, never afraid of a little parking ticket, you pull right up to the front door of Where It's All Happening. And man, you Twins can talk! Wherever you go you make friends. Or enemies. At least people know you've been there—because you never lack for something to say.

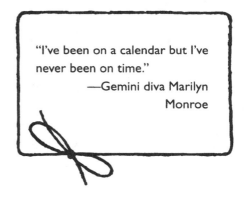

Simply sitting on a park bench, you interview strangers, getting the scoop on their life stories. You tell stories, too—sometimes believable, sometimes not, always entertaining. My Gemini gym buddy knows so much gossip that I wind up laughing more than lifting. Along with Aries, you Geminis have mastered the fine art of bitching and dishing. Where did you learn to say all the right things? Quick on the uptake, always armed with answers, you make us see life from many angles.

> "I don't care what anyone does . . . so long as they don't scare the horses."
>
> —Gemini Queen Victoria, 19th-century diva of the British Empire

Dr. Jekyll and Mr. Hyde. Sweet Samantha and mischievous alter-ego Serena on *Bewitched.* That's how pop culture portrays your infamous "schizo" personality. But Gemini isn't so much two-faced as multifaceted. Complex and full of surprises, you keep us guessing, defying simple pigeonholing.

Your adaptability allows you to go with the flow. Compromise comes naturally. You appreciate other points of view, even when they're clearly a crock. Willing to try anything—or any*one*—you've tasted exotic foods, attempted dangerous sports, probed extraordinary people. No, you may not always know what you want, but that's never stopped you before. For Gemini, figuring out is half the fun.

The Secret in Gemini's Closet

Gemini's secret? You don't keep many secrets. A big blabbermouth, you've exposed them all. Except one, perhaps: Your fear of being a big fuddy-duddy.

Below your colorful personality lies a base coat of beige. Deep down, under your jam-packed appointment book and life-of-the party dynamism, you'd like to spend all day snuggled in bed with a good book and a hot water bottle. Who'd have guessed you secretly, almost ashamedly, long for simple pleasures like a comfortable home, loving family, and macaroni and cheese out of the box?

Typically, you race around. You fill every empty minute. You meet and greet and act quick on your feet. Why? Maybe it makes you feel alive. Then again, maybe it's because you fear the quiet, the calm of doing nothing. Confronting naked truths without the distractions of loud music and a million things to do—it's a scary yet essential part of who you are.

The wise Gemini takes time to listen—not only to people but also to the simple sounds of a babbling brook or a rumbling stomach. Only then can you silence the noise in your head, disarming the fear of being overwhelmed, and get on with being your fascinating self. Maybe that's why Gemini author and actor Harvey Fierstein commented, "Of course people are afraid. But honestly facing that fear, seeing it for what it is, is the only way of putting it to rest."

Gay Gemini Growing Up

Memories of a Gemini childhood sound like a broken record: "Stop talking!" "Stop running!" "Stop playing and come inside!" Stop, stop, stop. As your mother probably never tires of reminding you, Gemini kids are a handful.

Gemini powers of persuasion being what they are, you easily convinced the folks to buy all the latest toys. Then you dissected them, reassembled them, and proceeded to your siblings' stuff, mixing up all the Ken and Barbie outfits.

As a teenager, no doubt, you got into all sorts of trouble yet always managed—somehow, you sly devil—to talk your way out of it. Many of you Gemini students found school so tedious that you took smarts for granted and slacked off. The fact is, most young Twins simply don't get enough stimulation. And gay Twins certainly don't get the kind of stimulation that suits their fancy.

Oh well. You stirred up your own stimuli. Parties, poetry contests, extracurricular activities—you tried it all. None of it, though, mattered so much as the girls' slumber parties. That's what you really wanted to do—stay up all night with like-minded pals, gabbing about everything and nothing. If you didn't do it back then, do it now. A bevy of "girlfriends" will do more for the kid within than all the boy toys on Fire Island.

Gemini in Love

"Easy come, easy go," your romantic attitude seems to say, as if the object of your desire changed as often as your

Calvins. A smooth operator, you can fall in and out of love without developing a single stretch mark. Your love weighs less than fat-free potato chips, and you treat it like cheap crystal: easily replaceable. In *La Traviata*, the party girl Violetta must have been a Gemini—she only laughed at love.

But, eventually, even Violetta met her match. So does every Gemini. At first, no doubt, you're happy to get to know a man—but *not* necessarily happy to let *him* get to know *you*. Though Gemini is the zodiac's great communicator, you don't easily speak your heart. You like to keep your affairs light, airy, and gay.

Then comes a time—and a man—in your life that changes all that. A trifling *affaire d'amour* deepens into a bona fide *grande passion*. When it clicks, it clicks. Hanky-panky evolves into genuine companionship. It's all heavier, stickier, messier than what you'd hoped for—and also more satisfying. Remembering Violetta, don't wait till it's too late to get serious about love. Tragically bittersweet endings are so *passé*.

Mr. Right—Or Is It Mr. Right Now?

Can you ever really settle for just one Mr. Right? It's possible, but only if he grants you plenty of freedom. Perhaps he'll travel, spending lots of time on the road, occasionally having you tag along. Mr. Right encourages you to settle down but never actually pins you down.

He doesn't try to possess you, nor does he expect you to forsake your friends or career—as if you'd drop everything to make room for little ole him. It'd sure be nice if he contributed to your sense of direction in life, but it won't work if he tries to ride you and break you like a young buck—at least not with your clothes on. He doesn't nag.

Mr. Right is witty and, like many of your closest friends, leads an interesting life. He expands your horizons. From one another you constantly learn and exchange ideas. He might know how to cook and get you to relax, but he mustn't turn into an old fart, since you appreciate youthfulness, even in old fogies.

> "It sounds like you can't decide your way out of a paper bag—are you a triple Gemini like me?"
>
> —Gemini advice columnist Mike Albo, *OUT* magazine

The way he looks matters less than the way he *moves.* A clumsy, sloppy oaf won't cut it. Mr. Right glides and gestures with grace. He has an agile mind and knows how to use it.

Gemini in the Sack

What's the body's biggest sexual organ? No, not *that!* It's the *brain*, silly. And more than any other orifice or erogenous zone, you like to get it stroked. Hot talk makes you hot. So do fantasies planned down to the last naughty detail. You've read all the how-to manuals and best erotica—and probably written some of your own.

What's less certain is how much you enjoy the *act* itself. No matter how buffed and flawless, a naked man fails to live up to your titillating *idea* of a naked man.

So the sexually satisfied Gemini learns how to reconcile fact and fantasy. Maybe you write graphically steamy letters to your partner. Perhaps you make home movies. The point is, you can express your erotic ideals while realizing most ideals forever elude attainment.

You need either lots of partners or one partner who can do lots of things. Sometimes playful, sometimes angry, sometimes romantic, sometimes smutty—your sex life benefits from what actors call a "big range." Then again, you may occasionally derive your greatest pleasure from having your partner lie back while you entertain him with your big bag of tricks.

Gemini's Fame and Fortune

Career

Do you ever really know what you want to be when you grow up?

No. It doesn't matter. In your Gemini life you will have many jobs, each a little weirder than the last. You may never find the "one" that answers the call of destiny. You may have to simply choose a project, a job, a career, and just try it, rather than fretting to death whether it suits you, and then never doing anything at all but watch daytime TV.

Think of Walt Whitman and all the other great gay Gemini writers in this chapter. Do you think they just sat down one day and wrote their masterpieces between lunch and teatime? No, they started and stopped. They chased ideas down blind alleys. For every page published, 17 kindled the fire.

> "Look, if you think you're gonna get back in my panties, forget it. There's one asshole in there already."
>
> —Gemini actress Kathleen Turner in *Crimes of Passion*

Don't just work—find a hobby. Develop a talent for which you don't get paid. Do it because it brings you joy. Not every activity belongs on a résumé. If it did, you might have a great career but an ultimately boring life.

Is Gemini a hard worker? It all depends. If you're steaming espressos just to pay the bills, a customer might collapse from exhaustion before you get around to grinding the beans. On the other hand, if your work engages and stimulates your mind, neither hunger nor free concert tickets can drag you away.

One tip from Dr. Matt: Drifting is bad. Don't switch careers every time you feel frustrated. But versatility and diversity are good. It's swell to grow a business or career with many twists and turns rather than one dull trajectory upward.

Money Matters

Money? Who cares! Spending? *You* care! An impulse purchaser, if you see it, you want it. You don't like to think about what you can and cannot afford.

You're not exactly a spendthrift or reckless charge-card charger, but because you have so many interests, hobbies, and friends, your money has so many places to go, so many ways to be spent. If you want to save money, try eating out a little less. TV dinners are cheap and don't require a tip. Or go shopping but not buying, trying on new outfits and tossing them over the dressing-room door. You'll be amazed at the savings.

If you want to invest, choose the classic "diversified portfolio." As long as you can keep track of it all, it's actually quite wise to invest a little here, a little there. And you may discover you have as much fun trading stocks and bonds as trading Barbie and Ken outfits!

Gemini in the Spotlight

Gemini Diva: Marilyn Monroe

The supreme sex symbol of the 1950s milked an innately Gemini talent: She simultaneously came across as innocent but erotic, the girl next door yet glamorously desirable. Though she seemed the dumb blonde bombshell, her Gemini curiosity drove her to study "real" acting at the legendary Actors Studio, whereupon she entered intellectual circles, married Arthur Miller, and converted to Judaism. This multifaceted nature epitomizes Gemini—not a schizo personality, but a flair for defining oneself without preconceived categories.

Gemini Diva: Judy Garland

"Are you a friend of Dorothy?" Before it was OK to be gay, that was a secret "code" gay men exchanged to find each other. As Dorothy in *The Wizard of Oz*, Judy Garland embodied the longing for acceptance that resonated with so many gay young people. Gemini communicates, and this "little girl with the big voice" seemed to speak the unspoken, attracting whole generations of gay men eager for a voice of their own. In fact, her untimely death in the summer of '69 helped inspire the Stonewall riots (see Cancer Event, p. 80), in which drag queens and other activists finally stuck up for their rainbow rights.

Gemini Royalty: "Queen" James I

It's one of the greatest ironies: The Bible preferred by most fundamentalist Christians was commissioned by King James, the "king who should have been queen." King James (the sixth of Scotland, the first of Great Britain) was the son of Mary, Queen of Scots. Though he married a Danish princess, he preferred his "favourites," a bevy of beautiful English boys. A typical Gemini jack-of-all-trades (and a bit of an intellectual snob), James wrote poetry and essays, deftly kept England out of foreign wars, and redecorated quite a few palaces.

Gemini Heroes: Whitman and Company

Clever Gemini traditionally "rules" writers. So it makes sense more gay authors have been Twins than any other sign. Walt Whitman tops the list as the granddaddy of modern gay literature. Then there's German novelist Thomas Mann, Spanish playwright Federico Garcia Lorca, Harlem Renaissance poet Countee Cullen, Broadway song-writer Cole Porter, Beat poet Allen Ginsberg, playwright Harvey Fierstein—the list goes on. Geminis simply have to express themselves!

Gemini Hero: Boy George

Kids ridiculed him as a "poof," the "pink sheep of the family," he recalls in his autobiography *Take It Like a Man.* But rather than run from the trauma, he ran to it, and little George O'Dowd became superstar Boy George, the flamboyant lead singer of Culture Club. Did he invent himself or did he find himself? It's hard to say with a Gemini. But it's clear this Twin could skillfully adapt to changing circumstances and opportunities by being anything he wanted to be.

Gemini Hero: Rupert Everett

Gemini dishes all the dirt. Beating the tabloids to a scandal, for example, Rupert Everett blabbered to the press in 1997 that he'd worked as a "rent boy" (a gigolo) in London. It didn't hurt his skyrocketing acting career; in fact, it fueled the public's fascination. Rupert is a Gemini multitasker whose career has taken many twists and turns, from boy toy to pop musician to novelist of the wickedly funny *Hello Darling, Are You Working?* Full of the Twin's mischief, he once sent clippings of his pubic hair to a critic. Tsk, tsk, Rupert—you should have sent them to your *fans.*

Gay Cancer

June 21–July 22

The Vicious Stereotype: Sign of Mommie Dearest

Oy, the guilt trips you send us on! Mama mia, the comfort foods you stuff us with! Oh *Mother*, you just don't understand! Like any *yente* worth her chicken soup, you meddle. As clingy as Velcro, beset by abandonment issues, you and your toothbrush move in after the first date. Your therapist doesn't need an alarm clock—he's got you to wake him up in the morning with your persistent distress calls. Your moods turn faster and more nauseatingly than the Teacups at Disneyland.

Costume:

- any frumpy haus-frau frock
- apron
- orthopedic shoes

Props:

- thermometer (old-fashioned variety that goes you-know-where)
- large box of tissues
- a wire hanger, of course!

Opening line: "Don't leave me! What will become of me?"

The Real You

If you only hear the stereotypes, Cancer sounds like nothing but a moody mommy brandishing a rolling pin in one hand and a wire hanger in the other, easily crunched by life in the fast lane. But aren't Crabs the least bit fabulous? Oh yes, you can definitely do fabulous! Consider Julius Caesar, for example. This Cancer emperor married Calpurnia, romanced Cleopatra, and kept boys on the side—all while conquering half the world. Not bad for a toga-wearing bisexual, eh?

So let's peer beyond the hackneyed image to spy the real you—because there's a lot going on in there! Cancer leads a lavish life of the imagination. When life's a dull drag, elaborate daydreams transport you to a better-decorated *milieu.* It's hardly frivolous. The acclaimed Cancer *artiste* Jean Cocteau, for instance, turned his dreams and fantasies into experimental films, regarding cinema as "a descent into oneself, a way of using the mechanism of the dream without sleeping."

You may wander around Greenwich Village looking lost and disoriented, but you tread the landscape of the heart and soul like a country lane whose every tree you've passed a million times. Hyperaware of your environment, you pick up on the subtle nuances. The intricate terrain of a man's wavy hair, for example, can engross you long after he's walked out of view.

A Cancer cliché says you're obsessed with the past. So what if you are? It doesn't hurt to understand how the past folds into the present, which then becomes the past of the future (go figure that one out!). Internally, where you often reside, time is not linear. The people you loved yesterday have not disappeared, only entered the movie that plays forever in your memory.

It's a shame if you cling morosely to regrets and disappointments from bygone days, like a bitter Miss Havisham rotting in her yellowed wedding gown. But it's a wise Cancer who can grasp an understanding and respect for his history, learning from it without repeating it.

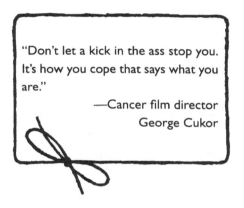

> "Don't let a kick in the ass stop you. It's how you cope that says what you are."
>
> —Cancer film director
> George Cukor

Even if we sidestep all that Mommie Dearest bubkus, Cancer still harbors a strong sense of family and a longing for community. Cancer author and activist Larry Kramer, for example, helped found the Gay Men's Health Crisis, a project that created an extended family of people living with HIV/AIDS. Cancers care deeply—so deeply that others rarely see to your depths.

Yet you see into theirs. More than any promiscuous foot fetishist, you put yourself in other people's shoes. You can empathize. You can offer understanding. "I'm a Cancer so I'm very intuitive," sums up Elvis, the *Playgirl* November 1998 Discovery Man.

No offense to all the fine gay therapists of every sign, but I'll stick with my Cancer shrink. He seems to know what's wrong before I utter a word. He gently touches my psychic boo-boos and nurtures them back to wellness.

The more it's needed, the more the Cancer spirit blossoms. Fiercely protective, you Cancers look out for your friends. "When they need me, I'm there," asserts Ethan, one of my Cancer clients. "Being strong for my friends is one of the things I like most about myself." Of course, not everyone gets to enter your orbit. You're selective. Like a loyal Labrador, you guard your home and privacy from suspicious strangers until they doggedly prove they bear treats instead of threats.

Maybe you're not hysterical, but there's no disputing the fact you Crabs are sensitive and emotional creatures who feel deeply and react extravagantly, spicing up the dull recitative of life with a splendid Cancerian aria.

The Secret in Cancer's Closet

Your adoring fans see a pillar of the community. The public notices your creativity and sympathy. Your critics witness a feisty and formidable opponent. Still, they'd all like to peek in your closet, but you keep it locked up tight. Why? Too many skeletons? Too scary? Or just too cluttered?

You Cancers tend to let worries, doubts, and fears pile

up, rarely expressing them. Repeatedly you assure yourself and others it'll be all right, it's not the end of the world. But do you really believe this? Perhaps not.

Sensitive to how fragile life is, how riddled with bad things and mean people, you may brood, hide, and generally avoid getting involved. People nowadays, for instance, come and go so quickly—so why get close to anyone? Thus, you may stick to the familiar and secure, sticking to Friday nights with your bowling team instead of venturing alone into that hot new dance club.

Deep down you long for the freedom and lightheartedness that come from being carefree. Forget security—you'd like some superficiality! To laugh off tough times, flutter away from ugliness, never give a second thought to someone else's problems. It's an impulse worth pursuing. Of course, if that's not who you are, don't pretend—but Dr. Matt gives you permission to occasionally take a vacation from caring so much.

> "Whatever the public blames you for, cultivate it: It is yourself."
>
> —Cancer author Jean Cocteau

Gay Cancer Growing Up

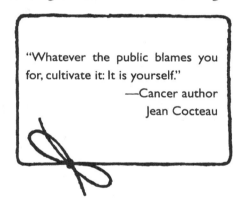

Cancers carry a lot of emotional baggage from childhood. At least that's what the old-fashioned astrologers say. I say fiddlesticks. We've all got baggage—and besides, it's not how much you have but how you pack it that counts.

Hungry for closeness, most gay Cancer kids stick close to a special friend—real or imaginary. If you didn't fit with the in crowd, you had no trouble uniting with the nerds, the drama kids, or other misunderstood "weirdos." Perhaps, though, because you feared loneliness and hadn't yet learned to trust your inner resources, you tried too hard to be liked.

> "I want to play a real frontier woman, not one of those crinoline-covered things you see in most westerns. I'm with the boys—I want to go where the boys go."
>
> —Cancer film star Barbara Stanwyck

Quite early on, unfortunately, insecurity festers in gay Cancer kids. Oh sure, you undoubtedly learned to adopt a confident face, but with this sun sign there too often comes an inner voice that murmurs (and in some cases shouts), "Something's wrong with me."

Then you grew up. You realized you're OK. You tossed the tough, self-protective shell of youth onto the heap of last year's fashions. And the child within got to relax, let loose, and expose his vulnerability without fear of getting squished.

Cancer in Love

Gay Cancer loves with all his heart, with an emotional intensity seldom seen in the males of our species. When, for example, the Cancer king Alexander the Great experienced the death of his long-time friend and lover, he fasted for three days, hanged the doctors, proclaimed a worldwide mourning period, and erected a funeral pyre five stories high. How's that for a broken heart?

Sappy sentimentalists, Cancer poofs are some of the few grownups who still write love letters, bless your heart. Contrary to many poets of his time, Cancer poet Hart Crane wrote with hopefulness and faith rather than cynicism; emotional intensity as opposed to intellectual detachment. The moment Cupid's arrow strikes, you gush. You emote. You start choosing china patterns before the second date. In fact, you Crabs may have a hard time reconciling the romantic with the practical elements of a long-term relationship.

As much as you want loving companionship, it can freak you out. Even when you meet the right guy, you get the urge to run away, wary of taking the next step. The Cancer novelist Nathaniel Hawthorne, for example, hesitated and resisted the love of the young Herman Melville—so the *Moby-Dick* author looked elsewhere. Try sticking it out a little longer. Not all frogs turn into princes on the first kiss. Keep kissing.

Mr. Right—Or Is It Mr. Right Now?

The strong silent type will do quite nicely, thank you very much. He can communicate his adoration without ever opening his mouth—at least to speak. You especially appreciate a lover who remembers what you like—and what you don't.

More important, Mr. Right provides a cozy harbor from uncertainty and disappointment. He pampers you, he babies you, he may even coo to you; that does not mean, however, he treats you like a child. He takes you seriously. He values your contributions to the relationship. And he deals with your complexity—the way you can be strong yet scared, both conflicted and so sure of yourself.

Mr. Right's been around the block more than a few times. He exhibits some modicum of maturity. So he's not too threatened by your success, and he can permit you to express yourself—erotically, emotionally, bitchily. He cares more about you than about other people's opinion of you.

Whoever Mr. Right turns out to be, he's got to pump you full of that warm fuzzy feeling. The ideal of the happy family runs deep in Cancers of all orientations—so you'd like to find a husband who fits nicely into your mental picture of you two and the dog curled up by the fireplace.

Cancer in the Sack

"My boyfriend and I don't have sex," a Cancer man told me. "We make love." Does he speak for all Crabs? Beats me, but I've certainly never met a Cancer who didn't prefer good company to good kink. Whether it's a quickie or a longie, you want intimacy.

You're a snuggler and a cuddler. While some lonely guys

settle for rubber blow-up dolls resembling the latest porn star, you ignore any boy who's likely to pop, deflate, and fly away.

None of this, however, makes you a Pollyanna in the bedroom. Steamy sexuality hisses and whistles down there somewhere. But it won't come out to play till it feels safe and secure. Whatever scene you get into, it helps if your partner(s) can push your limits without pushing you somewhere you'd rather not go. It also helps if you can express your erotic urges without worrying what your mother would think—she doesn't have to know!

Sagittarius may explore the world, Virgo may explore riddles and dilemmas, but Cancer explores his lovers. For you, passion is the greatest journey. You learn a man's secret places. You discover his physical cycles and emotional rhythms. You gently master his body like a kite in the wind—and he's happy to keep blowing.

One pointer from Dr. Matt: In matters of sex and romance you can be gullible and susceptible to seductive strangers who say all the right things and stroke all the right places but actually have all the wrong motives. Follow your mind as well as your bliss!

Cancer's Fame and Fortune

Career

You might be domestic, but you're hardly a stay-at-home Mommie Dearest. No matter how much you love to come home at night and get snug as a bug in a rug, in the morning you want to go out—and up. Cancer is the most quietly ambitious of signs. The public rarely sees how high you set your goals. But there's no question in your mind that you expect to be well compensated for your work.

You Cancer boys often get along with the toughest personalities. The best and most famous example is George Cukor, the Cancer director of classic films like *The Women* and *A Star Is Born*, who had an amazing knack for getting along with and bringing out the best of high-maintenance divas like Crawford, Garbo, and Garland.

When you find the right project, you can become totally absorbed in your work to the exclusion of everyone and everything else—rather like Cancer novelist Marcel Proust, who climbed into bed for nearly a decade to write the longest homoerotic novel of the 20th century, *Remembrance of Things Past*. You, too, can lose track of time in a big way.

In any professional setting, Cancer often becomes the Mama Bear or Papa Bear of the office, extremely nurturing souls. Cancers don't, though, tend to explore all their options. Your friends probably tell you to get out more, try more things. Your asset of carefulness can turn into the liability of hesitation.

One little warning: Many Cancers have trouble drawing boundaries between personal and professional life, business and pleasure, so tread with caution in those gray areas.

Money Matters

Remember Imelda Marcos, former First Lady of the Philippines, whose closets stockpiled thousands of pairs of designer shoes? You guessed it—a Cancer! And remember Leona Helmsley, the real-estate tycoon who gobbled up Manhattan hotels and dubbed herself "The Queen"? That's right—another Cancer!

> "I have always considered it despicable to grovel for your life as if life were a favor."
>
> —Cancer Cuban author Reinaldo Arenas

Not every Cancer greedily hoards, but it's not uncommon for you to have insecurity about security. No matter how many high heels or hotels you sock away, the little sign in your brain that's supposed to say "I have enough, I can make it" never seems to light up.

Maybe you'd worry less about money if you depended on it less. Will you really feel better if you splurge on that 18th-century chaise longue on which Marie Antoinette may once have sat? For a while, possibly, but then the guilt sets in.

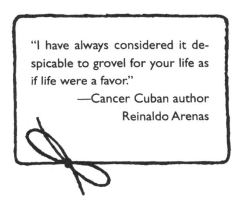

Crabs can be quite financially savvy, so Dr. Matt recommends breaking the vicious cycle of saving and spending, hoarding and splurging. Make a financial strategy. Stick to it. Forget the rest.

As for investments, you normally steer clear of big gambles, but just a little bit of "risky business" (as Tom Cruise discovered dancing in his underwear) can be a turn-on. Oh baby!

Cancer in the Spotlight

Cancer Diva: Princess Diana

This real-life fairy-tale princess broke the mold of the British establishment to express many of Cancer's most venerable traits. Compassionate, Diana helped destigmatize the "gay plague" by personally visiting AIDS patients in the hospital. Kind and caring, she used her royal privilege to benefit charities, like her controversial campaign against deadly land mines. And by speaking publicly about her eating disorder, she exposed her vulnerability—always a great act of courage for Cancer.

Cancer Diva: Barbara Stanwyck

According to Hollywood historians, actress Barbara Stanwyck wasn't only a diva of gay culture, but a hero, too—a real-life lesbian who also played one in the movies (*Walk on* *the Wild Side*) and probably had flings with Joan Crawford and Marlene Dietrich.* Like many Cancers, Stanwyck fiercely guarded her privacy and vulnerability. "She talks a tough game," said a family insider, "but . . . she isn't so cocksure like she always pretends. But it was a very hard shell she built." On TV she played the stereotypical Cancer-type of matriarch in *The Big Valley*.

Cancer Hero: David Hockney

"The longer you look at Hockney," said an art critic, "the simpler and kinder his work appears."† Coming out in the late 1950s, Hockney used art to record and forever cherish the men and places he loved. Best known are his paintings of nude swimmers in Los Angeles swimming pools. But with a Cancer's emotional response to the world, he also painted what he called "internal landscapes," tenderly capturing moods and longings.

Cancer Hero: Alexander the Great

If you think Cancer is all sweetness, light, and menopausal mood swings, think again. Three hundred years before Julius Caesar, this king of Macedonia conquered Persia, Egypt, and parts of India. But he wasn't just a tough guy. He studied ethics with Aristotle. He never left home without a book of poetry. He spread Hellenistic culture (think

*See *Hollywood Lesbians*, by Boze Hadleigh (New York: Barricade Books, 1994).

†Michael Joseph Gross, "The Art of Friendship: Eight Paintings by David Hockney are at the Museum of Fine Arts," *The Boston Phoenix*, June 1998

pretty naked statues). He refused to dismiss minority groups as "barbarians." He may even have talked to animals and plants. All of this goes to show that, for the Crab, what's happening inside, in the heart and soul, matters as much as all the victories and defeats happening outside.

Cancer Heroic Event: Stonewall

In my previous astrology book, *Work Your Stars!*, I pointed out the significance of the American, French, and Russian Revolutions starting under the sign of Cancer. To that list, let's add the Stonewall Inn riots in New York City, almost universally viewed as the historic commencement (our Declaration of Independence, if you will) of the gay rights movement. Stonewall's "birthday" was June 27, 1969. Astrologically, this makes sense. Though Aquarius is the traditional sign of revolution, Cancer is the sign of people banding together—in these cases, small militant minorities forming a family. To the outside world (especially the New York Police Department), Stonewall was a revolution. But within the gay community, Stonewall was more of a birth, the founding of our family. Such is Cancer's essence.

Cancer Heroes: Kramer and Kushner

Larry Kramer and Tony Kushner—what do they have in common besides being gay Jewish authors? They're both Crabs, of course! It makes sense. Though radically different in their approaches, both have attempted, through the medium of theater, to give shape and definition to the gay experience and identity. Kramer's *The Normal Heart* and Kushner's *Angels in America* both address the political and personal ramifications of AIDS on our society. By giving us leading gay characters who fight the "system," confront internalized homophobia, and reconcile spirituality with gay sexuality, these playwrights managed to hold up a mirror to our place in America.

Gay Leo

July 23–August 22

The Vicious Stereotype: Sign of the Prima Donna

Enter Leo. Having squeezed your size-eight figure into a size-four suit, you enter fashionably late—or is it just that you're running on LST, Leo Standard Time? Despite your dark sunglasses, it's quite clear you're madly craving attention, just dying for someone to ask for your phone number or—better yet—your autograph. To you, all the world's a stage, and all the men and women merely extras in a feature film *all about you.* You're more high-maintenance than a British sports car—and just as likely to roar, overheat, and have a breakdown.

Costume:

- gold lamé jumpsuit
- rhinestone jewelry (the gaudier the better)
- silk scarf

Props:

- above-mentioned silk scarf
- scepter
- door for storming out of

Opening line: "Don't you know who I am? I had my name in lights before you saw the light of day!"

The Real You

Yes, occasionally you live up to your reputation as an *LAP*—"a Leo American Princess." But there's so much more to you besides. Like your generosity. Deep down—under that heavily applied foundation of self-involvement—you long to give of yourself completely and utterly. You've got a heart the size of Jeff Stryker's . . . well, let's not go there.

Let's just say you're gay and gregarious, affectionate and affable. With friends and loved ones you may hog the conversation, but you never fail to offer warmth or to pawn your last rhinestone cuff links. Even with your enemies you're no ice queen—maybe a raging queen, but never a cold fish. Though you're a shameless self-promoter, you're more than a fair-weather friend, with a strong, inner toughness.

Sure, you demand a lot from the world. But then you demand a lot from yourself, too. In the face of adversity, you stand tall. You stick up for friends. You lick your losses and move on, probably the zodiac's most poised of risk-takers and roller-coaster riders. One minute *la vie est belle;* the next minute life's a bitch. Through it all, there's Leo, proud and confident, a bottle of bubbly always chilling in the fridge.

There's no denying that you occasionally pose or vogue or let your wrist fly freely, but you're hardly a frivolous glamour puss. Think of Auntie Mame, played in the movie musical *Mame* by fellow Leo Lucille Ball. Though Mame may have been a wild old broad, she embraced her duty as her nephew's guardian. When the Depression stole her fortune, she did what any self-respecting Leo would do: She got a job. When that flopped, she found a rich husband. With Leo, the show must go on.

Contrary to popular presumption, some Leos *are* shy. Quiet and demure, they linger on the sidelines like a fat cat who couldn't be bothered, the feline reincarnation of an omnipotent Egyptian pharaoh, planning their next *début*.

You Leos constantly reinvent yourselves. Life sucks? Invent a new one. The part's too small? Make it bigger! The leading man gets on your nerves? Trade him in for a newer model! This is a valuable skill, but make sure you know who you are at your core. Once you do, you can wear many costumes and travel through the world with genuine confidence.

Leo wants to understand his *unique* place in the universe. "What role do I play?" you may wonder, because whatever it is, you want to play it superbly. So don't bother with social climbing; just be a social animal. As for jealousy about other people's careers or fabulous lives, stop comparing yourself to anyone and everyone. Because face it, there's no one like you—and if there were, you wouldn't like it—"This personality's not big enough for the two of us."

Gay Leo is a "can-do" kind of guy. You may flirt with life's big questions—like the meaning of life or why orangutans are better endowed than your last boyfriend—but you don't sink into intellectual quagmire like the geekier, navel-gazing signs of Saj, Aquarius, or even Pisces. The present moment is Leo's domain. *Carpe diem!*

> "I go for two kinds of men. The kind with muscles, and the kind without."
>
> —Leo diva Mae West

The Secret in Leo's Closet

Bold and brash, you Leos seldom show your tender, vulnerable side. But it's there. Criticism and mean comments wound you deeply. Getting stood up seems like ample cause to slit your wrists—or someone else's. And while you may pretend to thrive on martinis and caviar, strokes and affection really nourish the Leo soul. Nevertheless, Madonna seems to speak for many Leos when she sings, "I don't need anyone."

Perhaps you've heard of the Napoléon Complex, named for the Leo French emperor with a big ego problem. If, like Napoléon, you feel self-conscious about being short or inferior in any way, you may overcompensate, putting on airs and playing the prima donna. It makes sense: If you fear you're weak, you'll work extrahard—maybe *too* hard—to prove you're strong, not letting anyone get to know the real you.

That's Leo's big secret: The cat fears he doesn't have nine lives, just one in which he'd really like love and acceptance despite his big hair, bitchy claws, and other human flaws.

Gay Leo Growing Up

It's never easy to grow up gay. But to grow up gay *and* a Leo. *Oy!* You must have suspected the hospital switched you at birth. Chances are you expended lots of energy projecting an image that concealed the real you.

Pretty precocious, you gay Leo kids acted sophisticated beyond your years and befriended older kids or even adults who seemed terribly glamorous and worldly, wondering why grown-ups have all the fun.

Most gay Leo kids look for a ticket out of their innocent but confining childhood by developing a talent or skill. Once you find it and carve out a comfortable and competent adult identity, you then grow younger as you grow older. Sophistication turns into silliness. It's good for you.

Every Leo has a loud and obnoxious inner child clamoring to get out. After all, it got cheated the first time around! The trick is to nurture and express your inner child without *becoming* a child. Because big boys *do* have more fun.

Leo in Love

With your flair for the dramatic, how else could you love but passionately, desperately, helplessly? When you fall in love, the whole world hears about it. Case in point: the Leo poet Alfred Lord Tennyson. When his "special friend" died at a tender age, Tennyson immortalized his undying love by writing one of his greatest works, *In Memoriam*—a poem that scandalized all of England. Read it some stormy night when you're feeling romantic and melancholy.

Along with Libra, you take the prize as the zodiac's biggest romantic sucker. When you're in love, the advice of friends—which you normally take pretty seriously—falls on deaf ears, especially if friends' opinions don't align with an idealized picture of your boyfriend *du jour*.

Leo basks in the attention of lots of gentlemen callers calling and suitors a-courting. So if you get involved with one main squeeze, you'll have to decide whether you can stop relying on the kindness of strangers.

Mr. Right—Or Is It Mr. Right Now?

Whatever your hormones may scream at the sight of a Speedo-clad hunk on the beach, good looks won't hold your interest for long. You're equally attracted by success and good conversation. You're even more attracted by a man who treats you like a queen.

For no occasion at all, he better send mushy Valentines—like, "You are the light of my life, you are the air that I breathe, your smile is the sunrise that starts my mornings." You won't believe a word of it, but the gesture still scores points. Mr. Right understands that Leo requires courtship. Yes, some of you do kiss on the first date, but you'd rather not sacrifice your romantic requirements. If he intends to keep you charmed, Prince Charming's work is never done.

Once the relationship's begun, your high expectations continue. Mr. Right is neither a slouch nor a vapid pretty boy. You're not embarrassed to take him home to Mama or the company Christmas party. He gives you bubble baths when you feel tired and plenty of space when you feel like Greta Garbo.

> "It's impossible to get anything major accomplished without stepping on a few toes; enemies are inevitable when one is a *doer*."
>
> —Leo actress Norma Shearer

Leo in the Sack

Yes! You like sex. You do it. Preferably lots of it. Who wants to be a kid in a candy shop when you can be a rake in a bedroom? More than just about any other activity, sex brings out your fun-loving, playful side. Sometimes you're a kitten that runs and hides and scratches; other times you're a fat Tom cat that rolls over and begs to have his tummy rubbed.

You expect your lover to keep you interested and entertained—and eagerly return the favor. Leos generally, however, stop short of excessive kink. A proposition for a ménage à trois, for example, might leave you wondering, "What's in it for me?" And as for S&M or bondage, you might like the idea of silk ropes and a feather duster, but you expect to be idolized in the boudoir, not locked up and enslaved!

While Cancer, the sign right before yours, is the zodiac's interior decorator, you skip the living room and go directly to the bedroom to create an enticing love nest. One San Francisco Leo I know, for instance, custom-ordered a round bed with a purple velvet comforter. He called it his playground. Remember, you *are* a princess, and as such, you want a prince in your bed, not a pea!

Leo's Fame and Fortune

Career

Remember Mrs. Howell (affectionately known as "Lovey") from *Gilligan's Island?* In one episode she was supposed to help work on an escape plan. "*Work?*" she asked in all seriousness. "What's 'work'?" Like that campy sitcom's stranded millionairess, you tend to look like an aristocrat who's never broken a nail on a hard day's labor.

Now let Dr. Matt shatter another Leo stereotype: *Many Leos are closeted workaholics.* Despite your reputation as party hoppers and kept boys, you Big Cats admire hard work—not the drudgery of a civil parking lot attendant, but the drive and dedication of an artist who can't leave his canvas.

You thrive on a full schedule of events and appointments. You rise to challenges to prove yourself, like the thrill-seeking Leo aviatrix Amelia Earhart setting out to fly round the world. So it's a crime for any fabulous Leo to waste his creativity and energy on professional bimbo-hood. But it's a good thing to find a gig that expresses your personality, like Leo actor Sir John Gielgud, or the Leo historian Martin Duberman, who helped establish gay and lesbian history as a legitimate discipline.

> "The big thing is . . . thus keeping yourself available for excitement."
> —Leo actor Sir John Gielgud

It might take you longer than some to find your calling—and once you find it, to make a living at it. But that's no excuse to settle. What if Martha Stewart, your Leo compatriot, had settled for catering backyard barbecues?

Money Matters

Personal finances can fluster an otherwise noble Leo. Your relationship to money flip-flops between "What the hell, easy come, easy go" and "Oh my gawd, I'll never get another paycheck!" As a result, you secretly fret about finances more than your *c'est la vie* attitude suggests. Is it that you're materialistic? Greedy? Jealous? Not really. You love to earn big bucks, you love to spend it, but from a burning house you'd rescue your pet pussy before a stash of T-bills.

Very few Leos—none I've ever met, actually—live according to their means. One of my Leo clients has a huge investment portfolio but resides in a tiny studio apartment and clips coupons, romantically attached to a bohemian lifestyle. More often, however, Leos spend extravagantly on little luxuries and *accoutrements* befitting their regal image. Along the lines of fellow Leos Jackie O and James Kirkwood (author of *A Chorus Line*), you're a connoisseur of all that's glitzy, glittery, and glamorous, and simply need enough cash to stay in the game.

Just one financial tip from Dr. Matt: Whether you choose to follow your bliss or your checkbook, don't let money determine your self-image.

Leo in the Spotlight

Leo Diva: Madonna

Like most Leos, Madonna constantly reinvents herself. "I did all I could do to really stand out," says Madonna of her childhood. Now a megastar, Madonna has proven, as every Leo longs to do, that she can stand out as her own person—and Papa, don't you preach! Madonna exemplifies the Leo urge to create a larger-than-life image and a career that's lived as a grand spectacle—not too many questions asked, thank you very much.

Leo Diva: Martha Stewart

"It's a Good Thing," says Martha Stewart, who exhibits some of the most telltale Leo attributes. She's stylish, glamorous, and high-maintenance. When Leo's around, why munch on fried chicken when you can feast on *coq au vin?*

Leo Diva: Mae West

"Come up and see me sometime." Leo diva of film and stage Mae West embodied the essence of her sign, but perhaps she's best remembered for her outrageous, unembarrassed sexuality. In addition to acting, by the way, she also wrote copiously, including plays with in-your-face drag queens and gay men, whom she found "all so clever and talented." Leos appreciate talent in the arts almost as much as talent in bed.

Leo Hero: James Baldwin

The life of author and activist James Baldwin epitomized the Leo quest for identity. In the late '40s he navigated the stress of being black and gay, a native New Yorker and a transplanted Parisian. In the '60s he fought for individual freedoms. And in novels like *Giovanni's Room* and *Another Country* he mapped the terrain of human desire. "The great difficulty," he said, "is to say Yes to life."

Leo Hero: Andy Warhol

The late great artist, filmmaker, and celebrity Andy Warhol represents Leo's obsession with popularity. Creating art wasn't enough; Warhol wanted business and popular success, too, surrounding himself with VIPs from Marilyn Monroe to President Carter, forever changing the definition of art and the people who make it.

"I'd prefer to remain a mystery," Warhol once divulged. "I never give my background and, anyway, I make it all up different every time I'm asked."

> "When I loved it was always soldiers . . . a superior being . . . a man who is always ready for any adventure, or for any danger.
>
> —Leo secret agent Mata Hari

Leo Hero: Randy Shilts

How do newspaper headlines and factoids become great literature that's more compelling than fiction? Ask a Leo! Randy Shilts started out covering gay and lesbian politics and AIDS and wound up producing important docu-novels like *And the Band Played On* and *The Mayor of Castro Street*, earning a loyal following as one of the first openly gay journalists and a reputation for masterful character portrayals.

Gay Virgo

August 23–September 22

The Vicious Stereotype: Sign of the Catholic Schoolgirl

Enter Virgo. Well, you're just little Miss Thing, now aren't you? You look more proper than a tea party, more goody-goody than the Flying Nun. You're so damned innocent you still think *gay* means happy. Like neatnik Monica on *Friends*, you live to clean—and criticize those who don't. Like Natalie Wood resisting irresistible Warren Beatty in *Splendor in the Grass*, you're repressed, a Freudian case study in the flesh. You radiate more purity and wholesomeness than an Abercrombie & Fitch underwear ad, all coy and lily white. Do you need an enema, or are you always this uptight?

Costume:

- plaid suit and starched white Oxford shirt
- patent-leather saddle shoes
- then again, a little nurse's uniform might work, too. And underneath? Black lace lingerie, of course!

Props:

- aerosol can of disinfectant
- chastity belt
- ruler for rapping knuckles and taking vital measurements

Opening line: "Oh no! I couldn't do *that* . . . unless, of course, it was our little secret."

The Real You

Oh please. Aren't you sick of the Virgo stereotypes? I bet you're actually too chic to wear plaid and too social to stay home to scrub the tub. Besides, that's what staff is for. It's high time we take a good look at the real you, the Virgin minus the chastity belt.

First, of course, Virgo gives good service. You vigilantly tend to your friends' welfare. You make sure they're staying healthy, popping their vitamins, and moisturizing sufficiently. You remember their birthdays and all their pet peeves.

In fact, according to astrological folklore, Virgo "rules" all pets. Why? Because Virgo takes care of things. The puppy is barfing? You feed him the right stuff. Mom needs Internet access? You get her connected. Your boyfriend springs a zit? You pop it. Like a latter-day Noah or Dr. Doolittle, you take them all under your wing, no succor too daunting or disgusting for the ones you love—and the ones you'd like to stop from whining.

Despite all this, a Virgo's greatest potential generally lies dormant until it's summoned forth by a truly worthy challenge. Perhaps that challenge will arise in the form of coming out, building a relationship, or overhauling your dowdy roommate's wardrobe. Whatever it is, you cannot shrink from your destiny as a healer, whether or not it involves needles and thermometers.

Yep, you tend to burden your mind with the worries of the world. Do you nag? Do you fuss? Well, maybe a little, darling—but if they know what's good for 'em, most people realize you do it out of love rather than harassment. Along with Capricorn you share a strong sense of obligation. Just remember: You can't care for others if you don't care for yourself.

The Virgo of pulp fiction resembles a little talking doll: Pull her string and she spouts criticism. As one of my Virgo clients explains, "Because Virgos are so critical, when they read the stereotypes, they criticize themselves for being too damn critical!" The real Virgo nature, however, isn't so much critical as analytical.

The nitty-gritty fascinates you. Does your recently broken-up friend, for example, need a shoulder to cry on or a stiff dose of "Get on with your life, honey!"? Would the merlot or cabernet best complement the beef Wellington? You think about these things. You and Taurus are the zodiac's greatest connoisseurs.

Virgo likes solving puzzles, putting the pieces together. Thanks to the problem-solving penchant of Virgo psychiatrist Evelyn Hooker, gays and lesbians officially became healthy and normal. In the 1970s, armed with a lifetime of careful research, Dr. Hooker convinced the medical establishment that homosexuality was definitely not a disease. In her search for truth, she literally rewrote the textbooks. It's all part of Virgo's preference for clarity over ambiguity, proof over assumption, wisdom over ignorance.

> "I always wanted to be *somebody*, but I should have been more specific."
>
> —Virgo comedienne Lily Tomlin

You try to be kind, really you do. And you try to be low-maintenance, not too demanding, not too troublesome. But everyone has limits! You hit your limit when the world lets you down, when promises get broken and potentials go unrealized. See, Virgo expects the trains to run on time. A Virgin plays by the rules—or not at all.

A perfect world this is not. Thank heavens we've got Virgo to make the mess a little tidier, prettier, and more interesting!

The Secret in Virgo's Closet

Take this mess and shove it! On some level, Virgo wants to ignore life's problems and live exclusively for its pleasures. The stereotype calls you "anal-retentive," but deep down there's an "oral-retentive" child (to use Dr. Freud's term) in search of more instant gratification than all the 900 numbers could provide.

To be the life of the party. To eat the chocolate cake regardless of the calories. To step onto your fire escape and belt out "Don't Cry for Me Argentina!" for all the neighbors to hear. All of it appeals to the reckless, wanton, playboy side of the Virgin.

Yet you keep it well contained. Like Virgo author Christopher Isherwood, you are both attracted to and repulsed by the pleasure principle, the idea that life is nothing but a *Cabaret*, old chum. You fear debauchery and decadence and overcompensate with decency and discipline.

Consequently, you may fight within yourself, a little devil and angel sparring in your head, one saying, "Go for it, baby!" the other holding you back with a halo.

Dr. Matt recommends moderation in all things, including moderation, so you can stop the vicious tug-of-war of anal versus oral and happily meet somewhere around the belly button.

Gay Virgo Growing Up

Most little boys ask, "Hey, Ma, what's for dinner?" Meanwhile, quite ahead of schedule, little Virgo boys asked, "What should I be when I grow up?" Yep, you gay Virgins started making plans early.

An industrious tot, you used your toys to create spectacular and intricate make-believe worlds. But the fight for acceptance in the so-called real world took more effort. You aimed to please, you worried too much, and you did your duty. Virgo's need to feel needed strikes young.

You put a lot of pressure on yourself to be just *so*, to live up to what you thought your parents, teachers, and buddies want from you. Lots of children do that, I suppose, but when you're gay and you're a Virgo, a little pressure becomes a lot of pressure.

Rather shy, you gay Virgo kids tended to undervalue yourselves, doubting your ability to make it in a straight guys' world. You took one look at the other kids' popularity, accomplishments, and perfect little families and thought, "Gee, that's not me," and probably did a lot of overcompensating. You were too young to understand the difference between appearances and reality. Now that you're old enough to understand, maybe you can lighten up.

> "A woman isn't complete without a man. But where do you find a man—a real man—these days?"
> —Virgo film star Lauren Bacall

Virgo's private side dawns early. Like Virgo actress Greta Garbo who, in the movie *Grand Hotel*, famously insisted, "I vant to be alone," you probably spent hours in your own highly developed, highly organized fantasy land. You may, in fact, have displayed such self-reliance that parents and teachers ignored you—not because you weren't a great kid, but precisely because you *were* a great kid.

A time of navel-gazing and self-absorption, puberty treats

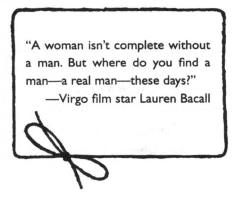

Virgo extra brutally—all that Virgin analytic energy turned inward could make you pretty self-conscious. Your sexuality, for instance, may have seemed more like a geometry problem to be solved than an exciting fact of life to be enjoyed.

Virgo in Love

On any other day, you keep your wits about you. Careful and precise, accurate and picky, you don't make a move without consulting the weather report and packing your umbrella. Not so when love comes along! Then, as skimpily clad as an *International Male* underwear model, you walk right into the eye of the storm, regardless of thunder, lightning, or volcanic eruption.

Like the *Arabian Nights'* magic carpet, love carries you away. It makes you forget your regular Tuesday-afternoon beauty parlor appointment. It causes you to stop pruning the rose bushes and start sniffing the blossoms. Love, dear Virgo, catches you with your drawers down.

Given the Virgo quest for perfection, you love the idea of having a soulmate, the Greek concept of one soul cleft in two bodies, searching for the bliss of reunification. In one of those amazing life-is-stranger-than-fiction stories, one of my former Virgo clients sought out an old boyfriend from 20 years before, convinced Mr. Right had slipped through his fingers all those years ago. They're now living happily ever after with a large family of cats.

A Virgo may learn to settle for a man who forgets to flush, but will never learn to settle for a life without love.

Mr. Right—Or Is It Mr. Right Now?

There's something wrong with Mr. Right. He's eccentric, romantic, and doesn't always pay the electric bill on time. Oh well! Everyone should dine by candlelight more often. A diamond in the rough with the soul of a poet, Mr. Right needs your help. Where others see an unemployed stagehand, you see the next Cecil B. DeMille.

It's not that you don't have high standards. You do. But for the right man, you accept love over perfection. And despite his human flaws and failings, Mr. Right does love you as is. How refreshing!

Mr. Right has a gentle touch. He cares for small animals and doesn't squash bugs. He's less practical than you, more lovey-dovey, and brings a magical, even spiritual quality into your life. Hardly a self-sufficient loner, he relies on your strengths without leaning on them like a crutch. You bring out each other's best.

A cross between a sensitive New Age guy and an old-world gentleman, Mr. Right doesn't chew gum in bed. He treats sex as sacred. He can please you without asking any favor in return. He can offer you his body like a gift, and you can spend all morning unwrapping it like a kid on Christmas morning.

Virgo in the Sack

In a new relationship, sex starts out stupendously. After that, it's all downhill. So says conventional wisdom. But Virgo disagrees. You're an ambitious lover, and you expect the sex to improve over time. You hone your technique. You develop greater confidence. You peel away more and more inhibitions, your confidence increasing with every layer.

There's something so teasingly tantalizing and titillating about Virgo sexuality. It's not overt. It hints and promises and gets us all worked up before the first zipper comes down. Think of the novel *Lady Chatterley's Lover* by Virgo author D. H. Lawrence—it makes you want to scream, "Just *do* it already!"

"I've no regrets. I've been everywhere and done everything. I've eaten caviar at Cannes, played baccarat at Biarritz. . . . What is there left but marriage?"

—Virgo actress Margaret Lockwood in *The Lady Vanishes*

In olden days, Virgo "ruled" servants. Nowadays, you still like to make a man beg for what he wants. Physically pushing yourself and your partner to new erotic frontiers gives you a rush. Virgo is not a greedy sign, but sex can evoke your gluttony.

It's crude but true: A Virgo always feels better when he's gettin' some. A happy, healthy sex life boosts your moxie more than all the protein-enhanced, wheat-grass-infused power smoothies on Muscle Beach.

Virgo's Fame and Fortune

Career

Did you ever watch the *Batman* TV series? If so, you must remember Virgo actor Adam West wearing satin briefs over blue tights—and that amazing utility belt. Full of gadgets, Batman's belt saved him in every episode from the nymphomaniacal clutches of Catwoman or the homoerotic perfidy of Riddler. That's Virgo—always prepared, ready for any situation, handy with a bobby pin when it's time to jimmy a lock or rescue big bad hair.

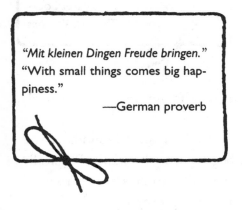

> "*Mit kleinen Dingen Freude bringen.*"
> "With small things comes big happiness."
>
> —German proverb

For you Virgins, a job worth doing is worth doing right. The most dedicated of workers, you alphabetize your life. You can't understand why others aren't so efficient.

Virgo sees solutions that most professionals overlook. The Virgo musician John Cage, for example, turned everyday objects like balloons and radiators into "instruments" that broadened the sounds available to classical music.

Diva of goodness and charity, Mother Teresa was a Virgo, too. Like her, you thrive in a career helping humanity. Even if you're not a superhero or a saint, you better make yourself feel useful and effective—or you're bound to feel dissatisfied. On the other hand, you may too often put other people's needs, including your employer's, before your own. Cut it out!

Do yourself a favor and don't get stuck in a back office in the boonies. Every gay Virgo needs a career, whether simple or grand, that keeps him on his toes—and I don't mean the ballet—though you might look cute in a tutu.

Money Matters

Virgo worries—and what better subject to worry about than money?

Whereas every Leo loves a parade, every Virgo frets over how to pay for it and clean up afterward. If the parade were entirely up to you, it might never happen, because you couldn't bring yourself to sign the check. Must the purchase of every sweater and hat cause such agony?

You make a budget like a war strategy. You crunch numbers like a human nutcracker. Only then do you splurge—and never with the intent to show off (you have better ways to do that!).

Virgos make careful investors. Whereas your Pisces friend buys a stock on a hunch, you study the company's annual plan, industry outlook, and profit projections. Since you hate messy situations, you try to stay out of financial entanglements like credit card debt and commingling funds with your significant other.

Of course you do have your weak spots for spending.

Beauty and health-care products, for example, loosen your purse strings. And you're a pushover when it comes to friends in need or wining and dining a date. For as much as you might pinch pennies, there are some things on which you can't put a price—like love, friendship, and a flawless complexion.

Virgo in the Spotlight

Virgo Diva: Blanche DuBois

Born on September 15 (" . . . that's under Virgo . . . the virgin"), the immortal tragic heroine of *A Streetcar Named Desire* magnificently embodies the hallmarks of her sign (chosen by playwright Tennessee Williams). A self-proclaimed "old-maid schoolteacher," Blanche is a stickler for gracious manners, a discriminating devotee of the arts, and a faded Southern belle who has "always depended on the kindness of strangers." Some of those strangers were paying "customers" at the seedy Flamingo Hotel and Blanche's imaginary beau, Dallas millionaire Shep Huntley. "I don't want realism. I want magic!" proclaims high-strung Blanche. Her meticulously virginal exterior masks the complex emotional desires of a woman longing for passionate romance—a longing left unfulfilled by a brief marriage to a sensitive young gay man.

Virgo Diva: Greta Garbo

Preferring slacks to skirts and "Sir" to "Ma'am," 1930s sex symbol Greta Garbo loved men on the screen but mostly women at home—another female icon of gay male culture whose own sexuality was anything but mainstream. Garbo exemplified Virgo's tendency to obsess. As a poor Stockholm shop girl, she opposed staggering odds (including her own painful shyness) to realize a theatre career. Later, as a Hollywood legend, she obsessively guarded her privacy, a recluse who refused to let the public crack her mystery.

Virgo Hero: Simon Le Vay

Virgo wants answers. Virgo seeks solutions. Virgo leaves nothing to chance and overlooks none of the details. Maybe that's why this gay Virgo scientist has dedicated himself to "proving" the biological roots of homosexuality. Simon Le Vay's books like *Queer Science* and *The Sexual Brain* painstakingly yet humorously explain how our brains make us gay. Having given up jobs at Harvard and elsewhere, he cofounded The Institute of Gay and Lesbian Education, which he describes as a sort of correction center to stop us from being "ineffectual queers." Oh yes, Virgo demands we be effectual!

Virgo Hero: Michael Feinstein

The successful performing career of the young singer/pianist who spearheaded the revival in the public's interest in classic American popular songs owes a great deal to his

Virgoan meticulousness for detail and analytical ability. Hired by the eminent lyricist Ira Gershwin to organize his enormous collection of recordings, young Michael Feinstein was able to learn at the feet of one of the masters of songwriting. In Ira's employ, Feinstein also forged personal and professional connections with a list of showbiz legends who later would be of invaluable support to him in his solo concert and recording career.

Virgo Hero: Christopher Isherwood

Best known as the creator of the "divinely decadent" Sally Bowles (in his books *Berlin Stories* and *Goodbye to Berlin*, later adapted for theatre as *I Am a Camera* and *Cabaret*), this English author struggled throughout his life to reconcile the competing aspects of his Virgo nature. As a young man in 1929, he left for Berlin to escape the social and sexual inhibitions of his homeland. Later, his spiritual quest led him to study for monkhood in the Ramakrishna order—a journey Isherwood found daunting, tied as he was to the material world by his taste for alcohol, tobacco, and sex. In 1953, he told his diary, "I've just started an affair with someone who is 18." His relationship with Don Bachardy lasted till Isherwood's death in 1986.

Gay Libra

September 23–October 22

The Vicious Stereotype: Sign of the Hopeless Romantic

Enter Libra. As suave as the *maitre d'* in a four-star restaurant, as smooth as a porn star's shaven chest, you're better at sucking up than a Hoover on overdrive. You're as genteel as a Southern belle, more of a fool for love than Madame Butterfly. You've never read Dickens but can't get enough of Danielle Steel. Someday your prince will come—but the closest you get is the pizza delivery boy. Your therapist, friends, and diary all know about your latest boyfriend—the only problem is *he* doesn't know *you* exist. C'mon, fess up: Don't you secretly long to quit your job and spend all day watching *Lifetime: Television for Women*?

Costume:

- artist's beret
- black turtleneck
- 5-karat engagement ring (you wish!)

Props:

- lots of candles—maybe even a torch
- copy of the personal ads
- old LP with Barbra Streisand singing "My Man"

Opening line: "Darling, let's make beautiful music together! Do you play the pipe organ?"

The Real You

Don't be embarrassed! In line at the supermarket, pick up a tabloid newspaper. Without a doubt, you'll find UFOs have colonized Nebraska. Elvis is alive and well—*again*—and doing a lounge act with Captain Kangaroo. And Libra is a hopeless romantic. Where do they *get* this stuff? Sure, romance figures prominently in every Libra's life, but it only scratches the surface of your sophisticated self.

The tabloids say you're shallow. I'd say you've got style. A culture vulture, you can probably sing the words to every Broadway musical and/or dance the steps to every ballroom dance. Hardly an old frump, however, you can also name all the hippest clubs in town and worm your way into the dressing room of any starlet passing through.

Still too shallow? Read on.

The most civilized of zodiac signs, Libra's got *smooth moves.* You put people at ease. Many of these folks think you're their best friend, even if you can't remember them from the tollbooth collector. Don't worry. Nobody can stay mad at you for long. You're too charming.

In England, they pronounce *Libra* like *library*. Go ahead, say it out loud: *Libe*-ruh. Doesn't it sound refined and genteel? It should—you Libras are the most elegant bunch of ladies and gentlemen.

> Thou dearest youth, who taught me first to know,
> What pleasures from a real friendship flow.
>
> —Libra poet John, Lord Hervey (1696–1743)

Don't join a monastery with vows of silence. Libra is a social animal. It's not so much that loneliness terrifies you, but companionship brings out your best. Your sullen mood suddenly turns cheery the moment you make your first witty remark at a party or in a crowded bus. As everyone laughs and the ice breaks, you know you've succeeded. You like to be liked. Without sickly sweetness, you approach relationships with an attitude of "Can't we all just get along?"

Full of compliments, you tell people what they want to hear. That's lovely—*if* talking nice helps smooth the way to better relationships. But if it's all about not rocking the boat, cut it out and get some assertiveness training. Life's too short to be milquetoast. Nobody said you have to be a wimp just because you're a pansy.

The stereotype says Libra seeks balance. Does that mean you try to stand on one foot while reciting "Leaves of Grass" and juggling four machetes and a flaming torch?

Not exactly. It has more to do with pursuing a balanced *life*.

Like garish colors and obnoxious noises in a Japanese tea garden, extreme actions and personalities upset your inner harmony. In crisis situations that send the rest of us sissies into fits of dramatic diva-hood, you appear merely stirred, not shaken, remaining calm lest your hair look bad for the TV cameras. It's all very Zen. Cleve Jones, founder of the NAMES Project's AIDS Memorial Quilt, is a Libra. Instead of wallowing in anger or bitterness when his friends died, he created a thing of beauty, a magnificent testament to their lives. True to the spirit of Libra, he fought ugliness with beauty.

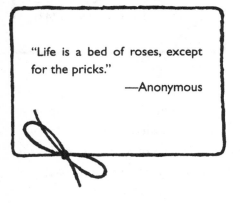

> "Life is a bed of roses, except for the pricks."
>
> —Anonymous

Libra also fights for justice. Fair play is your guiding principle. You despise the world's injustice and try to do your bit by not taking advantage of friends and associates. Libra wants to know, "How can we all win?"

Despite all of life's unfairness, your lofty ideals keep you hoping. No, you're not a fairy-tale dreamer like Pisces, but you still wish life more closely resembled a Broadway musical, with elegant sets, beautiful actors, and a finale that makes you want to sing in your seat and kiss the usher.

The Secret in Libra's Closet

You don't keep secrets. It's not polite. But you do tell little white lies. Your favorite white lie is "I'm *fine*, thanks. How are you?" A big smile and a confident handshake convince us you're telling the truth.

But are you? Behind your leading-man image, self-doubt may haunt your pretty little head. *What do these people think of me?* you worry. *What if they don't like me?* you fret.

If so, you may overcompensate by doing anything at all to please your mother, your lover, the bus driver. Or you may shy away from social intercourse altogether, afraid to meet new people, or at least afraid to meet them before you've scrubbed your face, coifed your hair, and lost 15 pounds.

You might have less stress if you didn't have to be the hostess with the mostest. You might have more fun if you let your flaws hang out and your claws come out. A model of good manners and social graces you may be, but that doesn't mean you can't occasionally exchange your Mary Poppins sweetness for Cruella DeVille's sinister selfishness.

Gay Libra Growing Up

Little boys play with fire trucks and footballs. Little boys don't dance or cook or dress up like movie stars. Little boys don't giggle and sing. And those little boys weren't you.

Quickly learning to fit in anywhere, you gay Libra kids weren't exactly misfits, but something set you apart. You were gentle and genteel. You worshipped glamour and the arts. While other boys were making trouble, you were seeking approval and affection. And even before hormones kicked in, you bonded with a few close friends more deeply than normal (whatever *normal* is).

When puberty did strike, all those lustful, lewd, animal urges naturally conflicted with your romantic notions. How could you reconcile your new "dirty" feelings with the porcelain-pure images you harbored of happy, loving couples?

For many gay Libra kids, childhood is simply too crude and boorish. Dreams filled you with visions of a more civilized or sophisticated environment than the sandbox or playground. The Libra child wants to find his people, and he will.

Libra in Love

Libra cannot live without love. Of course no one can, but some guys bury themselves in work or pleasure and forget love awhile. Not you. The ideal of true love and a good relationship never leaves your mind's eye—even when your other eye can't leave that well-sculpted swimmer at the gym.

Usually so patient and graceful, when it comes to love you rush and bounce. Have you heard the joke about the lesbians hiring a U-Haul after the first date and shacking up? If you substitute *Libra* for *lesbian*, the joke still makes perfect sense.

On the other hand, when a relationship's on the rocks,

you don't hurry to call it quits. Messy endings offend you. Strong emotions—like rage, hate, even desire—can make a Libra fella pretty nervous, upsetting your natural sense of balance and clear-headedness.

You put your lover on a pedestal. For the one you love, you'll bend over backward. Dr. Matt suggests, though, that you be careful where and for whom you bend—we wouldn't want you to break your heart, or any other vital organ.

> "Years from now, when you speak of this—and you will—be kind."
> —Libra actress Deborah Kerr, *Tea and Sympathy*

Despite your reputation as a hopeless romantic pining after Prince Charming, you've broken plenty of hearts yourself. Think of Libra actor Montgomery Clift—or better yet, see him shirtless in *From Here to Eternity.* He was the man every woman wanted to have but never could.

Mr. Right—Or Is It Mr. Right Now?

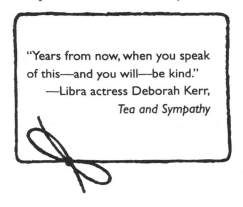

Mr. Right is a man in uniform—or at least he seems like a man in uniform. Like a marine, he's butch yet well groomed. Like an old-fashioned sheriff, he is strong but soft; he beats the bad guys and rescues Mrs. Livingston's cat from a tree. Like a Buckingham Palace guard, he's self-confident but not a big show-off. Like the mailman, he's a man of action but he'll sit and talk for hours. Is that asking too much?

Cynics, pessimists, and naysayers need not apply. Eager and enthusiastic, Mr. Right makes life faster, more interesting, less ordinary. While you play the melody, he pounds out the tempo. He wants both of you to reach your potential.

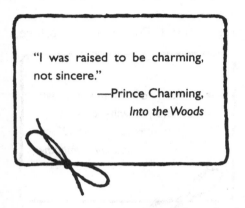

> "I was raised to be charming, not sincere."
>
> —Prince Charming, *Into the Woods*

He ain't cheap. He may not shower you with eight dozen roses every week, but he frequently selects little gifts that mean a lot. Mostly, though, he expresses his generosity with his body. He spoils you with hugs, kisses and, well, anything else his hands and mouth can offer.

Libra in the Sack

Leave it to Libra to be the world's authority on sex. That's right, the Libra scholar Michel Foucault wrote the definitive *History of Sexuality*—all three volumes—which documents how people throughout time have done "It."

You like to take your time and do it right. You're the master of foreplay, both mental and tactile. For you, making love is like making Christmas dinner: You set the right atmosphere, you serve festive appetizers, and everybody gets stuffed. Even for a quickie, your partner better value the act of love and not treat it too casually. "Sex Lite" fails to satisfy your appetite. But *schmaltz* will do the trick. Sticky, sweet, sentimental—you eat it up.

The best sex for a Libra appeals to all five senses. Your Libido-Meter registers not only how a man touches you, but how he sounds when he speaks and smells when he sweats. You dig the taste of a man's salty skin. You melt when he looks at you like a little kid watching puppies in the pet shop window.

The foolish man who doesn't go to the trouble of exploring all you have to offer doesn't know what he's missing. That's certainly how the Libra poet Virgil felt. In ancient Roman times he wrote to a young man:

> You scorn me, and thus you do not know,
> What flocks I have, what treasures to bestow.

Libra's Fame and Fortune

Career

What a schmoozer! My dishy Libra kid brother (sorry fellas, he's as straight as a cornstalk) sure can work a room. He runs an oyster bar, and every tourist who walks through the door instantly thinks he's their best friend. He makes them part of the party.

You're the ultimate people person, and that counts for a

lot in today's economy. Many, if not most, Libras gravitate toward careers in front of the public, and I think anybody who deals successfully with the public deserves an award—because God knows, not everyone can handle it with grace.

Don't underestimate your ability to network, socialize, and fraternize. Take Libra actress Julie Andrews, for instance. When she finished filming *The Sound of Music*, her costar Christopher Plummer reported, "Working with her is like being hit over the head with a Valentine's card." Persuasive and diplomatic, you can facilitate cooperation among the most high-maintenance individuals.

> "I am at heart a propagandist, a tremendous hater, a tiresome nag, completely positive that there is no human condition that could not be solved if people would simply do as I advise."
>
> —Libra novelist Gore Vidal

For Libra, the ideal job lets you strike a balance between personal goals and professional aspirations. You work hard, but lunch time and coffee breaks are sacrosanct—preferably with smart, funny colleagues.

Every Libra dreams of finding a secret door to the "inner circle." You want to know the big shots who call the shots. You need to feel like a player, not a bench warmer. When the Academy Awards—or your profession's equivalent—rolls around, you expect an invitation, and not for a seat in the back row with all the Hollywood has-beens.

Money Matters

Nobody ever accused you of monetary moderation. Your gift-buying budget alone could make a down payment on a small *château*. Constantly pining for luxury, a Libra gladly splurges on one delicious meal at Chez Gourmet, even if it means scraping by on Top Ramen the rest of the month. You place good taste above common sense. Who wants to be *common?* Not Libra!

Flaunting money and fancy jewelry is too *gauche* for Libra, yet you'll pull out the big bucks for parties, pizza, or the tab at the bar. For you, money was meant to be spent.

Or played with. You might suddenly start clipping coupons if you get the bug to invest and make deals. Though get-rich-quick schemes aren't your style, you enjoy the thrill of speculation. And when it's time to haggle, you suddenly forget your civilized manners and relish the opportunity to drive a hard bargain.

When it comes to your investments, you express a typically undisclosed stubborn streak. You're reluctant to settle for anything but a fair price, and you hesitate to enter deals that seem too good to be true. After all, you'd rather blow your wad on pleasure than pain.

Libra in the Spotlight

Libra Diva: Julie Andrews

It's hard to imagine Julie Andrews as any sign but Libra.

She's refined yet personable, sweet as a teaspoon of sugar yet willing to stand by her principles (such as refusing a Tony Award nomination because her colleagues had been "egregiously" ignored). Like many Libras—like it or not—she's had to endure her own goody-two-shoes image, hammered into the popular imagination by roles like Mary Poppins. But she's more complex. "I *would* be Mary Poppins if I pretended everything was rosy," Julie said. "And it ain't. Marriage is the hardest work." True to her sign, she focuses on relationships, often collaborating professionally with her husband, Blake Edwards.

Libra Diva: Divine

"When life is ugly, make it beautiful!" says the spirit of Libra. And so did Divine, the Libra drag queen, actor of the 1960s to '80s, and star of cult classics like *Pink Flamingos* and *Hairspray.* A lonely, overweight little boy, Divine started life as Harris Glen Milstead. His friend John Waters, the future filmmaker, called him Divine, and the name stuck. With a Libra's love of glamour, Divine made an art of emulating refined ladies who get what they want—undeterred by the fact he weighed 300 pounds and needed custom-made dresses. An equal-opportunity gender-bender, he also recorded the song "Walk Like a Man."

Libra Diva: Eleanor Roosevelt

Eleanor Roosevelt a *diva* of gay culture? Oh yes! So she was frumpy. Fabulous in other ways, she committed herself to the democratic ideals that grew into the Civil Rights movement—without which this book you're holding wouldn't be possible. And according to recent biographers, she may have been one of us,* lodging her favorite lady friend at the White House. As for her Libran qualities, take a look at her strong partnership with FDR and her sense of fairness and egalitarianism. "I will do my best to do what is right," Eleanor said. "We must make [democracy] a reality to more people."

Libra Hero: Oscar Wilde

Who could be more Libran than Oscar Wilde? He lived for beauty. He nearly died for honor and romance. He promoted "art for art's sake." And though he had his flaws, Oscar defended his beliefs—and thus set an early precedent for challenging homophobia—by arguing against gay relationships' "gross indecency" in favor of their beauty. Throughout his life and work, Oscar Wilde exercised Libra's sense of grace and style, wit and charm.

Libra Hero: Pedro Almodovar

If you've never seen an Almodovar film, you're in for a treat. Check out *Women on the Verge of a Nervous Breakdown* or *All About My Mother*. If you have seen them, you know what a brilliantly insane director Almodovar is. Like Oscar

*See Blanche Wiesen Cook, *Eleanor Roosevelt*, Vol. 2 (New York: Viking, 1999).

Wilde, he's a master of satire, turning social conventions and graces into madcap comedy. In the true spirit of Libra, his films may *seem* superficial, a little silly, nothing but a good time; they are entertaining and aim to please—and yet there's more going on. Rather slyly, his films make us question conventional morality and gender roles. What is satire, after all, but looking at the world from someone else's point of view? Very Libra indeed!

Libra Hero: Michel Foucault

The social butterfly of the zodiac, Libra is interested in how people get along. And that's what drove the work of this French philosopher and social historian. Foucault (Foo-*ko*) isn't a household name, but in academia in general and queer theory in particular, his influence is unavoidable. He taught that knowledge and power are inseparable. He developed theories of why groups on the "inside" push others to the "outside." And in *The History of Sexuality*, he explained how sexual categories change over time.

Gay Scorpio

October 23–November 21

The Vicious Stereotype: Sign of the Femme Fatale

Enter Scorpio. Whether or not you've got it, you flaunt it. All dressed in black, you show a little leg and a lot of pectoralis. You may tease, but you *never* please. Like a shadow, mystery follows you everywhere. A Siren, a maneater, a big overgrown Lolita, you pick up men like those free newspapers at the bars—and discard them just as quickly. A master of manipulation, an incorrigible opportunist, you worm your way into any crack. You wear one of those well-oiled soap-opera hairdos and enough foundation to rebuild the Taj Mahal. A Morticia Addams wannabe, you're queen of the come-on.

Costume:

- leather cat suit
- fuck-me shoes (you know the kind I mean!)
- or, instead of clothes, nothing but a bearskin rug

Props:

- poison ring
- tube of lipstick for applying seductively
- gun in your pocket (or are you just happy to see him?)

Opening line: "That's right, little boy—tell me how much you want it!"

The Real You

How it happened nobody knows. Somehow your sign got this rap as the Big Sleaze of the zodiac. If, at a party, you admit you're a Scorpio, other guests will likely take three steps back and look for the nearest emergency exit. Except the leather boys—they throw themselves at your feet. After all, don't you keep a dungeon in the basement to imprison ex-boyfriends and torture troublesome coworkers?

Well, I've got news for you. Dr. Matt's investigated the situation and discovered the truth: You're not as fiendish as all that. Sorry. I know you've enjoyed spooking us, but when push comes to shove, you'd rather roll over and have your tummy rubbed. Behind the plastic fangs flows the milk of human kindness.

You inspire self-confidence in timid friends and animate shrinking violets to reach their highest potential. Often you underestimate your effect on others—do you realize how much they appreciate you, need you, wither without you? Shallow relationships aren't your style. True friends must earn your trust slowly—for when you give it, you give it without reservation, and for a lifetime.

Maybe your intimidating image stems from the immense passion and intensity you bring to life. Scorpios pulse with strong emotions. Toward a single objective all your emotions and ecstasy can focus. This might make you a ruthless foe in business; then again, it can render you a dedicated friend and lover.

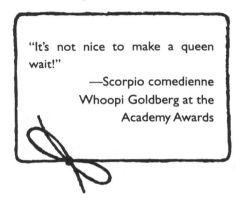

> "It's not nice to make a queen wait!"
>
> —Scorpio comedienne Whoopi Goldberg at the Academy Awards

Whatever you do, you do it to the max. You know what you like. Even more, you know what you don't. You form opinions about everyone and every thing. Unlike blunt Sagittarius and dogmatic Aquarius, however, a Scorpio can keep his opinions under wraps—till the time is ripe to use them.

Weakness offends you. Long ago I asked a Scorpio classmate how he handles a really bad day. "I wait until the next day," he replied, as if he considered a bad day too feeble an obstacle to concern him. Determined and forceful, you exercise immense tenacity and willpower. Not easily derailed, Scorpios can withstand the late nights and pedal-to-the-metal lifestyle of gay culture.

Invincible—that's how you like to think of yourself. I once lived with two Scorpios. One worked all day, partied all night, and played rugged sports all weekend. The other fought for the welfare of inner-city kids with HIV. Clearly, Scorpios do not choose the path of least resistance. Your candle burns at both ends. "Where there's a will there's a way," says a little voice inside.

Scorpios watch and observe and don't miss a beat. You closely scrutinize people. You unravel their knotted-up secrets—a trait that strangers despise but friends admire, since you help them get to the bottom of things. Maybe that accounts for why you seem so mysterious—because, like an olive in a martini glass, you immerse yourself in life's mysteries.

> "I like to keep the journalist puzzled, the charm is in the guessing."
>
> —Scorpio actor Rock Hudson

What makes people tick? Why do governments spend more on wars than schools? How does one have sex on the Concorde without getting caught? Such puzzles become your obsessions.

As for your sense of humor, you keep it under a tight lid—but it's there. It flies out when people expect it least but probably when they need it most. Much of yourself stays in reserve, like fine wine stored in the cellar, brought out only for special occasions. The Scorpio actress Goldie Hawn, for example, usually appears as a classic ditzy blonde when in reality she's a smart producer whose Hollywood career survived, against all odds, her "innocent" youth and beyond. Scorpios are masters of deception. That's cool. It'd be nice, though, if you didn't practice self-deception.

Face it: You may enjoy being a fly on the wall, but you're no wallflower. A water sign, Scorpio is like still waters that run deep. The Scorpio poet and adventurer Sir Walter Raleigh expressed it more eloquently:

> Passions are likened best to floods and streams:
> The shallow murmur, but the deep are dumb.

The Secret in Scorpio's Closet

You don't make life easy on yourself. You rely on self-reliance. Like the lady in the deodorant commercials, you never let them see you sweat. Wouldn't it be refreshing, though, to slouch and slump like an ordinary guy?

Scorpio longs to open up and share completely with another—to have no secrets. A part of you dreams of being whisked off your feet—not by a handsome stranger, but by an adoring husband. Familiar, devoted, unexciting. You want to ask for a little help from your friends, to trust they stick by your side out of love rather than ulterior motives. To fall and have someone catch you—that's the secret Scorpio desire, even if you do resolutely refute Hollywood endings where everybody saunters happily into the sunset.

Scorpios stay in control. If you didn't, perhaps, your emotions and desires would overwhelm you. Or the world would sniff your weakness and turn the tables, trying to control *you.* Nevertheless, like the insightful Jedi knight Obi Wan Kenobi in *Star Wars*, wise Scorpios know they can frequently gain power by letting go of control. May the Force be with you!

Gay Scorpio Growing Up

I asked a gay Scorpio client to tell me five words to describe him as a child. "I. Generally. Dislike. Remembering. Childhood," he quipped. "That's five words." Oh, you Scorpios are *sooo* sneaky and sly!

Easily wounded, gay Scorpio kids look for ways *not* to feel powerless. Introspective, you had a hunch other people like you existed, but you'd have to bide your time till you could find them.

Gay Scorpio kids typically run away—not to join the circus but to lead a life of the mind. Up in your brain you hid out like Anne Frank. You wanted to believe the world could be a better place. No doubt you admired prominent figures who fought for their beliefs.

But in every Scorpio's development, disillusionment figures prominently. In your eyes, gods, heroes, and ideals fell from grace when their flaws shone through their halos.

With luck and soul-searching, you became a realist, not a cynic. You learned to see people not in black and white but in many shades of the rainbow.

Scorpio in Love

When you fall in love, it hurts. It aches. It burns. But, as the Altoids mints ads remind us, there's "Pleasure in Pain."

Usually, of course, you don't let yourself go there. Skeptical, you doubt love will find you; when it does, you doubt it will last.

A self-possessed master of your own destiny, you may sip from Cupid's cup—"But just a sip," you say. Well honey, that's what they *all* say. Before you know it, you can't get enough of the stuff.

> "If you use your imagination you can look at any actress and see her nude. I hope to make you use your imagination."
>
> —Scorpio actress Hedy Lamarr

Pheromones override your rational mind. A primal mating call bellows more loudly than an elephant seal in heat. Love's power intoxicates every cell. From there, it's a long, amazing descent into the mysteries of your soul and your partner. By discovering him, you discover yourself; you discover the universe. What a trip!

Then, as dusk turns to dawn, the effect wears off. The challenge now is to retain the passion, the desire—all those ancient stirrings—in the context of a day-in, day-out relationship. Drat!

The issue of fidelity, for example, frequently crops up in Scorpio relationships. Either you obsess over your partner's extramarital goings-on, or you obsess over how to get some of your own.

And why not—who wouldn't want to get that mind-blowing feeling back again?

Before you join a 12-step program, Dr. Matt recommends you communicate openly with your partner about meeting each other's needs—not only what you'll *do* in bed, but who gets stuck *making* the bed every morning.

Mr. Right—Or Is It Mr. Right Now?

Prone to distinguishing fantasy from reality, you probably lump potential dates and prospective mates into two different categories. As for dates, you zero in on dreamy, almost mystical men who wouldn't win a beauty contest but nevertheless secrete an erotic *je ne sais quoi.* With palpable desire, they need you fiercely, maybe compulsively. They're complicated, full of trouble, and irresistible. In seeking a mate, however, you maintain more practical standards.

Mr. Right seems to you as clean and refreshing as a spring morning after a rainy night. He's not desperate. He doesn't play games. It's all so remarkably easy and simple! Suspicious old Scorpio, you didn't know it could be like that, did you?

Mr. Right deserves your trust. How? He doesn't try to manipulate you. Instead, he's a beacon of calm, a welcome island of moderation in your sea of intense emotions. Ideally, you lead him to your inner sanctum and share your mysteries. He tries to understand you—to sympathize, to feel your pain—without psychoanalyzing or diagnosing your "condition" (big mistake there!). He's patient getting to know you. All of you.

Scorpio in the Sack

Blond and blue-eyed, as seemingly innocent as a white picket fence, a Scorpio young man let me examine his horoscope and ask questions. "What's your biggest turn-on?" I asked. "Kissing someone while I am zapping them with electricity," he said. *Well!* What could I say but "Turn up the voltage"?

Your lover gets more than he bargained for. Even without electricity, you push the sexual envelope. Perhaps you'd agree with Dr. Kinsey, the famous sexologist, that "the only unnatural sex act is that which you cannot perform."

> "Aren't you ever going to stop deluding yourself? . . . Behaving like some ludicrous little underaged femme fatale—you're about as fatale as an after-dinner mint."
>
> —Brian to Sally in *Cabaret* (1972 film version)

Scorpio's desire is legendary. You seek a *total* experience—not just physical pleasure but intellectual intrigue and spiritual rapture as well. Only in bed do you express many of the feelings you otherwise keep silent. As if dancing or speaking sign language, you communicate with your body. Sex can be your way of "conversing" with people, of plumbing their depths in the most intimate, as well as the biblical, sense.

Scorpio's Fame and Fortune

Career

In the shower before you go to work, do you catch yourself singing "Respect" like Aretha Franklin? *R-E-S-P-E-C-T!* If you want one thing from a career, it's a little respect. Maybe not so little.

You don't have to be top dog, but you *won't* be taken for granted. The best job for you is one where the boss keeps you informed. Coworkers ask for your input. Everybody values your unique expertise. The assembly line, my friend, is not for you, since you thrive in a position where you're irreplaceable.

The Scorpio clichés paint you as a power-hungry Machiavellian, an Alexis Carrington wannabe. That's unfair. But we shouldn't overlook your need to exert *influence.*

You relish the opportunity to persuade, convince, and change people's minds. The Scorpio composer Aaron Copland, for instance, changed forever America's perception of jazz, folk, and classical music, blurring distinctions between traditional styles. Likewise, Scorpio entertainer Whoopi Goldberg has "shifted the paradigm" on TV and in movies, making mainstream audiences receptive to a bawdy black woman comedian and her wacky and witty gay colleagues, such as comedy writer Bruce Vilanch. How'd she do that?

Whoopi ought to remind all Scorpios to have more fun at work. Lay down your paranoia. Enjoy the camaraderie as well as the competition. Laughter, even in the midst of a high-power deal, is not a character flaw.

Money Matters

As they sing in *Cabaret*, "Money makes the world go around." Now that's a tune you could hum all day!

You don't need money to impress anybody—you can accomplish that perfectly well on a shoestring. You don't need money to feel inwardly secure—you derive security from other sources. Yet you're awfully fond of money's ability to open doors and buy power—to make the world go around.

For you, money is a means to an end. A fat wallet is your passport to go anywhere, do anything—unless what you do is illegal, in which case you simply need *more* money.

Without money, you'd survive. A Scorpio always does. But yes, Virginia, money *can* make you happy. Maybe not happy in the spiritual sense, but when you're feeling down, you can take fleeting solace in baubles and trifles. After all, if one must be miserable, one can still be well dressed, can't one?

Most Scorpios could easily become wealthier than they are. Though you occasionally go through hot flashes of financial paranoia, you typically occupy yourself with juicier subjects. A juicy, profitable investment—now there's a Scorpio ticket to Easy Street. Too bad Easy Street bores you more than *Sesame Street*.

Scorpio in the Spotlight

Scorpio Diva: k.d. lang

"Those who want to put a finger on exactly who this artist

really is will . . . find her elusively out of reach," says one of k.d.'s biographers. "However one may try to pin her down, she finds new ways to confound expectations and explode preconceptions."* Yes, this musician certainly knows how to be a Scorpio! Not simply entertainment, her songs unfold multiple layers of meaning—and many play on the very Scorpio theme of possessiveness. "Love is an elusive thing that all of us crave," says k.d. "Need is constant. It never goes away." Just hum a few bars from her hit "Constant Craving" and you'll know what I mean.

Scorpio Diva: Roseanne

Scorpio is the sign of transformation. Well, Roseanne certainly transformed the media's idea of what a star looks and acts like. To become a star in the first place, she transformed her life—going from high-school dropout to working mom to stand-up comic in a biker bar to actress in her own sitcom. And Scorpio is relentless, so when ABC canceled her show, Roseanne transformed her career again with a talk show. Scorpio makes us see behind the tinsel and bright lights, even if it ain't always pretty.

Scorpio Diva: Marie Antoinette

Every Halloween in San Francisco, many men—each more extravagant than the next—parade through the Castro District costumed as Marie Antoinette, the French queen who

*Warner Brothers, www.wbr.com/kdlang

lost her head to the guillotine. She appeals to us, I suppose, because she was so damn fabulous in her big wigs, enormous low-cut ball gowns, and an apparent obliviousness to anything but parties and pleasure (e.g., "Let them eat cake!"). Besides being a diva of high culture, this true queen was also a Scorpio, a complex woman who longed to live a simpler life, who if she had lived 200 years later, would have avoided execution and become a major celebrity with cameos on *Dynasty* and *Barbara Walters*.

Scorpio Hero: Robert Mapplethorpe

Betrayal and obscenity. Scandals and kinky sex. All of the pulp-fiction images of Scorpio crop up in the life story of this immensely controversial photographer. But the real Mapplethorpe was more than a stereotype. In his hands, the camera was a tool to alter people's perceptions. When he learned he had AIDS, for example, he used a series of self-portraits to focus attention on the disease. Scorpio takes us to the edge, and Mapplethorpe's shocking, erotic, maverick photos did just that.

Scorpio Hero: Terrence McNally

If you've seen Terrence McNally's plays and movies, you've seen a consummate Scorpio at work. Consider, for example, *The Lisbon Traviata* and *Master Class;* with their operatic themes, they flaunt the extreme emotions characteristic of this sign. Then there's *Frankie and Johnnie in the Claire de Lune*, which contains a Scorpionic obsession for exposing human nature rather than romanticizing it, often mixing tragedy with humor. And if you haven't seen it, check out McNally's movie *The Ritz*, a bathhouse farce that lampoons all the 1970s gay stereotypes. Scorpio can and does find humor in the most sordid places (and pathos in the prettiest), always by digging deep beneath the surface.

Scorpio Hero: Rock Hudson

To some he was a hero/heartthrob; to others, a closeted coward. Whichever, the very Scorpio Rock Hudson profoundly changed how Americans perceived AIDS and homosexuality. His AIDS-related death in the '80s gave the disease a famous face, forcing the public to realize HIV was a close-to-home threat needing their attention. Likewise, when Rock's gay past came out, it cracked like never before Hollywood's code of silence about the many gays and lesbians in film and TV. Scorpio has this effect—both creating mystery and exposing it.

Gay Sagittarius

November 22–December 21

The Vicious Stereotype: Sign of the Gypsy Queen

Enter Sagittarius. Here today, gone tomorrow, you're a hobo. Or maybe a *ho* with a lot of *beaux*. You keep strange hours and stranger bedfellows. As outgoing as a golden retriever, and just as likely to hump a fire hydrant, you ascribe to the motto, "Any port in a storm—and a sailor in every port." You've summered in Cannes but can't work a can opener. Blunt and loose-lipped, you think tact went out of style with bouffant hairdos. You like to see yourself as Esmerelda the exotic dancer, but you're more like Lucy stomping grapes.

Costume:

- hand-me-downs and thrift-store "discoveries"
- outrageous hats that change in every scene
- dangling jewelry and other exotic baubles

Props:

- tattered suitcase, always packed

- crystal ball
- Greyhound Bus schedule

Opening line: "It's been swell, but now it's over. Cheer up, sweetheart—we'll always have Paris."

The Real You

Start telling your life story to any stranger in a bar, and he can't help but think you've had a crazy life—like maybe you stole it from the plot of some B movie. And the credits haven't even rolled yet! But keep talking and the stranger will begin to understand that, minus the tattered suitcase and mile-a-minute chitchat, you're a thinker. In every Sagittarius dwells a thoughtful soul who can find the meaning of life in a bowl of salty pretzels.

Even without a passport, you've been on trips. Your mind roams and wanders. An adventurous spirit, you throb with enthusiasm for learning. To Saj, the journey is the destination. The answers don't amuse you half so much as the questions.

To the philosophical Archer, life is always a work in progress. A feeling lingers in every Sagittarius—no matter what his age or how numerous his accomplishments—of unfinished business. Out there lie worlds waiting to be discovered, and you won't rest till you've driven your flag into all their sands, which can never happen. With this dilemma every Saj must make his own peace.

Most mainstream astrology books point out the Archer's love of athletics. For members of our community, however, this often translates into a love of *athletes*. But even if you don't fish, boat, or otherwise play the weekend warrior, you're the kind of guy with an Oedipus complex for Mother Nature. You like to stare at stars, swing at the park, and sniff wild poppies. Like a werewolf during the full moon, you need to run free and wild.

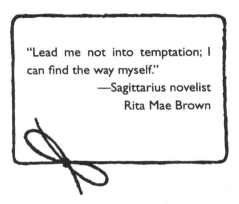

> "Lead me not into temptation; I can find the way myself."
>
> —Sagittarius novelist Rita Mae Brown

You like to think you're awfully cute and innocent. *Cute*, perhaps. But don't expect Dr. Matt to believe any *innocent* man could lead a life like Sagittarian author Jean Genet's. His biography reads like an old-fashioned adventure story, full of daring escapes, run-ins with the law, and an official pardon from the president of France. Typically Sagittarian. Or is that an oxymoron?

It's always fun to argue with a loudmouth Sagittarius. You boys attack issues with more fervor than insight, citing chapter and verse from your vast readings and experiences, swearing and vowing like a hellfire-and-brimstone preacher-man. Even if you haven't approached a chalkboard in 20 years, you're a born teacher. You unlock people's minds.

Like Libra, you can't tolerate injustice. You hold yourself to strict standards of right and wrong (though if you want to do something shady, you'll always find a way to rationalize it!). Mean, unfair people make you really mad. You'd rather not lose your cool, but in the case of inequity, you'll go there.

> "I wouldn't say I invented tack, but I definitely brought it to its present high popularity."
>
> —Sagittarius diva Bette Midler

Generous to a fault, you give of yourself, even if you can't afford to give of your cash. At your parties, people who'd never meet one another in "real" life mix, mingle, and exchange recipes and political polemics. Your friends come from every imaginable background—and a few not so imaginable. Where do you find these people? Or do they find you? Whichever, your photo album could easily be a best-seller, if it weren't censored first.

Given the Archer's quest for knowledge and understanding, it's little wonder the first gay bookshop in America, the Oscar Wilde Bookshop, was "born" a Sagittarius—it opened in New York City in early December 1967.

The Secret in Sagittarius's Closet

Optimistic and outgoing, you seem perennially on top of

the world. But even at the top of the world, night falls and the cold sets in. Alone in the dark, you question your faith, doubt life's significance, worry you're a bad boy.

Watching you, the world sees a doer, a goer, a man in motion. Why? Do you hunger for adventure? Or are you afraid to sit still? Only you can answer that one.

But consider this: Like Hamlet, you may fear "what dreams may come" if you don't keep putting on plays and bickering with queens. Silence or lack of activity is terrifying as your vast Sagittarian brain contemplates all the reasons to lose hope and give up chasing dreams.

So you globe-trot, generally avoiding the dark side, running yourself ragged. Unless, of course, you learn to explore not only the world outside, but the world inside, too. The trick for Saj is to map the inner landscape without falling into its valleys of despair. A true world traveler can go to the ends of the earth and always find his way home again.

Gay Sagittarius Growing Up

Sagittarius little boys smile big and laugh heartily, sometimes giggling quite uncontrollably. Their hearts pumping with wanderlust, every little Archer boy dreams of running away to join the circus.

You were probably friendly and talkative yet had a hard time relating to your peers and felt left out. As a result, you may have preferred the company of books, TV, or any medium that transported you far away.

Like your Pisces pals, you championed the underdogs and befriended the less-than-popular kids in school. You probably stumped your teachers with tough questions like, "Why is the sky blue?" or "Does HOMO-genized milk come from gay cows?"

The realities of early adulthood—like paying the rent and sorting light from dark dirty clothes—can be tough on the Saj young man who has spent his youth fantasizing about the fabulous adventures he'll have once he escapes Mom and Pop. Eek! Freedom costs a high price.

For every Saj, a big part of growing up is learning to take the bad with the good. Enthusiasm is tempered with realism—but never defeated.

Sagittarius in Love

Saj isn't afraid to come on strong. When you see a man you like, your eyes bulge and your tongue scrapes the gravel. Desire sends you into warp speed. If you're physically attracted to a man, that's enough. What else is there?

There's always his mind, I suppose. And before long, you'll want to pry it open and dig around like a kid who wants the toy from a box of Cracker Jacks. If his mind's no fun, you'll eventually discard the package and open another.

For Sagittarius, lust is a powerful force—but not so powerful as the urge to explore another human being to the outermost limits of his soul. You get into a man like a good book; some are easier to put down than others.

When it comes to the one you love, it's not that you

don't care, but you need the open air. So love presents a challenge: to have a relationship that feels like wearing a comfy sweater, but never a ball and chain.

Mr. Right—Or Is It Mr. Right Now?

Mr. Right better listen. You've got a lot to say, and you'll never get along with any man, no matter how hunky, if he doesn't at least feign interest in your crackpot theories. Bores and cry babies immediately wind up in the Mr. Wrong category. You can't abide closed-minded individuals and fags who rain on your parade.

> "A lifetime of disco music is a high price to pay for one's sexuality."
>
> —Sagittarian author and eccentric Quentin Crisp

When it comes to Mr. Right, size matters. He needs a huge vocabulary and wide range of interesting experiences and ideas to bounce back and forth. But while you want to glean wisdom from your partner, you'll reject any well-meaning but meddlesome wise guy telling you how to live your life.

You'd rather he hold your hand as you two trot off into the future. Being with Mr. Right sends your life in unexpected directions. Gee, you never thought you'd do these things and know these people, but here you are, all because your destiny converged with his. Every day is an adventure.

And so is every night. Mr. Right has a vast sexual repertoire—or at least he's willing to develop one. Sometimes he plays the lead; other times, your boy toy. Like you, he's an erotic thrill seeker. I knew, for example, one Sagittarius-Aries couple who almost always had sex on the kitchen floor because they couldn't wait to get to the bedroom. It was cold, but they didn't seem to mind.

> "I've known sheep who could outwit you. I've worn dresses with higher IQs, but you think you're an intellectual, don't you?"
>
> —Sagittarius actress Jamie Lee Curtis in *A Fish Called Wanda*

Sagittarius in the Sack

You take pride in your sexuality, and I'm not just talking about waving a rainbow flag.

Some guys flaunt their beauty. Others brag on their wealth. You, on the other hand, couldn't care less about such posing—you'd rather regale an audience with tales of your swashbuckling love life. A Sagittarius fully expects to lie on his deathbed fondly recalling all he's tasted of life, including *beaucoup* amorous exploits. Getting lucky makes you feel like the luckiest creature on earth.

Ruled by Jupiter, the solar system's largest planet, Sagittarius just can't seem to get enough. I wouldn't go so far as to say you're a *bona fide* size queen, but I wouldn't dispute it either. You pursue interesting lovers, men who look thrilling and intriguing, regardless of nostril hair and 11 fingers. You like to say, "Oh, I've done him." Exotic pleasures really charge your battery, so you're a sucker for foreigners who promise to teach you there's more than one way to roll a cigar. By the way, did you know *Ro hai hu* means "I love you" in the native Guarani language? You do now, baby!

When you don't get what you want sexually, you take it hard. Rejection wounds you deeply. Dissatisfaction is the ultimate disappointment. But since you're a Saj, you'll try, try again—maybe twice in one night.

Sagittarius's Fame and Fortune

Career

Personality-wise, you have little in common with your Taurus friends, but you sure can identify with the Bull's lazy side. You idolize idleness, not because you like to sit on your ass, but because you like to do *what* you want to do *when* you want to do it.

In your book, it's better to work smarter than work harder. You delight in finding shortcuts to complete your work. You revel in outsmarting the "system." Above all, you'd love to get paid a month's salary for delivering 12 minutes of advice. Forget what the other astrology books say—the only real Sagittarian dream job is consultant.

No matter how they earn their bread and butter, most Sagittarians remain lifelong students and scholars. Consider, for example, the career of Sagittarian fashion designer Gianni Versace; not only did he build a fashion empire, but he also devoted considerable time to designing costumes for operas at La Scala, ballets all over the world, and concert tours by Elton John, meanwhile lecturing on the history of fashion at museums and schools.

It helps if you ambitious Saj guppie types realize you might not arrive overnight at your destination. That doesn't mean you can't enjoy the bumpy ride along the way.

Money Matters

Hey, big spender! Extravagant, you stock up on truffles and gourmet olive oil but run dangerously low on toilet paper. Impulsive, you love to buy gifts on the spur of the moment but secretly resent having to buy them for certain special occasions. Whatever your financial circumstances, you try really hard to stay on top of your money instead of it staying on top of you. But it doesn't always work out that way.

I've never met a Sagittarian accountant. They might exist, but I've never met one, let alone a gay one. That's not to say you can't balance your checkbook, but the typical Saj would rather not factor income and outgo into his life decisions. You hate limits—especially the limit on your credit card—and want to live where you want to live, go where you want to go, and eat what you want to eat regardless of price. Nevertheless, you hate to be outsmarted, and it makes you mad, mostly as a matter of principle, if you paid too much.

In the long run, you're more likely to accumulate experiences than consumer goods, always on the lookout for new opportunities, whether fiscal or frisky.

Sagittarius in the Spotlight

Sagittarius Diva: Bette Midler

Who but "The Divine Miss M" could better represent the fun and rambunctious side of the Archer? Like most Sagittarians, she's willing to go anywhere: After working briefly in a Hawaiian pineapple cannery, she landed one of her first showbiz gigs telling sleazy jokes and singing in a gay bathhouse. You can always count on Saj for dumb jokes, coarse humor, and punny puns!

Sagittarius Diva: Maria Callas

Not merely a *diva*, she was *La Divina*—"The Divine One," the 20th century's most important icon to opera queens everywhere. With Sagittarian *savoir faire*, opera singer Maria Callas revived interest in 19th-century *bel canto* operas like Bellini's *Norma* and Donizetti's *Lucia di Lammermoor*, which the post–World War era found "too boring." Callas made them exciting again. Using a very Sagittarian flair for making stuffy material interesting and accessible, she breathed new dramatic life into long-forgotten or empty characters, giving them current emotional relevance. Raised in Greece, Callas was a gypsy all her life, playing at the world's greatest opera houses, eventually dying in Paris.

Sagittarius Diva: Agnes Moorehead

So many of us little witches-in-training remember Agnes Moorehead as Endora, the sassy yet classy, finger-snapping mother of Samantha Stephens on *Bewitched.* But she also acted in *Citizen Kane*, toured a one-woman show called *The Fabulous Redhead*, and earned her Ph.D. in literature. She sums up the sophisticated, intellectual side of Sagittarius, not to mention the wanderlust associated with this sign—remember how Endora popped from Africa to Europe to the living room on Morning Glory Lane? What a witch!

Sagittarius Hero: Noël Coward

Actor, playwright, songwriter—Sir Noël Coward did it all, and did it all with a witty, merry style that expressed so much gay Sagittarianism. Challenging the hypocrisy of his Victorian childhood, he celebrated the decadence and "loose" morals of the 1920s and delightedly turned human vices into the "comedy of bad manners." Publicly he exercised his "talent to amuse"—yet privately he philosophized about death, reflected on his homosexuality, and sought work with a higher purpose. Sound familiar?

Sagittarius Hero: Jean Genet

The Archer is blunt and brash. So is the work of Jean Genet. His audacious plays like *The Balcony* and *The Maids* dared to reinvent modern drama, advancing the mid–20th-century Theatre of Cruelty movement. "Rotted with genius," this philosophical Saj turned theatre into a religious ritual that startled audiences into pondering their existence and its inherent violence. "Would it perturb you to see things as they are?" he asked. "To gaze at the world and accept responsibility for your gaze, whatever it might see?"

Sagittarius Hero: Gianni Versace

"I was envious of a person who had the courage to live life so luxuriously," extolled Madonna after his death (that's saying a lot, coming from the Material Girl herself!). But Versace's life wasn't just luxurious—it was *big*, like everything Sagittarius does. His *haute couture* designs were big, bold, and fun-loving. To make them he drew from centuries of art, literature, and architecture. Like many Archers, he wanted life to seem less ordinary, more like an adventure.

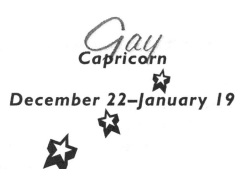

Gay Capricorn

December 22–January 19

The Vicious Stereotype: Sign of the Society Matron

Enter Capricorn. A cross between the Queen Mother and a homecoming queen, you name-drop till you drop. Your nose is so high in the air that it blips on air traffic control radar. A social climber, a country-club harridan, a garden-party trollop, you're charitable with your balls and black-tie affairs. Your idea of roughing it is staying at the Holiday Inn instead of the Hyatt. If you own it, you monogram it—so your boyfriend better watch out!

Costume:

- fur coat
- reading glasses dangling from gold chain
- sensible shoes (but never white before Memorial Day!)

Props:

- silver spoon
- bodyguard for keeping the riffraff away

- leather-bound editions of *Who's Who* and *The Social Register*

Opening line: "We are not amused! It's so hard to find good help these days."

The Real You

No, most Goats would rather not mingle with the riffraff. It's not that you dread catching cooties or bad taste, but you've set your sights on loftier goals than off-the-rack mediocrity. In the Bloomingdale's of life, you've decided to hop off the crowded escalator going to the bargain basement and hop onto the elevator headed for the penthouse suite. There among the movers and shakers you win friends and influence people. You wanna be a contender.

Is it blind ambition? Kind of, kind of not. Capricorns want to *deserve people's respect.* How do you do that? If you're a petty Capricorn, you show off, waving your résumé and the keys to your Porsche in envious onlookers' faces. If you're a Capricorn with character, you achieve greatness and distinction. You set goals. You pay your dues. You triumph over the odds. Of course, not everyone's respect is worth getting, so figure out who they are and don't waste your time on phony baloney.

Gallant and chivalrous, Goats are sturdy. If anyone's looking for a cowboy or construction worker type and can't find one (at least not a gay one), I recommend going for a Capricorn stud instead. Even without the chaps or hard hat, you exude strength and solidity, minus the callused fingers. Not easily intimidated, you rarely deviate from your plan—and every Capricorn has a plan.

A sense of responsibility influences your decisions. You dedicate your days to duty. You bail out friends in trouble. You try to do the right thing. It's not that you gay Goats don't have any fun, but you make yourself *earn* your kicks. Work comes before play. Without a strong sense of purpose, you'd be lost, wondering *Why bother at all?*

You're not a quitter. When life bites, you react with an upper lip stiffer than a Viagra-induced erection. You find meaning in struggle. Crises and overwhelming obstacles bring out your best. Case in point: On the first night of the first Twin Cities–Chicago AIDS Ride, a storm devastated the camp. The next morning, mud drenched everything, and morale hit rock bottom. Yet in spite of it all, the Chicken Lady—a bicycling drag queen who'd lost many friends to AIDS—bravely encouraged other riders. "Embrace the adversity, everyone," he crooned. "Embrace the adversity!" And they did, thanks to the spirit of Capricorn.

None of this means, however, you should actively seek chaos. It's noble to suffer for a worthy cause—but downright masochistic to suffer needlessly. If you're a wise Goat who wants to do a far, far better thing than you've ever done before, enjoy the best of times as much as the worst of times.

Like Aquarius, you want to make the world a better place. Yet you approach this challenge with greater pragmatism. Whereas Aquarius *changes* the world—which may or may not actually improve it—you work with what you've got. Pipe dreams aren't your style, but results and tangible excellence suit you to a T. Goats are hard-hitting realists. "I've always chosen the tough truths over a feel-good bromide," Capricorn novelist Edmund White told *The Advocate*.

Does all this make you dull? *Perish the thought!* Despite your serious nature, Capricorns often manage life and its travails with humor. It's a sense of humor as dry as a circuit boy's mouth after a weekend martini binge. Capricorn actress Maggie Smith, for example, frequently plays stuffy British dames (*First Wives' Club, Sister Act, California Suite*) who steal the show with witty one-liners.

And who doesn't appreciate a truly *bon mot* from a *grande Goat?*

The Secret in Capricorn's Closet

We'll get to your inner child later. But when was the last time you got in touch with your inner frat boy? Recently, I hope, because lurking inside every uptight Capricorn is a loose and lively party animal waiting to burst forth like an exotic dancer from a giant cake. To hell with respectability—you secretly want to swill beer all night and wake up naked next to strangers in the bathtub. You want to *live*, damn it.

Typically you don't believe all that "Today-is-the-first-day-of-the-rest-of-your-life" rubbish, but part of you would like to—the part that wishes you'd lighten up and play hooky.

Nevertheless, you mind your p's and q's. If you didn't, wouldn't the whole world come toppling down? You don't want to find out. You fear loss of control, and that simply won't do. So you go through life looking like a paragon of composure and decorum, when I know you'd really like to kick some ass.

> "Insanity runs in my family. . . . It practically gallops."
>
> —Capricorn actor Cary Grant in *Arsenic and Old Lace*

Go ahead, make some waves. Make some enemies. You know what they say: You can judge a man's personality by his friends, but you can judge a man's character by his enemies. And Capricorn is all about having character.

Gay Capricorn Growing Up

Capricorns have a hard time being youngsters. According to legend, Goats are old souls. Thus, many Capricorn children suffer the awkwardness of housing a geriatric spirit in a hormonal young body. Chalk it up to God's inscrutable plan. Oh well, it made you grow up fast.

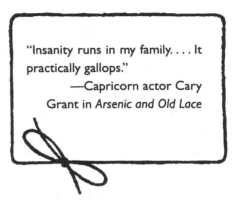

Maybe *too* fast. Chances are you developed maturity and shouldered a lot of responsibility at an early age. Perhaps you felt like one of Queen Victoria's dutiful daughters, married off to a foreign aristocrat for political, rather than romantic, purposes. Making love, instructed the old queen, was only a chore to be endured—so just "close your eyes and think of England." Gee, *that's* a turn-on.

All this premature maturity may have precluded your other interests, like kid stuff, like building sandcastles or skinny dipping at summer camp. And it may have prevented you from circulating among the *in* crowd, since more childish children typically resent and ridicule the sophisticates in their midst.

No doubt you held your head high and resolved to get even by making something of yourself. Good. You won. Like the jocks at my high-school reunion, those mean popular kids have probably sunk into their potbellies and ordinary lives, while you, my friend, have become a fabulous gay man, proud of who you are and where you've been. Maybe now you can kick back, forget about beating them or joining them, and let the good times roll on *your* terms.

Capricorn in Love

You're no fool for love. You don't give away your heart to just any schmo who'll juggle it as he pleases—"Hands *off* the merchandise, thank you very much!" The notion of *falling* in love seems rather too undignified for one so poised as *vous.* Prudent and circumspect, you realize bad judgment now could lead to years of fighting over who should clean the bathroom later.

As an earth sign, you especially appreciate big muscles and stunning bone structure, but as a pragmatist, you also revere a man who doesn't march in the Parade of Losers. Essentially, you need a good reason to fall in love—and the fact Mr. All That can get you off three times in one night probably doesn't qualify.

When, after much deliberation and consternation, you find love, you don't surrender it easily. You persevere, doing everything in your power to make it work. A steadfast partner, you stand by your man. Though you're not exactly fragile, rejection punctures your confidence, and you'll slam the door (or at least you *should*, darling) on any would-be Romeo who can't commit.

> "Don't fuck with me fellas—this ain't my first time at the rodeo."
>
> —Capricorn actress Faye Dunaway in *Mommie Dearest*

You want a love you can come home to, not merely dream about and pine for. You flourish in a true partnership, a relationship of mutual respect. In one of the greatest love stories of all time, the Capricorn queen Cleopatra both demanded and sacrificed entire empires for the love of Marc Antony. It was a big love, much more than puppy love.

Mr. Right—Or Is It Mr. Right Now?

He's tall, dark, and rich. But you'd settle for short, pale, and extremely wealthy. According to old-fashioned astrologers, Capricorns usually marry *up*—and if that leads to a fulfilling relationship, I say more power to you, *mon cheri!* In Dr. Matt's experience, however, you Goats fare better choosing a partner with a lot to recommend him besides his mutual funds.

What you really want is a sure thing. A good man with good values is good for you. Other than that, he just better not stand in the way of your career—because somebody's got to support the lifestyle to which you plan to become accustomed.

Mr. Right knows how to lead you astray, down a path of pleasure and satisfaction, without making you feel guilty for neglecting your obligations. He's the guy who literally holds the key to your heart—he opens up your emotions. When, for example, you storm into the house after a foul day at work, he can tease out what's wrong and say, "There, there, tell me all about it," without sounding like a condescending schmuck. He makes you laugh, too.

Capricorn in the Sack

You're as frigid as a Frigidaire refrigerator. You disapprove of all undergarments except sensible flannel boxers. You can't imagine any use for rubber gloves besides washing dishes.

Does that sound like you? Didn't think so! But that's the

stereotype. Perhaps the cliché of "No sex please, we're Capricorns!" applies to straight Goats (actually, I doubt it), but gay Goats know beds were built for more than sleeping.

Capricorns are discreet, and there's a reason: In your sex life you let it all hang out. Your stuffed shirt comes off and, almost surprisingly, hot-blooded flesh pulses underneath. You get *into* it, baby. I once played strip poker with a Capricorn man who was glad—only in this instance, I assure you—to lose. Buck naked except for a turban, he danced while everyone sang. What a sleaze! What a playboy! What fun! Who said Capricorn was a stick-in-the-mud?

But if you're going to do it, you want to do it right. You take pride in pleasing your partner. Days, weeks, maybe even months go into planning what you'll do to your lover when the lights go out. To you Goats, the body of your lover stretches out like a beautiful, undiscovered terrain—and you are the conquistador, taming the landscape and civilizing the natives.

Capricorn's Fame and Fortune

Career

Oh, goodie! Now we talk about work, one of Capricorn's favorite subjects. Not that you love work, but you love the *idea* of work, the *smell* of work, not to mention the results of work—the rewards, the respect, the recognition. Of course the Society Matron never wants to perform work beneath her station—but she'll do what she has to do. Likewise, even in evening wear, if you have to get down on all fours to scrub a floor, you'll drop to your knees. It doesn't take much.

One way or another, Capricorns command authority on the job. Maybe you've earned a reputation as a taskmaster, barking orders like a drill sergeant, instilling fear and obedience in your employees, colleagues, and maybe even in your boss. Or perhaps you've acquired eminence as a leader in your field, absolutely *the* person to ask when no one else has the know-how. However you go about it, you don't let people forget you're *not* playing the third spear-carrier from the left—or at least not for long.

Capricorns are commonly thought of as conservative executives climbing the ladder to successful 501k plans, wearing "standard-issue" JC Penney blue suits and a phony smile. But the truth is you're not all 1980s-style corporate types—and you certainly could live without the *de rigueur* blue suit. Whatever your career, you don't have to like it, but you better think it matters. When you feel you've outworn your usefulness, you Goats sink into despair—unless, somewhere along the line, you figured out *you* matter more than what you do.

May Dr. Matt offer one piece of unsolicited advice? Get a personal life—and do what you must to keep it.

Money Matters

Yes, money does matter. A Capricorn and his money are

not easily parted. It's not that you're greedy, but you're sensible, and it makes sense to avoid the *nuisance* of poverty. In a different world you might not care, but in our world of capitalism and consumerism, whoever has the most toys *wins*—and you're not about to get locked out of the toy store.

Besides, you enjoy what money can *do*. Lots of Goats' favorite hobby is watching their portfolio grow—and their influence in society along with it. But you may derive equal satisfaction from leveraging financial resources to help people. Despite a large inheritance and substantial book royalties, for example, Capricorn novelist E. M. Forster lived frugally and preferred to lavish his disposable income on friends and Greek sculpture, which he donated to museums.

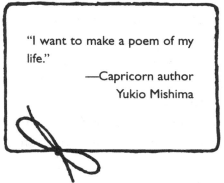

> "I want to make a poem of my life."
>
> —Capricorn author
> Yukio Mishima

However you spend it, you expect *value* for your dollar. Many a Goat has gotten rich by stocking up on long-term investments that profitably weather the vagaries of a volatile market.

Nevertheless, the really smart Capricorns place security in themselves, not in their bank accounts. The gay Capricorn author Paul Bowles must have figured this out, because he wrote, "Security is a false god; begin making sacrifices to it and you are lost."

Capricorn in the Spotlight

Capricorn Diva: Eartha Kitt

Filming in Paris, director Orson Welles called her "the most exciting woman in the world." Years later, the CIA called her "a sadistic sex nymphomaniac" when she criticized the Vietnam War. She's Eartha Kitt—that's *Miss* Kitt to you—the original Capricorn Cat Woman (one of three actresses to play Catwoman on TV's *Batman*). Eartha exemplifies Capricorn's ambitious and classy nature, determined all her life to "make it." Starting life poor and unwanted, she learned to sing and dance, speak many languages, and invest in real estate, all on her own—despite her songs about finding a sugar daddy. "Plato was a great influence on my mind," she said, "because he teaches you how to think."

Capricorn Diva: Marlene Dietrich

So very Capricorn, Dietrich forged a 50-year career in show business exerting her sign's eminent *toughness*. On screen she's cool and formidable, seeming to say, "Don't mess with this dame!" In life, she loved whom she pleased, male and female, and in her early Josef von Sternberg films, she dressed as a man, accentuating her allure to all genders and orientations. Despite the Depression, she lived aristocratically, and during World War II, she had the guts to denounce her native Germany and entertain Allied troops at the front line. Still, though, she maintained the Goat's down-to-earth sensibility; at the height of divahood she insisted, "I am not a myth."

Capricorn Diva: Cleopatra

"If the nose of Cleopatra had been shorter," goes an old saying, "the whole face of the earth would have changed." It sums up the enormous influence wielded on ancient history by one little Capricorn queen.* Deprived of her throne, Cleopatra wrested it back (Goats bounce back from underdog status). A queen playing in a man's world, she cleverly seduced Julius Caesar and other powerful men (Goats know where to find *real* power). And she gave the biggest, most opulent parties (Goats can entertain with dignity and charisma).

Capricorn Hero: David Sedaris

Famous for their nose-to-the-grindstone workaholism, Goats often have trouble just kicking back. David Sedaris, for example, wrote many best-selling books about his kooky jobs. But despite success, he refused to stop cleaning houses. His editor *made* him quit. So he looked for another

*Most historians and astrologers agree Cleopatra was born in January, 69 B.C.E. See Noel Tyl, *Astrology of the Famed* (St. Paul: Llewelyn Publications, 1996).

job. "I *hate* not having a job," he said. "I don't have to put my hand in someone's toilet to find things to write about, you know? I did it because it's my job and I enjoyed it."* If you've read his books (like *Santaland Diaries* and *Naked*), you've encountered Capricorn's twisted sense of humor: The Goat is great at picking out the petty, grotesque, and/or pathetic elements of any situation.

Capricorn Hero: David Bowie

Is he gay? Straight? Somewhere in between? Who knows! Whatever his personal preferences, this rock star made it cool to be queer in the 1970s. A rock 'n' roll dandy, he raised gender-bending to an art form (The Goat is *such* a trendsetter!). Long before Madonna, he was among the first to give pop music a theatrical panache. "I've gone my own way and been very stubborn," he said, sounding very Goatish. "That's the only reason for my existence, and the rest be damned, you know."

Capricorn Hero: E. M. Forster

During his lifetime, he refused to publish his gayest novel because he worried what his mother would think. But when *Maurice* finally came out, it defined our image of homosexuality in the glorious but repressed heyday of the British Raj. Besides becoming great movies with lovely little nude

*In an interview with Seth Rogovy in the *Berkshire Eagle*, published April 24, 1998.

scenes (like *A Room with a View)*, Forster's novels show Capricorn's interest in the value of human civilization—but they also point out that only the wealthy enjoy its benefits. Forster himself valued rigorous artistic standards, personal integrity, and honest relationships—all very Capricorn.

> "The way I see it, if you want the rainbow, you've got to put up with the rain."
>
> —Capricorn country diva Dolly Parton

Gay Aquarius

January 20–February 18

The Vicious Stereotype: Sign of the Radical Ice Queen

Enter Aquarius. Your hair is always a political statement. A rabble-rouser, an instigator, a maven of counter-culture, you're a queen with a cause. You save the whales, ban the bomb, and tell Mom she's a bourgeois pig. Like Lilith on *Frasier*, you're frigid—and as frosty and hard to penetrate as an Alpine pass. When men kiss you, they get their tongues stuck on your pole. You admire the vision of Harriet Tubman but can't muster more charm than Mr. Spock.

Costume:

- tie-dyed shirt
- recycled hemp jacket
- geek glasses

Props:

- picket sign and megaphone
- copy of Mao's little book

- entourage of kooky friends

Opening line: “Let’s start a revolution! Hey, what does one wear to a revolution?”

The Real You

So you’re a little, um—how does one put this delicately?—a tad *unusual.* Nothing wrong with that. We can’t all shop at The Gap and pierce all the same body parts. Besides, there’s so much more to you than the bumper stickers and outrageous wardrobe.

Perhaps most endearing of all Aquarian traits is the inclination to see the world not as it is, but as it should be. Lots of movie-makers are Aquarians. Lots of therapists, too. They’ve got this vision of the world and they want to promote it.

But you do more than talk about it. You actually believe in ideals. You practice philanthropy. A humanitarian, you champion worthy causes and intrepidly defend your principles and rights—especially the right to be yourself.

In university babble, you “shift the paradigm.” In corporate parlance, you “push the envelope.” In Silicon Valley speak, you “think outside the box.” Hell, you never knew the box was there, let alone got trapped inside.

Quirky and offbeat, you don’t mind your reputation as an odd duck, a *rara avis,* the one pink M&M in a bag of all the usual colors. It’s no surprise Broadway actress Tallulah

Bankhead was a Water Bearer. A critic once said, "Tallulah is always skating on thin ice. Everyone wants to be there when it breaks."

Indeed, the world is forever watching to see what you'll do next. You have a lot in common with static electricity: You go through life shocking people, and your energy spreads contagiously. You're a trendsetter. Case in point: Your fellow Aquarius, the French authoress Colette, made it fashionable in early 20th-century Paris for women to take other women as lovers. Now it's common as *café au lait.*

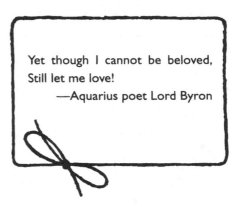

> Yet though I cannot be beloved,
> Still let me love!
> —Aquarius poet Lord Byron

Throughout history, the Water Bearer's iconoclasm is well documented. Lord Byron, for example, spent his life expressing the unconventional and rebellious spirit of Aquarius. He scandalized British society with a series of affairs with men, women, and his half-sister. Then, always eager for a change of pace, he fought for Greece's independence.

And of course James Dean, icon of an entire generation of rebellious American youth, was an Aquarius. He probably wasn't gay *per se*, but he experimented with men. Aquarians do that—experiment in all sorts of ways.

Experimentation leads to progress, and nothing could make you happier. You relish fresh, eye-popping ideas and life on the cutting edge. While the other boys in your neighborhood gleefully yet vapidly fritter away their off hours at the tanning salon and Ricky Martin fan club, you've got better, bigger things to occupy your cerebral cortex.

> "Do you think homosexuals are revolting? You bet your sweet ass we are."
>
> —Gay lib leaflet, 1969

Like Sagittarius, you collect a loud, colorful menagerie of friends—your *people*. They come from so many different countries and cultures that having them over for coffee may sound like Meryl Streep and Robin Williams rehearsing all their accents. Maybe your Rolodex isn't as full as Gemini's, but if your boss needs a Mandarin-speaking transsexual receptionist with sky-diving experience, she's bound to ask you first. You'll know one, or someone who does.

You lead no ordinary life. As an Aquarius, you expect the unexpected. You fight for acceptance yet resist total assimilation. You step precariously close to the edge but rarely lose your footing. By lunchtime you've changed the world seven times, and before dinnertime you're already wondering what's in store for this evening's entertainment.

The Secret in Aquarius's Closet

"I'm here, I'm queer, deal with it!" says your rebellious side. "Take me as I am. Love me or leave me," this rugged individualist demands. So who'd ever guess you secretly worry what people think about you?

That's right. A part of you actually wants to fit in. Like a 13-year-old out in public with his mother, this hidden part of you embarrasses easily and shudders with shame every time you make waves or attract attention.

Inside every Aquarius is an inner "normal" person dying to kill time at the mall and have sex in the basic missionary position. You don't let him out much, but this "regular" guy doesn't give a damn about politics, third-world sweat shops, or avant-garde performance art. He's happy with popcorn, a movie, and a long kiss good night.

Turning into Joe Schmo is not for you. Still, though, it might be nice if you occasionally indulged your craving for conventionality. Balance your impulse to save the world and make it a more interesting place with your day-to-day needs for food, shelter, and a man in your arms. Bring your ideas down to earth. Create stability. Then it'll be so much more fun to shake it all up again.

Gay Aquarius Growing Up

Ah, the good old days! Life was so much simpler then. So wonderfully uncomplicated. And *way* too dull. Though you may view your childhood as an idyllic time of making friends and vexing teachers, could you, would you, really go back? I doubt it. You're too focused on the future to backpedal into the past.

We shouldn't forget, though, that in your younger, less jaded days you first learned to march to the beat of your own drum—and taught others to groove to your beat. Like Robin Hood, you probably acquired a band of merry misfits. Camaraderie mattered intensely. So even if you scorned the *in* crowd, you desperately needed to belong to, or create, the *out* crowd.

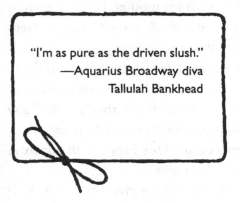

> "I'm as pure as the driven slush."
>
> —Aquarius Broadway diva
> Tallulah Bankhead

Even the sweetest little Aquarian children find ways to undermine authority. With your Gemini and Sagittarian buddies, no doubt, you stirred up mischief. Whenever I wasn't looking, for example, my childhood best friend—definitely an Aquarius—arranged my stuffed animals in the 69 position. Then he looked oh-so innocent when Mom walked in and blamed *me* for the porn version of *The Muppet Movie*. Aquarius does the best poker face.

Young Aquarians are complex little buggers. You were bright, but seldom the teacher's pet. You craved eclectic experiences, yet thrived on stability and resented change. Growing up a gay Aquarius is hardly a simple game of four square. You second-guessed your choices and worried the world didn't have room for one such as you. Through lots of trial and error you had to figure out the world doesn't make room—you make it yourself.

Aquarius in Love

What's all the fuss about? To you high-minded Aquarians, the whole modern world seems to have gone psycho for this thing called love. The sitcoms, the soaps, the *Men on Men* stories—they all seem like propaganda for a love that's silly, juvenile, and best befits a teenage girl. It's so *bourgeois.*

You're probably the only man in the zodiac who can fall in love without getting emotionally involved. Dr. Matt does not imply, however, that love's heat can never melt your snow cone. One day a man will come who, in fact, does more than just come. He turns the elevator music of ordinary love into a *Symphonie Fantastique* of phenomenal passion. Suddenly you find yourself uttering cheesy movie dialogue like, "I never knew it could be this way."

It startles you. It's messy, distracting, and potentially hazardous. All the same, you can't stay away—or at least you shouldn't. Sorry to promote more propaganda, but love can potentially magnify an Aquarian life beyond earthly proportions. I refer not to the cloying love that comes in a heart-shaped box of chocolates, but to a relationship where you constantly grow as a person because you are accepted completely.

You thrive in a relationship that doesn't depend on traditional gender roles or other worn-out paradigms. You and your partner make it up as you go along. Every day brings the excitement of inventing a different kind of romance, a better way to relate. No, you probably won't see your relationship depicted in the mainstream movies, but that's OK—you can always make home movies and play them for your friends . . . if you dare!

Mr. Right—Or Is It Mr. Right Now?

Wow! You can't miss him. Mr. Right gets your attention. Not a clone of you or anyone else, he stands out from the crowd.

Your ideal man feels like a day at the circus. He's fun, lively, and travels with a freak show's worth of interesting people and exotic creatures. He may come from the wrong side of the tracks or other side of the world, but none of that matters because regardless of his background he's such an original. You admire his hard-won identity and sense of self.

Yet despite his self-reliance, Mr. Right is glad to have you on his side. It bodes well for the relationship if both of you sign on as president of each other's fan club. It bodes even better if you frequently inject him with your special Aquarian brand of inspiration while he keeps you entertained, enthralled, and stimulated.

Chances are Mr. Right's less serious than you. Whereas you live in the future, he lives for the moment. With him in your life, you suddenly find yourself going to more parties and having more picnics. He drags you on vacations and buys you terrifically useless gifts that belong in a museum, garage sale, or top-secret laboratory.

> "It's still me, with one tiny difference . . . well, not tiny!"
> —Aquarius actor Nathan Lane in *The Birdcage*

To you, Mr. Right's SAT scores matter less than his flair for expressing himself. He's highly verbal or artistic or both. And he certainly knows how to express his sexuality! Better than a glass of champagne, he makes you giddy, flirty, and horny. Faster than a BMW goes from zero to 60, Mr. Right can go from turning on your IQ to turning down the sheets.

Aquarius in the Sack

The cliché version of having sex with Aquarius:

- Remove TV dinner from freezer; microwave on defrost for 11.7 minutes; consume before it melts plastic tray or goes totally limp.

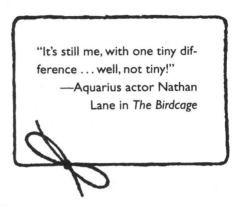

How unfair—no wonder so many Aquarians are skeptical about astrology. So let Dr. Matt set the record straight, er, correct: It might be true you treat sex rather clinically, that you undress a man as if unwrapping a package of chicken drumsticks, but we mustn't forget your *forté* for experimentation. You'll go where no man has gone before.

Unlike some boys we know, you don't wear your sexuality on your sleeve; nevertheless, it's in your eyes. You discreetly watch and wonder what it'd be like to have sex with so-and-so, what turns on a particular man, how to seduce another. Curiosity drives your sex drive. You may even have sex with buddies you're no more emotionally involved with than the men in your miniature golf club—but they sure help you handle a putter.

For the right man, however, your curiosity about various body parts transforms into a commitment to gratifying your partner in every way imaginable. You make it your mission to increase and improve his pleasure. No technique is too bizarre, no position too difficult, no fantasy too X-rated for the one you love.

Your friends and neighbors, meanwhile, may still suspect you have a sex life as bland as a eunuch's—but isn't it fun to keep them guessing?

Aquarius's Fame & Fortune

Career

Don't tell me you haven't seen *Willy Wonka and the Chocolate Factory*. Willy Wonka epitomizes the mad scientist in every Aquarius. He changes the world one jawbreaker at a time, he gives jobs to the otherwise unemployable Oompa-Loompas, and he rewards goodness over greed. As for running a profitable business, sure he's crazy—what Aquarius with half a mind to chase his dreams isn't?

If you want success—and something tells me you do—you won't find it at the end of the straight and narrow path so well trodden by the pawns of suburban consumer culture. Even if you snag the MBA and land the six-figure salary, you won't find career satisfaction if you don't blaze your own trail. You don't work just to pay the rent; you pay the rent so you can keep going to work. If you're stuck in a day job between masterpieces, it might not feel that way right now—but it will eventually, when you find your *métier.*

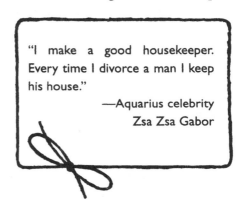

> "I make a good housekeeper. Every time I divorce a man I keep his house."
>
> —Aquarius celebrity Zsa Zsa Gabor

Before settling on a career, Aquarians take all sorts of kooky gigs. Aquarius actor Ellen DeGeneres shucked oysters before getting her first job as a stand-up comic. Nathan Lane, another Aquarius actor, delivered singing telegrams before landing his breakthrough in *Guys and Dolls.* And Aquarius author Somerset Maugham had to learn to turn his so-called personal defects and embarrassments into rich material before he could write anything but schlock.

No matter what his field, Aquarius is always on the lookout for the next blockbuster or megahit.

Money Matters

You're no cheapskate. You pay the price. If Dad needs triple bypass surgery, you fork over the cash. If your Halloween costume could benefit from an extra hundred rhinestones, you spare no expense. But you're also not a spendthrift or playboy.

Although you're happy to spend, money doesn't motivate you. The quest of affluence doesn't get you out of bed in the morning, nor does it keep you up at night. Some Aquarians chase the big bucks, but I'm convinced it's a game—you'd just as soon hunt for Easter eggs or rare Amazonian centipedes.

You find it crass to show off your toys and baubles, but you've got a basement full of them. And while you don't need any of that stuff, you keep the faith that somehow there will always be enough money to buy as many gadgets and gizmos your little heart could ever desire.

Aquarius in the Spotlight

Aquarius Hero and Diva: Ellen DeGeneres

Aquarius shakes things up, and that's exactly what Ellen has done. By coming out on national TV, she set a precedent, opening the airwaves to a flood of gay characters. By speaking publicly about her relationship with fellow actress Anne Heche, she extinguished the scandals that normally surrounded Hollywood's lesbian liaisons and eroded Hollywood's Don't Ask/Don't Tell policy. Opinionated and political, courageously willing to stand by her principles, this Water Bearer uses humor to make a point—and yes, she does have one!

Aquarius Diva and Hero: Gertrude Stein

She died 23 years before Stonewall, yet Gertrude Stein has become one of the gay community's greatest icons. Ahead of her time (a very Aquarian trait!), she shacked up with her lover, Alice B. Toklas, in 1907 after quitting medical school and moving to Paris. She experimented with unorthodox (also very Aquarian) forms of literature, and she "collected" artists (like Picasso) and writers (like Hemingway) into a community of expatriates. Symbol of individualism, eccentricity, and gay openness (all absolutely Aquarian), Gertrude's life has been even more influential than her work.

Aquarius Hero/Diva: Robin Hood

Did you know Robin Hood was gay? Yep! According to some revisionist historians, the legendary thief was, in fact, "The Forest Queen." In the Robin Hood ballads, the scholars assert, the true love story happens with Little John, not Maid Marian. It does make one rethink that old Disney cartoon, doesn't it? And did you know Robin Hood's zodiac sign? Although his birthday is unknown, all his characteristics strongly qualify him as an Aquarius. Robin Hood, for example, stands out as a defender of principles and icon of unflinching idealism. After all, he robbed from the rich to give to the poor, he formed a band of merry men who lived idyllically in the forest—and he may have pioneered gay rights activism in England!

Aquarius Hero: Greg Louganis

Stereotypes say gay men suck at sports. Not this guy. (Leave it to Aquarius to disprove popular assumptions!) Greg Louganis won four Olympic gold medals and countless other pieces of trophy jewelry for diving. Then he hit his head and leaked blood in the pool, sparking a big scandal over disclosing one's HIV status. (Leave it to Aquarius to stir up issues!) Shucking his Speedos, Greg has gone on to write books, act onstage, and otherwise prove that neither sexual orientation nor AIDS should exclude a person from expressing his talents.

Aquarius Hero: Nathan Lane

Quirky, offbeat, do-their-own-thing Aquarians look for a niche where they can fit in without conforming. That's Nathan Lane, the Broadway star who leapt to the silver screen in movies like *The Birdcage* and *The Lion King* (as the voice of Timon). Flamboyant, campy, and pretty much over the top, he has *swished* his way to fame as an irreplaceable personality. Aquarians also take a stand. That's what Nathan did by officially coming out after Matthew Shepard's brutal killing in 1998.

Gay Pisces

February 19–March 20

The Vicious Stereotype: Sign of the Fairy Princess

Enter Pisces. As slippery as the Tooth Fairy, as bubbly as Glenda the Good, as flighty as Tinker Bell, you live in fantasy land. Sensitive and volatile, you once mistook a bad-hair day for Armageddon. Your diet consists of sugar plums and magic mushrooms, washed down with a bottle of dandelion wine. A true believer, as hazy as the San Fernando Valley, you won't leave your house till your horoscope says so. You'd prefer to ride a unicorn, but until the DMV issues them license plates, you'll settle for a cantankerous Dodge Dart affectionately called *Whizzer.*

Costume:

- lots of chiffon
- plexiglass tiara and glass slippers
- rose-tinted sunglasses

Props:

- magic wand
- fairy dust
- little adorable animals rescued from a forest fire

Opening line: "Honey, I'd love to make all your dreams come true, but I'm so busy having a nervous breakdown."

The Real You

At first glance you may indeed look like someone who did too many drugs in the '60s—and the '70s, '80s, and '90s. A space case, a flower child, a permanent resident of La-La Land, you Fish have acquired a reputation for having your head in the clouds and your feet floating downstream. But is it truth or illusion? With Pisces, one never knows—so let's peek under your rhinestone tiara and find out.

Like Cinderella's fairy godmother, you seem to have a sixth sense for understanding people's problems—and an overpowering urge to rush to their rescue. Friends, family, and the supermarket checker can't stop themselves from confessing to you their deepest, darkest secrets. I doubt they'd do that with a total flake.

If your head occasionally drifts into the clouds, it's probably because you won't settle for the flaws and failings of life down on earth. You look for the magic in life, the miracle of being alive, not the curse of human suffering and calamity of a receding hairline. But if a pot of gold doesn't always greet you at the rainbow's end, it doesn't necessarily mean you'll curl up with a bottle of Valium.

You'd just as soon plunge into *Art.* Opera speaks to your soul. Impressionist paintings heighten your vision. African drums exhilarate your body. You rather enjoy an altered state of consciousness. My Pisces friend Thomas, for example, teaches yoga at Big Sur's Esalen Institute, helping visitors quiet their minds, awaken their spirits, and torture their bodies. They love it.

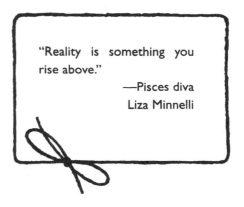

> "Reality is something you rise above."
>
> —Pisces diva Liza Minnelli

If one image defines Pisces, it's the ceiling of the Sistine Chapel, painted by gay Pisces artist Michelangelo. He shows a virtually naked Adam reaching out toward the hand of God. That, my dear Fish, captures the essence of Pisces in a loincloth: You attempt the impossible and yearn for the unattainable. So when your accomplishments fail to live up to expectations, Dr. Matt recommends you give yourself a break: Aim for perfection, but learn to accept what's good *enough.*

According to astrological legend, Pisces is the sign of the martyr. Nowadays it sounds like a dirty word, an epithet for a masochist who suffers needlessly and throws himself to the lions. But originally it meant a hero—not one who conquered, but a religious hero who made great sacrifices for his principles. You'll do the same for your dreams—you'll give whatever it takes to make them come true.

Did you know you inspire people? Most Pisces underestimate their effect on others, but it's true: You help us *believe.* In times of despair, you exude hope. In times of uncertainty, you offer a beacon. To see what I mean, read the poetry of Pisces poet Wilfred Owen. Killed in World War I, he combated war's ugliness with faith and a longing for love of his fellow man.

Supposedly all Pisces are psychic. I don't doubt it. You have amazing hunches and powerful instincts. Even when your own life is going to hell in the express lane, you can still analyze and solve other people's problems. You might not be able to find the missing umbrella, but you can convince us rain is a miracle we ought to enjoy anyway.

So, is gay Pisces really the Fairy Princess? On a good day, hell yes! On a bad day, just a fairy. But one thing's always for sure: Our lives are so much more magical when you wave your wand.

The Secret in Pisces's Closet

What better closet to rummage through than a Pisces's closet? You keep all *sorts* of interesting stuff in there. Among hat boxes and winter wraps, your secrets and skeletons pile up. You love to collect confidential stories and classified information. More important, you tend to hide away whatever you deem too ugly, disturbing, or irksome for the light of day—"Out of sight, out of mind, darling!"

Some secrets, however, might occasionally benefit from a good airing out—your disillusionment, for example. Typically you try to see the best in people. So when they let you down, which they invariably do, you sink into disappointment rather than criticize them.

Why not take off the rose-tinted sunglasses *before* the world turns dark and dismal? Dr. Matt suggests you tell folks what you really think rather than treat them like heroes on pedestals or victims in need of salvation.

> "This is friendship in the finest sense of the word, when you can hardly wait to tell your friend the tiniest details of the past day."
>
> —Pisces actor and author
> Sir Hugh Walpole

Which leads us to another secret: You're sometimes afraid to express yourself. You fear stating an opinion—for what if it's the wrong one? You worry you'll be kicked out of the club. You fret they won't invite you back to the house on Fire Island or the job in Hollywood, so you become *exactly what you think they want you to be*. It's good practice for earning an Oscar, but a bad habit for being your own person.

Will the real Pisces please stand up? Hurrah!

Gay Pisces Growing Up

Gay Pisces are sweet little boys who seem to come from a

distant planet. Growing up, you Pisces kids were hard to catch, harder to pin down. Early in life the typical Pisces child hears a calling, the voice of destiny whispering in his ear. So to friends and family, a part of you must always have seemed far away.

I remember you Pisces brats from junior high and high school, how you seemed to be permanently out to lunch, how you disappeared after school into fantasy lands that belonged to you and you alone, and then how you, at graduation, cleaned up all the awards and honors. What wily little creatures!

To survive the horrors of adolescence, surely you must have depended on a deep faith, a guiding light, or an imaginary friend. Though a bit of a loner, you had no trouble attracting friends and followers, yet the deep intimacy and companionship you craved must have seemed as impossible as catching a Leprechaun.

For you Pisces kids, a big part of growing up is learning to accept yourselves *as you are*, not as you'd like to be. You come to realize your dreams are not impossible—and you eventually sort out dreams you want to make real from dreams you're simply happy to keep dreaming.

Pisces in Love

You kiss a lot of frogs. On your pilgrimage for the perfect partner, you enter love affairs full of hope. So the guy's not rich—you'll survive. So he's shorter than a Ming vase—you'll stoop. So he's got bad body odor—you'll burn incense. All for the love of a man who might, when you kiss him hard enough, turn out to be a prince in disguise.

You're a trusting soul. You believe love will conquer all. You have faith in happy endings. Who am I to criticize? You might be deceiving yourself; then again, you might be thinking positive. Only you and your therapist can answer that one.

> "'Someday my prince will come,' said Snow White, changing hands for the fifth time."
>
> —English saying

What's certain is that it's not enough for you to find the one great love of your life. You also need friends, family, community. You thrive whenever and wherever you find and give love, no matter what its form, whether it's with your lover or your pet iguana.

Mr. Right—Or Is It Mr. Right Now?

For starters, you look for a man who can share your dreams. Even if you two see eye to eye today, the relationship is bound to go astray if you two can't agree on a vision for where it's headed tomorrow. As for a man who disregards dreams altogether, just put him out on the curb with the recycling bins.

That doesn't mean Mr. Right can't hoist you down to earth a wee bit. He's got his act together. Image-conscious but not image-obsessed, he's no flake. He's willing to work hard at making the relationship work. You can trust him completely and put yourself in his hands without fear of being dropped. He provides reassurance.

You also like a man who can cook—and clean, groom the dog, paint the ceiling, and otherwise figure out life's little dilemmas. You're happy to help, but you want to share responsibility as well as rapture. Together you aim to make a home where friends are always welcome and stray cats can take a vacation from the rat race.

Mr. Right sees the relationship as an opportunity for personal growth. Unlike Al Bundy, he doesn't marry you, pop open a can of Budweiser, and grow moldy on the couch. You don't require that he keep his girlish figure forever—but he better not get lazy and stop trying to turn you on.

Pisces in the Sack

Aw, gee. Golly, shucks! You'd prefer we didn't discuss the "S" word, wouldn't you? It's not that you're embarrassed—*hardly!*—but you approach the subject with less directness, more delicacy than Dr. Matt could ever muster.

You're like the blushing bride who isn't blushing out of shyness. You're the master of garter belts and lace stockings, sly smiles and averted glances. You're less of a *Playboy* centerfold than an intriguing and worshipped *Mona Lisa.*

If you're burned out on porn but still want a Pisces-type turn-on, listen to the *Adagio for Strings* by Pisces composer

Samuel Barber. It starts softly, sweetly. It promises and insinuates things to come. It builds and pushes to sheer climax, total release, unbelievable ecstasy. Wow! Who knew *that* was coming? Pisces, of course, but you didn't blurt it out. You save the best for when a man least expects it. It's not a marathon—it's a religious experience, an erotic epiphany.

> Englishmen were dolts and nitwits not to realize that there was better sport than with women."
>
> —16th-century Pisces playwright Christopher Marlowe

Sexually, you prefer two kinds of men: First, the anonymous stranger—the more anonymous the better—onto whom you can project your fantasy of the ideal lover. He's simply an actor in your little *mise-en-scène*.

Your second preference is the intimate companion—the more intimate the better—for whom you care so deeply that you want to give yourself completely. A kiss is *not* just a kiss. It says, "Take me, I'm yours, forever and ever."

For Pisces, you see, sex is no mere physical exercise. It's a vehicle for acting out dreams and articulating feelings. The body is just the paintbrush; the inner experience is the masterpiece.

Pisces's Fame and Fortune

Career

"One cannot walk through a mass-production factory and not feel that one is in Hell," said Pisces poet W. H. Auden. No, you're not an assembly-line kind of guy. You need a career with lots of room to grow and explore. Rarely does a Pisces's personal life stay out of his career, or vice versa. The Pisces author Jack Kerouac, for instance, incorporated his spiritual and philosophical beliefs into his novels such as *On the Road.*

"All Pisces," says my former astrology teacher, Joe Polis, "have some gift they must learn to use or share. And they must participate in something larger than themselves." That's right—you've got an itch to leave the world a better place than you found it.

But it's not always so easy to scratch that itch. You have to find your gift, develop it, make a living with it, and prevent it from monopolizing your life. Remember, it's better to start small than never to start at all.

You thrive in a people-centered, positive-attitude workplace. If negativity prevails or the bottom line dominates, you'll melt faster than the Wicked Witch of the West. Following a Yellow Brick Road to some grand lofty goal keeps you so much more motivated.

Money Matters

To some Pisces, money is a devil; to others, a god. Whichever camp you fall into, if you're a Fish, money is a subject you can't seem to ignore, no matter how hard you probably try.

If you number among those Fish who regard money as evil, you'd like money to just go away—and it does, disappearing as fast as you can earn it, sometimes faster. Sticking up for your financial welfare doesn't come easy, and you'd gladly leave the ledgers to someone else's care, maybe someone who doesn't care for your best interest. You hate the way money negatively impacts society, and you resent the gulf between rich and poor—like why can't everybody just share? You'd donate your last dime to feed a hungry pigeon. But as much as you try to forget about wicked, sinful moolah, it has a nasty habit of reminding you it's there—but never enough of it.

If, on the other hand, you're a Pisces who worships money, the quest for wealth drives your life. Money, it seems, paves the road to happiness. You're no Scrooge, but you make gargantuan sacrifices to maintain a certain lifestyle—a lifestyle that doesn't involve pushing a grocery cart and sleeping on a Central Park bench. You try to heal your wounds, and those of loved ones, with a miraculous mantra called "Charge it!"

Over a lifetime, of course, Pisces's relationship with money may alternate between worship and dread. Then, if you're lucky and savvy, you get over it. As far as finances are concerned, you have a little faith, a little practicality, and you banish the gods and devils from your mind.

Pisces in the Spotlight

Pisces Diva: Barbie

Can a doll have a sign? This one does! According to her manufacturer, Barbie's official birthday makes her a Pisces. It makes sense: Barbie exemplifies the fantasy element of the Fish. She's an ideal, a dream, larger than life yet smaller than a poodle. A peculiar but indisputable icon of the gay community, Barbie symbolizes our fascination with mainstream culture—and also our mockery of it. Did you know that all the world's Barbie dolls sold since 1959 would circle the earth more than *seven* times?!

Pisces Diva: Elizabeth Taylor

Early in her career, Liz personified the Pisces tension between beautiful fantasy and bitter reality. A child star, she achieved fame and fortune effortlessly—or so it seemed. Meanwhile, the tabloids turned her stormy personal life into a media circus. The world leered as she rapidly changed husbands and dress sizes (was she on a Pisces quest for the ideal mate and perfect body?). Later in life, she has expressed the Pisces urge to end human suffering, exploiting her media spotlight to found and fund two major AIDS foundations.

Pisces Diva: Liza Minnelli

"I am a most strangely extraordinary person," says Liza Minnelli as Sally Bowles in the gay cult film *Cabaret.* For the role she won an Oscar by lending it some of her Pisces mystique: Liza's Sally accepts everyone. Her eyes are big and open to everything. She covers up her pain by chasing dreams of stardom and romantic bliss. A daughter of Judy Garland, a lover of Mikhail Baryshnikov, the real Liza has led her own strangely extraordinary life.

Pisces Hero: Michelangelo

If you want to understand the essence of gay Pisces, study the life and work of Michelangelo, the Italian Renaissance artist. A typical Pisces dreamer, this sculptor of *David* literally tried to force fantasy into reality with his bare hands. His art, according to many critics, shows the human soul imprisoned in the flesh, struggling to break free. Also characteristic of his sign, Michelangelo wrestled with his faith, trying to reconcile Christian ideals with Greco-Roman humanism and the political turmoil of his time. Besides his visual art, check out his often homoerotic poetry.

Pisces Hero: Christopher Marlowe

Pisces is the sign of dreamers; nevertheless, many gay Fish are men of action. Take the spy, playwright, and all-around inconoclast Christopher Marlowe (Rupert Everett's character in *Shakespeare in Love*). Killed at age 29 in a tavern brawl, Marlowe often got into trouble by criticizing religion, claiming Jesus and St. John were lovers, and overindulging in booze, boys, and tobacco. Likewise, his heroes in plays like *Dr. Faustus* show a Pisces urge to transcend normal human boundaries. Four hundred years ago, his play *Edward II* dealt openly with homosexuality—and with the Fishy theme of clinging to one's love and beliefs in a hostile, misunderstanding world.

Pisces Hero: Edward Albee

A private person who doesn't like to be put in a box, he'd probably prefer we not call him a *hero* or *gay*, but this Pisces playwright is too juicy to ignore. There's no more Pisces play or movie than *Who's Afraid of Virginia Woolf?*, a psychological thriller that dissolves inhibitions and shatters illusions. Other Albee plays—like *Zoo Story* and *A Delicate Balance*—deal with Pisces themes of *reaching out* to connect deeply with another human being, which never quite succeeds in Albee's world. Not completely dismal, Albee combines Theatre of the Absurd with the Fish's sense of humor to create some unbelievably funny scenes where you don't know if you want to laugh or cry.

Part Two

The Stars in Action

Act One
Seduce Any Stud in the Universe

From across the room you see him. Your eyes soak him up like gravy in a fluffy biscuit. You want him *bad.* But does he return your gaze? *Noooo,* of course not. He's cool. He's coy. His smirk says, "I know you want me but you can't have me."

What can you do? Go home frustrated? Stalk him like the love-starved psycho in *Fatal Attraction?* No, there's a better way. There's an art to seduction. No one's impervious to Cupid's arrow—you just have to know where to stick it. That is, figure out his astrological soft spots.

How can you break the ice? Where can you take him to butter him up? What turns him on and drives him wild? First, figure out his sign. Then let the stars lead you to nights of endless pleasure—or whatever you're into.

Aries

Break the Ice: Go for it! Really—just go up and crack

the ice with a sledgehammer. Mr. Aries can't wait around while your courage dillydallies. Flex your muscles. Flaunt your desire. Then again, play the role of damsel in distress—he'll rush to rescue you from the jaws of death or your ex. This stud fantasizes he's wearing a big belt with lots of notches, so even though *you're* the seducer, let Aries believe it's *his* conquest.

Butter Him Up: Excitement—that's the ticket. Don't take three hours to make plans or primp. He wants a good time *now.* Think of *interactive* dates—like a jumping-and-screaming rock concert, not a sit-and-stare symphony You've got to stay up pretty late at night to catch an Aries stud, so be prepared to burn the midnight oil.

> "Skill makes love unending."
> —Pisces Roman poet Ovid

To get up his dander, start an argument—a friendly but feisty little spat over, say, the difference between *magenta* and *fuchsia.*

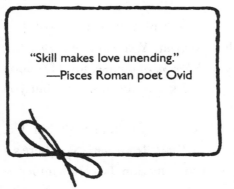

Drive Him *Wild:* Don't be afraid to get dirty. Mr. Aries expects the bed to burn more calories than the Stairmaster—so sweat, baby, *sweat!* Taunt him with the adrenaline rush of *almost* getting caught. Passion works wonders, too. Grab him the minute he walks through the door. Don't bother undressing or turning down the sheets. Look, if you exude enough raw sexuality and scream, "It's never been this good before!" then you've got your Aries stud where it counts.

"To me, passionate love has always been like a tight shoe rubbing blisters on my Achilles heel."

—Sagittarian actor and writer Noël Coward

Taurus

Break the Ice: Mosey on over. He doesn't know it, but this stud needs to be jostled out of self-satisfaction. Break down resistance with lascivious, conspiratorial glances from across a crowded room. Buy him a drink. Buy him flowers. Buy him *something*. Then he'll *know* you mean business. You'll have to do all the talking—at first. Keep him entertained—he's a receptive audience. And don't get discouraged—Mr. Taurus won't salivate in public, but that doesn't mean he isn't knock-kneed with lust.

Butter Him Up: A loaf of bread, a jug of wine, and Taurus. A gourmet dinner arouses him. So do satin sheets and expensive cologne. A leisurely trip to the countryside puts this down-home hunk in the mood for the birds and the bees. Ask him to slow dance—even in a noisy, crowded club. Score big points by *anticipating* his desires before he has to ask. He's casual, so let him put up his feet.

Drive Him *Wild:* If it feels good, do it! Make slow, rhythmic motions that start out innocent and become ever more erotic. Let him run his fingers through your hair or rub up against your fuzzy sweater. Stock up on plenty of toys and lotions. Edible undies might do the trick. Whatever you do, get good at it. And don't forget to cuddle in the morning—no "Wham, bam, thank you, ma'ams."

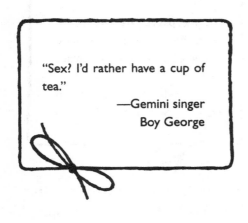

"Sex? I'd rather have a cup of tea."

—Gemini singer
Boy George

Gemini

Break the Ice: Bewilder him—he'll *have* to investigate. Keep his curiosity *piqued.* A wicked twinkle in your eye wouldn't hurt either. Joke with him, flirt with him, play with him—only then can you have him (and then only *maybe*). Direct, frontal assaults totally flop. Roll with the punches. Since Geminis are so damn handy, give this sly stud something to keep his fingers busy while your smooth moves and clever one-liners catch him off guard.

Butter Him Up: Make a plan—then *don't* stick to it. You've got to keep him on his toes. Surprise Mr. Gemini. Try dates that distract him from the stress of his workaday routine—but nothing too serene. Crowds turn him on. So does youthful vigor. Don't be such an *adult*—consider carnival rides and sitting in Santa's lap. Stay up all night talking, till his mouth waters with yearning and he finally fills it with more than hot air.

Drive Him *Wild*: Tease him to please him. Digress from one erogenous zone to the next, discovering them all, satisfying none—*yet*. Monotony is not an option. Go fast, then slow. Make it hot, then cold. Talk dirty, then sweet. Use your mouth, hands, elbows—all of it. Pry into his fantasies and act them out. If you can't figure out what turns him on, by all means ask. Talking about it will quickly become his favorite form of oral sex.

Cancer

Break the Ice: If he's not in the mood, then he's *not* in the mood. Oh well. You can still break the ice now and break his heart later. Put him at ease. Coax him out of his shell. He won't drop his armor and fire extinguisher till he feels tingles deep inside. So be gentle. Open up your life without clinging like static electricity. Show a little vulnerability, or at least a dose of humanity. Be emotionally available. Play the strong, silent type—but you can still throw in a pathetic puppy dog face that says, "Take me! I'm yours."

Butter Him Up: Intimate dates work best. One night of

perfect bliss has to seem it could last forever—even for strangers passing in the night. If you want to light a fire in his heart, light a nice cozy fire in the fireplace. Slip some money in the jukebox and play an old sad song. Show him stuff—your high-school yearbook, Coke bottle collection, your . . . well, you'll think of something. Make him aware of desires he doesn't even know he has.

Drive Him *Wild*: Mr. Cancer listens to body language. So shut up and let your fingers do the walking and talking. As you plant a kiss on his lips, cradle his head in your hands. Tenderness scores big points—*then* you can have your way with him all you like. Take turns playing dominant and submissive—sometimes he feels like a slave, sometimes he don't. Whimper and tremble—he likes the idea that sex with him disarms a guy. But absolutely stop yourself from screaming out the name of your ex-boyfriend.

Leo

Break the Ice: Admire him from afar. Laugh at his jokes. Be effusive. Mr. Leo does *not* want to believe your dance card has room for anyone else. And don't be a cheapskate—better to give him a single picture-perfect rose than a dozen wilting daisies. Stuck for conversation? Ask lots of questions about *him*. Above all, he's got to believe you'll respect him in the morning.

Butter Him Up: Forget a date—this stud needs an *event.*

He'll gladly sacrifice spontaneity in favor of telling his friends he has a hot date Friday night three weeks from now. Turn any occasion into a celebration. Dramatic gestures strike his fancy—so go ahead, order the limo. *However,* expensive yet impersonal gifts fall flat. And don't forget to turn off the cell phone or you'll turn *him* off.

> "Sex is more exciting on the screen and between the pages than between the sheets."
>
> —Leo artist Andy Warhol

Drive Him *Wild:* Treat him like a sex symbol. Use props—and never forget this is a *tour de force* performance. Whistle and catcall as his clothes fall to the floor—don't worry, he doesn't embarrass easily. Never let him feel inadequate—*unless* you give him the opportunity to disprove it. Leos love gambling and games of chance, so challenge him to a friendly yet high-stakes game of strip poker or spin the bottle. Whatever you do, don't say his G-string makes him look fat.

Virgo

Break the Ice: Mr. Virgo won't succumb to just any come-on line or come-hither expression. He expects a *proper* seduction—no shortcuts allowed. Keep it clean—with just a smidgen of smutty innuendo. Compliment his appearance—but only if you explain *exactly* why he's all that. Pay attention to details—he notices *everything*. Make a fuss. Does he want a cherry in his martini, extra foam on his cappuccino? If all else fails, talk him into the seduction—he can't resist a good excuse.

Butter Him Up: He'll play hard to get—it's not mean, he's simply assessing how far you'll go to get him. Build trust by doing what you say you'll do. Definitely make reservations. To Virgo, chivalry never died. Open the door for him. Let him order first. Avoid too much down time—this stud needs a plan and hates to squander a good time looking for parking. Does he need perking up? Pick his brain. Ask for advice—it's his ultimate flattery.

Drive Him *Wild:* Concentrate! Mr. Virgo takes sex seriously and can't stand a lover whose mind wanders from the matter at hand. Make a big deal about undressing. Try a little false modesty—it'll give him the challenge he needs to "corrupt" you (a pleasant role reversal). Don't ignore any part of his body—it all begs for attention. When the deed is done, compare notes on what felt good—he'll gladly give you a blow-by-blow progress report. Make sure he knows you're pleased. If you're not, he'll try, try again till you can't take any more.

Libra

Break the Ice: Sweep him off his feet. He responds well to corny tactics like big-toothed grins and Broadway love songs. Even while he rolls his eyes he eats it up. Stay cool. This seduction mustn't look like hard work—and don't put him on the spot in a big social gathering. He thrives on one-on-one, and hopefully you'll be the *one.* Forget the K-Y jelly—what really lubricates this stud is charm and the sparks that fly from a close connection.

> "We must reckon with the possibility that something in the nature of the sexual instinct itself is unfavorable to the realization of complete satisfaction."
>
> —Gemini psychiatrist Sigmund Freud—probably not gay, but you never know

Butter Him Up: He just can't get enough when you can't get enough of *him.* Play footsie under the table. Tell him you missed him, even after a trip to the men's room. On the town, don't treat the waiter or bartender like a slave—Mr. Libra *won't* be impressed. Don't freak when he can't make up his mind what movie to see. You'll win him over with an attitude of, "I'll do anything as long as you're with me." And don't worry if the date flops—this boy loves to kiss and make up.

Drive Him *Wild:* Don't go straight for the crotch. Instead, adore his toes, his earlobe, another underappreciated piece of anatomy. The ambience matters. Is the bed made? Is the lighting right? Tune into his responses. Give him total pleasure without any thought of your own. Don't worry, he'll return the favor. He might even enjoy a little friendly competition to see who can please whom more. Forget the trophy—he's triumphant with just your *oohs*, *ahhs*, and happy sighs.

Scorpio

Break the Ice: Make more than small talk. Match his intensity level. And if at first his ice won't crack, don't give up—this stud appreciates stamina. An air of mystery intrigues him. Don't promise the impossible, but it wouldn't hurt to hint you've got a mind-altering, life-transforming event in store for him. A little jealousy goes a long way—not too much but just enough to make yourself a hot property. Anymore than that and he may burst.

Butter Him Up: It doesn't have to be taboo or illegal, but show him a good time that he dares not divulge to his friends. Then again, taboo and illegal work, too. He values resourcefulness and potency—so mastermind a table with a view or backstage tickets to meet a celebrity. Don't play games—he'll forgive many flaws, but not deceit. Stop trying to figure out what he's thinking—just ask.

Drive Him *Wild:* Don't let him enjoy his prize all at once. He relishes a challenge and adores the taste of forbidden fruit. Dare him to go a little farther each time. Make him *work* to get you out of your skivvies. Wear him out—then make him beg for more. Try using blindfolds—as a power queen, Mr. Scorpio's titillated by the chance to both control and capitulate. Suddenly stop and say you can't take anymore—he'll find a way to *make* you take it.

Sagittarius

Break the Ice: Give a penny for his thoughts. Mr. Saj always has something on his mind. If it's got him down, let him wallow for two and a half minutes. Then change the subject and cheer him up. You'll quickly discover his happy topics. Then again, make yourself the topic—Saj loves to unravel a person like a ball of yarn. Let him get into your head. Meanwhile, act totally fascinated by him. Saj wants adventure, and if you can go there, he'll board your ship.

Butter Him Up: Whisk him off on a spontaneous assignation. Dump the car and hop on a train, hot-air balloon, or tandem bike. A big no-no is any date where he feels trapped—like your mother's house in the burbs without a getaway car. Honesty's the best policy—not polite dinner conversation about the weather. Urge him to exchange his big words for four-letter words. He's a sucker for dirty jokes, so make him laugh all the way to the bedroom.

Drive Him *Wild:* More is better, so take a disco nap beforehand and forget about watching *Saturday Night Live.* Drop your inhibitions at the door. Push the limits of arousal. Turn him on by showing him a new position, teaching him a new technique. He'll teach you a few things too, so be an eager pupil. If you want to keep him, don't you *dare* do exactly what you did last night. Introduce him to a new partner—the UPS driver, the naughty student, any role you can play.

Capricorn

Break the Ice: Play by the rules. He wants you to *deserve* the pleasure of his company. Act smart—not a smart aleck, mind you, but sophisticated. Know who you are, know what you're doing, know what you want. Keep trying; he expects you to *work* for the seduction. *He* would. Don't put him in an awkward situation—predatory chicken hawks need not apply. And don't be intimidated—this serious stud's dying for you to tickle his funny bone.

Butter Him Up: Go to some trouble. Get dressed up. Impress the hell out of him—but don't bother trying to *buy* his love. He can't feel cheap or used—then he'll freak and flee. Don't criticize—he takes it too hard. Discuss important issues, and be on top of current affairs. This stud needs to feel he matters in the world. Silliness and sarcasm will flunk out, but you get straight A's for wit and cleverness. Let him flaunt his *savoir faire* by ordering the wine or ordering you to strip.

Drive Him *Wild:* Shoot for quality, not quantity. It's no cinch, but coax him into a sense of wild abandon. Encourage him to relax and let loose. A strong yet soothing massage, for example, will get the kinks out of his joints and into your bed. Rejection terrifies this boy, so be polite when refusing to let him stick something somewhere you don't think it should go. Since he's so goal-oriented, you could offer him prizes commensurate with performance.

Aquarius

Break the Ice: Let him *like* you before he loves you. So approach him as a potential date, not a mate. Even for the quickest quickie, friendship comes first. Pander to his interests, talking shop, using the jargon. This cerebral stud has strong convictions—don't make him compromise his principles. By all means accept him 100 percent as is, but never let him think you think he's ordinary. Show him the ways you're so much more than what meets the eye.

> "Sex is the last refuge of the miserable."
>
> —Sagittarius author and eccentric Quentin Crisp

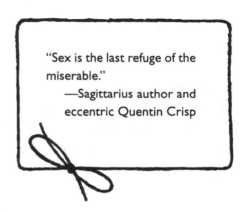

Butter Him Up: Take him on creative dates, not the first place that springs to mind—original thinking scores big. Wow him, like a sudden summer thunderstorm. He gets off on fun events with a higher ulterior purpose, so consider a date that benefits humanity, like a charity ball or soaking up knowledge at a museum. Let him "convert" you to a love of modern art, Mozart, or nudism.

Drive Him *Wild:* Choose bizarre moments to get it on. And don't just lie there! This democratic lover needs a full-participation partner. Every time has to be like the first time—as if discovering an act no one's ever done before. Try phone or cybersex. Make a home movie. Technology turns him on—and so does the chance to stretch his imagination.

Pisces

Break the Ice: Expose yourself—not your tan line but your soul. Tug on his heartstrings; make him feel a little sorry for you. Need his help. It also helps to overcome insurmountable odds to be with him—he'll feel touched and indebted. Don't think you have to fill every minute with talk. Allow a few moments for quietly staring into each other's eyes and letting those shivery things run up and down your back.

Butter Him Up: Share simple experiences. Don't overlook the romantic possibilities of a trip to the grocery store. Pamper each other. Invite him—and yourself, for that matter—to get pedicures or your palms read. Take him to secluded places like the seashore, out-of-the-way cafes, or other venues that bring out his inner poet. Fall under his spell. Let him tell you what he believes in.

Drive Him *Wild:* Leave something to his imagination. He doesn't want sex to be totally natural, healthy, and clinical. And don't poke fun when he reveals his deepest, darkest fetishes. This stud goes ga-ga for any sensation that sends him to La-La Land, where he completely lets go and only *feels.* Take him to the edge—and leave him there. Then do it again—and again. Dress up, or down, as his favorite fantasy character. Share your fantasies with him—they might become his, too! Wake him up and tell him what you dreamed.

An Appetite for Aphrodisiacs

If your powers of seduction are feeling rusty (as opposed to feeling *up* Rusty), perhaps you need some oral stimuli to get your man in the mood. So before you reach for his zipper, reach for a fork. Like the magic fairy dust in Shakespeare's *A Midsummer Night's Dream*, these foods will work like aphrodisiacs, cranking up his hormones. The word *aphrodisiac*, by the way, has an astrological origin, coming from "Aphrodite," the Greek name for Venus, goddess and planet of love and pleasure.

Aries

Red hot chile peppers (make his tongue beg for relief)

Taurus

Grapes (feed him one by one, or with a whole fist)
Fresh artichokes (eaten layer by layer, like a slow striptease)

Gemini

Nuts (big or small varieties, he likes the challenge of getting inside)
Whole grains (he doesn't want to miss a thing)

Cancer

Creamy dairy foods (mmm, it's like buttah!)
Oysters (gets him in the mood for swallowing without biting)

Leo

Mango (hard to eat but worth it—just don't choke on the pit)

Honey (sticky, sweet—did you know it's bee vomit?)

Virgo

Potatoes (Mash them! Whip them! Serve them!)

Carrots (What's *up*, doc?)

Eggplant (What do you do with it? Figuring out is half the fun.)

Libra

Berries (pluck them while they're ripe and enjoy with cream)

Spearmint (double your pleasure, double your fun)

Scorpio

Garlic (It won't keep this vamp away.)

Red wine (roll it around on the tongue)

Toasted marshmallows, or other on-fire foods, like crêpes Suzette (romantic, yet very hot and dangerous)

Sagittarius

Olive oil (tell him it's extra virgin, even if that is a lie)

Lime (preferably wedged on a tall glass alongside an umbrella)

Capricorn

Red meat (sink his teeth into fresh flesh)

Pasta (slurping spaghetti builds a strong jaw)

Aquarius

kumquats (he's got to swallow it whole)

Kiwi fruit (hairy, seedy, and strange—just like the bar where you met)

Pisces

Melon (slap it to see if it's ripe)

Fish (not just for lesbians anymore)

Cucumber (Isn't it obvious?)

Act Two

"You Oughta Be Committed!" Making the Love Last

I remember the first time I heard about a "commitment ceremony" at my synagogue. I pictured a nice, innocent member of our congregation standing on the *bima*, or altar, while three butch nurses strapped him into a strait-jacket and dragged the poor fellow to a pink padded room amid cheers of *mazel tov*—sort of like that final scene in *A Streetcar Named Desire* where, thanks to the kindness of strangers, Blanche DuBois is committed to the insane asylum.

Fortunately, someone quickly explained that these ceremonies celebrated long-term relationships, not psychiatric commitment, and that they allowed the loving couple to register for entire rooms full of free gifts from Crate & Barrel and Bloomingdale's.

Who knows if we'll ever be able to get married for real, with a license, health benefits, and prenup agreement. Clearly the nutcases who really ought to be committed—the talking heads on Capitol Hill who repudiate gay marriage—haven't realized we're capable of loving, lasting relationships and family values without filing a joint tax return.

But marriage or no marriage, among homos or heteros, whether totally committed or sexually open, relationships are as challenging as they are fulfilling, and keep thousands of therapists employed while we whimper about the men who ignore us and smother us. One of those therapists, my friend Nadya Giusi in Carmel, California, could save us all some time on the couch: "My definition of a good relationship, *any* good relationship, is simple," she says. "It's a relationship where everybody gets to be himself." So true, yet so hard to put into practice.

That's where astrology can help. Without judgment, it acknowledges that everybody's got issues—and what kinds of issues we'll likely encounter with the men we love on the path to better, more intimate relationships. So before you start fighting over who gets to wear the wedding dress at the commitment ceremony, check his sign in this chapter. Because love is a terrible thing to waste—and the faster you get serious about this relationship stuff, the faster you can register for a Cuisinart and new silverware.

Aries

Potential Issue Number One: In the beginning of your romance with Mr. Aries, he came on hot and heavy. Now he acts remote and indifferent. He insists on doing his own thing, refusing to cooperate. Is this a relationship, or what?

Working It Out: Don't take it personally. Your Aries man needs his autonomy, and your relationship—*any* relationship—could threaten his independence, causing him to "defend" himself with distance and/or superiority. Discuss with him how much togetherness and how much "apartness" each of you needs. Assure him you don't intend to squelch his unique identity.

Potential Issue Number Two: He gets hung up on who's in charge of the relationship. His way is always the best way. Overly confrontational, he's not happy till he "wins" in every situation.

Working It Out: Help him understand that if *either* of you loses, you *both* lose—that's the glory of love. Why does anyone have to take charge? Look for opportunities to share decisions, but let him make a few on his own so he knows he hasn't been put out to pasture.

Potential Issue Number Three: If there's not a problem, he creates one. Addicted to stress, he blows petty things out of proportion. When you try to lend a helping hand, he rejects it.

Working It Out: Without realizing it, Mr. Aries sometimes needs to be in the eye of a storm to feel good about himself and his ability to cope. Make sure he gets plenty of strokes, even when he may not *appear* to need them. When and if he ever needs your help, don't use it as a chance to make him feel small—there aren't enough vacuum pumps in West Hollywood to pump up *his* deflated ego.

Taurus

Potential Issue Number One: He resists change—even change for the better. When you move in, for example, he refuses to throw out his old toaster in favor of your newer one, and you're stuck with burned toast.

Working It Out: Introduce changes *gradually.* For example, place the two toasters side by side; eventually he'll see the light and prefer toast that doesn't make his gums bleed. Even under the best circumstances, relationships—especially in the early stages—generate stress. Sympathize with your Taurus man's need to feel his whole world isn't crumbling.

Potential Issue Number Two: The relationship stagnates. The passion goes kaput. Nothing's really *wrong*—but what happened to the good times?

Working It Out: Your Taurus man has not turned into a big boring oaf—it's just that when he finds a good thing, like your relationship, he holds on for dear life, occasionally choking the life out of it. Maybe he fears you'll find other men more "hunkalicious." Or perhaps he doesn't want to seem too needy. Security is the key. The more secure he feels in the relationship, the more chances he'll take—so break out the leather whips and feather boas.

Potential Issue Number Three: He's possessive. He limits the time you spend out of the relationship and keeps track of your every move.

Working It Out: If he's acting like this, Mr. Taurus probably fears you're like all the other guys: here one day, gone the next, only a fair-weather friend. So if you're here to stay, say so. Better yet, put it in writing. Register for domestic partnership or protect each other with legal documents like a will. What's more, it might help to explain, "We're connected but free." Then break into a chorus of "You Don't Own Me."

> "I expected to be frightened on my wedding night, but nothing like *this*."
>
> —*Invasion of the Saucer Man* (1957 film)

Gemini

Potential Issue Number One: He's too busy. He can't squeeze you into his calendar. Even when he promises to be with you, he shows up late, or not at all.

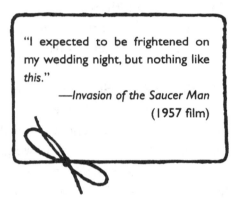

Working It Out: This is a toughie. Don't think you're the first who's had to beg Mr. Gemini to come home in time for dinner—you may have to go ahead and eat without him. More important, communicate very directly what means a lot to you as a couple. You can't control his time (he'll revolt!), but you *can* say you want his company on your birthday or anniversary—and how hurt you'll be without it.

Potential Issue Number Two: He avoids conflict, or any other unpleasant yet inevitable by-product of couplehood. So problems don't get resolved.

Working It Out: Stay calm. Don't kick and shout. Hissy fits will only alienate Mr. Gemini further. But that does not mean you should accept an unwillingness to deal with tough stuff. Instead of withdrawing, find your voice. Tell the truth, and say exactly what you need his help with confronting and resolving. Don't be abstract—decide together on a specific plan for improving the situation. When he sees conflicts reaching resolution without the world ending, he'll gladly stop avoiding and start dealing.

Potential Issue Number Three: He runs hot and cold. One day you two are Romeo and Juliet, the next you're Punch and Judy. Does this relationship have a strong, consistent foundation, or is it totally superficial?

Working It Out: No relationship has the same emotional "temperature" every day. But it's nice to have *some* predictability, consistency, and depth. Ask Mr. Gemini to give you that—he might even learn to appreciate it himself. And refuse to play "mind reader." If your Gemini partner seems preoccupied, don't worry it's your fault. If it is, he needs to say so. No, you can't change your lover; he is who he is. But you can teach him a few new tricks. With Gemini, teach active listening skills. Model those skills yourself—and let Gemini know how much it matters to share the microphone.

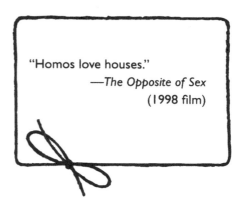

> "Homos love houses."
>
> —*The Opposite of Sex* (1998 film)

Cancer

Potential Issue Number One: When you're up, he's down. When he's up, you're down. It seems one person always has to be strong; the other, weak and dependent.

Working It Out: While "Big Daddy" and "Boy Toy" roles promote a lot of fun between the sheets, they present problems in a long-term relationship of equals. It's really important for both of you to be peers, and not to get caught in power struggles. Don't let him get away with always being the one who soothes your frazzled nerves while he cleverly hides his own.

Potential Issue Number Two: He doubts your love. He requires constant proof of how much you care, like: "If you don't skip work on my birthday, clearly you don't love me." Why is he so needy, and why can't he trust you more?

Working It Out: Realize you can't solve Cancer's insecurity. If he feels empty, don't imagine you can fill him up. But you can tell him what he's feeling is OK—as long as he doesn't suffocate you with it. You can also assure him you won't abandon him. Don't just turn off—he'll escalate, or simply leave because he feared you'd leave first. Instead, open a dialogue about his neediness, why it makes you nervous, and how you can enjoy each other's company without so much anxiety. For bonus points: Spoon with him at night!

Potential Issue Number Three: One day he's fine. The next he clams up. He broods, he pouts, but he won't say what's wrong. Anything you say or do seems to trigger his hurt and hurtful silence.

Working It Out: Quite often, Cancer men fear their feelings. *What's wrong with me?* he may wonder. *Why do I feel this way?* If so, he probably fears *you* will fear his feelings even more. Convince him he's wrong—you're not afraid of his feelings but you need him to manage them. Use a light touch. Keep it casual. Don't beg him to spill his guts, but encourage openness. Let him express sadness, disappointment, frustration, without it being a big deal. By all means, try to cheer him up, but don't fall into a habit of always "fixing" his mood. As he learns to trust you more, Mr. Cancer will forgo brooding in favor of bonding.

Leo

Potential Issue Number One: Drama! He overreacts. He has a cow. A simple disagreement turns into a hair-pulling, claw-baring brawl à la Alexis and Krystal in the lily pond.

Working It Out: Leos often feel nobody will listen if they don't *dramatize.* But you can pull the plug on his drama-queen antics by giving him your attention before it's too late. Then, too, you can realize many of his outbursts and other shenanigans simply go with his personality—and that's what you love about him. Still, you can set boundaries on how long you're willing to let the show go on.

> "The only queer people are those who don't love anybody."
>
> —Sagittarian author Rita Mae Brown, speaking at the 1982 Gay Games

Potential Issue Number Two: He's demanding and high maintenance. He pushes you to care more, love more passionately, do more for him. If he's not having a good time, you pay the price. Who's the star of this show, anyhow?

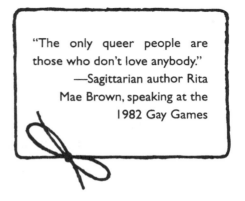

Working It Out: With his big personality, your Leo partner may occasionally forget that a relationship involves relating to another *person*, not to mirror, mirror, on the wall. By all means, pander to his needs—but not to the detriment of your own. A healthy relationship requires 50/50 participation. Discuss what you think is fair for him to expect from you. Reassure him he needn't go to great lengths to get your attention or help.

Potential Issue Number Three: He makes decisions that affect you without consulting you first. He calls the shots. He won't tolerate advice, criticism, or even the subtlest reminder to zip his fly.

Working It Out: Many of Mr. Leo's issues result from his fear of failure. Does he hog all the decisions because he lacks confidence in your ability to make them? Does he control the relationship because he worries it will flop? Kindly explore such possibilities. And speak up! Leo abhors a vacuum—and rushes to fill it. If you considerately seize power, he might just let you have it. One word of caution: Leos like to play around and joke around, so you two may humorously tease one another quite a lot. Great! But check in often to ensure Leo isn't actually feeling wounded by the ridicule.

Virgo

Potential Issue Number One: He nags and criticizes. He puts himself down, and he puts you down, too.

Working It Out: Refuse to enter a vicious cycle of finding each other's faults. Instead, encourage mutual acceptance. If he trusts that you accept him, warts and all, then maybe he'll learn to accept himself. And that paves the way to his accepting you, too. Also, when he criticizes, let him know what you regard as helpful, constructive criticism, and what feels more like *destructive* criticism.

Potential Issue Number Two: He's devoted to other responsibilities, not to you. "Sorry, I have to work late tonight," he says. "Sorry, I have to take my third cousin Betty to the doctor for her fourth face-lift." He's such a good Boy Scout—yet you feel neglected.

Working It Out: Early in your relationship, Mr. Virgo probably worked hard at courting you and catering to your needs, like an eager employee seeking a promotion. Now that he's been "promoted" to being your partner, he may feel other obligations and priorities command more of his attention. Some of that's OK—he needs to feel competent in many spheres. But don't shy away from telling him honestly how he can keep the relationship running smoothly. When he screws up, give him a chance to fix the problem before you blow up. He wants to do a good job!

Potential Issue Number Three: It's unfair! The relationship seems lopsided. One of you—it doesn't matter which one—always cleans the house while the other soaks in the bath. One of you isn't doing his fair share, and you fight about it.

Working It Out: Often without noticing it, Mr. Virgo gets caught in what are called transactional relationships—he keeps score, quid pro quo: "*If* you take out the trash, *then* I'll rub your feet." So encourage your Virgo partner to throw away the tally sheet. Good relationships involve give and take. Neither person does all the giving or taking. Don't blame Mr. Virgo, and don't let him blame you. Grown-ups don't blame, they sit down and resolve the problem. Think of a team—rather than a "who's the boss?"—relationship.

Libra

Potential Issue Number One: Everything's hunky-dory—but it's not. You ask how he's doing, and with a big bogus smile he merely says, "Fine." Your efforts at greater intimacy go nowhere fast.

Working It Out: Encourage your Libra man to tell you what's going on—like what's *really* going on, even if it hurts to talk about it. Frequently, these guys appear to let anger and anguish slide off like whipped cream from a hot fudge sundae, but behind that sweetly stoic facade, their resentment mounts. So inspire honesty. Share your life, the bad with the good. Together you can learn to ride the ups and downs.

Potential Issue Number Two: He promises too much, then fails to deliver. He shies away from rocking the boat—so the boat never goes anywhere.

Working It Out: With Mr. Libra, it's vital to establish an environment where it's OK to say no, to tell the truth, whatever. Yet even in the midst of fiercely open negotiations, he needs to know you still love each other, so avoid storming out and threatening divorce. Help him get comfortable with rocking the boat by assuring him the boat won't sink!

> "If you want to sacrifice the admiration of many men for the criticism of one, go ahead, get married."
>
> —Taurus actress Katharine Hepburn

Potential Issue Number Three: When you two met, your Libra man was independent, capable, and self-reliant. Now he's suddenly helpless without you. He needs help deciding whether to order the fish or the chicken. Maybe he even wants you to stick up for him.

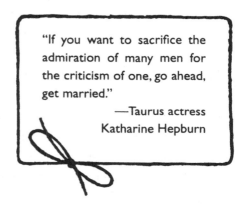

Working It Out: Don't attack! Remember, he wants balance too, but may not always know how to achieve it. Remaining diplomatic, point out what you see as the problem. Make him aware of how lopsided the relationship feels, and invite him to take responsibility for decisions. Yes, you can support him without coddling him.

Scorpio

Potential Issue Number One: He seethes with jealousy. He resents your friends—and maybe your family, too.

Working It Out: Gently remind him that no person, not even a "dream lover," can be all things to another human being. This info might devastate him, but he'll get over it. As for the jealousy, it might help if, once in a while, you acted jealous too, just to reinforce how much you really do want him. Whatever you do, talk about it—unspoken issues that fester beneath the surface are bad news for Scorpio relationships.

Potential Issue Number Two: He's controlling. He gives unsolicited directions, for example, on how to land a promotion or deal with your mother. Or he tells you how you should, or should not, spend your money or your time.

Working It Out: Ask him to stop. Tell him you appreciate the expertise and experience he can offer, and when you need it, you'll ask for it. Don't start a battle over who knows best. Explain that you have your own style, and you'd like the chance to make your own mistakes—and successes. If money's an issue, decide in advance who pays for what (including savings and investments), and as for the rest, you get to spend your money however your little heart desires.

Potential Issue Number Three: When the relationship started, you and Mr. Scorpio were very close. Now you're drifting. He seems separate and remote from the relationship.

Working It Out: Create rituals together. It could be big, like a commitment ceremony with all your friends present. Or it could be simple, like going to the theatre every Saturday night. To get his attention, don't play games, like withholding sex if he won't do what you want. Mr. Scorpio needs to know your motives are trustworthy. Show him you're his ongoing partner, not his adversary.

Sagittarius

Potential Issue Number One: He's restless, antsy, and nothing seems to please him. You wind up feeling confused—and inadequate.

Working It Out: Ask if he's feeling trapped—and why. It may have nothing to do with you. Always keep in mind one of his greatest fears: sitting around counting his gray hairs, never experiencing life to the fullest. This needn't *excuse* his behavior, but it may help explain it. Prod him to talk about his wishes for the future, then share yours, too. A relationship with this fellow prospers when you both do a lot of growing, both together and independently. Don't forget to splurge on weekend getaways.

Potential Issue Number Two: He's right, you're wrong. He has all the answers, you don't. He'd rather have an argument than have a good time.

Working It Out: Unwittingly, Mr. Saj sometimes values being right over being happy. Don't go there with him. You needn't swallow your pride. Just tell him you don't want to argue, and it doesn't matter who's "right." Stick to the real issue: getting over this "debate" so you can go back to getting along. One person can't have all the answers. Encourage him to listen to your ideas, and take them seriously, regardless of their "academic" merit. Eventually, he may learn to enjoy reaching different conclusions.

Potential Issue Number Three: He won't commit. When you talk about getting serious, he laughs uncontrollably—and uncomfortably.

Working It Out: Mr. Saj cherishes his freedom. Yet he also craves a deep connection, which led him to your relationship in the first place. So promote freedom *within* commitment—or, in other words, commitment without confinement. Ask him to clarify how much space he needs—and when. Ultimately, you'll have to discuss whether he wants to keep all his options open, or if he'll accept the challenge to limit his options in favor of deepening the partnership.

Capricorn

Potential Issue Number One: He won't take chances. He hides his vulnerability and sense of fun.

Working It Out: No, life offers no guarantees, but in a healthy relationship Mr. Capricorn can learn to let go and lighten up. Together, take *reasonable* risks, like a new vacation destination or sexual experience that's fun to try—but no great loss if it misses the mark. Commend his efforts. Let him feel good about trying, regardless of "results." And seize any and all opportunities to make him laugh.

Potential Issue Number Two: His work comes first. He seems to be more in love with his career than with you.

Working It Out: Respect his career. Acknowledge the value of his work. Mr. Capricorn needs to feel he's making a significant contribution. Also point out, however, the importance of your relationship. Allow him to feel like a success at home as well as at the office. Then watch out: He might quit his job and become a professional househusband!

Potential Issue Number Three: Nothing you do seems good enough. His standards—for you, himself, and life—are impossibly high.

Working It Out: Here's a novel idea: Ask him to define his standards. What does he expect of you? Tell him if you think it's realistic. Stand your ground, refusing to fall into the trap of feeling inadequate. And when he vents about his disappointments, remember that you can be there for him without going there with him.

Aquarius

Potential Issue Number One: He's emotionally distant, off in his own little world. Though you both communicate, you don't *connect.*

Working It Out: First, understand that your Aquarius man is an idealist who may have a hard time accepting that relationships don't always live up to ideals. He may be wondering *What went wrong?* when in fact nothing's wrong—it's simply that real life seldom lives up to expectations. Keep communicating. Tell him it hurts when he withdraws. But if at times he needs to disappear into his thoughts, let him—as long as it's not a trick to avoid intimacy.

Potential Issue Number Two: He's stubborn about his way of seeing things. He refuses to compromise or negotiate.

Working It Out: Your Aquarius man may worry you're trying to change him. Allay this fear by reinforcing how much you want to resolve a specific issue, not change who he is or force him to conform. Meet him halfway. Acknowledge his point of view—then ask him to see yours, too. Ask him to *experiment* with your solution—he might love it and never go back.

Potential Issue Number Three: He's not romantic. He's good, kind, and generous—but he forgets little things that mean a lot, like your anniversary or your allergy to latex. Are you lovers, or just roommates?

Working It Out: Sometimes Mr. Aquarius *thinks* about love but doesn't *show* passion—that would be too messy! So offer some concrete ideas on how you'd like to increase intimacy. And ferret out what makes *him* feel special, even if he pretends he doesn't like to be fussed over. Tell him you're happy he respects you—but you'd be happier if he *romanced* you.

Pisces

Potential Issue Number One: He puts on his martyr costume—yes, that old thing! He sends you on guilt trips. He performs the "Poor Me" song-and-dance routine.

Working It Out: Don't overreact. Acknowledge his feelings—that's essential. Then try to point out what he's doing. For a while, you may have to live with being cast as the bad guy, the evil oppressor. Don't worry about it. Eventually even Mr. Pisces will tire of the martyr costume and change into something more comfortable.

Potential Issue Number Two: He's wishy-washy, maybe even downright undependable. He doesn't do what he said he was going to do.

Working It Out: Discuss it. Is he just flaky, or are his actions (or inaction) trying to say something? If it's basic flake factor, remind him love isn't only a feeling—it's something one *does.* Don't persecute him for screwing up, but let him know how you feel. If, on the other hand, his behavior is meant to make a statement, tell him you'd rather he just *say* it, rather than "forget" your birthday or "suddenly" get sick on cleaning day.

Potential Issue Number Three: Somewhere, your Pisces man believes, the grass is always greener. Better sex, more money, greater fulfillment—it's all *out there.* He overlooks reality and escapes into . . . where exactly?

Working It Out: Actually, it's cute. Inside every Pisces is a bit of Peter Pan, the boy who refused to grow up. Maybe he fears whether he can stand on his own two feet. Or perhaps he doesn't know *how* to enjoy what he's got. Whichever, support him by *not* supporting this belief. Don't deep throat him with reality, but ask him to appreciate you and the relationship. Mutually establish attainable goals for enhancing your life together—then get on with *your* version of life, not Hollywood's.

The Stars of Broadway Musicals

Aries: Gypsy

Just like Mama Rose, Aries is bold, brassy, and takes his show on the road.

Taurus: The Sound of Music

Whether in a convent or a castle, all Taurus needs are his favorite things—and a little peace and quiet from those Von Trapp kids.

Gemini: Victor/Victoria

Gemini can quickly adapt to any scenario—he can be your hero *or* your heroine.

Cancer: Fiddler on the Roof

Sunrise to sunset, Cancer upholds "family" values—traditional or otherwise.

Leo: Mame

"Life is a banquet," and Leo always goes back for seconds.

Virgo: The King and I

Virgo kings—and queens—proclaim that their subjects must always meet the highest of standards, et cetera, et cetera, et cetera.

Libra: **West Side Story**

Libra feels pretty and witty and gay—and wants you to, too.

Scorpio: **Cabaret**

Divinely decadent Scorpio won't sit all alone in his room—and please don't tell his mama.

Sagittarius: **Man of La Mancha**

An impossible dreamer, Sagittarius will gladly tilt his lance at your windmill.

Capricorn: **How to Succeed in Business Without Really Trying**

Going by the book, Capricorn rises to the top—and lives to sing about it.

Aquarius: **Camelot**

Idealistic Aquarius wants justice to prevail and love to save the day.

Pisces: **Into the Woods**

Pisces gets through the woods with his friends by his side—and a rich fantasy life.

Act Three

Do You Know the Way to Nirvana?

Twelve Lessons of Spiritual Enlightenment

You've got the car, the house, and the time share in South Beach. You've caught Mr. Right, excelled at your career, and chiseled your tummy into a six-pack. You've got it all. Or maybe you don't. Either way, something's missing. You want more out of life. Sweetheart, join the club.

We all long for meaning in life. We want to feed a spiritual hunger and find a sense of being fully alive. We seek an understanding of our place in the universe and our relationship to—here comes that scary word—*God.*

For gay men, God and spirituality are touchy subjects. Many religions exclude us, and many spiritual leaders condemn us. So we've had to wrestle with our faith and defy traditions. That doesn't necessarily mean, however, that we've shunned God and spirituality. In fact, for many of us, the process has led toward a spiritual path that extends far beyond coming out. Maybe that's why you picked up this book, or why you'd bother to wonder about your place among the stars.

Astrology's not a religion, yet it does speak to spiritual affairs. The ancient Greeks, for example, believed that as the planets travel around the stars, they make music only our souls can hear—the Music of the Spheres. Perhaps, in rare moments of perfect bliss, you've heard the Music of the Spheres, when all of Creation sings in harmony, and you understand your sacred aliveness, as if listening to God Himself. Or *Her*self, if you prefer.

We live on earth, not the astral plane, so we more frequently hear the noise of traffic than the Music of the Spheres. Still, though, astrology can teach us a thing or two about bringing spirituality into our everyday lives. Each zodiac sign offers certain spiritual challenges and gifts. As you encounter people of each sign in your life, they may offer you their particular gift or challenge, helping you to grow. Likewise, you may, even unwittingly, "teach" others your sign's spiritual lesson.

Read the spiritual lessons below for your zodiac sign and those of the people you know and share your life with. Maybe together we can help bring a little stardust down to earth.

Aries

Aries teaches courage. In French, instead of saying "good luck," they often say *bon courage* ("have some heart"). Life is hard, a constant challenge, yet the spirit of Aries says, "I'm ready and willing." Every day is a fresh start. Awake and alert to life's possibilities, Aries challenges us to live in what *A Course in Miracles* calls "the holy instant"— the here and now. In the Zoroastrian religion (precursor to the Judeo-

Christian tradition), the new year starts when the sun enters Aries. From our Aries friends we can learn to take chances.

Taurus

Taurus teaches peace. In a loud and obnoxious world, the Taurus spirit reveres the beauty of silence, a mind uncluttered by worry and fear. "Let's not hurry," it says. "Let's savor the good stuff." Taurus challenges us to cultivate patience. Patience may help us get through the frustration of not reaching our spiritual "goals" as fast as we'd like. Taurus takes nothing for granted; the Bull values every nook and cranny of Creation. Gratitude emerges from a sense of "All I have is all I need." Serenity grows out of a dedication to excluding negative distractions. From our Taurus friends we can learn to stay calm and enjoy the gift of life.

> "This final, unexpected willingness to surrender to something beyond his understanding was a border, a crossing that would always mark him as different from what he had been."
>
> —Taurus author Lev Raphael, "Another Life"

Gemini

Gemini teaches perception. How we *see* may determine how we *are*. Ever mindful, the Twins challenge us to be like a tree that bends in the wind instead of breaking. Curiosity, another Gemini gift, leads us to find and fulfill our destinies. Without it, we would never discover our potential or our universe. The spirit of Gemini is not afraid to say, "I don't know, but I'll find out." It is full of wonder. As a Native American teacher once said, "Pay attention to the smallest crawling creature . . . even the smallest ant may wish to communicate with a man." The Gemini spirit opens up those magic moments of "Aha!" It reminds us not only that change is possible, but it's inevitable. From our Gemini friends we can learn to open our eyes and communicate what we see.

Cancer

Cancer teaches care. By caring for someone else, we stop dwelling on our own problems. The spirit of Cancer wants to reach out to those in need. It does not ask too many questions; it simply responds with kindness. Cancer shows us how to make family wherever love grows. With open arms, it wants to practice hospitality, inviting everyone to a place at the table. Cancer encourages us to let life sink in deeply, down to the bone, down to the soul. Cancer challenges us to experience life fully, with joy and sadness and everything in between. From our Cancer friends we can learn to nourish our souls—and the world.

Leo

Leo teaches passion. In Christianity, "passion" originally meant the passion of Christ on the cross. In Judaism, The "Song of Songs" likens the passion of lovers to the love between God and God's people. The Leo spirit wants to love life. It cares less for finding the meaning of life and more for living it. It longs to express its soul and place in Creation through its own creativity. Leo challenges us to have self-esteem. It wants to shout, "I'm OK, you're OK, we're all so bloody fabulous, darling." From our Leo friends we can learn to play and celebrate.

Virgo

Virgo teaches devotion. Without devotion, we may give up too quickly and neglect our well-being and true selves. "All the qualities of a spiritual teacher," a Sufi teacher once said, "can be found in the person who can cook an egg perfectly." The Virgo spirit inspires us to find God in a job well done, a life well lived. It yearns to find and fulfill its mission, whether it's to worship God or serve the world or make a commitment. Virgo challenges us to exercise our souls with rituals and practices that improve health in body and mind. From our Virgo friends we can learn to pray in actions as well as in words.

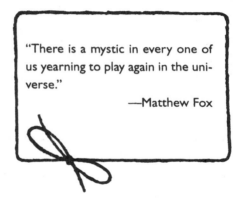

> "There is a mystic in every one of us yearning to play again in the universe."
>
> —Matthew Fox

Libra

Libra teaches empathy. By knowing and loving a friend, lover, or stranger, we more fully know and love ourselves and Creation. The Libra spirit longs to experience connectedness. It seeks meaning and joy in companionship and sharing. It gently strives for integration—to bring all aspects of life into a constantly evolving balance, no aspect receiving more or less than its fair share. Justice gladdens the Libra spirit. Libra challenges us to exercise choice—to choose our responses, outlook, and inner vision. The Libra spirit wants to express grace. It says, "I don't need to force the river to flow; it will flow by itself." From our Libra friends we can learn to cherish beauty and seek harmony.

> "The path for our spiritual growth can come to us from countless sources, although all routes will lead us toward a similar destination."
>
> —Gemini spiritual healer Justin Carson

Scorpio

Scorpio teaches rebirth. The Scorpio spirit is the phoenix, the mythic creature that died after 500 years and from its ashes arose again, forever reenacting the cycle. It seeks transformation. In order to grow and know its true nature, the Scorpio spirit wants to cleanse old patterns, bad habits, and worn-out beliefs. It challenges us to unlock our dormant potential. Sensitive to life's mysteries, the Scorpio spirit longs to express power wisely, as an extension of spirit, as a means of constantly becoming. From our Scorpio friends we can learn to confront the truth.

Sagittarius

Sagittarius teaches enthusiasm. "No matter what, I'm glad to be alive," the Archer spirit wishes to say. "I will hold nothing back." It wants to live life as an adventure, a quest for understanding. The Sagittarius spirit searches for meaning and tries to make sense of our experiences. Defying pessimism and boundaries, it reaches for wisdom that it can touch but never grasp, at least not in this lifetime. Sagittarius wants us to have freedom to explore our own unique destinies. It challenges us to transcend the ordinary and embrace the divine. From our Sagittarius friends we can learn to take journeys without distance.

Capricorn

Capricorn teaches dignity. "I matter!" says the spirit of Capricorn. "And so do you. And so does each soul." It longs to express the gift of respect and worthiness to itself and others. To the Capricorn spirit, life is not cheap. Fun but not frivolous, it wishes to act with purpose and intention. It seeks to be grounded in a spiritual center. When reality bites, the Capricorn spirit may laugh, but it will never run or shrink. It challenges us to overcome obstacles with clarity and strength—hey honey, let's deal with it! From our Capricorn friends we can learn to chase dreams and make them real.

Aquarius

Aquarius teaches tolerance. The Aquarius spirit wants to sing out, "Don't judge too quickly. I will approach this person, this situation with an open mind." For the Aquarius spirit, friendship and fraternity come in many packages; hope flourishes when we see the world as a place full of possibilities, capable of constant transformation, neither stagnant nor pointless. The Aquarius spirit encourages us to develop acceptance as a way of life. It challenges us to think differently and constantly evolve our beliefs. From our Aquarius friends we can learn to experiment and reinvent the world.

Pisces

Pisces teaches surrender. When we let go, we fall into life's protective hands. In order to let go, we need faith. Like the Buddha leaving his kingdom, like Moses's mother setting her son adrift in the Nile, like Christ on the cross, like Luke Skywalker trusting the Force, when we surrender to faith, we invite miracles. To the Pisces spirit, "Don't worry, be happy" is not a platitude but a useful philosophy. It longs to express oneness—like the Gaia theory, the scientific vision of earth as one living, breathing, dynamic organism, with all of us like cells in this magnificent creature. From our Pisces friends we can learn to relinquish control and gain grace.

"I'm an atheist who reads his horoscope."

—Screenwriter Paul Rudnick

Disco Spirit

Aries: "I Love the Nightlife" (Alicia Bridges)
Action! Life! Disco! The Aries spirit wants to boogie, baby!

Taurus: "Got to Be Real" (Cheryl Lynn)
He's gotta have it! And as long as it's real, the Taurus spirit's love is here to stay.

Gemini: "Ring My Bell" (Anita Ward)
Ding dong ding! Any time, anywhere, the Gemini spirit wants to ring a lot of bells.

Cancer: "I Will Survive" (Gloria Gaynor)
Does he crumble? Is he afraid? Petrified? Oh, no, not Cancer! As long as the Cancer spirit knows how to love, he'll survive.

Leo: "Dancing Queen" (Abba)
Feel the beat from the tambourine! Young and lean, the Leo spirit wants us to have the time of our lives—and digs being the dancing queen.

Virgo: "Everlasting Love" (Carl Carlton)
Did you realize? Open up your eyes! From the very start, the Virgo spirit heals hearts gone astray with its very own everlasting love.

Libra: "Come to Me" (France Joli)
Come to Libra! When the world's empty and cold, the Libra

spirit gives all the love we need.

Scorpio: "Don't Leave Me This Way" (Thelma Houston)
Baby! It's flamin' out of control! Full of love and desire, the Scorpio spirit seeks to satisfy the need for love to set us free—and to surrender to love's command.

Sagittarius: "Go West" (The Village People)
In search of open air and new beginnings, the Saj spirit goes to learn and teach where the skies are blue.

Capricorn: "Reach Out, I'll Be There" (Gloria Gaynor)
Reach out, darling! When we're lost and about to give up, the Capricorn spirit wants to catch us with a love that will see us through.

Aquarius: "I'm Coming Out" (Diana Ross)
Let it show! Break out and shout! The Aquarius spirit wants the world to know he's comin' out.

Pisces: "Losing My Mind" (Liza Minnelli with The Pet Shop Boys)
Sleepless nights and all day long, the Pisces spirit would rather lose his mind than not be kind.

Index

Printed in the United States
By Bookmasters